THE HEART OF MAN

Also by Jón Kalman Stefánsson in English translation

Heaven and Hell (2010)

The Sorrow of Angels (2013)

JÓN KALMAN STEFÁNSSON

THE HEART OF MAN

Translated from the Icelandic
by Philip Roughton

MacLehose Press
New York • London

MacLehose Press
An Imprint of Quercus
New York • London

Copyright © Jón Kalman Stefánsson, 2009
English translation copyright © 2015 by Philip Roughton
Published by agreement with Leonhardt & Høier Literary Agency A/S, Copenhagen
First published in the United States by Quercus in 2015

First published in the Icelandic language as *Hjarta mannsins*
by Bjartur, Reykjavík, in 2009

This book has been published with the financial support from
of Bókmenntasjóður/The Icelandic Literature Fund

Bókmenntasjóður
The Icelandic Literature Fund

Any member of educational institutions wishing to photocopy part or all of the work
for classroom use or anthology should send inquiries to permissions@quercus.com.

ISBN 978-1-62365-943-1

Library of Congress Control Number: 2015950134

Distributed in the United States and Canada by
Hachette Book Group
1290 Avenue of the Americas
New York, NY 10104

Manufactured in the United States

10 9 8 7 6 5 4 3 2 1

www.quercus.com

The trilogy *Heaven and Hell, The Sorrow of Angels* and *The Heart of Man* is dedicated to the sisters Bergljóta K. Þráinsdóttir (1938–69) and Jóhanna Þráinsdóttir (1940–2005).

And to María Karen Sigurðardóttir.

The three quotations on pp. 150–1 are from "Song of Myself," pts 21 and 44, by Walt Whitman (from his 1855 collection *Leaves of Grass*). The Icelandic poet Einar Benediktsson (1864–1940) translated parts of *Leaves of Grass* into Icelandic (*Úr grasblöðum*) and published them in 1892. The translations given here are of Benediktsson's text. The German phrase "*da ich ein Knabe war*" on p. 234, "when I was a boy," is from the poem of the same title by the German Romantic poet Friedrich Hölderlin (1770–1843).

A guide to the pronunciation of Icelandic consonants, vowels and vowel combinations can be found on p. 287.

THESE ARE THE STORIES THAT
WE OUGHT TO TELL

Death is neither light nor darkness; it's just anything but life. At times we keep vigil over folk who are dying and watch their lives fade away; each life is a universe and it's painful to see one disappear, see all become nothing in a single instant. Of course, lives are different; for some, they're humdrum, for others grand adventures, yet each consciousness is a world that stretches from ground to sky, and how can something so big vanish so easily, become nothing, not even foam left behind, not even an echo? But it's been a long time since someone joined our group. We're bloodless shadows, less than shadows, and it's bad to be dead yet not be allowed to die, such a thing does no one any good. In our day, some of us resorted to various means to try to escape—cast ourselves in front of oncoming cars, stuck our heads into the jaws of vicious dogs— but our screams were silent, the dogs' teeth cut through us like air; how is it possible to be less than nothing yet remember everything, to be dead yet sense life more intensely than ever before? Now you're sure to find us in the evenings, crouched in the cemetery, behind the church that's stood here for centuries, though not always the same building. Our church, where Reverend Þorvaldur tried, to little effect, unfortunately, to find forgiveness and overcome his weaknesses; a person's strength is measured only by his weaknesses, by how he faces them. The timber church paneled with corrugated metal is long gone and in its place is another one of stone, the stuff of mountains, which is appropriate; in such places the church should be modeled on mountains or the sky. The only times we find a trace of peace are here in the cemetery. Here we believe we can discern the muttering of the dead down in the earth, a distant hint of cheerful conversations. Thus can despair deceive. Yet these tranquil moments have multiplied slowly; they even seem to have lengthened, shifted ever so slightly from split seconds to seconds. We don't feel well, precisely, but these words keep us warm, they're our hope, and where there are words, there is life. Welcome them, and we exist. Welcome them, and there's hope. These are the stories that we ought to tell. Don't leave us.

AN OLD ARABIC MEDICAL TEXT SAYS THAT
THE HUMAN HEART IS DIVIDED INTO TWO
CHAMBERS, ONE CALLED HAPPINESS, THE
OTHER DESPAIR. WHAT ARE WE TO BELIEVE?

I

WHERE DO DREAMS END, WHERE DOES REALITY BEGIN? DREAMS
come from within, they trickle in from the world that we all have
inside us, possibly distorted, but what isn't distorted, what isn't dented?
I love you today, hate you tomorrow—he who never changes is lying
to the world.

The boy lies for a long time with his eyes closed. Uncertain whether
it's day or night, whether he's awake or asleep. He and Jens landed on
something hard. First they lost Hjalti, the farmhand who came with
them from Nes; the three of them dragged the coffin containing Ásta
over mountains and heaths. Then the boy and Jens landed on something hard. How much time has passed? And where is he? He opens
his eyes hesitantly; it isn't always certain what awaits you after sleep,
worlds change overnight, lives are extinguished, the space between
the stars increases and the darkness deepens; he opens his eyes hesitantly, nervously, and is lying in a moonlit room, is lying in deathly
white moonlight, and Hjalti's face is uncomfortably pale as he sits on a
chair and looks hard at the boy; Ásta is standing by the bed, emanat-
ing cold. You always escape, Hjalti says slowly. Yes, there are always
people ready to pull him to his feet, says Jens, who is sitting up in a
bed next to him, the moonlight having sewn a death mask on him.
But no one can help you now, Ásta says. No, says Jens; nor is he worth
it. What does he have to offer, anyway; what right does he have to live?

Hjalti says. The boy opens his mouth to reply, say something, but feels a weight on his chest, so heavy that it's hardly possible to speak, and then they begin fading slowly, they're slowly erased, and the moonlight transforms into endless snow and the room into a cold heath that fills the world. The sky is a thick layer of ice covering everything.

II

Is it safe for me to open my eyes? Maybe he hadn't slept, maybe it just takes such a long time to die. He hears neither the wind nor the hissing of the blowing snow, and doesn't feel the cold. I must have fallen asleep in the snow; this is the sleep that turns into a soft, comforting death. Nor can I fight it anymore, thinks the boy, and no one can help me now, Ásta is right about that, and why fight when all the best is finished? But I'm to be educated; Gísli, the headmaster himself, is supposed to teach me; isn't it a betrayal to die, mustn't I fight? And isn't he lying in a bed? He feels as if he is, in a soft bed, it's bizarre. Maybe he's just lying in his room in Geirþrúður's house and dreamt it all, the journey with Jens through storms and snow; is it even possible to dream so much snow, so much wind, so many lives and deaths; are dreams big enough for all of it? He can't open his eyes, simple as that; his eyelids are heavy stone slabs. Tries to feel what's around him, sends his hands off on a surveying expedition, but they prove to be as useless as his eyes, he can't even feel them, maybe they're dead, the frost has gnawed off his hands and they're lying there like old scraps of wood in the snow. Where are you, Jens? he thinks, or mutters, before sinking back into sleep, if this is indeed sleep, if it isn't death, sinks into rest, sinks into a nightmare.

III

Have you decided whether you'll live or die? she asks, this woman or girl. She has red hair, the dead are redheaded. I don't know, he says,

I'm not sure I know the difference, nor am I sure it's so significant. I'll kiss you, she says, you'll feel the difference, you're definitely dead if you don't feel a kiss. She comes right up and bends over him, her hair so red that it can hardly be true, and her lips are warm, they're soft. Where is life but in a kiss?

IV

Half-light surrounds the boy when he wakes, twilight, in fact. He's lying in a soft bed, beneath a warm blanket that smells like fresh spring air, and there are his hands, waiting trustily and patiently for him, the frost didn't gnaw them off, he can lift them and move his fingers, albeit stiffly, they're like befuddled old men but are in their places. Outstanding, he mutters. He can discern the outline of two windows behind the curtains and hears a deep breathing close by, gathers the courage and strength to lift himself up on his elbows and look around. He's in a fairly spacious room and there is another bed, a man is lying there breathing and it's Jens. So they're alive. How do you find out whether you're alive, not dead? It isn't always obvious. He thinks about it, then lifts the index finger of his right hand, bites the finger hard and feels the pain. Accordingly, his index finger should be alive; that's something anyway. On the other hand, it takes a considerable effort to get up, it makes him dizzy, he should just keep lying there, it was a mistake when man raised himself up onto his hind legs; that's when this tug-of-war between Heaven and Hell first began. The floor is cold and the boy hobbles over to Jens' bed, stands over him, watches him breathe, then sits down on the edge of the bed, relieved. Good that this difficult, silent man should be alive, then his sister Halla won't be tied down by strangers, she won't be kicked.

He hears movement and a short woman enters, her expression slightly sharp, as if she expects nothing good in this world. You're awake, then, she says. Can this be the woman from his dream, who kissed him, so sharp and at least twenty years older? What am I? he says. How should I know? I mean, *where*? In the doctor's house in Sléttueyri, where else should you be?

This isn't the voice from his dream, this woman isn't a dream, she's more like a length of rope, tough and steadfast. At Sléttueyri, he says slowly, as if to taste this name that had been their goal for two days, two nights, the tranquility and rest behind the storm. So he'd made it. He and Jens had made it. But Hjalti? She puts her hands on her hips, not much space between her eyes, has an air of impatience, maybe she knows that human life is short, the sky changes color and you're dead. So we made it, the boy says, as if to himself. It would seem so, the woman says.

But how did we get here, and . . . into bed? Jens and I, I mean. I don't remember anything.

You don't remember anything. Yet you've certainly talked enough. Did I speak?

You started as soon as you came into the warmth, half was unintelligible, and on top of that you wanted to go back out into the storm, buck-naked; you had to be restrained. Yes, buck-naked, your clothes had to be removed, of course, frozen solid as they were, and life rubbed back into the two of you.

She's gone over to the window, opened the curtains with one quick tug, and daylight streams in. Where's Hjalti? the boy says after his eyes have adjusted to the light. Hjalti, she repeats in the doorway, on her way out; I have no idea. Your jabbering sent ten men out into the night and they barely escaped an avalanche. Wait, the boy nearly shouts as she turns away. As if I have time for that, she says, and walks out.

Leaves the door ajar behind her, her rapid footsteps recede, short, quick steps, and soon afterward he hears the sound of voices. Jens breathes so slowly that it could be called peaceful, as if this big man is finally content with life; sleep can deceive us like that. How long have they slept, and was it night when they crashed into the house? Again the boy gets up carefully from the bed, his legs carry him, but they're in poor shape, have aged considerably, the right one by a few decades probably. It's fairly bright outside, maybe nearing midday; so he's slept for at least twelve hours, no surprise that he's muddle-headed. Cloudy, no sign of coming snowfall, a strong wind and cold, no doubt, the wind swirls up snow here and there as if it's bored, but doesn't block the view in any direction, and there's the sea, leaden, tremendously heavy, tossing and turning between the mountains, he looks to the right, where the ocean extends into the distance, calmer in its endlessness. The mountains are white, too distant to be threatening, entirely white except for the cliff-belts, which are pitch-black, like the door to Hell. He runs a fingertip over his lips, languidly, as if in search of a kiss. Was it a dream, the kiss, the voice, the red hair, the warmth?

It's cold to stand by the window, frost and snow breathe through the thin glass. He spies a few snow-covered houses, cold shells containing life. Leans forward and discerns the outline of the church; is Ásta inside it, waiting to be put into the ground? And where is Hjalti? The boy peers out as if hoping to see Hjalti dash from one snow-covered house to another, maybe in search of Bóthildur. Life is about finding another person to live with and then surviving that discovery, says a famous book, and that's fine, as far as it goes, because it must always be harder to survive alone than with others. We're born alone, die alone, and it's heartrending to live alone as well. The boy tries to think of Ragnheiður, the daughter of Friðrik, the factor of Tryggvi's Shop and Trading Company. She was going for a ride in the sunshine; but then someone comes up the stairs, stepping heavily. He starts back to bed, to get under the shelter of the covers, but stops, decides to return to the window but stops again, and is thus right between the two, or rather, nowhere, when a middle-aged man enters, the floor creaks beneath his heavy body; his build is robust, he's rather tall, nearly bald, but with big, bushy sideburns, wearing a wool jacket and vest, his nose is noticeably red, his steely blue eyes lie deep in his face, making his nose seem even bigger. You're awake, so it was true, the man says; his voice is deep but slightly worn, or hoarse, and he heaves a sigh. Good that you were able to rest, says a woman who appears beside the man, shorter by more than a head and younger, a difference of perhaps twenty years, thin, with thick blond hair and an expression so bright that the boy starts thinking once more about sunshine, about summer, about the blue nights of the month of June, will they ever return? The woman who's more like rope leans against the doorjamb, crosses her arms over her large bosom; well then, her expression seems to say, there you have it, so what now?

For several moments the boy stands defenseless in the middle of the room, wearing someone else's clothing of homespun wool, far too roomy; life seems to take great pains to belittle him. The man tucks his thumbs into his pants, says, Well then, and the woman, the bright one, says, You should get some rest, and he goes to the bed and lies down on it. Help me with the soup, she says, without taking her eyes off the boy, and the other woman unfolds her arms and is gone; she is footsteps receding. You should really lie down, the woman says to the boy, sitting down at the bedside and aging as she draws closer, faint wrinkles, furrows in her face made by the claws of time. Ólafur wants to have a look at you, and afterward we'd really like to hear of your travels, and of poor Ásta; folk here have hardly spoken of or thought about anything else since your arrival here in the village, with a bang, it's safe to say, you and this big man, and she glances at Jens. Have a look at me? asks the boy, without really knowing which way he should lie on the bed.

Forgive me, you don't know us, the woman says, this is Ólafur, the doctor in these parts and my husband; she waves one hand, a bit like a wing, toward the man, who bows quickly and smiles, as his eyes penetrate the boy. I'm Steinunn, she says, standing up to make room for her husband, who sits down heavily at the bedside, sighing slightly, as if he feels uncomfortable being upright, in this eternal, wearisome tug-of-war, and starts poking at the boy, asking concise, pointed questions; yes, I can move my legs, no, no numbness in my arms, yes, soreness in my neck, and fatigue, yes, and weakness. Well, Steinunn says, and her husband stands up to allow her to sit down again. He's so young, he says, and therefore can endure almost anything. Rest, decent food, water, avoid the cold, and he'll be good as new in about a week, ten days. You're so young, Steinunn says, or agrees. Nice to be young, Ólafur says; constantly changing. You're one thing today, something totally different tomorrow. We should all be young and never grow old, never let time catch up with us. You don't want change, his wife says, shaking her blond head slightly, you detest it.

Is Jens alright? the boy says softly, suddenly feeling faint.

Jens, so his name is Jens, the big one, Ólafur says, well, oh, he's worse off than you, no denying it, he's suffered frostbite.

Worse off? the boy says hesitantly, so he's not out of danger? Out of danger, when is a person out of danger? Ólafur says, I did what I could, but he will likely end up walking with a limp. Maybe worse.

They all fall silent. As if they're contemplating the final words, "and maybe worse"—what they mean; how bad is worse, how far is death from life?

The boy hesitates, then asks, So you didn't find Hjalti? Finally daring to ask because people are alive as long as we don't ask; they're safe in the silence, and then we start talking and someone is dead. Hjalti, says Ólafur, glancing at his wife, and then out the window; you said a lot about this Hjalti, that's why we sent the boys out into the storm. Ten of them. Álfheiður rounded them up in no time. Night and a storm, and an avalanche, that's how it was, he says, looking back at the boy and repeating, That's how it was, let me tell you! As if he didn't know that, his wife says softly, looking at the boy; she has beautiful eyes, they're like old, warm stars, it was the same night and same storm that drove them here. Ólafur goes to the wall and pulls over a wooden chair, sits down, nods, of course, quite right, drove them, literally threw them, against the house, startling me so much that I spilled the winter's last glass of sherry; there went that drop, there went that taste. He drums on his knees with relatively short fingers and starts whistling a meandering tune. Ólafur and I, Steinunn says, as if in explanation, were up late writing letters when you arrived . . . boisterously, interrupts Ólafur, yes, boisterously, she agrees, boom, Ólafur says, giving his thigh a quick slap and startling the boy. But judging by what you said, Steinunn says, you weren't traveling alone, so we sent men up the mountain. Out into that crazy storm, Ólafur says, and they found Ásta from Nes, a sled, remnants of a coffin, but nothing more.

The boy closes his eyes, overcome by a sudden faintness, and the image of Hjalti outside the farm at Nes comes to him, fills his consciousness; the man rolls an ever-expanding snowball ahead of him, holding the youngest boy like a sack beneath his arm, the other children skipping by his side. Could this big but slightly sorrowful man have died of exposure? He'll manage, Jens had said, and Jens knows these things. He has to know them. Maybe Hjalti simply returned to the children, to the place where he belongs, in the bay behind the world. The children need him, the world can't be so ghastly as to take that big man from them. You should eat now, Steinunn says. Her voice is as soothing as a warm embrace; there are some people who should simply sit next to you and speak, ease fatigue and pain with their voices. He opens his eyes. The woman, the short one, the length of rope, has returned, carrying a steaming tray; her name must be Álfheiður, and it is she who'd gathered the men to search for Hjalti. And Ásta, except that she was dead, and it's pointless to search for the dead, you don't search for what no longer exists. He hears a faint sound of child's laughter from downstairs, life goes on laughing despite death, it's so unbearable, tasteless, it's so important, our mainstay. Steinunn has him sit up, props a pillow in the small of his back, Álfheiður places the tray on his lap, steaming soup, bends over the boy to adjust the tray, a heavy, slightly sweet smell from her collar. The boy looks down at his dish for several long moments. Eat, dear, Steinunn says. Hjalti, he then says to the soup, is a farmhand of Bjarni and Ásta, was, or is, he says, confused about the tense, should he speak in the past or the present, will Hjalti die if the boy speaks about him in the past tense? I don't remember any Hjalti, Steinunn says, but I always forget names, and people as well. And besides, some people are just hard to remember for long. Some people are better wrought than others, Ólafur says.

Álfheiður: I knew a man by that name, but he drowned many years ago.

Ólafur: The sea, damn it all, that's tough; did he have a family?

Álfheiður: Four children and a wife.

Indeed, Ólafur says, sighing softly, it just isn't right.

Álfheiður: So justice does exist in this world, was what his wife said when she learned of the drowning.

Ólafur: What?

The boy, resolutely, to his soup: Hjalti didn't drown, he was . . . he's Bjarni and Ásta's farmhand . . . or was . . . I mean, she's dead, of course.

The soup is thick, hot and hearty, he eats without realizing it, as if in a daze.

Álfheiður takes the tray; again that warm, cloying smell. Shall I bring him coffee as well?

Ólafur: Bring a damned great lot of coffee, Þórdís dear. The boy glances up; it's so strange when people change name from one moment to the next. Þórdís mutters something almost inaudible, but the boy shuts his eyes and envisions Hjalti clearly, so unbearably clearly, sees his eyes, etched with disappointment, maybe sorrow, hears the last thing that Hjalti said before the sled ran off with the coffin and the three of them lost each other: Damn it, does a man come into this life just to die? And then he says it, opens his eyes and says, Can they be sent again to search for Hjalti?

Ólafur: What, again, for the third time?

Third time? the boy asks. They were able to search better yesterday, the doctor says; that makes twice, the weather wasn't quite as bad, it wasn't blowing hard enough to knock you down, but they found nothing. We presumed that there were more of you involved in transporting the body; it takes more than two to bring a coffin over a mountain.

The boy: We'd come to the ravine.

Steinunn looks at her husband; standing straight to have a proper look around is possible now, she says, and the doctor lumbers to his feet, goes out and shouts in a booming voice, Álfheiður! Gather some of the boys and tell them to go and search for this Hjalti! Tell them to follow the ravine! They'll have me to answer to if they so much as grumble! They won't be happy, the poor boys, he says when he returns. It's impossible to be happy all one's life, Steinunn says; no, Ólafur says, it would be damned depressing in the long run. Do you feel up to telling us the story of your journey? she asks the boy. Yes, Ólafur says, it wouldn't be bad to have a story, and here comes the coffee, he adds when Þórdís returns with coffee for the three of them, and the boy realizes that he can hardly avoid telling the story, that it's more or less expected of him. There should be a woman in one of the houses here, he says slowly, by the name of Bóthildur? Bóthildur, no, the couple doesn't know anyone by that name, why do you ask? She was apparently here three years ago. We've been here for twenty years, Ólafur says, and have never met anyone by that name, why do you ask? No reason in particular, the boy mutters, feeling his stomach knot up. He looks at the mailman, watches the cover rise and fall with his breathing. Those who breathe are alive, whatever that might

mean. And then he starts telling his story. The reserve mailman Guðmundur had become ill; that's how it began.

V

Jens awakes in the evening.

The boy had dozed, tired after telling the story of their journey,
it can take some effort to recall past events, we find then that life is
never a continuous thread except occasionally by coincidence, which
is as savage as it is beautiful. Some of the incidents pass through us
and are gone without leaving anything behind, but there are others
that we constantly relive, because what is past dwells in us, colors our
days, transforms our dreams. The past is so interwoven with our present that it's not always possible to distinguish between them, words
you speak today will return to find you five years on, come to you like
a bouquet of flowers, like a consolation, like a bloody knife. And what
you hear tomorrow transforms an old, cherished kiss into a memory
of a snake bite.

He'd told the story, relived the events, but didn't tell all of it, didn't
betray Jens, told neither of the mailman's defeat in the dory nor of
what he'd said about Halla and their father, the boy didn't stray so close
to Jens' heart, but he told of the little girl, she who coughs so badly in
Vetrarströnd that the thread of her life nearly tears apart. He told of
the priest in Vík, poor old Kjartan, Ólafur muttered, not to mention
Anna, Steinunn said, it's bad to lose one's sight, worse to lose one's
lust for life, Ólafur said. Are you certain, Steinunn had then said,
that the darkness around Anna isn't caused by lack of love rather
than impaired vision? Don't be ridiculous, people don't lose their
sight from lovelessness, it simply isn't possible, blindness is biologi-
cal, it's scientific. What do we know about it? Steinunn said, what do
we know about people? Perhaps not terribly much when it comes
right down to it, Ólafur admitted, and the boy told about the snow,

about the storm, the heath, about a farmer and a teenage boy on a heath, that he'd lost Jens, but then it was as if Ásta had appeared to him and led him to the mailman, through the dark storm, maybe it was just my imagination, said the boy when he noticed the looks the couple gave him, when will she be buried? Tomorrow or the day after, Steinunn said, depending on Reverend Gísli's health, and how long it takes to dig a grave, it's tough going digging frozen ground. How far down do they dig? the boy said apprehensively, with some vague idea that the deeper she lay, the greater the likelihood that she would find peace. It's one-and-a-half to two yards down to bedrock, Ólafur said, the dead lie shallowly here, but hopefully we can cover her better in the summer. Hopefully? A lot is forgotten in summer, young man, in the birdsong, the flies and all the fish. It's hard to remember the dead when the sun is shining, and it may be unnecessary, as well.

Þórdís had come in at the end of the story, with a new hot water bag for Jens. But who are you? Ólafur said, after Þórdís replaced the hot water bag, and both women looked automatically at the boy, who said nothing; what was he supposed to say, anyway? How does one explain one's existence, who am I, are we what we do, or what we dream? You have, said Steinunn when nothing was forthcoming from the boy, given us a great deal of cause for speculation. You were wearing well-made, expensive snow boots, Norwegian, I suppose, and warm clothing, cited poetry, we couldn't make out everything you said, almost none of it, really, but I thought I recognized Shakespeare and he's not what you'd call common, yet your hands suggest you've done your share of labor. People are either hardworking or they're not, said Þórdís, lifting her chin slightly. I'm staying with Geirþrúður, the boy said, as if that explained things. Geirþrúður, repeated Ólafur, do you mean *Geirþrúður*, Guðjón's wife? The boy nodded. Well now, Steinunn said. Is she keeping you for breeding purposes? Þórdís asked. No, said the boy, before adding curtly, almost before he realized it, and anyway, I prefer sensitive

women like you. I would smack you, Þórdís said, if you weren't
lying in bed.

After they left, the boy nodded off, his fatigue from the journey like
a heavy drone within him, a deep-rooted pain that reared its head
as he relived it in his narrative. Nodded off, slept, and it's evening
by the time he stirs. Jens is standing at the window, looking out, his
rough-hewn face deathly pale. For some time the boy doesn't dare
say anything, because words can reveal who is dead, who is alive,
one word and Jens dissolves and is a dead body in the next bed. But
we've got to know the difference between life and death, and this
is why the boy says, We're in Sléttueyri. Jens doesn't move, as if he
hasn't heard, what words do we need to use for the dead to be able to
hear us, so that God can hear? I know that, Jens says. In the doctor's
house, the boy adds, that is to say, when he's able; as soon as he heard
Jens' voice the grief welled up in his throat, unexpectedly, as if with
a will of its own, welled up and moistened his vocal cords. I know
that, Jens replies, continuing to look out into the world, which is full
of moonlight, this big man doesn't need to fight back tears, he just is.
Voices can be heard outside, male voices. Probably the men who went
to search for Hjalti, and for the third time, says the boy after listening
for a moment, trying to distinguish the words. I know, Jens says. We
crashed into the house and woke those who were sleeping, startled
the others badly. Jens says nothing. Just in time, says the boy, says
it softly. Yes, Jens agrees, leaning against the window frame to take
the weight off his legs, to help steady himself, to support his bones,
muscles, memories, betrayals, and the thought of what awaits him.
They hear light footsteps approaching, exchange a quick glance and
Steinunn walks in, hesitates when she sees the big man by the window. You're not only awake, you're on your feet as well, she says with
that voice of hers, which is placid, like lukewarm water. Jens looks at
her, I don't know about that, he says a bit dryly, before hobbling over

to the bed. You didn't find anyone? Jens says after lying down, says it calmly, suppresses pain, fatigue, the humiliation of not being able to walk upright, of being barely able to support himself. No, she says, the visibility was decent, but we've had a lot of snow, making it hard to guess what lies buried beneath it. The boy looks at them in turn, Steinunn is speaking differently now, as if mulling over every word. We're never the same, the presence of others changes us, draws forth different features and only rarely all at once, within every person are hidden worlds, some of which never reach the surface. He could hardly have gone back to Nes, Jens says. We have to hope for the best, she says, looking neither at Jens nor at the boy. Hope is fine, Jens says, but it does little to help a man more dead than alive in a foul storm. I know that, my boy, the woman says, fixing her eyes on Jens, who looks down, as if his head has suddenly grown unbearably heavy.

Jens is given porridge with a slice of blood sausage and a cup of freshly brewed coffee. How is the frostbite? he asks Ólafur, who came in soon after Þórdís, the three of them, the household, stand there watching Jens, it doesn't appear to have the slightest effect on him. Ugly, Ólafur replies. Frostbite is never pretty, Jens says, in a low voice. As I well know, the doctor says. Will it heal? I've seen worse. To this, Jens says nothing, but he doesn't take his eyes off Ólafur. The doctor looks away, shrugs, will it heal, what heals? A man is punched in the face, the face might forget the blow, but the man does not. Jens starts eating, as if he can no longer be bothered to look at the doctor. I'm fairly sure he wasn't asking about philosophy, Steinunn says, but about whether he'll get to keep his extremities intact. Right you are, Ólafur says, but with a scowl; there's a reasonable chance you'll get to keep everything, undamaged. But only just reasonable; several of your toes, possibly one or two fingers, are doubtful, it might depend on how good a patient you are, that may be the biggest uncertainty of all. Quite the quandary.

Þórdís: The best thing for frostbite is to wade through snow twice a day. It's always proven best. No one grows strong on tenderness.

Yet you seem strong enough, the boy says.

I'm not bringing this thing any more food, Þórdís says, and her light-blue eyes pierce the boy, while Steinunn mumbles something and goes to the window to look out.

Hjalti deserved better, the boy says when they're alone again; outside the window the sky holds the moon like a dim lantern. Yes, Jens says, nothing more than this one word, which isn't always a word but rather something akin to a sigh or even less, a breath, says it in such a way that for a moment all the boy's energy goes into trying not to cry. One of the worst things we can do to another person is cry in their presence, that's why we cry alone, in secret preferably, as if in shame, yet there are probably fewer things purer in this world than tears born of sorrow, of regret, civilization often takes us in peculiar directions. How will it go now for the children at Nes, the boy says finally, and Bjarni? But this time Jens makes no reply, or, yes, it's almost as if he says, Mmm, perhaps meaning that life is a hard mountain to climb. The mailman's eyes are shut, and then he's asleep. Sunk into a world so deep that it reaches almost all the way down to death, he sleeps and tries instinctively to clench his fists in their dressings, defenseless in dreamworlds.

VI

It's daytime, calm, clear, and Jens is not in the room. The boy sits for a long time at the window, looking out. Watches a group of giggling, screaming and laughing children playing between the houses; they've tramped a large circle in the snow and three of the biggest are trying to pull the others into the circle. He watches for a long time, thinks about what's gone, rubs his chest, the place of his heart, which ages faster than the other organs, except perhaps for the eyes. The number of children within the ring increases, and they hop and shout warnings and encouragement to those still outside it, pursued by the three giants. Once we were all children, the summers were warmer, longer, the world was endlessly wide, incomprehensible and full of promise. Once. I lived once. You loved me once. Once upon a time. Is there a sadder phrase than this: once upon a time? Once upon a time, but not any longer. Once upon a time I was a child. Once upon a time our days were fairy-tale palaces. Then they sank into a dark forest and were lost, we let it happen. We still let it happen. We let life stagnate, grow harder. Where do you go, life, where are you, kindness?

There's someone in the room. He turns and finds himself face-to-face with a slender woman wearing brown, well-worn clothing, a cardigan and dress, and a brown headscarf that hides all of her hair. She's entirely brown except for the pallor of her skin, except for her green eyes.

I was told to check whether you were dead, this woman says.

Where is Jens? he says, trying not to look into her green eyes.

Downstairs.

He managed to go down?

He'd hardly be there otherwise.

The children outside shout and the boy feels that he should say something about Jens, or the children outside, or something general about the day, but instead he says, You have green eyes.

You should come down and eat.

Is your name Álfheiður, by any chance? Yes, Álfheiður says. She has freckles that lie like a dense galaxy across her face, over her nose and out onto her cheeks.

You have freckles, he says, almost as if explaining something embarrassing. But when she says nothing, he adds, Were you the one who kissed me?

I thought that you were dying.

Which I didn't, he says, semiapologetically.

It doesn't matter, she says, and he isn't certain whether she means the kiss or his survival. You should come down, she adds, and leads the way.

We in Sléttueyri are deprived of food, Steinunn says; the boy has come down, there's Jens, bowed, distant, an empty coffee mug in front of him. There's enough, to be sure, it's just that there's little variety; eat as much as you can, and there's no shortage of milk here, dear boy, Steinunn adds. Ólafur is nowhere in sight, nor Þórdís, she's outside, the doctor's residence is also a working farm, two cows, thirty sheep, eight chickens, plenty to do. Álfheiður lays the table for the boy, once brushing against him, arm touches arm.

And these are the world's tidings; this is how the newspaper's front pages read:

No break in the angry grumbling between Japan and China, and the Japanese possess great military might.

Earth's population is 1 billion, 479 million, 729 thousand and 4 hundred, to boot.

Arms brush against each other at Sléttueyri in Iceland.

She has red hair. The scarf nearly covers her entire head, but a few locks escape from beneath it around her ears. He's served smoked seabird, she leaves and he takes a bite, chews. Red hair, green eyes, smoked seabird, Hjalti dead, no longer breathing, no longer thinking, no longer feeling, he never needs to pee again, spit, let alone cry. Steinunn puts down the paper, sighs, this is the tenth time she's read this particular edition, or eleventh, or twelfth, the papers are delivered late or never, winter slows all the news, there are a lot of people in this world, she says.

* * *

I can't make it upstairs without help, says Jens when they're alone in the kitchen. You probably shouldn't have come down, the boy says. I realized that when I was halfway. Then why didn't you turn around? I don't turn around, Jens says, and they go to the staircase, plod up the stairs, the boy needs to pause twice, Jens hangs onto him, breathing and cursing in his ear, and then lies down on the bed, the boy leans against the window frame, recomposes himself after his exertions, the burden on his sore legs. So he didn't make it back? the boy asks the daylight. No, Jens says. Maybe he dug himself a snow cave, waited out the worst and then headed home. Maybe. But highly unlikely? Jens does not reply, and the boy continues to look out; it's good to look into the daylight, we should all look toward it, even though it will never revive anyone. Neither of them speaks. There are many kinds of silence. Sometimes people say nothing to each other because something has happened in their lives, something for which words do not suffice, something that the tongue cannot manage to touch, and that's why these two men are silent now. One is standing, the other is lying in bed, the third died of exposure, nodded off in the snow—he is silence. There's so much taken from us, in the end everything. Death seems at times to enclose our lives just as the blackness of space encloses the earth, this blue planet, this blue cry in the vast expanse of space, a cry for God, a purpose. I feel sorry for the children, says the boy, breaking the silence, at Nes, he adds. Yes, Jens says. No one here knows Bóthildur. No.

He may have confused the names: a lapse of memory?

Bóthildur: it's hard to misremember a name like that.

Then what?

I don't know.

Maybe, the boy says hesitantly, extremely cautiously, she simply didn't exist. He looks out the window as he says this, but Jens says nothing, nor does the windowpane, nor does the daylight. I once knew a woman named Bóthildur, and she kissed me. Why do people lie about such things? Because we can't live otherwise? Or, when it comes down to it, is it the reality that lies but the person who tells the truth?

He has stopped looking out, it's become overcast, as well, as if it will soon start to snow. And Jens appears to be sleeping. The boy sits down on the bed, it will be good to get away, complete this terribly long journey that stretched from life to death, and a bit further, get back to the Village, to Geirþrúður's house, although of course he doesn't dare think the words "to get home." *Home* is far too big a word, it's saved many a man in the turmoil of life, those who have a home somewhere are less likely to give up. I'll just lie down, shut my eyes and think about Ragnheiður, about the softness of her lips, about how she trembled. He shuts his eyes, but immediately reopens them, because standing there is Álfheiður, and she's begun speaking to Jens, who apparently wasn't asleep, unless he woke to those green eyes, which isn't unlikely; how is it possible to sleep in their vicinity? But it doesn't matter, he's thinking about Ragnheiður, who trembled and who is going for a ride in sunshine, best to shut his eyes in the meantime; he who shuts his eyes is gone.

But then he's standing by the window and she's still speaking to Jens, the doctor this, the doctor that. This brown-clad, pale person seems to have some poise; yes, she might indeed, and it may even be somewhat appealing. But let's not forget that there are poised women throughout the world, in China alone there are likely an incredible number of poised women; he could easily believe that they amount to several million, so what does one slender maid in worn clothing matter, on the upper floor of a house teetering on the brink of the world; if the world were to sneeze, they would fly off it. He leans against the window frame, crosses his arms and looks forward to getting away. The doctor is making a house call, will come this evening or during the night, Jens should rest. Yes, says Jens, and adds something, he suddenly knows how to speak, and could he actually be smiling at

Álfheiður? But are you alright? she says, addressing the boy, who simply says, Yes, yes, calm as can be. But why has he uncrossed his arms, and what is he supposed to do with them now? Hopeless to let them hang stupidly by his sides like that, heavily and awkwardly, wouldn't it be best to open the window and toss them out?

The window can't be opened, it's frozen shut, she says, because the boy is now attempting to open it, muttering something about heavy air, he pushes at the window angrily. Not unless you want to break the windowpane, she says, and smiles. He glances at her quickly, she appears to have a more or less full set of teeth, though some of them are crooked, like tired people leaning against each other. He tucks his hands into his armpits, holds them there tightly, they can't do anything wrong in the meantime. There are people all over the world, he says, particularly in Russia and China, and in some places trees grow. Jens is in bed, she is standing, they both look at him, just watch, and for that reason he adds, They grow tea in China.

And sometimes it rains in the mountains there.

On the mice as well.

And on people's hands.

But that's alright if you're in China, because sometimes the rain there is warm.

VII

It's strange to come out into serene, clear air, to step outside without putting yourself in mortal danger, it's almost difficult to keep your balance in such calm. He follows a path that leads down to the nearest houses and winds around drifts. The boy looks around and is alive. Probably forty or fifty houses in the village, unevenly distributed in a large circle, the church towering over them on a low hill at its center. The doctor's house is located higher up, at the foot of a steep slope, the same one that he and Jens hurtled down, while above it the ravine cuts the mountainside like a dark, gaping wound. It's around two hundred and twenty yards down to the nearest houses, which form a fairly dense cluster. The boy stops before he comes to them, turns around and looks up at the mountain. Six days and nights since he set off, pushed the dory into the sea below Sodom, the headmaster Gísli and Marta watching. Was it only six days? Not six hundred?

The cold assails him as he stands there motionless, maybe he's not allowed to go out, he snuck down, unseen, heard Þórdís' voice, hard as rock, then Steinunn's gentle voice, maybe he should rest, gather his strength, go easy on himself, but Jens fell asleep soon after Álfheiður left, she took her eyes with her, their greenness. Jens asked nothing about the rain in China, whether rain could be warm in general, nor did he ask about the mice. The boy had been listening to her footsteps recede when Jens said, This was my last postal trip, which was followed by a long silence, as if the boy hadn't heard his announcement or, more likely, as if he simply didn't care. What did it matter to him, anyway, whether Jens were carrying mail between mountains or sitting safe at home; a person's life isn't anyone else's business. Jens shut his eyes. Everyone is responsible for his own life and shouldn't share that responsibility with others; why does a person have legs if he can't support himself on them? Is it because of Salvör? asked the boy out of the silence into which he had retreated, and Jens started as if stabbed by a knife. It's none of your business, he said curtly and gruffly, and two, three days ago that would have been more than enough, but not now, there's been too much snow, too much wind, too many mountains, too much death, uncertainty and fragile life in the last few days between them. For this reason, the boy said, Yes, maybe, but I'm asking anyway. And it was good of him to ask. If no one asks, we shut ourselves off in the silence, with all the pain that transforms over the years into loneliness, bitterness and a difficult death. Jens cursed, sat up with difficulty, like an old man. You see how I am, he said, as if that sufficed as an explanation for his announcement, but the boy asked again, for the third time, as if he didn't know any other words, understood nothing, Is it because of Salvör? Jens said nothing, what could he say, anyway, how are words to contain all that's within him? The boy remained standing by the window, leaning against the window frame, and waited tranquilly, knew that he needed to wait. Her husband drank and treated her badly, Jens said, looking down at his hands, because how do you distinguish hands that harm from those that don't harm? How do you distinguish someone who betrays from someone who doesn't betray?

The boy looks up at the ravine, he's the only one outside and all is silent, the children are gone, and with them their voices, their vivacity and maybe the daylight as well; doesn't it seem as if the sky has started to darken over the mountains? Gusts of wind ripple the sea beyond the harbor, lift the snow, transform it into veils that fall to the earth almost immediately. I know you, he says aloud to the wind, you transparent devil. He looks out over the mountains, toward Nes, where four children miss Ásta, miss Hjalti, miss and wait for him who cannot return. Where Bjarni sits on his bed, occupies himself with some work, bathes his mother, she's lost so much, her husband, friends, siblings, youth, most of her life, memories, thoughts, she opens her mouth, that black hole, when her body calls for food, and a slight tremor seizes it when she remembers something, when consciousness stirs beneath the weight of forgetfulness, she trembles slightly. But she also trembles when she passes a stool, when she longs for coffee and Bjarni lifts her like old hay, he has strong hands and can save lives in storms, at sea, but they're not strong enough to hug the children, not strong enough to console.

The boy has come to the houses, a cluster of eight of them, somewhat separate yet close enough to have an influence on the wind, on how the snow piles into drifts. A little house and so frosted over that the windows can barely be seen, like strange creatures that have died of exposure in the harshness of winter. Yet one of them stands out; it's the size of the doctor's house, two stories, is nearest the shore, and the icicles hang like large canines from its eaves. The boy doesn't see the red-painted sign until he's come right up to the house, is on his way down to the shore, but stops when he catches a glimpse of it above the door, barely makes out the yellow letters beneath the snow, SHOP. And then he remembers the slip of paper from María on Vetrarströnd. The note stating that he, the boy, could purchase books to the amount of 5 *krónur* at the shop in Sléttueyri. Remembers—of course he hasn't forgotten the note. How could he possibly have forgotten María, her passion for books, and also how she looked at her husband Jón, a bit as if the world were beautiful while she looked, can it be beautiful when human life is buried in snow, when one child is dead and another coughs too much, far too much, can the world be beautiful then, whence does she derive the strength not to give in? But he's lost the note, he's been entrusted with a great deal, but has failed. He walks down past the house, stands at the crest of the beach, looks out over and along it. It's a gravel beach, handy for landing, easy for pulling up the boats, a number of which are lying there, two sixareens, several smaller ones, and some had been at sea last night, or early that morning, a few seagulls fight and screech over the little that is to be found among the rocks after the gutting of the catch, one of the gulls takes flight, soars high and cries out twice. Gusts of wind have begun streaking the sea with gray and he spies a ship approaching, likely a schooner, although it's too far away to be certain, at least an hour until it reaches land. He gazes out over the sea, which breathes heavily between the mountains—behind the mountains and the sea they await him, Geirþrúður, Helga and Kolbeinn, the blind skipper, maybe even anxiously; his and Jens' journey took much longer than anyone expected, they encountered a storm, lost their way and took a longer route because Jens needed to think. And Hjalti died. The gull cries again. Somewhere it's written that he who dies of exposure doesn't die a real death but changes into a seagull, becomes a cry in the sky. The boy has returned to the shop, slip of paper or not, surely he'll be allowed to choose a book or books for María and have them sent to her at the first opportunity, whenever that may be. He pushes at the door.

It's stiff, he has to put his shoulder into it, even force it, it takes an act of will to enter, meaning that it passes no one's notice when someone comes in. Now I'll be stared at, he thinks after shoving open the door and stepping into the shop, but the door shuts behind him, strangely effortlessly. This shop isn't big for someone who's accustomed to Tryggvi's Shop, and who was even going to start working in Leó's Shop in the summer, before Bárður forgot his raincoat and the world changed forever. We never know which way life will go, don't know who will live and who will die, don't know whether the next greeting will be a kiss, bitter words, a hurtful gaze; someone doesn't take care, forgets to look to the right and is dead, and then it's too late to take back harsh words, too late to say sorry, too late to say what matters, and what we wanted to say but couldn't due to annoyance, the weariness of everyday life, time constraints, you forgot to look to the right and I'll never see you again and the words you spoke to me will reverberate within me all my days and nights, and the kiss you should have received dries on my lips, becomes a wound that rips open every time someone else kisses me. The boy sniffles as if to break the silence, it's barely three yards from the door to the counter, the shelves look bare. To the boy's right, in a partially lit corner, is a little table with four chairs; on one of them sits a man who doesn't take his eyes off the boy, startling him terribly, having seen at first only a table and empty chairs out of the corner of his eye. The man sits there perfectly motionless, the back of his chair leaning against the wall, the chair's front legs suspended in the air; he's wearing brown-colored clothing and his hair is brown, like the wall behind him. Good day, says the boy, having recovered from the shock, before repeating himself when the man makes no reply, good day. The man's eyes are open, his thin hair is parted neatly in the middle, and he sports a hefty, drooping, well-trimmed mustache; he appears to be tall and thin, although it's difficult to judge from the posture of a man who's sitting, while his neck is unusually long, as if his head, with its sharp, apparently carved facial features, is perched on a stem. Good day, the boy tries for the third time, no response, is it possible that the man is newly dead? The boy doesn't dare move closer, but leans forward a bit more, and no, the eyes don't have the glassiness of a dead man's, yet it's as if they are fixed. You are, the boy begins, I mean, it's my understanding that you have books for sale? Didn't one of his eyelids move? The boy moves closer, involuntarily, the floor creaks beneath him; some floors are more loose-lipped than others and reveal every movement. The corners of the man's mouth move, but then no more, and he's just as lifeless as before. The boy swallows, has started to perspire, he's dressed for the weather and it's uncomfortable having those big, brown eyes staring at him, lifeless yet not glassy, and to have no idea what to do; should he run up to the doctor's house and get help, maybe the man is in danger, death is assailing him while the boy asks whether he sells books! Would you like me to get some help? he says, leaning forward, now look-ing directly into the man's eyes, is everything alright? he finally says, point-blank, like a fool, because everything is obviously not alright, it would be an exaggeration to claim that, particularly when a woman's voice answers, No.

She's standing in the doorway behind the counter, the corridor at her back so dark that it's as if she has stepped out of the kingdom of death itself. Sorry, says the boy, still startled by her arrival, good day, he adds. Are you certain it's so good? says the woman, step-ping out from behind the counter; she's tall, big-boned, her face too rough-hewn to be called beautiful, something harsh in her expres-sion. The boy says nothing, and indeed knows nothing. You must be one of those who delivered the mail. He nods. And you're asking about books. Yes, the boy says, apologetically, in fact, because it may not be good to have barely escaped death, to have lost his traveling companion, the third one lying bedridden, and then to ask about books, unless now is precisely the right time to ask about them? He's drunk, she says, crossing her long arms. Oh, yes, drunk, the boy says, as if that clarifies everything, as if everything becomes apparent, everything is answered, he looks at the man, who has begun to smile beneath his hefty mustache while his eyes, as well as his face, are just as distant as before, as if the smile has been painted on him as ironic decoration. Drunk, yes, although dead-drunk would be more fitting, he was afraid that the liquor would run out before the first spring shipment arrived, so drank what was left in the shop; I need to get him into bed, she adds, and the boy takes off his hat and mittens and is ready.

It takes a considerable amount of time to haul the man up. She lights a lamp in the hallway, a dim glow, and the heavy darkness turns into gray, opaque air; the boy notices that the stairs are rather steep, the topmost ones in semidarkness. The man isn't exactly heavy, but his powerlessness makes him heavier, those who do nothing are always a heavy burden, and besides that, he's tall, is constantly bumping his shins against the wall, the handrail, and halfway up the stairs he mutters something. Wait, the woman says, or rather pants, and the boy stops his slow, labored ascent, gripping the man under his armpits as the woman holds his legs, and a few moments later the man starts, his long body contracts as if in pain, as if he needs to vomit, but nothing comes out except a deep moan. I usually lug him up here alone, says the woman after they've settled him in bed, but I suppose it's better having help, thank you. She adjusts the man's limbs, pulls off his shoes, removes his jacket, having to raise him up partway in order to do so, at which he opens his eyes, just a crack, and mutters one word. Did he say Hell? the boy says. I heard Hildur, she says. Who's Hildur? says the boy without thinking, and immediately regrets it, of course; this Hildur might be someone who mustn't be named in this house, a woman whom he loves but can't win, who is dead, gone into the blue, and he drinks because he misses her so terribly much, feels the longing and emptiness that make us fragile. That would be me, the woman says, straightening up with the jacket in one hand, I'm Hildur, though he's called me by various names, and not always good ones; for that matter it may as well have been Hell. She lays the jacket aside, covers the man with a blanket, strokes his head like someone running her hands over something she's fond of, and the boy looks away. Hildur opens a drawer in a commode locked with a key, pulls out a rope, ties one end around the man's leg, the other around the commode's stout legs. That's a tough knot to undo, says the boy after she's finished tying it quickly, securely. Sigurður's all thumbs with knots, she says, straightening back up; she regards him, sleeping, bound. Do you find it strange that I should bind him? Yes, I do, the boy says; they both look at the sleeping man, dead-drunk. But you aren't asking about it? You're not curious? she says when the boy says nothing, or are people generally tied down where you come from? No, at least not with ropes, anyway, except for dogs and half-wits. The woman looks askance at the boy; they're the same height, the corners of her mouth no longer curve downward, lending her an almost beautiful air despite the fatigued lines of her face. When he wakes up, Sigurður wants liquor, and he'll do anything he can to get it, no one here in the fjord has any liquor nowadays except for the Norwegians at the whaling station, he would dash straight there, day or night, regardless of the weather, and those Norwegians always seem to have endless amounts of some sort of damn moonshine and enjoy pouring it into him when he's in such a state he couldn't care less how he's treated, last time he crawled home in the pelting rain, it's two miles and there wasn't much skin left on his knees, they'd drawn a dog's snout on each cheek of his rear end, a lot of people found it funny. I know a few men who would have laughed, the boy says, thinking of Einar from the fishing hut, his pitch-black beard; the boy's hatred of him makes his voice tremble. Yes, she says, looking at him again, and then they both look at Sigurður, who has turned his face away, as if in shame. I feel, says the boy, after taking a long look and gathering the courage to ask, as if I recognize his face, Sigurður's I mean, feel that I've seen him before, as if I know him, which, however, I don't—not at all, he concludes, biting his lip. Hildur looks at him suspiciously, you mean you don't know who he is? No, just that he's your husband and probably the shop manager here. So you need actual books? Yes, he says, surprised. She stares at him, brushes a lock of hair off her face, her hair is starting to turn gray, I thought you were trying to butter up Sigurður, people are constantly doing that, trying to soften him up by pretending to have an interest in books, it works well, so well that it won't be long before he's let go, Friðrik doesn't take such things lightly, so you came solely to get books? He nods, preferably newly published, recently, I mean, and poetry. There's little of that, the doctor and his wife are the only ones who purchase such things; there's only this volume that Sigurður's brother published, I think there's one copy left. And then it comes to the boy, the face, why he recognizes the face; Pálsson, he shouts involuntarily, excitedly, now I understand! He stares at the inebriated man as if captivated, drinks in his presence, the brother of Gestur Pálsson; he's never come as close to a poet before. Sigurður mumbles something vague and twitches, Hildur is quick to the bed, has a bowl to hand and manages to steer the spew toward it, most of it anyway. Sigurður vomits with his eyes wide open; Hildur, he says weakly, or whimpers. Yes, she says, is it bad? Yes, rather, I would say. He lies back down; have you tied me down? Yes, Sigurður. It's unnecessary. I wish that were true. He sighs. I dreamed a young man, he then says, shutting his eyes, he was young, he adds, opening his eyes, searching for Hildur but apparently seeing nothing, shuts them again, mutters something about the place whence the darkness comes, opens his eyes again, I was once so young, do you remember, Hildur? Vaguely, yes. I don't know what happened, he says, before dozing off, sunk once more into the shelter that drink provides.

Hildur accompanies the boy downstairs, reaches for a thin volume, I'm giving you this, as thanks for your help, and he gently strokes the binding, Gestur Pálsson, *Three Stories*. I need to go back up, she says, almost pushing the boy out, he barely manages to stow the little volume under his coat, reaches for his cap and mittens. I have to keep watch, he's going to throw up again and it isn't nice to suffocate in your own vomit. Do you really need to tie him down now? the boy says doubtfully, even pleadingly. She smiles, causing a dimple to appear on her right cheek, smiles briefly, but the smile soon extinguishes, the dimple becomes shallow and disappears. He's fine now, but won't be after a few hours, when he'll shout and curse at me, call me the worst names, his words will reek of smoke, but then he'll cry and implore me like a little child, except that no child cries for liquor, but thank you for helping and try to live in such a way that a woman doesn't need to tie you to the bed, it's so disgraceful, she says, locking the door behind him.

VIII

The boy wastes no time going up to the church; he takes the shortest path, having lost interest in the village, its other scattered clusters of houses, the snow-houses, ice-encrusted mounds containing lives that he'll never come to know about. First he threads a half-trodden trail, the land rises gently toward the church, which perches on a low hill above the village and cemetery full of vanished lives, bones and rotting flesh, we store death below ground and it slowly transforms into soil, the abode of earthworms, and into vegetation. During the summers the grass is a green song, and perhaps that song is man's eternity. The boy thinks of little but makes haste as if he's late for a date, yet no one awaits him except a dead woman inside the church and the dead know how to wait, they have to know how, there's nothing else to offer. Now and then he steps off the path to plod through the snow and the struggle frees him from the image of the shop manager Sigurður tied to his bed, the brother of the poet, the boy feels the volume inside his coat, plans to read it several times before sending it to María. Where is happiness, fulfillment, if not in books, poetry, knowledge? First it's Headmaster Gísli, then Reverend Kjartan in Vík, now Sigurður; whence comes their unhappiness, their frustration, and why isn't knowledge a comfort, what does it take to find happiness? he thinks, and feels anxiety spreading through him, fear in the face of life.

The sky is rather overcast, the clouds grow darker, a snowstorm is starting, but it's not as cold as on the previous days, tomorrow or the next day the snow could change to rain, spring is approaching, blessed spring, it comes to us with daylight, small birds, colors, yellow flowers and birdsong, it arrives with a rapid thaw, turning the mass of snow into several days of unbearable slush; the turf farms, some of which are covered in snow, even buried in it, become miserably soggy, beds become wet, it will be cold to sleep, cold to wake, the humidity works its way into one's bones, and how will it go then for a little girl on Vetrarströnd who coughs and coughs? The boy stops just below the church, thinks about the girl, looks out over the snow-covered houses, the wind-ruffled sea, the dark ship approaching, the sheer white mountains with their rough, pitch-black cliff-belts. How is it possible to survive in a country where the redeeming spring kills the vulnerable? Where the dark, long winter lies like a dead weight on people's dispositions and the brilliant summer so often brings disappointment; who survives such things? Durable people, assiduous, sometimes soft with self-pity and given to selfishness, but to strong dreams, as well?

The church is newish, fairly large and built of wood. Two slender dogs loiter uneasily by the door; they whine softly, don't look up though they doubtless hear the boy, it's unusual, maybe they're religious, he thinks, but then they stop whining, perk up their ears, fix their gaze on the doorknob and try to slip in as soon as the door opens. It's the priest himself who steps out, an old man who curses the dogs, tries to shoo them away, but when they don't heed him, wanting only to enter God's house, the priest kicks his right foot at the more eager of the two. Damned cur, he says angrily, but his voice is old and hardly bears the strain, nearly breaks apart. Let the children come to me, thinks the boy as the priest shuts the door tightly behind him, but leave the damn dogs outside. The priest looks away, doesn't see the boy. Is she ready, then? he asks the two men rounding the corner of the church, one holding a shovel and the other a pick, while the dogs saunter over to the boy, those who aren't allowed into church have little better to do than investigate new scents. The dog that the priest kicked looks up at the boy, wags its tail cheerfully, seemingly having forgotten what happened; is it a gift or an affliction to be able to forget humiliation so quickly? The two men mutter something in reply but have their eyes on the boy, and then the priest turns to look, is surprised at first, even confused, judging by his expression, but soon he works things out. Yes, he says, you must be one of the two delivering the mail, the younger one, and the boy nods, pulls off one of his mittens to scratch the dog behind its ear; and it starts snowing. Big, downy-soft flakes float dreamily to the ground, filling the sky with white dreams, and the priest's dark garment whitens. They were digging a grave for blessed Ásta, says the old man, nodding toward the two others, broad-faced men with somber expressions who both stare at the boy, but the priest comes over to him, lays his hand on his shoulder, and the boy smells old age blended with the odor of tobacco; the priest's blue eyes are peculiarly bright, some old eyes take on such blueness, perhaps because they're so much closer to death

than life and absorb the light of the world before their owner enters
the night behind life. The priest gazes at the boy's face, mildly and
with compassion. Have you come to pray for her? he asks, and the
boy nods, feeling it safest to lie. So very kind of you, says the priest,
patting the boy's shoulder wearily, she's going in tomorrow morning,
perhaps it would have been better to delay until the thaw, until the
spring softened the frozen ground, but Ásta is eager to get down into
it, I've dreamed about her twice. Twice, my boy, says the priest, his
hand still on the boy's shoulder, perhaps relieved to have a place to
rest. First, the night that the two of you came down, when I knew
nothing about her, and then last night. Sometimes the Lord speaks to
us through dreams, and man lives to obey the Lord. What's more, it's
quite impossible to keep her much longer in the church, and be careful that the dogs don't get in, there's not much of an odor yet, though
enough to rouse them, why doesn't someone toss some scraps to the
creatures?—kick them away if nothing else works. The priest raises
his hand, lets it drop again to the boy's shoulder, repeats twice what
he says about the dogs, says, Yes, yes, the boy should just kick them
away, and then ambles off between the two men, who have toiled for
two days digging a grave in the hard ground. The boy watches the two
diggers, the shovel and pick against their shoulders like rifles, walking close to the priest, perhaps to support him or prevent him from
being lifted into the air and vanishing into the snowfall, the old man
having turned completely white between them, looking more and
more like an old angel the further they recede, although his dark shoe
is visible each time he lifts his right foot. The dogs stare expectantly
at the boy as he grabs the doorknob, he smiles at them, opens the
door quick as a flash and slips in, outside they whine and scratch at it.

The church is tidy, but the windows are so blind with hoarfrost that
the daylight barely sifts through them. Six rows of pews on either
side, space for sixty people, is Mass ever held for a full house? Perhaps

when the Norwegians from the whaling station come out here, thirsting for the presence of God. The coffin is next to the altar, a quality wooden casket, the smell of smoke is mild yet noticeable. Hello again, the boy says softly, sitting down in a pew, it's been a mere two days since they were with her in the storm. The three of them. He, Hjalti and Jens, dragging death behind them, at times telling of their lives, sharing memories like morsels of bread, Jens least of all, he said practically nothing, and now it's just the two of them, Hjalti is lying somewhere in the snow and can no longer speak. It's uncomfortably silent in the church after the dogs stop scratching at the door; why did he come here? The boy looks around, it's a beautiful, unassuming church, with little to capture the eye, and this is how, it says somewhere, all of the world's houses of worship should be, so unassuming that they attract no attention, and thereby come not between God and man: "God dwells everywhere but in material grandeur and magnificent buildings, which are raised to the glory of man and thus divert the mind from Heaven."

The boy breathes in the cold air, the faint odor of smoke, and goes over to the coffin, feels he should say or at least think something suitable, but what is suitable? She died and left four young children and a husband, the children cry themselves to sleep. Feeling slightly agitated, he reaches out to make the sign of the cross over the coffin, stops and instead draws an incomprehensible symbol in the air, then looks around perplexed, as if expecting to find an answer, finally fixes his eyes on the altarpiece and moves closer to examine its details. Jesus is walking on the water, the apostle Peter is sinking with his hands stretched out to his Lord, and five men watch from the boat, their bearded faces displaying surprise, fear, hope. The boy looks at this image for a long time, at first somewhat distractedly but then with growing interest, because there's something unusual about it. He steps closer, and then it comes to him; he recognizes the surroundings. Recognizes the boat, and the six men manning it. And the sea. It isn't a body of water far to the world's south but the Polar Sea, here, just beyond the harbor, and he recognizes the mountains as well, white, vague in the background. The boat is rather large for a sixareen, but its shape and construction are Icelandic, and the fishermen are all wearing raincoats and woolen mittens, except for Peter, who has taken one off and is reaching out with a large, calloused hand toward Jesus, who is beardless, his face soft and affable, his delicate hand just about to reach Peter's. The Redeemer is wearing a light-colored gown and flimsy shoes, and his feet are bluish, probably due to the cold; the six men have frost in their beards.

He hears the dogs again, whining softly and a bit bitterly, as if they're lamenting, see how the world treats us, those who are nearest to God kick us, yet you call us man's best friend; how, then, do you treat your enemies? Then they stop, a woman's voice says something, the door opens, the dogs slip in eagerly, she behind them, with those green eyes of hers.

The dogs don't give themselves time to sniff the boy, yet come so close that one of them brushes against him, it's the coffin that attracts them, the smell of smoke from Ásta, they follow their noses, and their hunger, place their front paws on the coffin, lift themselves up and stand there nearly upright, like caricatures of men, sniff, wag their tails. Álfheiður has come over to the boy, they stare at the dogs. I don't know if this is right, he mutters; we hardly ever do, she says, before calling softly to the dogs, who obey, come right over to her, look up, their eyes full of guileless faith, and sure enough she reaches into her coat pocket, takes out two nice bits of blood sausage, tosses them into the aisle, and the dogs attack them, devour them so greedily that it approaches desperation, growling a bit as they do so, then look at her and wag their tails. They're starving, he says. Yes, old Arnar doesn't let them in. Who's Arnar? Their master; he hasn't let them in for two days, so they usually loiter here by the church in the hope that God might toss them some scraps. Why does he treat them so

badly? God is no friend of dogs, nor perhaps a friend of man. I meant
Arnar, says the boy after some silence; he'd tried to look at her without her noticing, but she was only interested in the dogs. Yes, well,
they quarrel regularly, which ends with Arnar throwing them out,
no matter what the weather, says that they're unreasonable, damned
slobs who think only about their own behinds. They both look at the
dogs. They know you, the boy says. I often give them something, it's
easy to make friends with dogs, you give them something to eat and
don't kick them, that's all it takes, yet it's still too much for most of us.
She pulls off her mittens, her cap and her scarf, and most definitely
has red hair. It had to be so red, of course, instead of being normal,
ash-blond, for example, or flaxen, something proper; of course it had
to be fiery red, albeit short, bobbed, in fact, but indisputably red,
probably better that she puts her scarf on again, quick as she can,
otherwise she might set the church on fire, and maybe something
else, as well. Álfheiður goes over to the coffin, stepping lightly, ever
so softly, as if effortlessly, like snow falling to the earth in still air; the
dogs follow her. Why did you come? the boy asks, he'd decided to say
something else, for example something about the dogs, that they're
from a particular family of predators, but then asks this, a highly
dubious question that could solicit a dangerous reply. I followed you,
she says, running her hand over the coffin, ordering the dogs with a
gentle gesture to sit; they obey, look up at her with their soft, broad
tongues hanging out between strong-looking, sharp teeth, you're so
beautiful, and you believe that dead folk can and will go out into
storms to seek the living, or maybe you don't believe it? I don't know,
have I said that? Yes, in your delirium, and in fragments. What one
sees and hears doesn't necessarily exist, he says. Well, there's comfort
in that. You followed me? There are several yards between them, yet
it's as if she's standing right next to him, very close, almost as close as
Ragnheiður at the hotel. What sort of man is the big one? she asks.
Jens, he says, surprised, what do you mean? Is he good, she asks,

and has suddenly become someone else; she even looks down. What do you want from him? the boy asks testily. You can't answer? The boy looks at her and breathes, it's a simple question; is the rain wet, what sort of man is the big one? He puts his hands behind his back, where he can clench his fists if he wants to, vent his feelings quietly, all of his consciousness and perception having become a battlefield upon which affection, devotion, disappointment and hatred seem to be engaged in a life-and-death struggle. So what if this red-haired girl is interested in Jens, all the women are interested in him; he's so big, so powerful, his voice is as deep as the sea, he seems so strong in his indifference. Yes, the boy says slowly, he's a good man. He says this almost against his will, his affection and devotion are the victors, though narrowly, very narrowly, his fists are transformed into sweaty palms marked by his nails. Does he beat women? this girl asks. So what if she wants to climb into bed with Jens? Or no, she absolutely mustn't do that, Jens mustn't betray Salvör, they traveled all this way together, through snow and death, only and just so that Jens might come to her, have the courage to come, find the words that would lead him to her. Jens doesn't beat anyone, the boy says, he has good hands, he has a sister who's much better than we are and his mind is on another woman; we traveled all this way, in fact, through storms and death and Hjalti died so that Jens could have his mind on her, just for that.

There she stands, by the coffin holding Ásta, if only Ásta could say something to him now, how she felt, how it was to be dead, whether she could travel over difficult ground and stroke the heads of her four children with transparent hands, could tell him whether she was completely alone in death, saw no one, heard no one, received no news, whether God existed, but this girl stands there straight as an arrow and stares at him and the dogs stare as well, and she seems on the verge of saying something, but then the door is opened and a man enters, snow is sucked in behind him, a white gust that he then shuts the door on, takes big steps, approaches them with one finger wagging, his hands bare, I knew it, he says angrily, I knew you would let the creatures in, you have no respect for anything! Someone should do himself the honor of teaching you a proper lesson!

The man brought the snow in with him, he is himself entirely white, yet he's shaken most of it off, revealing his dark form beneath the whiteness, and the snow slowly melts on the floor. It's impossible to defeat the winter; you can only survive it, or live with it. The dogs have instinctively sought shelter behind Álfheiður, who says, Yes, and you just happened to be passing, Vigfús. Hello, Vigfús says to the boy, I'm Vigfús and I live here just above the church, you're one of them? Yes, the boy says, admitting his identity for the third time that day. I'll get rid of the dogs for you, Vigfús has come over to the boy, tall, slim, his face scored and drawn by the storms of time, his highly expressive face and eyes rather large, they're as blue as holes in the sky in summer. No need, the boy says. Not a need, Vigfús says, but a necessity, as he moves toward Álfheiður and the dogs, I saw you heading this way and knew that you'd take the beasts with you into God's house and disturb this boy here in his prayers, some of us still have respect for this house, and that doesn't include you. You know, Álfheiður says, you're quite beautiful when you're angry. I'll throw the creatures out! And I'll sic them on you. Vigfús hesitates, his head wobbling slightly. *Bad man*, she says to the dogs, which immediately start growling. Don't you dare, you hussy! I'm both conscienceless and heartless, you never grow weary of telling me that, so I can hardly behave myself any differently, and the dogs don't like you, either. Why do you treat me like this? he says, his anger suddenly gone; it simply vanished, to be replaced by a sort of pleading look on his hard, scored face, what have I done to you? There, there, she says, either to him or to the dogs, who calm down, stop growling, one of them even sits down and yawns, the other stretches its snout in the direction of the coffin, sniffs, whines softly. No, that's not allowed, Vigfús says, looking helplessly at the boy, before sitting down in the front pew and staring at the altarpiece. I was here when Bjarni painted this. You're in the boat as well, she says, and then the boy notices that one of the fishermen is a spitting image of Vigfús, it's just the beard that threw him off; the same scored face, the same blue eyes. You're one of the apostles, he says, and Álfheiður laughs softly. Vigfús smiles apologetically, shyly. When I sleep, he says quietly to the boy, I'm in the boat, watching the Redeemer pulling Peter from the sea, see, he's in up to his knees and continues to sink up to his armpits, but then the Redeemer pulls him up so lightly, together they walk over to us, and then, as we haul in the fish, plump and handsome cod, he tells us beautiful stories of benevolence and sacrifice. What stories, she asks, those old ones? No, stories that I've never heard any priest tell, but I forget them just as soon as I open my eyes. Can't you start to tell them before you open your eyes, even just the beginning of one? I always wake up alone, as you know, and I have no one to talk to; I told you that you shouldn't have brought the creatures in; are you angry? The dog that sat down and yawned has started to sniff the haunches of the other dog, which must be a bitch, at first distractedly, bored, but then the smell excites it, it whines, tries to mount the bitch, its mouth hanging open with excitement, and the bitch turns away while still sniffing the coffin. This is a church, Vigfús says, looking on, and this is a dead woman! But this is the only real way to defeat death, she says, and smiles. I feel sorry for you, says Vigfús when he sees the smile, you're in darkness, this boy here risked his life to bring the woman over here and you let dogs fuck under the coffin. *Damn you!* shouts Vigfús at the animals, who stop abruptly; the bitch sits down, the dog turns in circles before sitting down, as well, giving the humans what seems like a half-apologetic look, as if wishing to say, But it's just so good. Álfheiður had sat down beside the boy, putting him between the two of them. You should move in with me, Vigfús says, and the boy opens his mouth to reply, without having any idea what his reply should be, why on earth should he move in with this man? You're married, she says. It's not my fault. Did you get married in a dream? She tricked me, Vigfús says. You still live in the same house; am I supposed to sleep between you?

We don't sleep together, you know that.

But why do you live still with her?

It's bad to be alone; so many things dwell in the darkness.

Get a dog.

You don't understand the Lord, you don't want to sail with Jesus.

Yet you still want me.

Those eyes of yours, Vigfús says hopelessly, staring at the altarpiece. The Devil has green eyes, she says. I know, sighs Vigfús, I just can't help myself. The bitch has curled up in a ball, tries to sleep, the dog looks from the bitch to the people and back, stands up, sits down, whines softly, poignantly, poor me, it says, this is so difficult, it says, and then starts in again sniffing the bitch's rear, sticking its snout as closely to it as possible.

Vigfús: This isn't good.

The boy, softly: He thinks it is.

Vigfús: Jesus is with us, he sees us, he judges us. We can't allow this. Did you come to pray or to watch dogs fuck?

The boy: I didn't come to pray, I just wanted to talk to Ásta.

Vigfús: She's dead, my boy.

So is Jesus, the boy says, blurting it out, as if the Devil were inside him, spitting something into his blood. Dear God, Vigfús says, God help you, saying such things. Everything would be better, and different, Álfheiður says, watching the dog, which has started licking the bitch, if Jesus had been a woman. God sent his Son, says Vigfús resolutely, but he watches as well. The boy glances over to get a better look at her, at the band of freckles, her lips, the lower one broader, as if it's holding up the upper one. No, get down, Vigfús says hopelessly as the dog remounts the bitch, who acts as if she can't be bothered to resist any longer and simply accepts him, the dog whines with joy and its rear end starts pumping madly, like an independent body part, its jaws gaping. If God had actually wanted to change the world, Álfheiður says, he would have sent his daughter, not his son. The daughter of God would have brought out all the worst in humankind; she would have been beaten and disgraced and humiliated, and the Romans would have raped her before her crucifixion. She would have exposed the worst in us and it might have worked to change us. You men wouldn't have been able to avoid trying to understand what it means to be a woman, what we've had to endure, what it means to be the underdog, always, what it means to be born second-class. But God doesn't understand women, and therefore sent his son.

This is what she says, with the boy sitting between her and Vigfús and the dogs humping beneath the coffin. And then it's done. I don't feel well, says Vigfús outside the church; the dogs run around them happily, won't you come with me? I'll tell Kristín to leave; she sleeps in the kitchen anyway so won't be in our way. You don't desire me, just the sin, she says, stroking this tall man, stroking his cheek; she has thin, work-swollen fingers, and a shiver passes through Vigfús, he feels something but it's not clear what, while her hair is so red that the boy daren't look, then she puts on her scarf and her cap, and the two of them walk off toward the doctor's house while Vigfús plods home, the dogs remain behind at the church, hot from the sex and the running. In the doctor's house lies Jens; he's big and she's thinking about him. An old Arabic medical text says that the human heart is divided into two compartments, one called happiness, the other despair. What are we to believe?

IX

When the boy returns, Jens is sleeping, trembling slightly, as if dreaming of loneliness. There is no Hell, just loneliness, all else pales in comparison to it, the grasses of life wither, and we tremble at the thought. The boy sits on his bed and watches this big man tremble. They'd walked quietly side by side, she walked like the woman you dream of, but was thinking of another man, of course. Luckily. She's a penniless maid with a child, he has nothing and would betray his parents, their lives, dreams, if he went and lived with green eyes, red hair and a child, destitute, every single day would be a grind, both on land and at sea, he would haul in the lines in frost and rain, watch his hands age, swell, crack, transform into old stones, no education, knowledge, just toil and hardship, the hardship that has narrowed horizons, reduced dimensions. Just as well that her mind is on Jens and not me, thinks the boy, yet that isn't particularly good either, all it does is hurt, hurt very much, in fact, and then he can't bear being inside any longer, goes back out into the snow, vanishes in the snowfall, hides himself among snowflakes that carry silence and cold between them. He doesn't consider where to go, or in what direction, and he hasn't gone far when the snow starts to turn into sleet, the weather is warmer, the snow wilts, becomes wet, it turns as gray as hopelessness, and the boy finds himself on the mountainside above the house. That's how spring arrives. What was white and soft becomes gray and wet. If the snowfall is the sorrow of angels, sleet is the Devil's spit; everything becomes wet, heavier, the snow becomes an abominable slush. The boy stands on the mountainside, his head bent, like a horse, recalls his journey with Jens, from the time he was informed of it in Geirþrúður's parlor; he was promised an education, adventures, and then sent off on a long journey with a man who doesn't know how to talk. He stands there and becomes wet. Little by little the whiteness fades around him, spring is arriving and he recalls the entire journey. Stands for a long time on the mountainside, there's so much that happened yet he's precisely the same there on the slope as when he set off, still with uncertainty in place of blood. Nothing had happened, except that a child had coughed badly on Vetrarströnd; he'd been given an unexpected glimpse into the dreams of the child's mother, María, the book that he got for her, short stories by Gestur Pálsson, is in the house by his bed, but what accompanies books besides death and gloom, what do they do but remind us of what we don't have? Bárður is in the ground in the countryside where he grew up, he who was everything is no longer anything but a name on a cross, nothing left of that world but regret and memories, and Reverend Kjartan goes out into the night, hears a peculiar sound, as if something from Hell has come to fetch him, unless it's God calling to him from a great distance, and Anna, his wife, is nearly blind and maybe that's why he's stopped touching her, and all their dreams are dead, extinguished. Dreams light man's way, they're the brightness around him, without them it's darkness, and if you stop dreaming, you know what happens; you'll know where the darkness in man comes from. Sleet blows over the boy, who does little else than think about red hair, green eyes, how she walked, no one can walk like her, who had a child out of wedlock, and besides that thinks of Jens, who is very big but trembles in his sleep. The boy looks up into the sleet and toward the ravine, focuses his mind on Hjalti, with whom he lived for two days and nights, hardly knew him at all yet perhaps knew him better than most, and now Hjalti is lying dead somewhere in the sleet, spring will thaw his frozen body, ravens and foxes will be drawn to the smell, a large amount to eat in such a big man. The boy shuts his eyes yet nothing comes to him except for what she said about the world being different if Jesus had been a woman, disgraced by man before ascending into the light, dear God how he longs to love a person who thinks like that. He opens his eyes and weeps a little. It's sleeting, everything turns wet, gray, the sea churns and the drowned talk about spring, the nights when all is bright, when the world has changed into blue eternity, and somewhere, at a depth of eighty yards, sits his father and lets the fish nibble at him, shuts his eyes and imagines that he's still alive, not drowned, not at the bottom of the sea, and that she's kissing him, cold kisses at eighty yards deep, his skull creaks beneath the weight of the sea, the same weight that holds him down at the bottom, in the loneliness of death, through eternity, throughout black eternity, unless the boy begins to live.

X

Ólafur's unlikely to come before tonight, says Steinunn to the boy when he's done eating, although he ate almost nothing, just picked at his food like a baby bird, and for it faced Þórdís' reprimands, he who eats little is less of a man, he who's always looking down at his lap lacks pluck. He wanted to go upstairs, lie down, fall asleep, flee into his dreams, to sleep is to escape, but then Steinunn says that Ólafur's unlikely to come before tonight and asks whether the boy wouldn't like to come and sit in the family room with her, it's boring to be alone, and he goes in with her, feels that it would be rude not to, doesn't dare refuse though shyness is like a constant drone within him, what could they possibly talk about?

Here's where we were sitting when you crashed into the house; she points at a sofa and wide chair, almost as if showing him to a seat, but he's drawn to the book cabinet, a heavy, carved cabinet holding around a hundred books. Mostly old sins from our life in Copenhagen, she says, we lived there for eight years, I occasionally miss the commotion that comes with crowds, I miss the spires, the theaters, the concerts. She looks thoughtfully at the boy, then asks about Geirþrúður, although cautiously, as if not quite knowing how to ask. How is it to live there? she tries. It's nice, is all he says, desperately longing to touch the books but feeling uncomfortable about doing so while she's looking at him as she is. But what business is it of mine? she says, after asking her third or fourth question, listening to replies that are hardly replies, the woman can have her own life as far as I'm concerned, but one is instinctively curious about such a woman, about those who are different; go right ahead and look at the books, she adds, and that's what he does, those old sins from the city of Copenhagen, which Steinunn misses, and instead of asking more about Geirþrúður she starts telling the boy about her life with her husband in that city, thirty years ago. She sits on a chair with her back to the organ, speaking about a past time that she and her husband have recalled on many an occasion when the winter was longest, the darkness so heavy that the lamps smoked as if they were on the verge of suffocation, it was then that they'd spoken of a bygone era, relived the moments, some repeatedly, and so often that they're slowly turning threadbare, like a Sunday dress that is inadvertently worn too frequently and loses its charm. But now she has new ears, which changes everything, almost as if she'd never recalled some of it; if only Ólafur were here to relive it as well. She talks and he listens, and then she plays the organ.

Turns around, works the pedals, plays notes that seem descended from a distant night, warm twilight, music creates more space in our breasts, it can create new skies, new hope, without it human beings are impoverished. Oh, it's such a cursed wreck now, Steinunn says, after time has passed and the boy has sunk into a Russian story in Danish, he understands barely half of it but can't stop, cursed wreck, she repeats, stroking the organ affectionately, it has to be taken to the church from time to time and in all types of weather, such journeys aren't good for organs. I'll play a bit tomorrow for your Ásta; it can certainly do with loosening up a bit, she says, before playing more, while he continues to read about a highly neurotic young man, they may be peers, but this one seems to be starving, in wretched shape and poor. People out in the world suffer as well. They're poor and starving; life is a long and difficult road. Outside the sleet turns gradually into rain, dense rain, the May evening is nearly dusky and the hour is late. I hope Ólafur doesn't catch cold in this wet weather, she says, and stops playing, shuts the organ, it becomes a box around silent eternity. They leave the family room and there she sits, on the lowest stair, with a sleeping child, a three-year-old girl who lies there breathing open-mouthed, with fine, light-colored hair and small fingers that hold onto Álfheiður's brown dress, not letting go even in a dream. You're sitting here, girl, says Steinunn in surprise, why? I thought she might fall asleep quicker to the music, says Álfheiður, rising gently to her feet so as not to wake the child, so as to torment the boy who has a hard time falling asleep; he tosses and turns in bed, she stood up so softly, glanced at him with her green eyes, hopefully I'll get away tomorrow, he mutters to his pillow, gets out of bed, looks out into the rain that darkens the evening, just barely makes out the outline of the schooner anchored outside the harbor, and then comes night. Night, night, night.

XI

Spring and its light come through the rain and wake the boy. He stands at the window for a long time, barefoot, cold timber beneath his feet, gazes out into the rain-gray light, at the transparent drops that penetrate the white snow.

Jens is nowhere to be seen, someone has made his bed, Þórdís or Álfheiður. My salvation, thinks the boy, for knowing what I want. Then he goes down and there sits Jens, prepared for travel, no matter what Ólafur says; everything opposes your leaving, all common sense, but Jens says nothing, just drinks the coffee that Þórdís brings him, touching him as if by accident, this big, silent man. But of course it's rarely been thought useful in this country to heed common sense, Ólafur says, unusually sharply, but it doesn't bother Jens and Þórdís says, there is such a thing as manliness, it hasn't completely disappeared yet, and in the meantime we're not going to die, and she touches Jens again because it's good to touch what's big and solid; Steinunn notices it and looks away. I was hoping that manliness had already killed enough people, Ólafur says wearily, leaning his head against the wall; it's done a lot of that. That's right, the boy says unexpectedly, and so enthusiastically that he's on his feet, he'd just sat down but stands up as if he's about to make a speech and everyone looks at him in surprise, these four people, the doctor and his wife, Þórdís and Jens, who smiles faintly. I'm leaving today if I can manage it, says Jens after the boy sits back down, it's urgent, he adds, and Þórdís reaches over but doesn't dare touch him again, without a pretext; she withdraws her hand, catches Steinunn's eye and the maid's face hardens, turns to stone. Ólafur sighs, having just returned home from a difficult house call, a young woman in labor. He went north with the woman's husband, along the entire course of the ravine, through a difficult pass, they climbed high, the sleet turned to snow, the snow back to sleet, they crossed high heaths in the uncertain darkness of the spring night, but heard a plover on the way down, two plovers, which was so unexpected that Ólafur had to stop and sit, overcome as he was with tears. He kept his head lowered to hide his tears from the farmer, who stared uneasily through the sleet toward home, as if to send his gaze ahead, let it brush the little window above his wife's bed, opened and closed his hands inside his mittens, could barely refrain from shouting at the doctor that he could rest later, that rest for him here on the mountain could mean death for his wife, and then two children would be motherless, the newborn possibly the third, leaving him alone with his ailing mother, stared through the sleet and again they heard the plovers. Ólafur leaned forward, as if to crouch down on all fours, sobbed softly, the first plover song of the year, unusually late, even here, a few bright, slightly melancholy notes through sleet and snow, maybe life never gives in and perhaps is nowhere as strong as in birdsong during a cold spring. Ólafur opens his eyes in the kitchen, he managed to save the woman, and the child, but then had to go to another farm, spent four hours there, where practically the entire household was bedridden, undernourished, the farmer almost blue in the face, no food left but spoiled seabird, and nothing else had been eaten there the past few weeks; as soon as he returned, Ólafur sent men out, seven in number, with a large sledge to carry the family down to the village. One man would have to stay behind to tend the livestock, slaughter the beasts that were at the end of their tethers, the other six would return with the family and would hardly be bored along the way, the farmer and his wife know loads of verses and stories and ballads and thrive on sharing them, the fellowship energizes them.

We're leaving today, then? asks the boy. Yes, it looks as if we are, on board the schooner that came here to pick up some things.

But use is to be made of the boy before they leave, to help them move the organ onto a custom-made pallet and carry it over to the church. Through the rain, the snow, the slush, it's eight degrees outside, Steinunn says, having entered the figure in the weather log that she's kept for eighteen years, recording wind direction, wind speed, temperature, cloud cover, the condition of the sea, facts of which we have desperate need, using them to explain the world, to endure life, these nearly empty facts that explain nothing. Nor were these purely weather logs except during the first two, three years, before she gradually yielded to the urge to scribble down a few events of the day and sometimes, as if by the by, how her heart was beating as well. Tomorrow she'll write about the boy, something about the way he stood next to the bookshelf, something about his eyes, that it might be difficult to forget them, about Þórdís, who had to watch Jens leave without getting to touch him again, how Þórdís had missed out on so much of life that her heart had hardened, perhaps from bitterness, perhaps in order to survive. Sometimes it's intolerable that I should feel so sorry for her that I'm incapable of letting her go, writes Steinunn, before adding something about birdsong on a mountain, what it can do to a person; she writes, she's filled a total of nine books, and there will be more, sixteen in all, and they won't be lost, the life that words preserve in them will find its way to us.

Bringing the organ out is time-consuming, the space is so constricted that there's only room for two people to carry it, the boy and a man called upon from next door, the boy forgets his name as soon as it's mentioned. A silent man who keeps his head down, perhaps to conceal his sarcastic look; he kicks twice at the organ, but stealthily, as if to express his disapproval. Jens has to settle for watching, which is difficult, to be so useless; he's hardly capable of more than standing on his own two feet. The boy hears Þórdís say something about himself, he doesn't know what but her tone doesn't escape him, and it makes him angry, fills him with curses and energy, and he's sweaty but relieved when they finally manage to coax the organ out. Yes yes, Ólafur says into the air, while Steinunn is quick to spread a cover over the instrument. We should perhaps get two more men to help, Ólafur says, clutching his broad lower back; you take the lightest corner, Steinunn says, and be careful of your back. They position themselves at the corners, the boy, the silent man, Ólafur and Þórdís, who has a foul look on her face. It's quite a way to the church, over wet snow, they bend to lift the pallet but then notice a big man trudging up to the house, bareheaded, gray-haired, with a full, hoary beard and eyes that are nearly black; he shouts something, sounding extremely happy for some reason. Þórdís looks around, perhaps in an attempt to locate the source of his happiness, yet lacking the right eyes for it. Holy shit, says the boy in surprise, because it's Brynjólfur, the skipper of the *Hope*, the schooner owned by Snorri the merchant, and Brynjólfur doesn't reek of alcohol as he grabs at the boy and lifts him up as lightly as an empty sack.

Now the carrying will be easier. The skipper replaces Ólafur, who again clutches his lower back as if to excuse himself, and Steinunn runs her hand over his shoulder, it's alright, says her hand, it's not muscles that make you a man, and they never have done. But the organ and pallet are heavy, they feel it, the boy and the silent man who spits regularly and breathes heavily, Brynjólfur looks around as if to kill time, feels no weight, Þórdís stands straight-backed, no change there, Jens follows at a slight distance and feels the humiliation in every step, pain and weakness. They've come a good way when the boy sets eye on Álfheiður; there's a man with her, carrying the child on his shoulders, his strength is apparent even from this distance, and he grows more handsome the closer they come, chatting, smiling, and it's good, of course, that someone still knows how to smile in this world, a smile can rend the darkness, it lights up the world, but the boy's heart contracts into a pebble; afterward he'll go down to the shore and skip his heart across the surface of the sea, watch it skip several times before sinking, and then he'll be free from that idiotic, disturbing organ.

It's a Norwegian from the whaling station, one of the main voices in the choir; Álfheiður, sent to fetch him, didn't mind doing so at all. The little girl is delighted on the man's shoulders, grinning broadly and holding on tight to his full head of hair, but her smile fades and then vanishes when she's put down in front of the church, everything grows unreasonably large and people change into giants, she hangs her head, too shy to look up and reveal her eyes, which is a pity, because if anything can save us it's the eyes of a three-year-old child, the most valuable things that humankind has; the most sensitive, the strongest can be found in their glance, we should never make important decisions without looking into such eyes. Her mother, on the other hand, doesn't hide her green eyes, but prefers to squander them on this Norwegian, who is both tall and sturdy looking, limber, with clear blue eyes thick dark hair, all of his teeth are in perfect condition and he displays them unsparingly, his voice is pleasantly deep. I've probably always hated Norwegians, thinks the boy. They carry the organ into the church, leaving the rain and the dogs outside.

Ásta is lying in her coffin, she's dead, misses her children, but the boy sits down quickly and concentrates on hating all Norwegians and everything Norwegian, the mountains, forests, animals, the finger that Headmaster Gísli sometimes carries around with him, the whaling stations and whaleboats scattered around the fjords here, whale carcasses and decaying viscera on the beaches. Then Steinunn starts pumping the organ. To get the chill out of it, she says, as the priest scratches his head, surprised at the absence of so many choir members. Yes, Ólafur says, they're fetching some people for me, and Sigurður can't go anywhere right now. What, why not? the priest asks accusingly, because Sigurður's absence is bothersome, he's the lead singer, the most important voice, beautiful as twilight or silver in shadow. He's drunk, the wretch, Þórdís says. I'm afraid so, confirms Ólafur. He's a wretch, repeats Þórdís, and has hardly done a decent day's work in his life. Could we have expected anything else? she adds, while Steinunn plays to loosen up the organ, to work the uncertainty out of it. Work ennobles a man. Proverbs, idioms, contain the wisdom of the ages, the results of the lives of many generations, a mishmash of messages from the past to the present, carved and polished into the right words so that they aren't forgotten, aren't lost, don't slip away over time, and where would we be without knowledge of the past? Work ennobles a man, too true, but it's also dubious nonsense. Work has kept us alive, but what ennobles us is the sacrifice, being able to overcome our egos, what ennobles us is being there for someone else, taking hold of an outstretched hand. Where are we without song? the priest says, after they've listened for some moments, and he stares into space as if he's suddenly remembered everything that he's missed out on, remembered that life is passing, that he'd been given his life, but it's turned out as it has done. Where is the beauty, the grandeur, the adventure? Perhaps he's thinking of his wife, lying at home, decrepit from old age; some days, the worst ones, she seems to emit a slight odor of decay, lying there day and night, humming old verses that she's known for seventy years or more, having sung them when she was two years old and living safe and sound with her mother, in the never-ending world of childhood. He once loved her, it's true, but for a short time, just one or two years, loved her long, fair hair, resembling sunshine, the light of spring, loved her full lips, so perfectly soft for kissing, her smiling eyes, small breasts that fit so well in his hands, how her nipples swelled at the moment he touched them, which he did often, feeling as if he could never have enough of doing so, yet it had happened: he'd had enough, more than enough. Who stole the love? he thinks, and why so quickly? Just a few months, one or two years, and he'd gone back to looking at other women, his life one long struggle to restrain his eyes, too cowardly to do anything other than look, or else he had too powerful a conscience, we sometimes confuse these two, conscience and cowardice, which isn't a good thing. I let life go by, never grabbed it, except for a short time ages ago; it's cowardice not to dare to live, paltriness, what will the Lord say to me? Is someone calling for me? he thinks, looking up hesitantly, having lost track of time and place, he'd sat down in the front pew, next to the coffin, breathed in the smell of smoke, Þórdís is standing before him and saying something, she's energetic, that's certain, and has lovely breasts, nothing lacking there either, but look her in the eye, he admonishes himself, she's a parishioner and needs guidance, I mustn't fail others though I've failed myself. And he lifts his old head, his cloudy eyes glance out from beneath his bushy gray brows. Þórdís, can I help you, my dear? he asks, his head clearing in that same moment, his surroundings open up to him and he remembers everything, gets ponderously to his feet, we can survive without a voice, he says, trying to make his own voice clearer, pretending not to notice the others' glances. I can sing, I have a voice, Brynjólfur says loudly, as Jens steps back instinctively.

The ceremony isn't long, just a few words about life and death, a few familiar old words, far too familiar, nothing happens if we always use the same words, if we take the same route, the gap between life and death grows no larger, we don't cleave the darkness any better, we find no solutions but rather stop and gradually change into dim shadows. Ásta deserves so much better, thinks the boy, than old, worn-out words, blunt thoughts. Then, unfortunately, he can no longer think, because she sits down next to him, with those eyes, that damn hair, which is as short as it was yesterday, sits down next to him along with her daughter, though there was plenty of room elsewhere, Jens sits in a different pew off to the side, the silent man with the sarcastic expression in the rearmost pew next to the aisle, the boy shuts his eyes, tries to doze, as if to demonstrate that this is of no interest to him, not the people, living or dead, not the words, not her short hair, even less her earlobe, which he sees when he glances over quickly at her profile. Glances quickly at her, then looks down at his fingers, which tremble and mutter to each other, we've never experienced anything like this. The choir does its best to keep in tune, but it takes the organ a long time to regain its composure, before running off with the choir in hot pursuit until it turns piercingly false, at which point the choir halts, and then nothing is heard but the unruly music, the sounds as Steinunn, concentrated, pumps the organ's pedals. For a time however it's as if the instrument gives up on the music and can only complain about its lot, to be so distant from a pristine tone. Álfheiður leans against the boy, who for some reason has a lump in his throat; such sounds, she says softly when the organ complains the loudest, would be made if God used us as organs.

Was that the reason for the lump in his throat, that man is an imperfect instrument, a poorly tuned organ, and therefore rarely attains a pristine tone in life?

Brynjólfur, however, smiles the entire time. Happy in his singing, in the great depths of his bass voice, giving fully of himself, caring only about the sound he himself makes and thus carrying the tune, his eyes fastened on Steinunn as if she's the best thing he's ever seen. He can sing, Álfheiður says. The Norwegian? asks the boy, almost aggressively, but she smiles. No, or yes, Jan can sing, but I meant the skipper, that big man. His name is Brynjólfur, the boy says, and I'm

leaving on his ship later today. Yes, you're leaving, she says, looking at the boy, but nothing more. And then the daughter, who has
been regarding him for some time and has come to the conclusion
that there's no need to be shy with him, says, My name is Salvör, are
you going far away, do you have a home somewhere? And he, who'd
once had a little sister who sometimes laughs and cries in his dreams,
says, Salvör, what a beautiful name, but I'm not sure if I have a home
anywhere. Me neither, whispers the girl in return, as the singing
stops. The priest has stopped speaking, he's put aside the old words,
the old implements, the gap-toothed rakes that rake badly, and then
Steinunn starts pumping the organ's pedals once more, she's soaked
with sweat, plays a two-hundred-year-old song, forgets everything in
her zeal to achieve a tone pristine enough for the woman lying in the
coffin, who died and left her children and husband behind, died and
left life, the least that the living can do for the dead is achieve a passably
pristine tone, the least and the most. Álfheiður glances at the boy, just
a quick glance, but one glance can easily make the difference between
happiness and despair, that's how it is, this is what we have learned: it
is, first and foremost, the minor incidents, nearly invisible in time, that
make the difference between nothing and everything.

It's a pity that no one wept, says the priest when everything is finished,
the coffin down in its narrow, shallow grave, although the dogs had
to be scolded as it was borne out, not much dignity in that, and Ásta
shifted slightly in the coffin, which was too wide and too long. None
of those present will ever forget her, not because of the sorrow she left
behind, the children, the flickers of light in her life, not because of her
industriousness, but because of the smell of smoke, the excited dogs,
because she shifted in her coffin as they lowered it into the grave,
and because the Norwegian merrily hummed a Christmas tune to
himself, without realizing what he was doing. I'm going to remember
you differently, thought the boy. The Norwegian is at least six feet tall

and carries himself so well that all the Icelanders seem to pale beside him. The boy notices Álfheiður fiddling with a red lock of hair, pushing it behind her ear. It's always better when people weep at funerals, the priest says, but no one had wept. They'll be weeping for her somewhere else, perhaps for a long time, Steinunn says, and then the organ is carried back, someone escorts the old priest home. How was it? asks his wife, turning in bed in the vain hope that it will alleviate the pain and the weariness. Oh, she smelled so much of smoke that no one wept, he says. I have the feeling that we were all thinking of smoked lamb, no better than the dogs, and he sits down ponderously at his wife's side and strokes the back of her hand, not that he necessarily wants to; he simply has no other place in the world.

XII

The human body is a stupid beast that we drag along through time, like a heavy memory.

The boy's heart has hardly beaten since she sat down next to him in the church, yet many minutes have passed. He's holding onto the corner of the pallet supporting the organ, it's raining, and she walks away with the Norwegian and her daughter; the doctor's house draws nearer. It's a fact that the human heart has two chambers, which is why it's possible to love two people at the same time. Biology makes it possible, demands it, some would say, but our consciences, consciousness, tell us a different story, which can make everyday life unbearably burdensome. As they say goodbye to the doctor and his wife, the boy considers asking Ólafur for a gun so that he can shoot himself through the chamber suddenly and mercilessly occupied by the girl with green eyes and hair that's far too short. Wouldn't he then be made whole, and shouldn't everyone else do the same thing, eliminate one of the chambers of their hearts, cut it away?

Þórdís bids Jens farewell with a handshake, firmly, presses her palm solidly into his, as if to gain a piece of him, his life, presses hard, be with me, says her palm, perhaps, don't leave me behind, and Jens presses back, but not as hard. Steinunn hugs the boy, it's impossible not to embrace this boy, she'll write later that evening, following an undemonstrative description of the rain, the wind, the temperature, the look of the sea and how the clouds change, how the organ sounded, how the people sang, impossible not to hold, squeeze tightly and protect, because sometimes he's like an infant who can't speak yet, and sometimes also something completely different that I don't understand. Damn it all, I don't know whether such people belong in this country in the first place. I don't know whether they're a mistake, or an attempt at a correction. Remember to discuss this with Óli.

But there goes the boy, his idiotic body between two giants, Brynjólfur and Jens. The skipper is cheerful, summer is on its way, and he'll sail and the sea is his friend, it never betrays you, is whole and pure, whether conditions are calm and still or there are storms and death. All that cast a shadow was his inability to procure liquor. Sigurður's tied up and can't come, his wife had said when Brynjólfur had asked after the tall shop manager who'd previously provided the skipper and other honest men with liquor when everywhere else was dry. Liquor, the woman had repeated, mimicking Brynjólfur, almost as if she didn't know what he meant and needed to say the word out loud, at least twice, to understand it; well, no, we ran out ages ago, you're going to sea, anyway, and hardly need liquor in the meantime, I'd have thought. You're absolutely right, Brynjólfur had said, although he'd come here only for the liquor, and decided to sail right away to the whaling station, the Norwegians probably had some moonshine, but then he stopped, had the feeling that she was standing at the window, watching him. I'll survive a couple of days, he thought, anything else would be pitiful. He changed course and immediately felt as if he'd won a victory, headed up to the doctor's house, saw a crowd of people there and something that resembled an organ, strange as that might be, beneath the open sky.

They walk down to the shore, a bit too quickly for Jens, although he manages to keep up and even tries to pass the boy, but every step hurts and he's nearly lurching his way forward by the time the boy realizes how fast he's going and slows down, coughing to restart his heart, get it to beat normally instead of quiver like a peculiar little animal. Brynjólfur goes to find someone to row them out to the ship, and then who should happen to be on the beach but her and her daughter, not a Norwegian in sight, they're looking for shells, and she comes over to them. The mountains can't be seen very clearly in the rain, their outlines are grainy in places, and they quiver as well, in rhythm with the little beast in his chest, he has to fight against dizziness and nausea, hears little, senses little, except that all five of them are in a little boat, it happened somehow, the three of them, her and her daughter, and Álfheiður rows. They both smile—the mother at the effort, the daughter at life. The former is speaking to Brynjólfur, but it's impossible to hear anything beyond the restlessness in the mountains. The boy is the last to board the ship, he smiles at the little girl and is smiled at in return, so beautiful and pure, with even a hint of dimples, that his dizziness subsides a bit, he hears the sea once more, its surge, notices Álfheiður hand Jens a letter while saying something, softly, and Jens hesitates, no, is startled, which is understandable, there's nothing pleasant, naturally, about being loved by such green eyes and short red hair, let alone when he should only be thinking of a woman who waits beyond mountains and heaths.

Men are beasts, she'd said to Jens, weeping, can I trust you? she'd asked, and Jens had answered, Yes, with great conviction, but the human heart is divided into two chambers, it isn't unified.

Jens barely manages to make it up onto the ship, the boy has to help him carefully, so that the boat doesn't capsize, and then he follows him up, but she says something and looks at him. I can't hear anything for the mountains, he says, or thinks, there may not be any difference, and he adds, in thought or words, the mountains are quivering and filling the air with their whine.

He's come aboard, she rows away, fast.

XIII

A ship sailing on a fair wind is like music. The ribs creak, the salted timber, the sails are swollen with wind, this air that moves beneath stars and sun, and it has stopped raining. The *Hope* sails, leaves Sléttueyri behind, there's a boat on shore and she rowed it, the hands that could have been his beginning and then a heavy end, held the oars. Man is born to love; the foundation of life is that simple. This is why the heart beats, that strange compass, and because of it we're able to make our way easily through the densest fogs, with danger at every hand, because of it we stray and die of exposure in beaming sunshine.

He watched her walk up to the doctor's house with her daughter, they held hands and it was beautiful. Then they disappeared into the house. She who thinks of Jens, a beautiful Norwegian, I'm going to forget her, the boy muttered to the wind, which gripped his words and scattered them throughout the blue air, which the *Hope* cleaves like music. They leave Sléttueyri behind, that sparse village, a few snow-beaten houses that the spring has started to thaw, and he goes down to Jens. Jonni, the bald cook, had taken it upon himself to nurse the mailman; a cheerful man, this Jonni, so open and vibrant that he can seldom conceal his emotions, unlike his shipmates, who never display them, not knowing how to, not daring to do so, except when drunk, at which time their tough skin is stripped off and emotions appear, uncomfortably naked. It was plain that Jonni was none too happy about the condition of Jens, who was brought down to the forecastle, wrapped in a blanket, given a warm drink, some nasty concoction of Jonni's. Damn disgusting, admitted the cook, but it does the trick, my grandma raised my grandpa from the dead three times with this, and regretted it each time. And Jens empties the mug, shivering from the cold and horror at the taste, and then lies down. Are you cold? the boy says. One chamber of his heart hates Jens, the other is so fond of him that the boy feels like crying, they traveled together through Hell, to the end of the world, saw life, found death, the tie that binds them will never be broken, fate tied them together and no one can unravel the knot, neither men nor devils. I feel like I'm lying in a glacial crevasse, hisses Jens, having to hiss in order to get the words out in one piece. You're not going to die, says the boy, one of the chambers of his heart; it isn't allowed. Do you think I'm a fool? Jens says, and then they say nothing, while the ship is music; they need no words. Do you think I'm that much of a fool as to go and die on you? Because beyond the snowy heaths where it's raining now awaits she who had asked, What will you do when you return?, who had bid Jens farewell with those words, and now he understands, lying in an icy crevasse, that she was in fact asking about a beginning or an end, she was saying that there was no in-between anymore. Kiss you, he'd answered, like a fool, and could almost have added, he sees it now, sinking deeper into the crevasse, kiss you and die. Die and leave her behind, alone, and even farther away, beyond more heaths, awaits his father, old, tired, with half-clouded eyes constantly filling with tears, without warning, for no apparent reason, maybe a memory that's begun to quiver, and his sister Halla, with her cloudless questions, when is Jens coming?, why hasn't he come?, and his father moans in his sleep, moans with fear and anxiety because Jens should have come long ago, without him they're lost, paupers, the human world is unjust to those who are weak, it's corrupt with cruelty and greed. Jens is lying in an icy crevasse, stringing together curse words because he intends to live.

Bárður also intended to live; he was going to go to Copenhagen with Sigríður, who has dark hair and a warm laugh, she laughs like a night in June, or laughed that way, that is, before the frost and the sea turned everything cold. Now Bárður is down in the ground, Sigríður put the raincoat that he forgot into the coffin, in case another sea voyage awaited him on the other side. He left, cheerful and strong, in the winter, returned, dead and destitute, in the spring. The boy has come up on deck, settles himself in a sheltered place, looks, thinks, as the sky starts to cleanse itself and the sun arrives, not a white and cold winter sun but a yellow spring sun. Now the winter is retreating, leaving behind a huge amount of melting snow; the boy looks northwards, somewhere there, beyond the horizon, the ice stretches endlessly, it's there that the winter retreats, waiting patiently for the short summer to pass.

MAN'S HEAVENLY STRING?

There are very few things that man needs: to love, to be happy, to eat; and then he dies. Yet there are over six thousand languages spoken in the world—why do there need to be so many in order to make such simple desires understood? And why do we manage it so rarely, why does the light in words fade as soon as we write them down? One touch can say more than all the world's words, that's true, but the touch fades with the years and then we need words again, they're our weapons against time, death, forgetfulness, unhappiness. When man spoke his first word he became the thread that quivers eternally between evil and goodness, Heaven and Hell. Words were what hewed the root between man and nature, they were the serpent and the apple, what lifted us from the beautiful ignorance of beasts into a world that we still don't understand. History says that once, near the beginning of time, the difference between a word and its meaning had hardly been measurable, but words have worn down over the course of man's journey, and the distance between words and meanings has grown so much that no life, no death, seems capable of bridging it any longer.

But words are simply all we have.

Here we've wandered, pale specters, for almost an entire century, dead, invisible, alone. Others who died were put into the ground and didn't come up again. It could be painful. Lips that we'd kissed, hair that we'd stroked, hands that we'd protected, all this went into the ground, did not come back, turned to nothing. But we neither sank into the ground nor ascended to the sky. You wouldn't think it nice to see us now, a crowd of pale, distorted creatures. For a time, despair was the only human part of us, and then we found an out-of-the-way attic in a big house, a forgotten place, remained there in the vain hope that time would erase us, the scum of the world, tormented by memories, regret and self-pity. We were hardly aware of time, out in the world raged war and death, peace and mundanity. Many years passed in static eventlessness, decades, but one day a black cat crawled into the darkest corner where we were keeping ourselves and gave birth to five kittens. At times it went out in the evening in search of food, and something happened on one such trip, the cat didn't return, perhaps it was run over, and those blind, motherless kittens that it left behind remain the only living creatures that have sensed us. Five creatures that crawled to us trembling with fear, hunger and loneliness in the hope of warmth, comfort, neither of which we could provide. One of them was pitch-black, but with a front paw white as snow, uncomfortably resembling a kitten that a foreign skipper once brought here. It finally died, whimpered like an infant for an entire night, alone in the world, without understanding why these creatures that it sensed did not allay its loneliness. We tried; that was the most painful thing of all, but between it and us was the unnameable, which we couldn't overcome, couldn't get through. A blind kitten, black but with a white front paw, died, and that's why we crawled out to you again, crawled out of our dark hiding place, because we couldn't comfort a dying kitten, is that how God works or was it merely coincidence that a cat gave birth and then disappeared; is compassion the only thing that can save a person, is it man's heavenly string? We crawled out to you because it matters to us, and because we long for liberation and understanding. Paradise, is it the place where understanding is unnecessary, or is that perhaps the description of Hell? But this is our final attempt; a crack has opened between us and you, the dead have entered your existence, forgotten storms, vanished eyes, we whisper to you stories full of silver, regret, smiles and cruelty, so that you remember. This is war against oblivion, in the hope that hidden within the stories are words that free us all from our fetters. You as well.

LIFE, THAT GREAT MUSICAL INSTRUMENT, IS NEITHER SONOROUS NOR FINE-TUNED BY THE LORD

I

ICELANDIC SUMMERS ARE SO SHORT AND UNPREDICTABLE THAT IT seems at times as if they don't exist. Here snow can fall as far down as the bottom halves of the mountains in June, even in the settlements, and birds can freeze between tussocks on August nights. But nothing in the world is as bright and clear as the month of June, days and nights merge, all the shadows vanish and the sky is blue as eternity in the middle of the night. Is it because of the light that time seems endless in the summer, and summer thus seems considerably longer than the calendar indicates? Today is the 101st of June, we might say, when the calendar indicates the 15th. The 101st and the light expands our lives.

Yet it's still only May.

Snipes dive over fields and moors, making summer sounds with their tail-feathers and filling us with optimism. The sun draws closer with each passing day, but there's snow on the mountainsides, great heaps, the bleeding remnants of winter, the earth everywhere wet and slushy from the snow, and the drifts at the bottom of the fjord are shrinking rapidly. The boy runs there several times a week, in one damn rush, from Geirþrúður's house to the drifts at the bottom of the fjord. He runs this course for no apparent reason in a single burst, without stopping, eyes bulging, startling the horses and sheep,

especially the sheep; a running man must mean round-up and they
hustle off as soon as the boy comes in sight. Helga asks him to choose
a time when the fewest number of people are out and about, early or
late, if he really feels he needs to be doing this, and more often than
not he chooses the evenings, before the readings, when the light has
faded slightly over the earth, fatigue has settled on beasts and men
after a long day. He runs down to the bottom of the fjord, six miles,
and then back, though not straight to the house, instead makes his
way above the cemetery and down to the shore, the inlet, sits on
the same rock and looks out at the sea, though seeing little, at first,
due to the shortness of his breath, the pounding of his heart, but is
quick to recover. The shoreline there is gentle, soft, a strip of black
sand that's prominent at low tide, and the beachy crest behind the
boy obstructs his view of the village; the one house that he's able to
see is a crooked mound in which old Mildiríður and her son Simmi
live. Simmi often comes out and waves happily at the boy, as if all of
life is good, existence a vale of bliss, and the boy waves back, but otherwise looks only at the sea as he recovers from his run, as the taste
of blood dwindles in his mouth, he looks out over the sea, which he's
almost completely stopped hating, it's pointless, anyway, like hating
the sky for the frost. He sees Vetrarströnd, that long glacier, the only
glacier in the world that has hayfields and grazing sheep on it. There,
in many places, the snow still reaches down to the beach, although it's
begun to retreat, revealing green grass beneath its whiteness. There's
no spring here, and there hasn't been for seven hundred years; summer takes over from winter. The boy sits on a rock, thinks about
the lives that he came into contact with along the white coast; is the
girl still coughing, does she look from time to time at the pieces of
paper that Jens left behind, which she and her siblings have probably
covered with drawings and words, does she cough or has the worst
happened, and she's lying there patiently while her father, so afraid of
words, builds her coffin, fastens coarse planks together with nails and

despair, builds a little box around the biggest and most delicate thing that the world has ever seen? Live, says the boy on the rock, he always says it, each time, live; he says it to the waves, which whisper it to the fish, which tell it to the seabed, which repeats it to drowned men, live, he says to the sky, which is too far away to hear human words. Vetrarströnd obstructs the view of Sléttueyri. What we don't see has the tendency to vanish, dissolve or recede so far from the commonplace that it doesn't touch our existence. Yet sometimes it's exactly the opposite; it doesn't vanish at all, but grows, becomes unmanageable, precisely because the commonplace doesn't reach it, because nothing tarnishes it. In short: her hair is so red that it's clearly visible through the mountains. These mountains, of course, are no affectation, they're bulky and severe, yet her hair color slips through effortlessly, comes to him and changes everything. Changes earth and sky; they turn red as blood. The sea, the sky, the clouds, if there are clouds, the snipe becomes a drop of blood in the air, Simmi turns red as he stands there by the lopsided mound of a farmhouse and waves, as do the farm itself and the smoke wafting from it, the boy's fingers, the words that he says to the sky; he gets up to pee and his penis is fiery red and his urine as well, why has everything turned so red? mutter the drowned men down at the bottom of the sea, as the boy groans like a wounded animal and stares at an eider duck out beyond the harbor, stares at the bobbing bird until the red begins to fade and vanish, and all becomes as it was, just more impoverished. He sits down again and stares at the bird, knows that he needs to hurry home for the reading, that Kolbeinn must be impatient, cursing the run, cursing the boy, apparently he feels the need to run, Helga says, he's so young, she tries to calm the skipper and defend the boy, feels the need, Kolbeinn says, it's just horniness, he needs to get himself a girl, damn run, damn perversity; yet out on the sea, not far from land, the eider duck will soon take on its normal color, it's started to chatter ceaselessly, as eider ducks have done since anyone can remember, which isn't such a short time, compared to a human life, why does it have so much on its mind? Is it reciting a verse about the eternal life that steps lightly over death, is it rattling off ancient wisdom from the depths of time? Should we, before we proceed any further toward the end, which might not be an end at all, because nothing ends while the sky hangs over the earth, hovering like a blue note in black space, learn the language of birds, set aside the tired words, those worn-down farm implements, and start chirping and singing and twittering like birds; what wisdom about the wide expanses of life does the eider duck rattle off? Or does it harp continually on the one line of poetry that it has composed over the millennia, its simple, heartfelt ode to life: fun to eat! fun to eat! Falling silent just as it dives down after food, popping up to the surface half a minute later like a cork, happy, munching; it swallows, looks contentedly at the boy, who has got up off his rock, and then starts in again: fun to eat! fun to eat!

II

May!

So much bustle that no day seems long enough, there are never enough hands, there's never a vacant moment or a spot of silence, and it's tired people who go to bed beneath towering mountains, who wake in light and fall asleep in light. Everywhere there's shouting and movement, laughter and energy! There are few who wander about, contemplating the distance between God and man, the grand purpose, the justification for man's existence. He who wanders about during these busy weeks full of light is simply knocked over by the commotion, shoved aside, there's no room for that sort of thing here, and his thoughts are pulled hither and yon by this bulging life, the unrestrained zeal for work.

The school is closed, all the children have vanished into the flurry of activity, there's no time for Danish verbs, and absolutely not for ancient Latin poetry, the air above the Village quivers, it's like being in Hell. The headmaster Gísli, a member of one of the distinguished families, is too restless to remain inside; the hubbub reaches all the way over there, deep into the Old Neighborhood, into the pretty little wooden house with an ordinary female saltfish worker in the basement, who pays such a low rent that it's hardly possible to write such a tiny figure, in exchange for cleaning for Gísli, occasionally cooking for him, the hubbub reaches all the way into the parlor with its hundreds of books, its heavy desk, not even half-crazed French poets or Greek heroes manage to keep him at home, the confusion of light and bustle drives him out, where the grind welcomes him, the people's excitement, the work, the saltfish, the endless sky. Doubtful that anyone will take the time to chat, and those who pause to stretch, to rub their sore lower backs, have little interest in wasting time talking to an unoccupied headmaster, unless he chooses to talk about saltfish, the blessed, cursed saltfish, we build our lives upon it, the Devil invented it to stupefy us utterly; as if I care what schooner or wretched little cutter catches the most fish, thinks Gísli, as he enters Hotel World's End, not wanting to stay with Ágúst and Marta at Sodom, which is occupied only by sailors, who speak of almost nothing but fish and women's crotches, and who make dirty remarks to Marta, who sometimes replies so coarsely that holes are singed into the blue May sky. Marta, who hugged the headmaster three times this winter when he brought her books about mythology and the history of humankind, about all the killings, kings and revolutions, hugged Gísli, giving him the chance to hold her close and feel her large breasts fully, which made him squeeze even tighter. But now Sodom is awash with fishermen and Marta has no time for Gísli or history, the light drives me out to the end of the world, he says to Teitur, the hotelkeeper, who always manages to smile with unfailing courtesy even though he's heard from Gísli about the light and the end of the world numerous times before. Inside the hotel, the quivering of village life can be forgotten, many things can be forgotten amidst the heavy furniture, where foreigners sit, now and then, a traveler or two driven to this godforsaken hole, no one knows why, skippers of big sailing ships that sail between the world and us, of steamers, of the Danish king's coastguard ships, and where there are occasional animated conversations and perhaps even such vehement bursts of laughter that Hulda, Teitur's daughter, keeps her distance if possible. But the beer is expensive at the End of the World, where everything costs more, the whisky, the cognac, the food, you have to pay for the shelter and the comfort, and if this summer develops like the last few summers, which it will, of course, because life here is like Hell, stifled by repetition, then Gísli will have to seek the assistance of his brother, Friðrik, even in early July, and borrow money from him in order to keep going, until the sky begins to darken once more and the berries turn blue on the hills and mountainsides. It's a damned disgrace to have to bend a knee to Friðrik in his office, but what can be done when the light hovers over you with its gun barrels?

III

If only it were winter, when the days drag themselves along like a mortally wounded beast, the darkness so dense that people can barely make their way from house to house, and the nights so murky that you lose your hand if you extend it without thinking, to find it again only after many hours of searching. Delightful is the darkness, a shelter to think in, a cave to crawl into, a bed to read in, although it can of course be so heavy that some things break in such a way that they can hardly be put back together again. Still, the darkness is a thousand times better than the light, which weighs so little that it provides no support, neither thoughts nor dreams can lean up against it. The light stretches over the length of the sky, as raucous as a great black-backed gull, and it seems as if everything living has been sentenced to sing praises to life; those without voices search in vain for shelter. The summer is spent waiting for the darkness.

IV

Andrea, Pétur's wife, the Custodian of the fishing huts and friend of his and Bárður's, was waiting for the boy when he came from the end of the world, from Dumbsfirðir, in tatters from the storm, memories, red hair, green eyes, but also with a draft, in his mind, of a letter that he'd promised to write for Oddur, the snow-shoveler, before he and Jens set out on their epic journey. Oddur's marriage proposal to Rakel, who works long hours salting fish and is the best and most wondrous woman who has ever been born here on earth, or at least in Iceland, Oddur said that he didn't know much about foreign countries, hardly anything, really, and maybe not much about Iceland either, yet had once gone all the way south to Dalir. The letter is meant to be a cry of life, of simple, pure life, and the boy had composed a draft of it in his mind, on the deck of the *Hope*, in the cool May weather, but with the sun hanging over him, larger in fact than all else that man can encounter, the eye of God, it's called in one poem, and it fits, God is one-eyed, which explains a great deal, the one-eyed don't see as well as the rest of us, they lack the comparisons provided by two eyes.

The boy was pleased with the letter, could hardly wait to come ashore, go up to the house of the trinity, Geirþrúður, Helga and Kolbeinn, get hold of a sheet of paper and a pen, but Jens was down in the forecastle, lying in a glacial crevasse, suffering bouts of shivering, coughing, and at times completely helpless, the big man. Yet he wouldn't hear of being helped up onto the deck, pulling himself up with his own hands when his stout legs threatened to betray him, and then they were standing together, watching the Village come closer, the mountains grow taller and cast shadows on the world, the boy feeling pleased with himself about the letter, although it was merely words in his blood at that moment, but hopefully later would do the most important thing of all, bring two lives together, combine two notes into a chord, into the rough outline of a tune that we could then whistle happily and by doing so make the world a slightly better place. What are you going to do? he asked Jens, after rejoicing enough in the moment on his own, go straight home? Yes. Straight home, without stopping? A man stops when he needs to, and then keeps going. Jens swayed clumsily with the waves, his face pale, his gray eyes hard balls. You know what I mean, the boy said. They could make out the buildings, saw Sodom, which reminded them both of the dory that they'd borrowed from the couple the previous week, a hundred and twelve years ago. We've got to get the dory, said Jens; do you think you can take care of that? Yes, the boy said. They fell silent and the mountains grew taller. The *Hope* crawled into the channel, the narrow strait between the islands and the mountain, no movement around Sodom, and then Jens was suddenly standing before the boy, his hand outstretched, his paw outstretched, and for several moments the paw hung there like a misunderstanding, until the boy realized what was happening, smiled, held out his hand, and his slender palm disappeared momentarily into the mailman's paw.

It clearly took a great effort for Jens to walk; putting one foot in front of the other was no longer a sure thing. First they went to retrieve his horses, Krummi and Bleikur, from Jóhann, Geirþrúður's bookkeeper, Jens letting fly with several profanities along the way, as if he were spitting black stones. The boy avoided them and asked again, What are you going to do? I thought I'd already answered that question, Jens said. No. You ask a lot of questions as well. Do you remember what Hjalti said? He said a lot of things. If you do nothing, he said, you betray everyone. Jens glanced at the boy. I remember that, he said, almost sharply, and then he refused to lie down to rest in Geirþrúður's house, though he did accept something to eat, wrote a brief message to the doctor and postmaster, Sigurður, by way of a resignation, using big, bulky letters, a bit as if he were scratching in the sand with a pole. Take something for your cough, Helga said, and I don't like that trembling. I'd rather die than take any of Sigurður's medicines. To tell the truth, I didn't think you were so stupid. It isn't stupidity, I'm simply not far enough gone to ask him for anything. Then Jens was sitting straight-backed on his horse, looking down at the boy. So here we have it, he said, grabbing the reins. The horse, Krummi, lifted its head. I don't know what we have, the boy said, except for life, of course. Jens said nothing, but kept his eyes fixed on the boy, which prompted the latter to add, and now we no longer have each other's company and I don't know whether you can handle that. Jens smiled and rode off; night led death by the reins.

And evening fell.

The four of them sat together in the parlor until eleven. Now we'll hear a story, Geirþrúður had said, and that's what they got, part of a story; we should send you back out on another journey soon, said Kolbeinn when the boy stopped, too tired to go on, they'd come to Vík, and would continue tomorrow evening. But before they sat down in the parlor, and before the boy was given something to eat, he went to Sigurður's, returned the bags, one of them half-full of letters from Sléttueyri, mostly dry accounts concerning money, merchandise, business, upon which the human world turns without helping it one bit; it heals no wounds, alleviates neither loneliness nor regret. Sigurður himself received Jens' resignation letter. Should I be able to understand this, he said, is this what's supposed to be called handwriting? Yet he understood what he wanted to understand, muttered something about it not being the proper way, but smiled as well, though nearly invisibly, looked through the boy as if he hardly existed, waved his hand at a middle-aged woman when the boy said, excuse me, I know it's evening now, but I was wondering whether I might be able to buy three books, and pulled out some money as proof, feeling it to be safer, for some reason.

Books, said the woman dryly, broad-faced, tilting her head backward as if she felt it a nuisance to have the boy so near; books, now, this late? Yes, he said, instinctively showing her the money. You have nothing else to do with that money than buy books? she said, yet grabbed the money anyway, and the boy bent over the bookshelf, having had to press himself sideways between the shelves of medications in order to get close enough; he stroked the books' spines slowly and tenderly, moved his lips as he read the titles. I have other things to do with my time than stand here watching you, said the woman, and so late; it isn't normal. The boy said nothing and breathed in the concentrated pharmaceutical smell, thinking, Just the smell will protect me from the flu for the next ten years, before finally selecting three books, *Hamlet the Prince of Denmark: A Tragedy*, translated by Matthías Jochumsson, a book about death and doubt; the *Odyssey* by Homer, who was apparently blind like Milton when he wrote *Paradise Lost*, two poets who searched for words to replace their eyes, to replace the light that was lost to them. The third book was *Swan-White, Several Foreign Poems in Icelandic Translation*, by Matthías Jochumsson and Steingrímur Thorsteinsson. The cost was slightly higher than the amount specified on María's lost credit bill, but the boy had anticipated this and got money from Helga, hastily explaining why he needed it, how María was when she talked about books, about poetry, told of what he saw in her eyes, that he'd lost the bill. Helga had just said, Well then, and let him have what he needed. So María is getting four books, the fourth being the volume of short stories by Gestur Pálsson, whose brother is occasionally tied down upstairs in a house some distance from here. What use is this? said the woman, grabbing, as if at random, the poetry translations. What use is life? the boy said in return. No one loses sleep over books, the woman said angrily, as if poetry had done her a bad turn at some point, and of course she was wrong, the boy stayed up half the night copying the poems, yet he still needed to sleep, was still tired, half-paralyzed from fatigue, turned out the light around three, sank instantaneously into sleep, plummeted into it like a shot bird and dreamed of Hjalti lying frozen in snow and bad weather. Damn it all, the big man said, I had to go and die, then, so everything's finished, I would have liked to have been with a woman first, once, it's so warm, much warmer and softer than death, but have you seen my dog? No, the boy said, and as he did, everything around him became empty and desolate. Then the tussocks began to grow. Low humps that shot up from the ground and she with green eyes strolled through these tussocks, glancing to one side as if uninterested in anything, but the other was there as well, the one with blue-gray eyes. I'm going for a ride this summer, in sunshine, she said. Yes, but I'm just looking for Hjalti's dog, the boy said, that's why I'm here, and for no other reason. The next morning, when the boy finally came downstairs, having slept in, it being just past eight o'clock when he appeared, Helga said, We didn't want to tell you last night, felt it unnecessary to wake you, but there's a woman here who wants to meet you, who has been waiting for you.

V

Andrea arrived in the Village at around the same time that the boy and Jens lost Hjalti in the storm above Sléttueyri; it was easy for the storm to swallow such a big man, wipe him off the face of the earth, leaving little but impressions in the minds of the boy and Jens, regret and memories in a little weather-beaten cottage behind the world's mountains, out on the heavy Polar Sea. But what is a person, anyway, apart from a memory?

Andrea had searched for and found Geirþrúður's house, which wasn't exactly difficult, but still, she was practically a stranger to the Village, her and Pétur's shop being in a different village, smaller and farther south. She came into the café, asked softly for coffee, then sat there with her bundle in her lap, at first looking around as if in search of something, twice seeming about to ask Ólafía something but changing her mind, and then she stopped looking around, simply sat there as her coffee cooled in front of her, turned ice cold, inside the cup it was black and still, as if someone had poured a touch of death into it. Finally she got up; there were quite a few people in the café, lively, too, but her face was gray, even white, and she bumped into two sailors on her way out, as if she could no longer see, was losing her sight. Come over here, said one of them, I have something that might cheer you up, but she left and had reached the bottom step when Helga called after her. They'd been watching Andrea, she and Ólafía, it's rare for women to come here alone, and what's more, she sat there as if the world had completely forgotten her, it hurts when everyone forgets you, really hurts; your shoulders sink, your eyes dull, solitude enters your body and starts killing your cells, that's how Andrea was sitting. It was why Helga stepped out onto the stoop and asked, Can I help you?, startling Andrea, who gripped her bundle tighter, at first said no, but then asked about the boy.

There was a room for her in the big house next to the school. Geirþrúður had bought it some years ago and rented it out to family members; the little basement room was unoccupied, it had sheltered an old woman who'd died recently of loneliness and influenza.

Andrea had gone home to her basement room before the boy returned from his journey, except that it isn't a home, of course, but rather, a shelter, refuge, despair. You'll just work for us to start with, said Helga, when Andrea had explained who she was, why she'd come, to meet the boy, to start a new life, if that were possible, if another life existed for her. I don't know what I'm doing, she said.

There's a woman here who wants to meet you, said Helga, before going down with the sleepy boy to the café, no patrons, just the three of them, Ólafía, Kolbeinn and Andrea. Helga sat down and began immediately to talk to Kolbeinn and Ólafía, while the boy and Andrea stood opposite one another. Don't forget me, boy, she'd said to him in the fishing hut a month ago, said good-bye with a kiss, Bárður lay right beside them and would never be kissed again. I got your letter, Andrea said. I left Pétur, Andrea said, but the boy remained silent, swallowed his shame, felt no joy at seeing Andrea, on the contrary suddenly became angry; he really felt so filthy inside, then. There she stood, so awkward, entirely unlike the woman he kept in his memory and to whom he'd written the letter, her appearance so plain, ordinary. What have I done? he thought, trying to hide the pettiness, the filthiness inside him, managed to do so but not entirely, perhaps, Andrea looked away, it was as if someone had cast her aside. Then the filthiness vanished, the boy took several precious steps and embraced this woman whom his words had torn away from a barren, secure life, embraced the woman who'd once made his life a tiny bit warmer, a tiny bit softer, the bitter odor of the fishing hut still clung to her, he put his arms around her and she trembled slightly.

She'd had her hair cut. Helga cut Andrea's hair short, like a boy's, making her look several years younger; maybe you're not so old, said the boy when he saw her up close, and she laughed. Little is as important for a person as laughter, and crying; it's far more important than sex, let alone power, let alone money, that spittle of the Devil in our blood, those who never laugh gradually turn to stone. She laughed, and the ravine that life had, through its unfathomable ruthlessness, sliced open between them closed up, nearly disappeared, but not entirely. Andrea does the work of two at the café, at times the place certainly needs it, some days there's a steady stream of customers, and the sailors are eager to have Andrea serve them, admiring her speed, her unhesitating, effortless movements, her boy's haircut, drawn to the warmth that makes humans beautiful, many of them sit there motionless, hoping for words from her, a glance, and Kolbeinn becomes almost cheerful. You should move here and marry me, he says, because what's the point of hanging around in a room in a basement? She smiles, although he doesn't see it, and pampers the old wolffish with his useless eyes, he doesn't see her smile, or the shadow on her face when life tracks her down in idle moments, with all its importunate, cruel questions.

I'm leaving, she'd said to Pétur. Leaving, you're not leaving anywhere! I forbid you to leave. I decide for myself, she said, slightly surprised, not knowing where the words came from, as if someone else had spoken for her, in fact, and Pétur's heart turned to stone. You're not going anywhere, woman, and just where are you planning to go, what's got into you, don't we have everything, don't I do everything that needs doing? There aren't many who catch more fish than me, and soon, this summer even, I'm going to renovate the farm, you didn't know that! No. I didn't want to mention it too soon—one shouldn't talk about things but do them. Despite that, Pétur, I'm leaving, and I'm leaving tomorrow, in the morning, while you're at sea. They were out in the salting shed, the saltfish stack had grown so high that he had to stand on tiptoe in order to thrust himself in properly, but it's just so good to do it standing, it's so damned good, and he spoke her name as the moment approached, spoke her name while trying to speed up without losing his balance, spoke her name twice, heatedly, and her eyes moistened a bit because he'd never done that before, not during sex, just panted, and he had to say it now, far too late, as if to make it all more difficult, despite it already being difficult enough. After finishing, he immediately began to fix the stack, as if ashamed of his chatter, the sentimental nonsense; Andrea wiped and tidied herself carefully, and then said that it was over. I'm leaving, and he knew immediately what she meant, but it's easiest to pretend not to understand anything while life is crumbling into a thousand pieces around you. What are we supposed to eat when we return from sea? he finally asked, almost snidely, you can hardly expect us to go hungry? Guðrún can look after you to start with; I'll speak to her. Guðrún, are you out of your mind? She's your niece, you know, your own blood. She's not coming into my hut—I'd sooner die than give Guðmundur that weapon. So you'll die of starvation? she asked, unable to check her sarcasm, but then you'll have to, she said when he made no reply, simply continued to punch lightly at the stack as if focused only on arranging it better, then you'll just have to cook for yourself, at which Pétur stopped fiddling with the stack and looked at Andrea as if she'd finally lost her mind, maybe it would be safer to tie her up during this damned fit of hers. What's the poor girl ever done to you? I'm absolutely positive that you and Guðmundur no longer have any idea what your quarrel is about. I know what I know, and besides, all it takes is a glimpse of him out here for me to know—it's better to know than to recall. You'll have to see to your own food tomorrow, then, there's no other way. What do I look like, a woman? You can set fish aside as soon as you land, Guðrún will take it and boil it and be back in her own hut before you've gutted the rest. What am I supposed to tell my crew? You'll growl something at them, if I know you right, she said, without having intended to say it, hadn't intended to speak like that, but suddenly became so angry, so fierce, and it knocked all the wind out of Pétur, all the fight. You can't just leave like that, was all he could say. Nor can you live like this, she'd said, no longer fierce, almost adding, dear Pétur, actually wanting to comfort him. But then Pétur straightened up and said, sarcastically, Just go, then, you'll come crawling back before spring is over, what's wrong with people nowadays? To which she didn't reply, what was she supposed to say to that? And set off the next morning, had come to the Village by nine, but the boy wasn't there.

The boy's eyes aren't useless, he's seen the shadows clouding Andrea's face, she leans against something, stares into the distance and looks almost old. Leave him, he'd written, leave, if you want to live, if you want to feel life. What right did he have to write such things, what right does he have to combine words that could change someone's life, what would his responsibility be then? Those who fire guns are responsible for the bullets, the pain that they may cause; doesn't the same apply to words? I should ask her, he thinks, I should talk to her about something other than ordinary things, the things that speak for themselves. Of course I should talk to her, he mumbles to himself during the day, says it to himself before he sleeps, but retreats cowardly at every opportunity, Andrea looks at him sometimes, as if waiting for him to say something; he who knows nothing, is nothing, who loses the little that he does know and understand as soon as he looks in someone's face.

Yet he's going to write another letter. For Oddur. Once more gather words to change a life. He makes a trip, more than once, out to the spit where Rakel cleans saltfish, from morning to evening, carefully, with a steel brush, rinses, trims, washes away the blood, removes the membrane, works energetically, her ash-blond hair showing beneath her scarf, she's short, thick-set, has strong arms, is probably thirty years old yet giggles like a girl, and giggles a lot, is never downcast. The boy watches Rakel and thinks, Life probably isn't complicated or wearisome, it's just me who's so stupid. Five times in as many days he's feigned an errand, in rain, a chill wind, sunshine and calm, the women standing there shuffling their feet beneath the open, windy sky, on the exposed spit, there's still snow on the mountains, and sometimes they need to break the ice off the washing tubs, splashing in cold water all day, from six in the morning, in cold breezes, sleet or perhaps rain, which would deaden most people's joy, but not Rakel, she giggles and works, hops like a little girl to warm herself, such a bright disposition, can one buy it, plant it, let it grow into a person, is it a godsend or just unbearable folly? You've obviously never lost a child, one woman says to Rakel, after she's stopped hopping childishly and has started to sing, there's sleet in the air and the ice that they broke off this morning is still lying there on the ground, it isn't warm enough for it to melt; you've obviously never lost a child, you don't know how it is, don't know life, don't know hardship, and then Rakel looks down and stops singing, the boy notices her blushing. Have you nothing better to do than disturb working folk? says the foreman, appearing at the side of the boy, who goes back to the house and writes the letter that was composed in his head except for several sentences he jotted down, writes it quickly, puts it in an envelope, takes it to Rakel, who lives in the old neighborhood, in a dark basement apartment, two little rooms, it's the basement of Headmaster Gísli's house, the door is unlocked, the boy puts the letter inside, and then he's done it again, sent out words that are meant to change a person's life.

VI

Andrea is often seated at the table, her exhausted hands holding the coffeepot, deriving warmth from it, when the boy comes down to the kitchen. It's good to feel the heat from the coffee spread into her palms, incredibly good, yet it's also painful if you only have a coffee mug and not a hand to hold. Pétur, of course, wasn't much for holding hands, and never when others might have seen, although sometimes beneath the covers, on dark nights, when she felt the heavy loneliness that seemed to come from the darkness outside, incomprehensible, cold loneliness, her hand would reach instinctively for his, her palm for his, and press. He would either act as if there were nothing out of the ordinary or perhaps press gently in return, almost imperceptibly, yet still press, and this "yet" is no small thing, it's quite a lot. All too often he'd stiffen up, as if he were uncomfortable, and she would take her hand back. Does he never put his arms around her? Never of his own accord, Andrea says, but he does sometimes when I ask him to, late at night when I'm certain that everyone else is asleep. Then I ask him to hold me.

Helga: And does he?

Andrea: Not always, of course. He's sometimes half asleep when I touch him, and then he gets angry.

But now and then Pétur puts his heavy, warm arms around her; he's very strong. And is it nice?

Andrea: Yes, it's nice, and sometimes I say, Let's fall asleep like this, and it's terribly nice to sleep snuggled against him, he's so warm, you see, but he can't always bear feeling me so close to him and becomes excited and doesn't stop until he's satisfied. Then he falls fast asleep, but I often lie there a long time, unable to sleep myself. Well, it can be good, of course, you know, but sometimes I'm not entirely ready for it; sometimes I just want to be held. And then I have to listen to Einar's panting.

Einar, the grumpy one, with a black beard?

Yes.

What panting, you don't mean . . .

Yes, he always seems to wake up if we do anything, as if he's on alert, and then waits for Pétur to fall asleep before starting, you know, and then I have to listen to him panting while he finishes, what a pest that man is.

The more intense the spring light, the more crotchety Kolbeinn becomes; he's always been averse to the light, he's said, and that's why his sight was taken from him. More often than not, the boy comes down before he does, walks in on the whispering of Helga and Andrea, who instinctively stopped the first several mornings, but no longer do so, as if it's pointless to hide things from him. He eats, reads from the book that he brings with him downstairs, or from the pages that he filled with poems from *Swan-White*, loses himself in poetry, but listens now and then and hears this about Pétur, from the beginning, in fact, and about Einar, how he lies in his bunk after Pétur's asleep, panting with one hand beneath the covers, what a damned bastard that man is, it's only beasts who do such things, he thinks, looking at his hands, which are perhaps resting on the table, as if they were criminals.

The letter that his hands wrote is read in the evening in the basement of Gísli's house, read extremely slowly, Rakel is barely literate, takes a good hour to finish the two pages and then has to start again, convinced that she'd misunderstood everything. She slept badly that night, showed up for work red-eyed and silent. Where did your joy go? someone asks, because it's as if Rakel's heavy mood dulls the light over the tubs, but she says nothing, breaks the skin of ice off the water and starts cleaning the fish.

In the meantime, Oddur, along with Lúlli, works at unloading, three ships have arrived in the space of as many days from way out in the world, where everything happens, beyond the sea and the horizon, loaded with wares from hull to deck, with salt, coal, sacks of grain, barrels of kerosene, wood rough and planed, to be used for boats, buildings, farm implements, coffins; and tar, mortar, whisky, beer, figs, linen, stoves, shoes, many varieties of hand soap, boiled sweets, red wine, cigars, coffee, chocolate, we need a dreadful amount of things to live, and all of it has to be unloaded quickly, during the night, in fact, those who don't like it can go back to idling at home, there are plenty of hands eager for work, and no need to take breaks to eat. Those who are married bring food from home, the wife lays aside her steel brush or leaves the fish for half an hour, hurries home, feeds the children, goes to her husband or sends one of the children who is old enough for the task but too young to work. It's always the woman who has to run around and tend to many things at once, while the men shovel food into their mouths, just standing there, leaning against something, it's a virtue to eat quickly, the manliest of them eats the quickest, food is meant to be consumed quickly, not enjoyed.

Lúlli and Oddur have brought provisions, the two of them live together, without women; we haven't seen such a beautiful friendship between two men since the brothers Núlli and Jón were alive. Lúlli and Oddur sit down to eat, chew slowly and sit there looking peculiar, like old men with worn-out legs or like foreigners, but oddly the foreman refrains from making a fuss, although he wants to sometimes, wants to desperately, it boils his blood to see those bastards, he wants most to shoot them, in fact, when he's most vexed. But the snow-shovelers are a class unto themselves, the merchants covet their energy when it comes to unloading, when they work together as one man, closely and efficiently, never complaining, never stopping until the job is done, and because of this they're allowed their quirks. It would still be good to shoot them, even just one of them, once or twice, mutters the foreman, his name is Kjartan and he belongs to one of the important families, albeit not the inner circle, yet he's related to Friðrik and chews so much tobacco, especially in the spring when there's suddenly plenty available after the lean winter, that it often looks as if his mouth is bleeding, which gives him a frenetic air and makes the workers feel they'd be safer heeding him on the double, preferably before he opens his mouth to issue an order. Kjartan stares angrily down at Lúlli and Oddur, chewing their food tranquilly like damned ruminants, sitting there like imbecilic parliamentarians. Damn it all to Hell, he says loudly, and has to turn away to avoid bursting.

The letter is read, a day passes, then another, and it's evening. Dusk hardly falls between the mountains, yet the light diminishes enough for Mercury to ignite in the sky, just over Vetrarströnd, that little planet scorched by the presence of the sun, it can go badly for those who love too much.

The boy and Andrea walk in the direction of the old neighborhood. They say little, hardly anything, sunburnt Mercury above them and the earth still wet from the frost. The weather is warming yet isn't warm, 7 or 8 degrees at noon, it could be higher, the sun would truly be welcome to come closer and breathe on the wounds that winter left behind, on shattered hopes, breathe on the frostbite of life.

Andrea and the boy come from Lúlli and Oddur's house and head toward Rakel's, this is the first time they've been alone since saying goodbye in the fishing hut, Bárður frozen on the baiting table, the wind howling out on the sea, the mountains lost in the snowfall, she'd hugged him, kissed him, he'd wept, maybe they came too close to each other, it can take time to recover from such a thing. Quiet amidst the houses, most people at work, cleaning saltfish, unloading, fishing, and the children, those who are too young for work, are out and about in search of adventure. They hear hens in a back garden. Have you written many letters? asks Andrea, trying to sound nonchalant, but her voice is sharp. Yet the boy is glad, the letter exists between them once again, no longer lies in silence. Lúlli had come to the café toward evening to see the boy, worried, at a loss because Rakel apparently hadn't shown up at work today, had been unlike herself yesterday, and Oddur was devastated—perhaps she'd taken the letter badly? Perhaps the boy's tone had been too enthusiastic? He mustn't misunderstand, the letter was very beautiful and Oddur was proud to sign it, but perhaps it was too enthusiastic? Or something? Might the boy consider checking on her, just look in on her, huh? His heart beat faster; had he done it again, then, thrown life out of whack by writing down words? If so, it would be cowardice and treachery to retreat once more. He took Andrea with him, she'd heard most of his conversation with Lúlli, anyway there was little to do in the café at the moment, just before closing, she'd been standing next to the boy as he sat opposite the perplexed Lúlli, had stroked the boy's hair as she'd done sometimes in the fishing hut, but withdrew her hand when she heard about the letter.

Now she asks whether he's written many letters. Only to you, the boy says, louder than he'd intended, and to Rakel for Oddur. He asked me to. Is this the one? she asks, stopping in front of Headmaster Gísli's house. Yes, mutters the boy, startled when he sees Gísli at the window. And this Rakel is in the basement? Yes. You know each other? No.

You've spoken to each other? No. What did you write? Might you have told her, as you wrote to me, to question life, did you tell her that she would betray life if she didn't marry Oddur, did you say that the way to a secure life, to numbness, is not to question one's situation? He looks away, clenches his fists inside his mittens, then Andrea sighs softly, just tell me what you wrote in the letter. The boy rattles off its contents to Andrea, eagerly, as if he'd been waiting for the opportunity, knows the letter by heart, down to every last comma and full stop. Then he's finished. And do you think you have the right to write such things? she asks, without taking her eyes off the house, and the boy looks at it as well; nothing wrong with doing that for a moment.

Gísli had the house painted red when he moved in just over ten years ago and has occasionally had the paint refreshed, moved into the middle of the old neighborhood to the considerable annoyance of his brother Friðrik, who'd sent word to Gísli in Copenhagen to come back and take over the newly established primary school. The news that Gísli was returning home found its way into *The Will of the People*, and, along with the announcement, the paper published a photograph of him, with the caption "Our Highly Learned Headmaster," his thick hair slicked back and his expression suggesting that he was on the verge of thinking something grand. With six years of learning under his belt, the man must surely know everything. Six years of natural science and poetry, Gísli liked to say, with top marks; fished out of the gutter, some say, out of the lice-infested beds of prostitutes, returned penniless, destitute and wallowing in debt, having sold off all he owned while abroad. Friðrik had intended to have Gísli live above the school, but their mother, Karólína, the matriarch who is still alive, unlike her husband, the cruel bastard whom the Devil swallowed in one bite many years ago, declared that her Gísli might, if he wished, buy himself a house of his own choosing. And although Karólína is bent double with old age and has been unable to straighten her back for years, no one contradicts her, not even

Friðrik, and Gísli expressed his gratitude by buying this house, this hovel, in the middle of the old neighborhood, among the populace, the screaming children, cackling chickens. You defy me, dear brother, from beneath our mother's wing, Friðrik had said, so coldly that frost clung to his words, such are the terrible effects of the French Revolution, Gísli had said, and painted the house red to enliven the area, which was also considered newsworthy enough to make its way into the pages of *The Will of the People*, for many years it was the only painted house in the Village, and it stands there red among the black, gloomy houses, red as a ruby, as a cry of desperation, a bleeding heart.

I wanted to help Oddur, the boy says finally, softly, looking away from the house.

That's fine, but you didn't consider how Rakel might take it; words can affect people, you should know that, not least written words, they get into you somehow and don't leave you alone, it isn't easy and in the meantime you've got to attend to life as if nothing is out of the ordinary.

Andrea is right. What's more, written words forget nothing and remember everything; they might lie somewhere between oblivion and darkness, but they start to shine as soon as someone looks in their direction.

Why did you send the letter to me, with Simmi, why did you write as you did, who gave you the right?

The boy doesn't dare look at Andrea, but does so anyway. Her lips are thin lines; where's the mercy gone that makes her beautiful, that softens the world, that causes people to seek it out, the blind as well as the sighted? You're too good for Pétur, he says. Who gave you the right to write such a thing? I don't know, I just had to. That's no answer. I care. About what? You. That's no answer, either. But it's the only thing that I seem to do better than others, to write such things, I mean, it's practically the only thing I know how to do in life, and I care about you, you're too good for Pétur, he never says anything beautiful to you and it makes you unhappy, life is too short for unhappiness. My God, boy, what do you know about happiness and unhappiness between man and wife? Probably nothing, he admits. Yet I've still witnessed happiness, he says, and you left him, do you regret it? I don't know anything anymore, she says, her anger seemingly having subsided, along with her ferocity.

Should I not have sent you the letter?

Maybe life would be easier if I hadn't met you and Bárður; you confused me, and then he dies, and then this letter arrives and makes me feel as if I matter, and now I'm standing here and know nothing.

But you've left him, that's something.

Is it? And have I left, is it possible to leave one's life, aren't I just visiting town, what use is it for me to dream, I'm married, I'm a woman, people will say that I've failed and what do I do then? I can't stay with Helga and Geirþrúður forever, any more than you can, at some point we've got to make a decision, or some sort of decision, is that the headmaster there at the window?

The boy looks up, sees Gísli at the window, he appears not to notice them, raises a glass to his lips, he's drunk, mutters the boy, has more or less been that way since school let out. Alcohol is his sea wall, Andrea says. God, how I miss Bárður, Andrea says, it would be easier to live if you hadn't written me the letter, Andrea says, though I thank you for it, I think that no one will ever send me anything as beautiful. Then they go up to the house. Knock on the basement door, twice, thrice, four times. Are you sure she's at home? asks Andrea, but the boy doesn't answer, doesn't need to, someone fumbles with the door, it opens, Rakel looks at them, she doesn't appear to be feeling particularly well.

The ceiling is low, Jens would have to bend over, Hjalti as well, of course; the memory of these two men renders the boy unable to speak, to get his bearings. Where is Hjalti lying, with his huge, lonely body, have they found him, where is he with his sad memories and nostalgia for his vicious dog, and maybe for a woman who loved a Norwegian, if the woman in fact existed? It hurts to love someone who doesn't exist, it's a great misfortune; and Jens, is he alive, did he make it home on his horses or did they carry a dead man to his farm, the end of the world for Halla and their father? The longing for the presence of the silent man, grouchy and unsociable but indispensable in some incomprehensible way, when life has entwined them so completely, fills the boy's veins, he nearly forgets his bitterness about how she with the green eyes thinks about Jens, that she let Jens have some sort of letter, probably a declaration of love; come back, my big, strong man, and fetch me. He leans against the wall, could easily touch the ceiling with his fingers and sense Gísli's footsteps as he paces the floor up above, his voice drifts down to them, rising, falling. No, no one is with him, Rakel says, he often talks to himself. It's exceptionally tidy here, says Andrea, who has started making coffee, because everything seems to be easier in the vicinity of that black drink, less weight lies upon the words, a smaller pile of rocks, coffee and the Gulf Stream make this land, this remote island, scorched by volcanic fire and blasted by wind but with green valleys like dreams amidst the rock, barely habitable. Rakel sits on her bed, her swollen hands like little dying animals in her lap. She's slept badly for two days and nights, has eaten little, forgot to go to work today. In fact yesterday as well. You forgot to go to work? Yes, she says, knitting her brows as if in surprise. It's so spic-and-span in the apartment, marvelously tidy, ragged and sleepless Rakel seems not to belong here, a visitor in her own life, she watches numbly as Andrea makes the coffee, takes out some rusks. Andrea doesn't ask, Why don't you reply to Oddur, why are you sitting here instead of working, just look at you, what sort of way is this to behave? No, instead she says, It's so wonderfully tidy here. She says, Oh, where did you get this tablecloth, I haven't seen this pattern before? She says, Are you from here in the Village?

I'm just here out of negligence, she says, I really don't know what to do with myself, it's so strange to have to make a decision about it, about how I should spend my life, I mean. She says, I always thought that the wife should do her husband proud, have a good home and children, yes, have children and not question things that are self-evident, not be like a skittish sheep. I'll be damned, she says, there we are, the coffee's ready.

Then they drink their coffee. Two women adrift without a purpose. The boy doesn't move. He'd written two letters and that's why the two women are here now, yet he doesn't belong there, is a distraction, it's best not to move, not to draw attention. Upstairs, Gísli shuffles his feet, a little more than a foot above the crown of the boy's head.

I've never missed a day's work, says Rakel, having drunk half her cup, I've gone to work sick, dead tired, have always gone and never missed a day. I can well imagine that, Andrea says. I feel ill if I don't work, beside myself, yet here I've been sitting for two days, like a wretch.

It's strange.

This morning I wasn't even sure that I wanted to live.

No one should disdain life, it's a gift from God.

They stop talking. Nothing can be heard but Gísli's footsteps, as if he's dragging his feet behind him, and his voice, which quavers up and down; he's alone up there, Rakel says. Yet still talks so much. He's usually alone. That's not very good. No, probably not, Rakel says, I clean for him, most often when he's not at home, he's very learned. We just came from Oddur's, says Andrea, pouring more coffee into Rakel's cup. He's not in good shape, and that's putting it mildly. So, was he in an accident? says Rakel slowly, having sat up, staring into space as if expecting to see something interesting; she has a long neck and such a small chin that it's barely possible to find room for anything on it, except for one kiss perhaps. Accident, it might be called an accident. Hopefully nothing dangerous, Rakel says, still looking around for whatever it is that's so interesting. Well, I understand that it can be fatal. That's too bad, but people have got to be careful, of course; Þorsteinn wasn't at all careful last year, was toiling away madly and fell into the hold of an English ship that was half-full of coal. Was he badly hurt? He wound up on the parish, he and his family. Oddur didn't fall into the hold of an English ship. Well, I just hope he doesn't end up on the parish, says Rakel, who's done looking around, having given up on discovering anything interesting, perhaps there's nothing interesting to see anymore in this world, maybe all such things have departed, like Þorsteinn's life and luck. Her mouth quivers slightly, not at all noticeably, but the boy has a good eye, her lips protrude just a touch, almost as if they're asking the world for a kiss, the body does what it wishes, that's man's fortune and misfortune. He didn't have the courage to come here himself, Andrea says. Why should he come here? says Rakel, who stands up abruptly and says, I should get to work now, and then sits back down and starts to whimper. Sits there at her little kitchen table, her shoulders hunch, her head droops, her half-clenched, swollen hands rise to her face and her body trembles, and then the boy remembers the five kittens that he was ordered to drown when he was ten or twelve years old, they were blind, he took them away from their mother, pulled them from her teats, put them carefully into a canvas sack, carried it down to a brook, the whole time holding the sack tightly, as if to keep them warm before darkness swallowed them, felt them trembling, heard them whimpering, before he plunged the sack into the brook, chill as spring, and held it there until his hands were blue and numb with cold, and now Rakel trembles and whimpers as if she expects fate to walk in, put her in a canvas bag and drown her.

Andrea: He wanted me to tell you that he meant every word in the letter.

Rakel: I've never received such a letter before.

Andrea: I know.

Rakel: I like being happy; it makes it easier to exist.

Andrea: It's a gift from God, joy, and it's handed out sparingly.

Rakel: Some people find it difficult to start washing the fish in cold weather. We start by breaking the ice off the top, and then we have our hands in cold water all day. Sometimes there's snow on the mountains or it's raining or there's sleet and maybe even wind as well, but I can still be happy. I can't help it.

Andrea: If only I were you.

Rakel: They're not always happy about it.

Andrea: Who, and with what, joy?

It's mainly two of them, says Rakel, stroking her swollen hands as if to calm herself, that are angry with me sometimes. They say I've never experienced anything, that I'm all alone and never have to endure anything. They sometimes say, You've never been beaten, you've never lost a child, and that's why I'm so cheerful. And that's why I'm so foolish. It's probably true that you need to be a little bit foolish to feel cheerful when you start the day by breaking ice off the top of a tub of fish, when there's snow on the mountains and they're terribly high and the wind can be so cold that we're chilled to the bone, even to our brains. Many times, they'll say bad things to me, too, those two. No, not often, I mustn't be unfair, but sometimes. Some people are beyond help, Andrea says, don't listen to them, there's so much spite and malice in people. It isn't right, Rakel says. Of course not, Andrea says. I too have experienced a lot, Rakel adds.

Andrea: Pay no heed to those old blatherers, if only they knew of the letter you received!

Rakel: My father had very heavy hands; I've never told anyone that. No, Andrea says hesitantly, reaching for the coffee, pushing the rusks toward Rakel, who takes one, raises it slowly to her lips, stops before taking a bite, her hand sinks back and her palms cover the rusk, protecting it. I'm almost certain that the Devil controlled them when my father was drunk; my brothers left as soon as they could, Björssi's in Winnipeg, or somewhere nearby, I think, where a lot of trees grow. Illugi's in the sea, you can't reach him anymore, I said to Father when Illugi drowned. Mother never did anything; maybe she was relieved to have some rest while it was going on, he had very heavy hands, he was very strong and did what he wanted and . . . Björssi told me to come to him and I wanted to because I'm sure it's fun to watch trees grow into the sky and see the birds sitting in them, but I couldn't betray Mother, and then I didn't dare when she died, I was going to go but Father forbade it and it was as if he could, I mean, what he said seemed to be stronger than I was. But once, during a bad winter storm, he strayed too far from the house and wasn't found for many days. Then I came here. I sold the livestock and came here and haven't managed to go any further. Anyway, I think that America's too big for someone like me, she says, before stopping, sitting absolutely still, having crumbled the rusk as she spoke, covering her lap with crumbs.

My dear child, says Andrea, pouring more coffee into Rakel's cup, brushing the crumbs from her lap, my dear child, she says, stroking her cheek once, lightly. They're probably the same age, yet she's so much younger, younger than me, really, thinks the boy, looking at Rakel, who's taken another rusk, breaks it in two, dips one half into her coffee. Yes, she says, her head trembling slightly, and her lips as well. I thought, she says, but so softly that the other two lean forward automatically to hear better, Gísli's footsteps and muttering nearly drown out Rakel's soft voice, I even thought that they'd got someone to write the letter to tease me, and got Oddur to agree to it and play along, which I found horrible because I know exactly how Oddur is. He's eyed me sometimes, but beautifully, making me dream. I'm more than likely foolish, but I think that foolish people also have dreams. They're just more foolish.

I wrote the letter, the boy says. Overhead, Gísli raises his voice, stamps his feet, and the ceiling trembles like a threatening sky. He asked me to, Oddur, and no one else had anything to do with it, except of course Lúlli. Everything written in the letter is true, I was just trying to say . . . to describe how his heart beats when he thinks of you, when . . . he looks at you and when he dreams of you, when . . . Aren't you the boy who's staying at Geirþrúður's? Rakel says. Yes. Your handwriting is very fine, the letters are quite slender yet they hold a great deal, how does that happen? I don't know, mutters the boy, looking past Rakel, at the rusk dissolving in her coffee. Didn't your friend die because of a foreign poem?

The boy: No, he died because fish mean more here than life.

The poor boy, says Rakel with a sniffle, and the boy isn't sure whether she means him or Bárður. His name was Bárður, Andrea says, he forgot his raincoat, Andrea says, his raincoat lay next to the book that he was reading, Andrea says, he forgot his raincoat because he was thinking too much about the book. The ceiling above them resounds; it's as if Gísli has started to dance. Gísli reads a lot, Rakel says; her eyes are red. Life expands when you read, the boy says, there's more to it, he says, it's as if you acquire something that no one can take from you, ever, he says, it makes you happier. Gísli isn't happy very often, Rakel says. Once he said to me, All of my books for your joy, otherwise he says little to me, and why should he? He's the headmaster and brother of Friðrik and Reverend Þorvaldur.

Andrea stands up, pours the coffee and the dissolved rusk out of the mug, and fills it again halfway, places it on the table before Rakel, but now you know that it was Oddur who sent you the letter, not any spiteful old blatherers from the drying lot, and that it's a proposal of marriage. I'm told that Oddur's a handsome man, a good soul. He has a steady winter job. You can't find a better man; now drink your coffee.

But you know what they can do to us, says Rakel, so loudly that it startles them, her lips quiver again, her swollen hands grope the air, as if they're searching for something to hold onto, but sometimes there seems to be nothing to hold onto in this world. Andrea glances at the boy as if she doesn't recognize him, as if she's seeing him for the first time, and it's not very comfortable. How, Jens had said several weeks ago, up on a mountain, in a storm, in the dubious shelter of a coffin, how does one distinguish hands that injure from those that don't? Yes, Andrea says at last, I know what they can do. It's good to be alone, says Rakel, sniffling, it might be a bit tiresome sometimes, you get lonely, but no one can do anything to me and no one can forbid me anything. When I'm alone I don't need to fear anything except the darkness.

VII

Headmaster Gísli occasionally takes slow walks down the fjord, to escape the houses, the people, to escape life or whatever it's called that buzzes around him and rarely gives him any peace. It's summer and the greenness emerges from the earth where blind worms live their lives and keep life in the soil, see to it that it doesn't suffocate, we have them to thank for the greenness, the multitude of flowers. Gísli starts his walks early, not necessarily well rested and perhaps hungover, his mind heavy and infertile, no blind worms that keep life in it with their tireless labor, yet without hope of any reward other than that which is contained in life itself. Gísli has a walking stick that he bought on his last voyage overseas, when he traveled through Germany many years ago, but where can he get the money to go abroad again? It's buried as deep as the purpose of life, yet he can spend long moments thinking about his last trip, reliving it, and it's an excellent walking stick, made of oak that grew in the light and darkness down south in Europe, Gísli calls it Heine, who was a German poet inclined to sins of the flesh. Both of us are, Gísli says to his walking stick, feeling better to be able to talk to someone, walks out of the Village into the bright light of summer, no cover anywhere, no darkness to plunge into, no children to distract him. Over the last few days Gísli has tried to be disciplined, refraining from drink after eleven at night and thus feeling tolerable when he sets out on his walk at four in the morning, bright and silent, it's necessary to set out early to avoid seeing people, those disagreeable, banal creatures, admirers of saltfish. This nation will never amount to anything, he says out loud, to himself, to the light, to his walking stick, it will never choose education over fish, never put faith in the power of the mind, a thousand years of living on this island has crushed the nation, it believes in the hands, not the mind, in work, not thought, and will never acquire the patience to accomplish anything grand.

He's come to the cemetery, props his walking stick against the cemetery wall, unbuttons his coat, the walk has made him warm, the weather is calm and so tranquil that Gísli can hear the small, gentle waves lapping at the sand of the beach where the boy likes to sit on his rock, recovering his strength after his vigorous runs. This nation, says Gísli—it's nice to talk to yourself, you're always right, then—is always just barely scraping by, patching together planks to float on; it will never have ships in which to sail the world. He looks at his stick as if expecting it to answer, but walking sticks rarely say much. Gísli sighs softly, mumbles, I should write an article about this, it would please Skúli, that bastard. Sighs again, sits down on the wall, reaches into his jacket for a French picture book, a fine edition, 24 photographs of scantily clad women, they're young and smile at the headmaster, who gazes at them, lost in his imagination, looks up as if to regain his composure and sees people walking by, yet it's barely four in the morning. Never any peace and quiet, he thinks, squinting to see better, having to squint because everything regresses, everything dwindles, the sex drive, dreams, sleep, vision. It's a man and woman, both looking down, there's a gap between them, four arms hang irresolutely at their sides. Why, if it isn't the headmaster, Oddur says, at which Rakel looks up. The man's always reading, Oddur says, and Rakel nods; then they stop, unsure of what to do next. Oh, it's you, says Gísli, putting the book back beneath his coat. He stands up, fumbles for his walking stick. Yes, Rakel says rather quietly, we're just out for a walk, Oddur says apologetically, so you know each other, Gísli says, well, says Oddur hesitantly, glancing at Rakel, who has hooked her hands together behind her back and is indescribably beautiful like that. Well, a bit, says Oddur, just a bit, and before he knows it finds himself bowing to Gísli. Splendid, says Gísli, nodding, simply splendid, and are you going to walk any further? I'm heading this way, he says, pointing with his stick down the fjord. No, I don't think so, says Oddur, too loudly, and Rakel shakes her head, turns around and walks back toward the Village; Oddur bows again, and then they recede, side by side, four awkward arms. I'm no good at speaking to such distinguished people, says Oddur, whose forehead is sweating slightly. I don't think he feels well, she says, looking down, a lock of her ash-blond hair falls over her eyes, which also makes her look so beautiful. Oddur sighs softly, it's difficult to have two hands and a longing to touch her, but he senses how she starts, sees her eyes grow dark and frightened, when his hands touch her, but now she looks down, which is undeniably wise, there are around thirty cows in the Village and they're herded morning and evening along this road, in and out of town, cowpats can be big and the human foot small; Rakel, for instance, has small feet and it wouldn't be much fun if one of them sank, even disappeared, into a cowpat from last evening.

They must be bored with each other, mutters Gísli, barely discerning them in the distance, but noticing that they both have their heads lowered, and that there's a gap between them. Then he sets off down the fjord, passes the Village's cows, which are all lying down, chewing their cuds, their big, tender, vacant eyes shut, shaking their large heads now and then to free them of flies, otherwise making no move even when the headmaster, this man from a finer family, thirsty for a drink of milk, kneels down next to one of them, grabs a teat and squeezes several lukewarm jets into his mouth. These are the only breasts I get to touch nowadays, Gísli says out loud, glancing over his shoulder, though they're long gone, of course, Oddur and Rakel, doubtlessly fucking each other somewhere, maybe even in the headmaster's basement. Damn it, he's getting his pleasure, that ridiculous, ungainly snow-shoveler; if only I had the money to escape from here. But I should just marry Rakel, mutters Gísli, having set off again and talking to himself or to his walking stick; hurry up and do it before that imbecile gets her, he has a snow shovel, that's enough for him. God help me, to have the opportunity to lie against a warm female body, it's utter nonsense that people need to love, love is overrated. How many times have we heard the saying that love never lasts? It is truly just a flash in the pan.

The birds are awake. Two plovers run ahead of Gísli, up and down tussocks, singing a note or two, so pure but also poignant because the summer is short, the sun is sometimes so excessively far away and ravens wait on black cliffs for you to leave, it's good to eat eggs, good to eat warm chicks, and the snipe climbs into the light, dives, spreads notes over the moors. I can always visit Reverend Kjartan this summer, thinks Gísli, stay there for several days, it would be good for my soul. He's come to the bottom of the fjord, which cuts like a dagger into the land, just beyond it is a decent stretch of land, moors, fields, meadows and a capricious river, and then the mountains rise, higher than life; damn mountains, thinks Gísli as he walks past two farmhouses, one a cottage, a mere tussock with a door, the other more stately, built partly of timber. The first folk are awake, Gísli walks so near to the cottage, to avoid a swampy patch of ground, that he hears a woman humming. It's cooler here at the bottom of the fjord, and everything's dripping with dew, but Gísli is from a distinguished family and is wearing good shoes, unlike the people on the farm, whose feet remain wet from the time the frost leaves the earth until it returns. Right now everything is so dewy that it's impossible to sit down in a soft hollow, gaze back up the fjord, think about eternity and the purpose of life, perhaps look a bit at the picture book. A cursed agitation in his flesh that's been there since he sat down on the cemetery wall with the book, man's life is a long, exhausting struggle with the agitation of the flesh.

Gísli has found himself a large, flat rock out of sight; he wipes it off, peruses the photos in his book and does what he needs to do, and the fjord is mirror-smooth on this tranquil morning, so tranquil that everything becomes beautiful. A farmer and a dog emerge from the cottage, both yawn, shake off sleep, pee, the woman comes out with the nightsoil and spies her husband, puts down the bucket, sneaks up behind him, puts her arms around him, let me aim it, she says, and the man laughs softly. Her palm, hard, calloused, wraps around him and directs the stream. They've been married for more than twenty years, life has worn them out, yet it's still fun to be alive, they both giggle there in front of the cottage; she begins moving her hand quickly and he spreads his feet wider because it's better like that. Afterward he kisses her withered hair and says something that none but the two of them would feel worthy of writing down and keeping, yet that is possibly worth more than the entire fleet of ships belonging to Tryggvi's Shop and Trading Company. Of course, that's a brazen assertion. Tryggvi owns numerous ships, nineteen in all, a great empire. Friðrik owns a share in four of them, Karólína, the hunched matriarch nearly bent double by time despite still having considerable fight left in her, owns a substantial share in three of them, which Gísli will inherit after time has finally succeeded in its mission, or at least that's what the headmaster hopes and Friðrik fears. Freedom, thinks Gísli. A waste, thinks Friðrik. Everyone sees life with his own eyes and that's why it's never possible to speak of one life, one world.

Gísli returns. Looks out at the fjord, nearly white with tranquility and silence, not a cloud in the sky, and the morning sun lifts itself high enough to light the mountains, which then shine like music. Gísli wades through the dew, the tranquility, free of agitation, walks back past the cottage, that overgrown tussock, dark inside, the folk there wake and sleep in heavy air, in confinement. Damn it, mutters Gísli. The dog is outside, wanting desperately to sniff this man, perhaps finagle a pat or two on the head, it's so good to be scratched behind the ear, almost as good as getting an unexpected piece of meat, but he doesn't dare go over to the man, is afraid of the walking stick, it hurts to be beaten. Gísli goes over to the spot where the couple stood before, but is at a loss. He thinks many a remarkable thought about life and poetry; there are few who think as deeply beneath these high mountains as our headmaster, he also knows incredibly much about human beings, how they are, where they come from, what they desire. At times it's as if his eyes see more than others', he looks down from above and can see our lives in unexpected contexts; even Friðrik avoids debating with his brother, unless the topic has to do with the laws of ledgers, the laws of the powers-that-be. Unfortunately, there's a huge gap between thinking and living. It's possible to know more than everyone else, to understand life, to be able to describe it in moving words, distinguish between cause and effect, yet have no idea how to live an ordinary, everyday life. A bit like knowing all the notes but being unable to whistle a simple melody.

Yet the stillness of the morning, the walk, the moment on the flat rock, put Gísli in a good mood, and he decides to stop at the print shop; Ásgeir, the manager there, always has something up his sleeve, and it's also good to breathe in the smell of ink, listen to the sound of the press, which the youngest printer works with his feet, sitting on the windowsill, printing the words, the blessed, cursed words. On the printing schedule today are the poems of the Icelandic-Canadian poet Jóhann Magnús Bjarnason, poems that might not save anyone from distress yet are fine enough. Gísli smiles, breathes in tussocks and the morning, walks around the verge of a hill and sees the boy coming toward him at great speed, his eyes bulging, running so swiftly it's as if he hardly touches the ground, as if he's floating, and he passes the headmaster with such energy that the air vibrates around him. They're several yards apart when the boy runs by, he turns his head in Gísli's direction, and for several moments it's as if life, none other than the world's youth, the eternal spring, trembling with pent-up energy, sheer power, fervor and possibilities, gives the headmaster a glance. The boy runs past and is gone and everything becomes uncomfortably still; not a fly to be heard, let alone any bigger animal, because it was time itself that ran past, in the guise of the boy, ran past the headmaster and left him behind, old and useless, an abode of shattered dreams.

Gísli plods laboriously toward the Village, well above the beach, finally finds himself some shelter amidst tussocks, sits down. The most burdensome thing in this life is never to be able to escape oneself, one's own existence, shut up inside a compartment, in a world that never gives you any space, except perhaps in particular dreams, but that comes to you as soon as you open your eyes; how can it be tolerated? The most burdensome thing is not to know how to live, to know the notes but to be unable to sing them. Gísli sits among the soft, moist tussocks, watching seagulls glide past the cliff face on an updraft, they know how to let themselves glide, rest their wings, know how to live, yet have never thought anything. There they glide. The sun is over the eastern mountains and the seagulls gleam in the light, the sun illuminates them, they can be seen from a great distance, even Gísli sees them with his rather weak eyes. He watches. Then a cloud draws over the sun and it's as if a light goes out inside the birds, they disappear, but not Gísli, he doesn't disappear, unfortunately; he sits there and has to tolerate himself.

VIII

You run, says Gísli. Yes, says the boy, I run.

Why?

Why do I run?

Gísli doesn't reply; this learned man stands there looking into the light that streams in through the big window and upsets him. The boy scratches his head, I just have to, he says, but Gísli looks and waits, I like it, Gísli still waits, I feel free when I do, the boy adds. Free, Gísli repeats, stuff and nonsense, and looks out once more. Write this, he then says to the light, the twelfth article of the constitution, quote, the king pardons men and grants a general reprieve, full stop, unquote. The boy writes fast yet hasn't managed to cap the sentence with the closing quotation mark when there's a knock at the front door, and since Helga is out at the café, the boy goes to answer it. He hears a soft murmur from the café as he steps into the hallway, quite a few people there now, the world is thirsty for beer, the sun fills the sky like birdsong, and two foreign ships arrived late last evening, a big sailing ship that slipped so quietly down the fjord, into the Lagoon that no one noticed it, but in its wake came a hissing, wheezing steamer, the clamorous future.

I heard a steamer in the night, Helga had said at the breakfast table, so it could be busy today; which turned out to be the case, sailors from the wheezing steamer, the silent sailing ship, a considerable crowd that needs to kill time, needs something to drink, English and Danish sailors, and Andrea feels a bit insecure and vulnerable as she watches Helga deal with the foreigners. She'd brought one book with her from the fishing station, Jón Ólafsson's English-language textbook, and reads it in the evenings, in her basement room, alone, all alone, the next person nearly four hundred thousand miles away, like the moon that the spring light has wiped clean from the sky. It's difficult to aim for a place that's gone, difficult to reach those who no longer exist. What do you want with this? She'd asked the boy and Bárður when they brought the textbook to the fishing hut just over two months ago. So that we can say I love you and I desire you in English, Bárður had said, causing her heart to skip a beat, skip a beat so stupidly, and now she knows how to say I love you in English. But of course it's rather silly of her to sit over a book in the evenings, learning these words by heart, this brief sentence that has nothing to do with her, neither in Icelandic nor in English, nor in any language, for that matter.

More knocking. Heavy, determined blows. Yet not impertinent, far from it, these blows don't say, Damn it, why is it taking so long? Open up immediately, time is precious! That's not at all what they say, meaning it could hardly be Friðrik doing the knocking, bringing new threats, albeit what he calls offers, contracts, those in power use language differently. This knocking says, It's very important to me that I be heard. They say, as well, which the boy sees when he opens the door, I've traveled a long way to this house, over an ocean bigger than life, I sailed aboard my ship for days on end just so that my knocking would be heard, I sailed swiftly, and the wind that filled the sails is named desire, even love. The boy opens the door and greets the one knocking in this way, greets the ship's captain whom he saw for the first time at the very start of April, just after Bárður died. Then the boy had greeted the man with a nod, while the foreigner had looked at him with a kind of warmth, with friendliness. Now the captain, who arrived a day and night ago and spent most of yesterday in the house, greets the boy with a smile and English words as the light streams over both of them, into the hallway where it embraces Geirþrúður, who has come downstairs, wearing a thick green sweater, her black hair falling over the greenness, and she smiles, not much, yet discernibly, and her slightly crooked teeth remind us of imperfection. She says something in English and the captain says something in return, laying one thick hand over his heart before raising both hands, smiling broadly, handsome, his blue eyes possessing a certain magnetism. Gísli enters from the parlor, appearing behind her, and looks at them.

Geirþrúður goes over to the boy, stands very close to him, chooses to stand there as she introduces the two men, Gísli and the captain. We're going to, Geirþrúður softly informs the boy as the two men speak to each other, we're going to, she says softly, a bit animatedly, get horses from Jóhann, go for a ride, I'll likely not be back before evening, but wait for me for your reading, and how do I look? The last item, the question, she says in such a way that it's as if his reply matters. You're beautiful, he says, before adding, because one should always tell the truth, men in foreign countries would go to war over you, poets would compose poems. He receives a kiss from her, soft lips, her warm breath on his cheek, I told you you would be danger-ous, she says in his ear with a soft laugh, a bit like a girl, if you lost your innocence. Try to hold onto it a bit longer.

It's an unexpected relief to get a chance to speak the language of cultivated people, it allows you to escape, to catch your breath for a moment and feel invigorated, this captain speaks almost like a man of learning, married, of course, unclear what his wife would say to this, her husband being here, at the edge of the end of the world, heading off somewhere with a woman whom some say is marked by sin and immorality; it's rather refreshing to see a woman in pants. Gísli raises his coffee cup to his lips, his hand trembles, he hasn't had a drink since the day before yesterday, perhaps that's the reason. You run, he then says, hastily, takes another sip of coffee, stands at the window, looks out, then glances quickly at the boy, run like the Devil himself is after you, why do you run like that? The boy rocks in his seat, as if he's being asked about something uncomfortable, but then Kolbeinn walks in, as he usually does when Gísli is teach-ing, sits down on the sofa, leans forward on his cane, waits, listens, turns his better ear toward them. Well, Gísli says, gazing at the blind skipper for a moment with a distracted expression, grants a general reprieve, full stop, unquote, did you get that down? Yes, the boy says. Where will Geirþrúður go with the captain and what will they do? As if you don't know, he thinks, looking at the quotation mark that concludes the sentence, that clumsy symbol. Well then, Gísli says, and whence does the king derive this vast power to pardon criminals; you've committed a crime, killed someone, stolen valuables, but I forgive you, how can he say this, whence does he derive the power? I don't know. That's no answer, you should try, never give up, try! From God? From the Devil? Splendid, Gísli says, just splendid, what do you say to that, Kolbeinn? I'm not here, the skipper says curtly, I don't see you. Splendid, Gísli says again, just splendid, but can you name a person, a living human being, who has more power than the king? No. Well, here's a question to wrestle with: If a king possesses this incomprehensible power, can he pardon someone who betrays his trust, can he pardon someone who goes back on his word, can a king pardon someone who betrays himself? Is this what you call instruction? says Kolbeinn, despite his not being there; he pounds his cane on the floor, had hoped for a continuation of the last lesson about the Greek world, Gísli had lectured on Athens, on the Greek state, an empire of culture, an empire of thought. There were 115,000 slaves in Greece, they did every task imaginable, allowing the Greeks to think with clear heads, unfatigued, never needing to bounce around the Aegean in boats, didn't die of exposure between houses, didn't toil in dust and heat, hardship couldn't diminish them, they came near to Heaven by standing on the shoulders of slaves. Man is cruel, we mustn't admire those who rise highest before we know what they stand upon, their own two legs or the lives of others. Is this instruction, is this scholarship? Kolbeinn asks again, did you get this from Copenhagen? You certainly talk a lot for someone who's not here, Gísli says, but I suppose you wanted the Greeks again, you wanted facts, just wait, they're coming, I know very well what it is that people call education, know what people take as valid, and I will teach it, shall not fail, am too craven to do otherwise. But I would just like to spoil the boy a bit, he's well suited for it. I'll get back to the Greeks, you can count on it, what does it mean to betray oneself? Gísli asks the boy without hesitating in his monologue, questions the boy, who struggles to follow what Gísli's saying, while at the same time pushing aside thoughts of Geirþrúður, this old woman who is, in any case, not at all old, now she's riding astride Jóhann's horse, away from the Village. Listen to this, Árni had said in the fishing hut this winter, reading from *The Will of the People*: Gentlewomen in Paris, London and New York have stopped riding side-saddle, they now ride like men, astride the saddle. Ride astride the saddle! Einar had exclaimed heatedly, what's next, huh, what's next, where is this damn world heading?

The boy closes his eyes as if to make a quick escape: To dare not.

Gísli: What, oh, well, but what, to dare not what?

The boy: Live. To dare not speak. To dare not be afraid. To attempt not to overcome . . . the dark storm inside you. If you do nothing, you betray everyone who matters. If there's anyone left who matters; alive, I mean. But maybe it doesn't matter whether people are alive or not, I mean. Nor should you betray those who are dead; we should live for them, as well, they mustn't be left in the dark and cold, and they mustn't be forgotten at the bottom of the sea. Look here, Gísli says, what book did you take this from? The boy looks down, says nothing, it's so petty to be proud of having said what matters. What do you say about this, old fisherman? Gísli says, looking at Kolbeinn, who doesn't reply; no, you're not here, of course, mutters Gísli; overcome the dark storm inside you, hmm, yes, was that in the twelfth article of the constitution? It was Hjalti who said it, about the dark storm. What Hjalti? He helped Jens and me transport the coffin from Nes, he was a farmhand there, the weather was foul and he didn't make it all the way. There aren't many people who do, Gísli says, looking out the window.

IX

The cod that had swam in the depths of the sea the entire winter, far from the world of men, as happy as its cold blood allowed, now lies flattened, spineless and gutted on the Village's drying lots, transformed into saltfish. Saltfish everywhere you look, the smell forces its way into every house, every room, the saltfish is shaped like angel wings and covers the entire spit. Seen from above, it looks like a graveyard of angels.

Gísli walks away from Geirþrúður's house, his lesson finished.

What does it mean to betray oneself, what is the greatest treachery, the most heinous crime, so heinous that the king can't pardon you? To dare not to live, the boy had answered.

Cursed boy, thinks Gísli, before meeting his brother-in-law Sigurður, doctor and postmaster, outside the print shop, where he'd been looking in on the second printing of the booklet *On Breastfeeding and the Use of Glass Bottles with Rubber Nipples*, which he'd had printed three or four years ago, written by Gísli, according to Sigurður's prescriptions. The booklet had saved the lives of numerous infants, and now the two brothers-in-law stand there, Sigurður slim, impeccably dressed, Gísli somewhat taller, yet so drooping, torpid, that he seems shorter, his pants stained. Where have you come from? the doctor says. From Hell, the headmaster replies, were you checking on the booklet? It'll be ready tomorrow, Sigurður says, you should have dinner with us tonight. Can a king pardon those who've betrayed themselves? Gísli says. You're always welcome, the doctor says, but you'd better not show up drunk. Gísli shrugs, which can mean many things. Hmm, says Sigurður, hmm, he says again, perhaps, yes, perhaps better for you to know it—Friðrik has mentioned sending you away for the summer. Because I ask whether a king could pardon those who've betrayed themselves? It's neither pretty nor appropriate for one of us to be staggering drunkenly through the streets, spending hour after hour at Sodom or in Geirþrúður's parlor. Where will he send me? You have close kin in Eyjafjörður. Don't we have any kin in Paris? They don't necessarily need to be good. Stop by this evening, around six, if you're presentable, says Sigurður, patting his brother-in-law amicably on the shoulder, and Gísli goes into the print shop, the youngest printer is sitting on the windowsill, his foot pumping the apparatus that prints the booklet. Why am I here? Gísli asks Ásgeir, the print shop manager, they stand at Ásgeir's desk, which is untidy, everything on it in a jumble, the headmaster momentarily free from the light, the sky, his brother-in-law, why am I here, when there are places with names such as Paris?

Yes, why? Yet it's undeniably beautiful to hike up a mountain, look out over the spit white with saltfish, white with dead angels, and see all the ships that sail into the fjord, loaded with fish, with cod, sail in, unload the fish, take on provisions, water, sail back out, some up to seventy tons. Well over two hundred sailors work on the ships outfitted by Tryggvi's Shop and Trading Company, the summer is hectic as well, long working days for the company's bookkeepers, for Friðrik, and soon Tryggvi will come, leave his mansion in Copenhagen, the bustling city life, and stay with us for six or eight weeks, come on his sailing ship loaded with wares, unless he's bought a steamer, contrary to the advice of Friðrik, who prefers prudence in everything, to welcome new times slowly, yet vague news has been spreading about Tryggvi and a steamer, something to talk about, wonder about. The schooners stream to and from the Village, Friðrik goes three or four times a day out to the spit to visit the drying lots, in which the company has a share, goes down to the ships, inspects the catches, determines whether they've been unloaded properly, not tossed ashore carelessly; it's important that the fish be undamaged when they're flattened, the salt adheres to them better, producing a higher quality, more valuable product. Friðrik checks on everything, trusts no one completely except himself, he strolls around, sits in his office and meets with workers and fishermen who bring him reports and receive a tiny bit of goodwill in return, provisions for the future, individuals whom Friðrik has chosen to be his eyes and ears on the drying lots, on deck out at sea, in the cabins, what's spoken of, how the men behave, who is shirking, his eyes and ears are everywhere, he wants to hear everything, nothing is too small, insignificant, the company has just under five hundred people working for it in the summer, the personnel must be kept track of, the most must be got out of them, slacking off prevented, otherwise things would go badly, there would be a breakdown of discipline, dawdling, complacency, and the quality would drop, the prices fall, the company would suffer losses and with it the Village, and thereby us, and everything would darken, little would separate us from deprivation, even death, a huge weight rests on Friðrik's shoulders and he does what he needs to do. Those in charge can't allow themselves pedantry, sensitivity, this is a merciless country, complacency kills, concession kills, and dreams can also kill. Just under five hundred people, at sea, here on land, shop clerks, men and women to process the saltfish, numerous itinerant workers, from Snæfellsnes, from Húnavatn County and farther away. They come in groups aboard the coastal ships, step ashore, some wobbly, it's not always pleasant at sea, they look around, look at the mountains, steep as a scream, level ground is almost nonexistent, and these people ask in surprise, Where are the meadows?

X

Words are not lifeless rock or gnawed, wind-whitened bones up in the mountains. Even the most mundane of them can grow distant over time and be transformed into museums that house the past, what is gone and will never return. Meadows, manured hayfields, we're moved to tears by these words, something snaps within us, as when we unexpectedly come across old photographs and see faces long since lost in the earth or the sea. Where are the meadows? We recall tranquil summer mornings, so still and deep that we could nearly hear God, but we also recall the toil, the wet feet, the wet grass, newly mown, we recall the tremendous fatigue, we recall what's gone and will never return, recall so poignantly that we were once alive, that we could once hold hands, that there were once childish questions. Once we were alive, had names, and they were sometimes spoken in such a way that the deserts of life began to flourish with greenery. Once we were alive, but not any longer, what surrounds us is called death. Where are the meadows?

XI

Is your heart still beating?

And how does it beat?

Damn it all. The boy receives a letter in which he's asked about his heartbeat. As if living isn't enough of a trial.

He awakes each morning just before six, reaches out and grabs a book, poems to read as he emerges from his dreams into the delicate morning, connecting night and day, dreams and waking with poems, there may be no better way for a person to wake up. Yet the questions don't go anywhere, what is he supposed to do with his life? Does he love Ragnheiður, whom he's met twice since returning from his journey with Jens, a journey that went all the way to the end of the world, through gloomy weather, through life and death? The first time, they met on the street and she looked at the boy as if he were nothing, even a bit less than that. The next day he was about to enter the German Bakery when Ragnheiður stepped out with Danish pastries for her father, Friðrik, warm pastries were practically the only luxury he permitted himself, and Ragnheiður was the only one who was allowed to buy them, and then she deigned to recognize the boy,

I heard you nearly killed yourself on your journey with the drunkard, how could you ever think of dying before I left for Copenhagen? Jens is not a drunk, he said, feeling mildly dizzy, her eyes are somewhat wide-set, those gray eyes that can be cold as frost, as the blood of a cod. Between them dwells my fate, he thought, couldn't help doing so. This sweater is new, she said. Yes, he said. It's beautiful, they know how to clothe you. There's lint on your shoulder, said Ragnheiður, brushing his right shoulder.

Is your heart still beating? And why?

Life is strange; as far back as he can remember, education had been the promised land that echoed under and over his mother's letters—his only education until now had been in preparation for his Confirmation, and one month of lessons with an itinerant teacher when he was ten or twelve years old. Yet he was able to read and write fluently by the time the sea claimed his father, and he practiced writing whenever he could, scratched letters on ice, on moldering rafters in the roof of the cowshed, in the snow, at first without constraint, neglected his chores, the rafters barely held up against the weight of the words, and one morning when people came out of the farmhouse it was nearly impossible for them to step into the snow due to the sheer amount of words, the boy hadn't been able to sleep because of the moonlight, had gone out while it was still night and started to write. Twelve strokes of the switch for three days in a row and no dinner brought him to his senses. He was beaten not out of malice but out of necessity, for, in the first place, writing words in the snow or dirt is bad luck, and second, chores go unattended in the meantime, and how are people supposed to live in this land if they neglect their work? And what would happen to you, who would employ you if word got out that you wrote in the snow instead of worked? You'd soon end up on the parish, you'd be kicked like a dog, so welcome these twelve strokes, let them teach you, they're not given out of malice but out of necessity, even care. Now he gets up, does light chores, takes lessons twice a week from Gísli, the most educated man in the village, the county, even this quarter of the country, the headmaster himself, has English lessons twice a week with Hulda, occasionally arithmetic with Helga, wakes up in the mornings, connects dreams and reality with poems, reality where he's encouraged to get an education, what is distant has come to him, yet he asks, Why am I alive, where is life heading? And then the boy receives a letter.

Is your heart still beating?

If so, how?

It's beating like that of a drowning man, a wingless bird, how the hell should he answer this? Of course it's important to receive a letter, to have a person consider it worthwhile to sit down and assemble words and have you in mind the entire time it takes to write the letter, to receive a letter indicates that you exist, that you're closer to being light than darkness. Admittedly, not all letters are good, and some should perhaps never have been sent, never have been opened, read, some are full of hatred, accusations, they're poison that will deprive you of your strength, they bring darkness and disappointment.

There's a letter for you, said Andrea with something of a mischievous look. Letter, he exclaimed in surprise, because who should be writing him a letter, his mother sent him eleven letters, he has all of them, the twelfth never came. It might be from Reverend Kjartan, he said nonchalantly, and absurdly, of course; why should Reverend Kjartan send him a letter, why should such an educated, intelligent man, the owner of large numbers of books, show any interest in his existence? Might be from Reverend Kjartan, he said, having just come into the café after an English lesson with Hulda, two English lessons behind him, singular, plural, the definite and indefinite articles, a table, tables, an apple, apples. Have you tasted an apple? asked the boy as he wrote down the word for this spherical, exotic fruit, as far from our everyday existence as Jupiter. No, said Hulda curtly, telling a lie.

Teitur sometimes gets apples from foreign sailors who've come here often and might be called acquaintances, but it's easier to say no; it's safer, no is a fort protecting her. No, she says, and you can't get any closer. No, said Hulda, glancing at the boy through the battlements, and he said, unable to stop himself, Is there a plural form of love in every language? A love, she said, loves. With a "v"? Yes, a "v," but you shouldn't write it down, it's not in the curriculum. Love isn't in the curriculum? No, just apples, she replied, looking down to hide her smile.

Reverend Kjartan? Andrea said. He's in Vík, remember, Jens and I stayed there our second night, his wife's name is Anna, and she's nearly blind. Yes, no, the letter's not from him, it's from a woman, or at least a woman has addressed the envelope. A woman? he said in surprise, umm, oh, then that would be María, from Vetrarströnd. He took the envelope, gave it a quick look and was taken aback when he saw the letters, their ardor, as if they were all running into each other. They're fighting, he added, the letters, he explained, when Andrea asked, What? So she's that ardent, is she? Andrea said, smiling at the boy, who hardly heard anything over the pounding of his heart. María would never write like that; she's ardent, of course, fires burn inside her, she cries sometimes about something she lacks without knowing what it is, just feels as if she's lacking something, and then Jón holds her, his embrace is warm and strong, yet doesn't encompass the horizon. No, María would probably be more meticulous, she produces only the best and would have made the letters smaller, to save space; she doesn't know how else to do it. He looked at the envelope. Yes, he said, she's ardent. How does her heart beat? So ardently that herbivores in Africa look up, so ardently that the birds of the air are knocked off course. We can go over my English a bit, the boy said to Andrea, who smiled broadly, warming the boy with her smile, warming him so much that he was able to sit at the table, go over singular and plural in English without going insane with impatience, he sat calmly, now and then leaning closer to Andrea, she has such a warm scent, blended with a faint musty smell from her basement room, and twice she stroked his cheek with her weary fingers, these two people far out on life's sea of uncertainty, surrounded by heavy currents. He breathed in Andrea and the letter quivered as it touched his flesh.

But now he's sitting in his room. Is your heart beating?

XII

"Is your heart still beating? And if so, how? I'm sitting by the wall of the house, the one you crashed into, you and the big man, Jens. It's sunny and everything is very wet. Your feet get wet just by looking outside. But now the sun is warm. You can give it that. The frost melts into the ground. That's why the ground is wet, as if it's weeping. I'm sitting on a stool. I brought a book to read, I wasn't going to write you a letter, the book is a quite long. It's called *The Odyssey* and is ages old. Steinunn said it was a 'classic,' I expect that you know of it. That's how you are. I noticed it immediately. That's why you know it's about a man who's trying to get home, but who ends up in all sorts of adventures and catastrophes. In the meantime his wife has to wait there, albeit in a palace and with enough to eat, it's warm there and no one gets buried in snow. Yet it's probably no easier to exist there, it's probably no easier to wait in uncertainty even if the weather's good and the house has no leaks. I shouldn't think it's any easier. She has to wait and doesn't know whether he's dead or is being unfaithful. She just waits, composed and patient and faithful, while he experiences adventures, and then a book is written about him. No need to tell me about women. No need to tell me about men. Then it crossed my mind to write you a letter. I guess I'd thought about you, I must have done, but that doesn't have to mean anything. For example, I also think about the frost that melts into the ground and makes everything wet, makes all our feet wet. Not yours, you who had such good shoes, people here still talk about it, and then there are those American boots that apparently keep one's feet eternally dry. Not many people here believe it. But even if I think about you, it's absolutely meaningless. So much has been thought here in Iceland, ever since the country was settled a thousand years ago. Yet some people never seem to think anything, simply never. Have you noticed? The expressions of such people remind me of rotten, useless hay. I'm going to stop now. Sometimes I also think about a horse trailer, about kittens and about Jupiter, which is a very big planet yet is still just a tiny speck of light in the sky. I also think sometimes about the rain in China, which I suppose you're familiar with. I think about all sorts of things. So even if I think about you, it's nothing remarkable. I'm sitting on a stool, no, I'd already mentioned that. The snow is melting on the mountain above me. You see how little happens here. Life here is just melting snow and frost. Is it any wonder that it crossed my mind to write a letter? I'm lying, though. Life here isn't just melting snow and frost. For example, the shop manager Sigurður is drunker some days than others. Yesterday he couldn't stand on his own two feet. The day before yesterday he was so lively that his wife had to lock him in the house. She seems to have some trick or other for keeping him inside when it's necessary. That Hjalti who was with you still hasn't been found. The doctor and his wife sent some men over to Nes. What a place that's supposed to be. The men said that when they got there, they found no Hjalti, but that everyone was doing well. People can be so stupid. They might have been standing upright, but of course they weren't doing well. Maybe I should go there and never come back? I wonder if you've recovered? You two didn't look very well when you left. There was still a chill in you, and particularly in the big man, Jens. He made it all the way home. His sister was terribly happy. She's considerably better than us, from the sound of it. You see that I've come to the end of this sheet of paper, there's no more space. Nor can I spend more time on it. I know that I can't write, you don't need to tell me. My letters are as ugly and tattered as old hens."

XIII

I think about you sometimes. It's good to walk up over the Village where the tussocks are soft, you lie down between them and it's as if they embrace you. The boy is lying among them, looking up at the sky. I think about you sometimes. Then it crossed my mind to write you a letter. I guess I'd thought about you. He lies there so long that the birds have become used to him; even the redshank has calmed down. But I also think sometimes about a horse trailer, about kittens and about Jupiter, which is a very big planet yet is still just a tiny speck of light in the sky. I also think about rain in China, I'm sure you're familiar with it.

Helga bristles when he returns; what's the meaning of disappearing like that, things need doing here. The boy replies with an indecipherable mutter, so pale and muddle-headed that Helga says, Well then, and sends him to the café. It's as if she knows how he feels, as if she understands his sensitivity. Sensitivity is my truest dream, says an old poem, a line that shines through time, and it's true, the essence of man is sensitivity, we feel it so desperately in the spring when existence is at the needle-point of life and death. The song of the plover, that poignant sound, reminds us of it, and now and then we're startled to hear it, it's why Ólafur sat up on the mountain, in sleet, and wept; he had to weep, he sensed man's truest dream while realizing the distance between his dream and the world that he's created. Then it's evening.

It's evening, and the weather is bad, those who are able to be at home are at home, listening to the wind, reading *The Will of the*

People; Icelanders, it says, appear to have sworn a solemn oath to live beyond their means, controlled by merchants, and then die in debt. Merchants rule our days where we allow them to. People believe that it's an immutable law. Consequently, we don't stand together; everyone lives for himself. As a result, we nearly always fish using their hooks rather than our own.

Skúli owns a share in a schooner, his father-in-law is a wealthy farmer in a bountiful area south of the mountains, Skúli can afford to provoke us with his pen, having little to lose, which is different from us, we depend entirely on merchants and their goodwill. Still, it's fun to read such things: it's titillating, exciting, a bit like when children go off somewhere to say bad words. It's good that someone's giving them what for, making them tremble a bit.

Dogs have to have the chance to bark now and then, says Friðrik; then there's less chance they'll bite. It's evening, terribly windy, pelting with rain, out of the question to open the windows, the cigar smoke hangs thickly in Friðrik's master bedroom, so big it's nearly a parlor. There are six of them: Friðrik, Reverend Þorvaldur, Dr. Sigurður, Jón, the factor of Léo's Shop and Trading Company, the magistrate Lárus, and Högni, the head bookkeeper at Tryggvi's Shop and Trading Company and director of the savings bank, which opened three years ago; it's open for business an hour every day, five days a week. Lárus had started talking about one of Skúli's articles. He's becoming more and more aggressive, said the magistrate, before listing various other articles, and Friðrik simply let them talk, allowed them to worry. He's become dangerous, said Sigurður, who always sits up so damn straight. Yes, Jón says excitedly, sucking on his cigar, Skúli's what you call in Danish a *skadefugl*, a curmudgeon, and the others smile at the word, as if Tove were speaking through him, but then the door opens and a maid enters with more coffee, refills their cups, tops up their cognac glasses; she's young, moves lithely, like a herb in water, never looks up, they don't get a good look at her eyes, those blue stones, and she isn't perturbed by their looks, watching her as the fire works its way up their stiff cigars with a low hiss, but she's glad to get out of there. A fine piece of work, mutters Lárus. To say the least, agrees Sigurður, while Þorvaldur says nothing, he'd watched as well, that was his sin. Then Friðrik says, waving his hand as if to brush the girl aside, her youth, the agitation that they all felt, Dogs have to be allowed to bark, then there's less chance they'll bite. But Skúli hit the nail on the head, albeit in reverse; most people spend beyond their means, as witnessed by the trading companies' ledgers, far too many people die in debt, which is why we must keep a firm hand on things, otherwise society as a whole will resemble the ledgers of its people— full of nothing but debt. But never mind Skúli, he's not a problem; it's Geirþrúður we need to worry about. Skúli hides nothing, is out in the open, but she's underhanded, shrewder, causes a stir and is a corrupter of morals, no less. You remember how she got her hands on Kolbeinn's share when he lost his sight, acquired a majority in one of the Village's best ships by inviting him to live with her? It doesn't cost much to feed a blind wretch, a wretch with plenty of money of his own; where's it supposed to go when he breathes his last, huh? She's clever and takes advantage of situations. She got hold of Snorri's share in the ice house at a bargain price two years ago, tossed him a pittance of a payment, he was and is no man to stipulate conditions and was surely overjoyed to get at least something for it, while she tightened the noose around the poor bastard's neck, and is probably lying in wait now for his schooner, the *Hope*, if she hasn't already secured it. In her own opinion, adds Friðrik. Has Tryggvi got his eye on Snorri's company? asks Jón; he has to ask, has been ordered to ask. Friðrik looks at him, smokes, the rain beats down on the house, it's a June evening.

It's the very start of June, yet it's still dusky between the mountains. Gloomy weather. The wind picks up, the saltfish stacks are tied down tightly. There's hardly anyone out and about in this tempest, compared to how beautifully the day began, the sky full of sun and blue promises of calm and comfort, birdsong audible far and wide, nothing to dampen it in the transparent, motionless air. Flies buzzed over flowers and grass, saltfish covered the spit, the drying lots, much had turned green and beautiful in the mountains. In the Village itself, all was astir, naturally; there were shouts and cries and laughter and cursing and moving hands. Lúlli and Oddur were on a tear down in the hold of a ship, its captain rode off with Geirþrúður. I could love this country, he said. They rode up onto a heath, down into another fjord and into an empty, grassy valley.

There's good cover here, Geirþrúður said, and he gave her a long look before saying that he could love this country. Everything was turning green, and it was still and quiet between the tussocks, between the blades of grass, between the mountains that gathered sunshine and shone. On such days it's as if birdsong can heal the wounds within us. They lay in the grass for a long time, found a hollow, those who find good hollows during an Icelandic summer can't complain, bliss awaits them, if the flies let them be, that is. The blades of grass moved almost imperceptibly, like rows of venerable statesmen, and the birdsong healed wounds. I could easily love this country, said the captain, before adding, I could easily love you. Men say the most incredible things before satisfying their desires, or while doing so, all that's been whispered, breathless phrases, profound promises that prove to be shallow and worth little when all is said and done, the orgasm done and gone, the penis no longer erect and quivering with ardor and the lust for life, but slack, a dangling rag of skin between the legs. But when he said he could love her, that moment had already passed. They'd lain down and stripped off whatever clothing got in their way, it was unbridled passion, it was vehemence, the sky witnessed it, the blades of grass felt it, the mountains heard it and it startled birds nearby; they were like wild animals, they were beautiful, but now it was over. They smoked, sipped from a flask, regarded blades of grass, the sky, the mountain, birds, and the captain said that he could love her.

He lay with his head in her lap and she stroked the hair back from his forehead, his eyes, those pure eyes, from that strong, beautiful face, stroked the lips that knew so well how to kiss, knew how to speak words that were good to hear. I know, she said. You could love me, he said, he asked, he entreated. A woman in love is defenseless, she said, and I can't take that chance, and besides, you're married, you love your wife; continue to do so. Are you cruel, perhaps? No, but life can easily be so. Then he was sad, a bit like a child, this big foreigner, captain of a substantial sailing ship that Lúlli and Oddur worked at emptying while he lay with Geirþrúður among tussocks, beneath the blue sky. Did you get to put your arms around her? repeated Lúlli, having to press his friend hard to get an answer, and finally Oddur answered; he smiled.

Can a man love two women? the captain said. I expect so, she said, her long fingers in his thick hair, and perhaps even more if there's an ocean between them. But you don't know me, John, I'm just a diversion, a little adventure on a long sea voyage, a little dusky adventure that awaits you here at the end of the world, in among such steep, high mountains that no one can see us. You couldn't love me, not if you knew me, were with me every day, my heart is an organ that beats because that's all it knows. I'm a sea, John, and as the sea grants you freedom for a little while, I offer you adventure, a touch of sin, yet those who venture too far out onto such seas, and for too long, find little but loneliness and death.

A snipe whinnied close by, a plover replied with a poignant cry. Are you so unhappy? he asked softly, he asked tenderly. You need to experience happiness to understand unhappiness, and don't look at me like that, no one needs to comfort me, there's nothing to comfort, life is either victory or defeat, not happiness or unhappiness, and I'm going to be victorious in my own way. How can you be victorious without happiness? said her captain, John Andersen, stroking Geirþrúður's eyes with his broad hands, stroking tenderly, stroking as a man strokes something that matters a great deal to him. She took his hand, bit it gently with her predator's teeth, I'll tell you tomorrow, or whisper it to you, but now it's getting cold. They looked up at the sky, the blueness had darkened, the storm pounding Friðrik's house was approaching. But if you want, she added, and if you can manage it again, I'm ready. Only if I may love you, he said.

You may; but then leave your love behind when you sail away, leave it here amid the mountains.

Love is not a thing that one lays aside.

Yes, this love is, she said, unbuttoning her blouse. She unbuttoned her blouse and he beheld her gleaming white breasts, those breasts that he could gaze at endlessly, that pursued him far out to sea, all the way to England, those breasts, that skin, that scent, those long legs that locked around him, and the pitch-black hair that flowed like darkness over green heather and grass, those hoarse words that she muttered in his ear. If I could only love you, he whispered happily, he whispered despairingly, it would just be unhappiness and death, she whispered back, before forcing his head down to prevent him from seeing her face, seeing the black eyes that looked up at the sky. The sky that was growing restless. The sky that is so distant that it seems at times to have sentenced man to solitude.

Now this sky is heavy and restless, with dark, rushing clouds. It's summer, yet dangerous weather hangs over us. In June, which at times is so bright that it seems we can see down to the bottom of existence, to see eternity, friendly and huge in the distance. A storm, but in June; it could certainly treat us more fairly.

The wind breaks up the sea and everything that isn't fastened down blows away: handcarts, shovels, promises; forgive me, but I don't love you anymore, the wind tore my love from me, blew it away.

Horses stand on the moors, in some places completely exposed, turning away from the wind that lashes the creatures, they let the tantrum pass over them, stare in front of them, look forward to grazing again. The rain pounds them violently, it pounds the big parlor window in Geirþrúður's house, all four of them sit in the parlor, the boy beneath a dim lamp, you've got to have light to see the pages; whither went the light, who took it, bring it back, we don't deserve this.

He has to raise his voice somewhat for the three of them to hear, because all the words have to make it across, that's how poetry is, those are the rules, that's how it should be, must be, writing is a war and maybe authors experience more defeat than victory, that's just how it is, Gísli had explained, losing himself in his explanation, there was a gleam in his eye, as if he were really alive. He'd read over the five pages that the boy had translated of Mr. Dickens' story *A Tale of Two Cities*. It was the best of times, it was the worst of times. In this story there are few mistakes, few defeats, making the job of the translator more difficult yet happier. The boy said nothing, had the five pages in front of him, some of them heavily marked up by Gísli, the translation, the tireless work, anguish, sweat, joy, delicate movement between languages, shredded by the comments of the headmaster who talked and talked, the boy looked at the pages and the anger welled up inside him. It certainly would be nice to wad up the pages, make a big ball and stuff it into Gísli, deep into his throat, that dark tunnel. No need to let my compliments go to your head, pride is poison, Gísli said, his voice suddenly prickly. Compliments! the boy exclaimed, smiling without realizing it, his eyes still on the marked-up pages; compliments, he repeated; can it be called a compliment to rip apart a work into which you've put all you've got, your heart, lungs, breath? The boy looks in astonishment at Kolbeinn, sitting next to him, his eyes closed, as if sleeping, though with his left ear turned toward them, catching every word. Yes, Gísli said, I call it a compliment to say that you've done quite a good job, in some places very finely done indeed, quite unusual for an uneducated person, I would call that a compliment, wouldn't you call that a compliment from me, Kolbeinn? He raised his voice, looked over at the skipper, who said nothing, didn't react at all. Absolutely right, Gísli muttered, you're not here, what a wonderful talent to be able to vanish like that, a rare talent, you should give me lessons. I didn't hear it, the compliment, I mean, the boy said apologetically, I just saw that you'd marked up everything, thought that it was no good. Is that so, did you think that? Yes. But what was that smile of yours supposed to mean, then? I was just thinking. Thinking about what, what was so amusing? Well, the boy said, embarrassed, that it would be fun to stuff the pages down your throat, at which Kolbeinn laughed, or at least emitted a noise like an old, crotchety dog that suddenly encounters something interesting, unexpectedly: a nice piece of meat, an extinguished sex drive.

The boy reads the pages, had managed to rewrite them in time, followed Gísli's suggestions, corrections, for the most part, reads them as the rain pounds the world, pounds the house, pounds the horses, and the wind tears up the sea. He reads and tries to forget that right now the sea is breaching the embankments, flooding the earth in torrents, and to top it off there's this gale, as if to punish us for having enjoyed the light, the gentleness of summer.

There's power in this text, says Helga after the boy has read the five pages, these words that he found in the language and used for bridge-building so that both he and others, could seek out remote worlds, seek out life, feelings, seek out what exists in the distance of which we weren't aware. Translations, Gísli had said, it's hardly possible to describe their importance. They enrich and broaden us, help us to understand the world better, understand ourselves. A nation that translates little, focusing only on its own thoughts, is constricted, and if it boasts a large population it becomes dangerous to others, as well, because most things are alien to it except for its own thoughts and customs. Translations broaden people, and thereby the world.

They help you understand distant nations. People hate less, or fear less, what they understand. Understanding can save people from themselves. Generals have a harder time getting you to kill if you possess understanding. Hatred and prejudice, I say to you, are fear and ignorance; you may write that down.

He did so, wrote it all down, then went up to his room and corrected the translation, and has now read it over; he read it as the storm pounded the house, the rain lashed the Village, the horses, the sheep, the earth, and turned the June light to dusk. He concludes his reading. There's power in this text, Helga says. Yes, Geirþrúður says, yes, there's power, and she looks at the boy. Even Kolbeinn seems to mumble something that might be interpreted as a compliment, that curmudgeon who still hasn't let the boy into his room to view his library, four hundred books, let alone loaned him any, and although the boy hopes that that might change every single day, he would never ask out of the blue, never in his life, a man has his pride. He sits in the parlor, having accomplished something. Done what's important, something besides pulling fish from the deep, digging up peat, stacking hay in the barn, and now, while the sky quakes with the storm and ships fight against death, the boy feels as if he matters. He who has been called a variety of names ever since his father drowned ten or twelve years ago, who forgets everything, remembers nothing, hardly notices anything, forgets and loses things. You would have lost it a long time ago, said the old women on the farm where he grew up after everyone died who was supposed to have lived, you would have lost it ages ago, that thing hanging between your thighs, if it wasn't attached to you. He's been called an idiot, a dolt, a muttonhead, a lout, a moron, a wimp, a wastrel, a wimp, a scoundrel, a poltroon, scum and loafer, the language is rich with such words, it's so easy to scold and humiliate, it takes neither talent nor intelligence, let alone courage. It could undeniably be difficult at times to believe that a physically fit urchin, later an adolescent and young man, could take so long with certain chores, could hardly remember anything that his hands were supposed to learn; he might have learned to tie a knot in the evening, and then came night and when he awoke his hands had completely forgotten how to tie it. Chances are you're just an imbecile, an old woman said to him once, not out of malice, but rather astonishment. Yet now he's been complimented, which is no small thing for one who's been called many difficult names throughout his life; words have influence, they can sink into you and cause a stir, get a person to believe things about himself; to receive such a compliment, and from these women—the boy is close to sobbing. Another five pages in a week, can you manage it? Geirþrúður says, raising her wine glass to her lips, those lips that were kissed today, and that kissed; then she was alive, in the deserted valley, she existed, she burned, the birds were startled and the mountains took note of her. Yes, the boy says, convinced, confident, happy, I can manage it, there's zeal in his eyes, while outside the storm rages and the world trembles. It would probably be safer to tie it down so that it doesn't blow out into the darkness of space. Andrea lies in her bed in her basement room and listens to the storm, it's not her bed, admittedly, but Geirþrúður's, as is the entire house, she lies there and can't sleep, tosses and turns, doesn't know how she should lie, how she should live, the wind pounds the house, tears up the sea, which is dark and heavy and restless, even the Lagoon, which is usually calm even when breakers beat outside it, is tumultuous, and J. Andersen's ship rolls upon it frighteningly, its hold empty.

Lúlli and Oddur had worked tirelessly, along with some others, to empty the ship's hold of sacks, bags, barrels, and they succeeded, continual work, many hands, things are often urgent here between the mountains, life is in a rush, or, put better, people, not life itself, which simply exists, is just there, like a flower, like music, like a dagger, like sleet, an abyss, healing light. But whatever life is, extraordinary or commonplace, it was urgent that Andersen's ship, the *St. Louise*, be undocked. Saint Louise. We don't know why she was made a saint, this Louise after whom the ship is named, why she deserved it, what torments she had to suffer, does a person have to suffer torments to deserve the name of saint; can't she be happy, isn't it difficult enough in this world, beautiful enough, noble enough? But it was urgent that the *St. Louise* be moved from the pier, another ship was waiting on the Lagoon, laden with salt, salt is needed to salt the fish, and the *St. Louise* needed to be unloaded in haste, yes, now the men had an opportunity to show what they were made of, work like devils and never quit; if their hands dropped off them with fatigue, they should just screw them back on. The foreman, Kjartan, was in his element, he's a great shouter, great at goading men, sometimes they work at night, even until morning, and if someone grumbles, wants to go home, it's fine, do as you please, but you won't need to return anytime soon. Skúli has written pointed articles in opposition to this labor fervency, an energetic man, that Skúli, not a stylistic adept, his sentences aren't daggers but rather, hefty cudgels. It's heartening that Skúli should stand up to these devils, but it's not at all heartening to lose your job, to fall out of favor; then it's a struggle to survive—are you supposed to watch your children starve in the summer, drop dead from cold in the winter? No, unfortunately, it's better to swallow your pride and work, labor on as you're ordered to do. The *St. Louise* was emptied of everything that foreign countries have: figs, Akvavit, cotton, planed choice timber, coffee; there were even crates of apples. Oddur dexterously managed to open one without being seen, hid two apples beneath his coat, and now, as the storm tears the June light apart, howls over the houses and makes the mountains rumble, the three of them sit, Oddur, Rakel and Lúlli, at Oddur and Lúlli's, they've sliced the apples and slowly eat this fruit that has drunk in the sunshine and tenderness of faraway worlds. Rakel smiles; dear God, how delightful it is to see her smile up close as the storm shakes the little house furiously, the world has turned into one continuous roar. Whence comes this savage power, now, when the month of June should be plover song over our existence?

Oddur had stopped in to see Rakel toward evening, after they'd finished unloading the St. Louise; we saw what was coming, the darkening clouds, rising wind, a rumble or two from the mountains, as if it were too much to restrain their suppressed wrath. Oddur wanted her to join them, what with a storm in the wings, well, or at least foul weather, and he also had a little something that he and Lúlli wanted to share with her; nor is there any need for you to be alone in such foul weather. But she's often been alone in foul weather, malicious winter storms, and she's never been afraid, the only storm that she fears is the one in people; to be more precise, in men, which is worse, infinitely worse, when it's not enough to dress warmly, take shelter, it penetrates you and fills you with anxiety, fear, fills your blood with a maddening drone. Rakel said nothing, of course, about the storms in men. She said, Stormy weather is just wind in a hurry, there's little to fear. Still, Oddur said, it would be nice to have you visit, and she went with him without having meant to, without having dared to, something inside her made the decision, and Gísli watched her leave with Oddur, saw how they walked side by side. Well, now I'll lose her, he thought, she'll leave the basement and then there'll be nothing more between me and the Devil, perhaps I should rent you the basement, he said to his walking stick, which was leaning against the wall by the door and naturally has no mouth, no eyes, no heart; it doesn't matter if you give it a name, names don't change death into life. But the three of them, Oddur, Rakel, Lúlli, eat apples, and she smiles and Oddur's heart takes many an extra beat, while out on the Lagoon the St. Louise rolls horribly.

Rolls with men and rats and the ship's cat, which is still basically a kitten, afraid of the rats, afraid of the storm, and stays with John Andersen in the captain's cabin. Rolls and pitches horribly, the Lagoon is unrecognizable and the wind wails in the mountains, a wail that can practically burst your head if you aren't used to it. The crew can't sleep, so they might as well drink, take the opportunity and get roaring drunk, cheers friends, cheers brothers, we've all got the sea in our veins and that's why we're brothers. Andersen doesn't drink with them, he's on the verge of falling asleep with the purring cat next to him. The storm terrified the creature, the wailing, the rolling. It's alright, the captain mutters soothingly, we're closer to being on land than at sea, you terrible fool, he says, smiling when the cat finally sleeps, carefree as long as it feels the hand of its master, who strokes its small head with his thumb. Charming animal, this cat, more or less a kitten, eternally happy, glancing around in search of something to play with, something that moves. Andersen had told Geirþrúður about the kitten, its *joie de vivre* is so abundant, he said, you should get yourself a cat. That would hardly please the ravens, she said, smiling. He looked into her dark eyes, nearly black, and felt as if he caught a sudden glimpse of those big, black birds. He reached to stroke her face, her nose, eyes, lips, reached out his hand as if to pull her up from the loneliness that he could sense so strongly that tears came to his eyes. Even now his eyes are moist, as the ship rolls and he pets the purring cat. His younger daughter gave him the cat, then nearly blind and helpless; the girl's name is Olavia, just thirteen years old, bright and quick to laugh and a bit delicate. Olavia gave me the kitten, he told Geirþrúður, had to say it, she's the youngest, she laughs so wonderfully, and then, before he knew it, he'd said the names of the other children, Thomas and Ivylin, both have left home. He talked, spoke of and forgot the agreement he'd made with Geirþrúður—not to speak of his family.

I start to love you, Geirþrúður had said four years before, when a power stronger than the two of them began to draw them together, as soon as you behold the land rise from the sea, as soon as you behold it rise from the depths, then I start to love you, then you begin to exist. Where you come from, whoever you are there, what life you have, that doesn't exist between us, with me you're someone else, with me you're mine. It was good to have it that way, easier, but no one can keep silent, in the long run, about his life, sooner or later memories rise to the surface, it's a law of nature, even Jens had to speak, though he barely has a mouth. Captain John Andersen spoke of his children, but mostly of Olavia, followed by his wife, spoke her name. Geirþrúður said nothing, just looked up at the sky, her fingers fondled his hair, she didn't stop him, didn't silence him with a kiss, which is the gentlest way in the world to tell someone to hush, I shut your lips with a kiss because your words torment me. She allowed him to talk, she listened, though it hurt, maybe because this man, a foreign ship's captain, means so much to her that it frightens her sometimes. They lay on their backs in the hollow, his head in her lap, his eyes were shut but she looked up and the sky sank into her dark eyes.

Now Geirþrúður is asleep in her big bed.

He couldn't be persuaded to sleep with her; I'm sure I could bear having you with me tonight, Geirþrúður had said as they approached the Village, the breeze that barely stirred the blades of grass would become this storm, and now they all lie leveled, completely overcome, they have no chance, but will rise again as soon as the storm subsides, as if nothing had happened. Andersen couldn't have stayed with Geirþrúður though he wished to, longed to fall asleep to her scent, fall asleep to her black hair, but because of the storm he had to return to his ship. The cat, the half-adolescent kitten, is glad of his presence, so big, with a strong, soothing voice, because the ship is rolling so horribly. It mewed several times in fright, but Andersen calmed it, the big hand calmed it and the cat fell asleep purring. The *St. Louise* rolls, it rolls unnaturally, and Andersen sits up, in careless haste, forgets himself, wakes the cat, which complains a bit, opens one eye a crack, mews softly. Where is your hand? it asks, and Andersen extends his heavy arm without a second thought, soothes, comforts with gentle strokes. Something had awakened him, torn him from the sleep into which he was sinking. He strokes the cat, stares into space, at first thinks only of Geirþrúður. Simplest would be to cut all ties with her, simplest by far; it would also be more convenient for dealing with the people in this remote village, the merchants for whom he sails, their behavior toward him changed, cooled, when he began to be drawn to Geirþrúður. But sometimes, even the simplest, most obvious course can prove impossible to take. I'm putting a stop to this now, he's thought at times, setting sail to the north in the spring, sailing in the direction of cold and light, but as soon as he sees the land rise, emerge from the unfathomable depths, his desire grows so strong that he could kill, his longing so great that he could weep. Sometimes in the winter, as we're sailing in the Mediterranean, perhaps, I wake up to your scent and have difficulty breathing and miss you so unbearably. It's dangerous to miss someone, Geirþrúður had said, but smiled, smiled beautifully, smiled as if she couldn't help it. The ship rolls. He'd lost himself in his thoughts, the longing, the lust, the love, all of it sedated his vigilance, his responsibility. The ship shouldn't be rolling so terribly. The damned imbeciles have forgotten, or haven't bothered, to add ballast, didn't take the possibility of extreme weather into consideration, it being summer; no space for storms in all this light. I don't like the look of this, Andersen mutters, spreading the covers over the cat like a child, even kissing it with a faint smile, and the cat emits a tiny whimper of bliss. Andersen sits up and perhaps it's then that the boy looks out the window, having been unable to sleep, yet not having cared, not having the heart to do so, sat there and translated Mr. Dickens, enjoyed being alive, the praise and recognition from Geirþrúður, Helga and Gísli within him like a song, and it's impossible to fall asleep with blood singing in your veins, he sat there for four hours, then opens the curtain. What a tumult, he mutters in surprise, having hardly noticed the frenzied weather, forgotten about it, the rain that pounded the mountains, the howling wind, he sees the Lagoon between the houses and the *St. Louise* rolling. God damn, he thinks, feeling nauseous, draws the curtain, lies back down, smiles, shuts his eyes and thinks about his brother, where might he be, and how might he find out? Sleep approaches, he hears a faint rumble, a heavy echo in the mountains as a terrifying wind blasts across this speck of the world, this nook that is our universe. A violent gust, almost like an explosion, and the mountains resound over the sleeping Village. Then the deafening noise passes and for several seconds all is silent, even the rain stops falling, the drops stop and hang in the air like thousands of transparent eyes, as if the storm had finally found an outlet in the squall, and now stops, looks around to see whether it's had any noticeable effect. I'm falling asleep, the boy thinks, I'm falling asleep in the silence, after the storm has stopped and the raindrops are no longer raindrops but transparent eyes. What the eyes see, they tell the sky.

XIV

Horrific accident, reads the headline in *The Will of the People* several days later, the storm having long since passed. All storms, or nearly all, are forgotten, which is incredible, as imposing as they are while they rage, lord it over life, terrifying and enveloping all existence, tearing up the sea, rocking the sky, an empire of violence and power, we crawl into our houses like mice into the tussocks. Then it passes, is forgotten, the grass rights itself, the breeze knows nothing of the howling wind, and no storm has managed to shatter everyday life so thoroughly that it hasn't been able to grow back together. The commonplace is the grass of life, it says somewhere; without it nothing exists. It's true, everyday life is like the grass, you scorch it to the roots, but over time it grows again, blasts its way up from the darkness, and suddenly there are flowers, as well. The storm certainly threatened us while it lasted, saddened us and frightened us because it's June, the abode of light torn apart by the wind, the heavy rain pulverized it. Horrific, this weather, declared Jón, the factor of Leó's Shop and Trading Company, at Friðrik's; they coughed, drank within the cigar smoke, drank more than they intended, powerful men who control the Village, where the houses will stand whether we stand up straight or not, yet when storms have the world in their clutches these men are just ordinary people, they too missed the light and because of it had another glass, loosened up, said all this about Geirþrúður and considerably more, how she was, they no longer stopped talking when the maid came in and felt her way through the cigar fog, heard the things they said. She doesn't get enough, Sigurður said, women who aren't fucked regularly become filled with illusions, they become troublesome, they should send her a few healthy boys, that would put some sense in her. Sigurður was drunk, there were creases in his suit jacket, Friðrik sucked his cigar fervidly. Don't be so stupid, he said, and his fingers brushed the girl's hip. Horrific weather, this, she heard Jón say, having almost escaped them, it's wild, he added when they didn't respond, said nothing, stared into space with drunken eyes, and Reverend Þorvaldur struggled not to think about the girl, the movement of her hips; the storm pounded the house, threatened ships, and Jón stood up hesitantly, wanting to leave. Storms and disease were the only things in this world that Tove feared. It's worst of all when it rumbles and echoes like that in the mountains, as if they're standing there howling at us, having had enough of humankind, and who can blame them? Tove had most likely drawn all the curtains and shut herself in the northernmost bedroom, which is windowless, on the sheltered side. She waited for him, impatient, afraid, and he wanted to leave immediately, said this about the weather, so horrific, but Friðrik gave him a derisive look and Jón felt his face grow warm, muttered something that resembled an apology, escaped from the cigar fog, escaped into the storm. It's good to be important, incredibly good to be able to comfort someone stronger than yourself, to embrace that person. At one point he needed to take shelter beneath a house gable, otherwise the gusting wind would have taken him with it, and he caught a glimpse of the Lagoon, saw the *St. Louise* rolling and pitching so violently. Horrific weather, he groaned.

Horrific weather, *horrific accident.*

"English schooner, *St. Louise* out of Hull, 113.47 tons, Captain J. Andersen, arrived here on May 29 carrying wares from England for the trading company of the merchant Magnús, capsized in the harbor in violent weather on the eve of June 2, with all hands lost, 8 in number. The ship had been unloaded and was to be cleaned the next day and loaded with saltfish, which the merchant had stored here this past winter, owing to the fact that his own ship, which was to take on the fish, had sunk the previous autumn on its way from England. The *St. Louise* lay at anchor in the harbor, completely empty, and the crew had not taken care to ballast it, making it hardly surprising that things went as they did in such a violent storm, unusually bad for this time of year. No one witnessed the accident; it lay capsized here in the Lagoon when people awoke, with little more than the keel breaking the surface of the sea. The bodies of the deckhands and helmsman have been found washed up at Eyrarhlíð; the captain's body has not been found.

"Difficulties have been encountered in righting the ship, it being fastened in place by one of its masts, stuck in the seabed."

Thus it was, the mast stuck in the seabed, the sea refusing to release its prey. So many things are strange. Of course we're familiar with the sea, we live on an island, the sea is our only neighbor, the only thing with which we can compare ourselves, and it's dangerous, it quickly and mercilessly kills everyone who is careless, who forgets himself. That this cruelty, this absolute lack of leniency, to sentence foreigners to death for having forgotten or not taken care to ballast the ship for the night, too tired, most likely, after the unloading was finally completed, too tired and the captain still away, which lulled them into forgetting, into yielding to carelessness, that this lack of leniency should reach so unconditionally into the Lagoon, which is often so incredibly tranquil, surprised even us. Admittedly, people have fallen into the Lagoon and lost their lives, left them behind in the sea among the fish, oblivion, silence, just last spring a bookkeeper and two clerks from Magnús' Shop rowed out onto the Lagoon, the herring had come in and the men were given permission to leave their work indoors; they rowed out in a dory, hauled in herring, happily, their raucous laughter could be heard onshore, and then the shouts when the bookkeeper lost his balance and plunged into the tranquil sea. The dory capsized when the clerks tried to save him, people on land were quick to launch boats to come to their aid, yet it was too late, the clerks hung cold and silent on the keel, while close by the bookkeeper floated half-submerged, face down, as if he were trying to read something on the bottom.

It's difficult, and far from encouraging, to have a capsized ship before your eyes, keel up, like a thick knife used to cut the light. All the dignity that comes with ships is gone, the freedom that dwells in the sails, the music as it sails, it's gone, a capsized ship in the sea is disgraced, it hurts the eyes, troubles the heart. Almost total calm when we awoke the next morning, and news of the incident spread rapidly, astonishingly rapidly. When Helga steps out onto the stoop with Andrea, who points, as if it were necessary, as if one needs specifically to point out humiliation and death, it wasn't much after six, yet at least three boats had gone out to the ship, bobbing there like laundry tubs in comparison with the huge keel. Almost total calm, yet the sea was still restless, its hatred not entirely used up, and when Helga raises the spyglass that the boy had fetched for her, she sees a man pounding the keel of the ship with his fists, as if he's knocking on a door; hello, is anyone there? Yes, death says, I'm always here, you'll never find my door shut, you're always welcome, my embrace is larger than life.

Is he? begins the boy, they're all standing on the stoop, he himself on one of the steps to make room for the three women, Ólafía by the door, Helga holding the spyglass, Andrea leaning on the handrail, her right hand grasping her left elbow, there's a gray sheen to her hair and her lips are pursed. She looks out at the Lagoon, squints to see better what she doesn't want to see, what appeared to her when she came out of her basement room and heard that no one had survived. Is he? begins the boy once more, and then Andrea looks at him, their eyes meet, she looks so beautifully at the boy that tears come to his eyes, the lump starts at his heart and lifts itself up to his throat, dissolving his words. He has to stop and swallow to continue, get the words out unjumbled, oddly happy at how Andrea looked at him, but also shamefaced that he should now, when death appears before their eyes on the Lagoon, the keel a knife cutting life asunder, when men have drowned, when their existence has been wiped away and somewhere on the other side of the sea people will miss them and weep, a child will ask for him who shall never return, a life transformed into a memory, a touch into regret, that he should feel this deep, happy affection. Did he go, begins the boy, trying again, did he go out to the ship or spend the night here? Helga lets the spyglass drop, Ólafía takes a step or two farther out onto the stoop, her big, swollen hands grasp Andrea's arm, remain there, for some of life is an abyss, and where is there an arm to save me from falling? No, Helga says, letting the spyglass dangle, the man stops knocking on the keel, addressing death with his fists, and the boats bobble around the ship, irresolute, he went to the ship; John, she adds. Ólafía starts whimpering. That beautiful man, she says, and Andrea puts her arms around her, here is my shoulder, say her arms, and Ólafía weeps. She simply sobs, though she didn't know Captain John Andersen well, he drank coffee in the café, had joked with them and Helga had interpreted, smiling unusually much, he'd told them about his cat, more of a kitten, actually, told about it with delicacy and humor, it's only good men who do that, with those beautiful eyes of his and now he's surely dead, the sea took him. Ólafía sobs. Helga, who esteemed John Andersen, hardly changes her expression, she strokes Ólafía's shoulder, knowing, in all likelihood, that it's not sorrow for the captain that sets loose this flood of tears, it's not a wound that opens there on the stoop, opens wide, but her life, her existence, the children who went to America, the grandchildren who are growing older and whom she'll probably never get to see, their little children's fingers will never get to touch and feel her plump face. And she sobs for Brynjólfur, that big man who held her in his arms for more than twenty years before gradually stopping, as if she'd become ugly and boring, it's all so unfair, so infinitely painful. Come to us, Mama, writes Áki, their son, but she can't leave Brynjólfur, he drinks so much, he's unhappy, it's impossible to leave him behind and soon she'll have the chance to hold him in her arms once again, surely she will, absolutely, absolutely. Andrea holds the clumsy body tightly, understands barely half of Ólafía's broken mumbling, but understands tears, understands them extremely well. Yes, absolutely, she whispers, stroking the sobbing woman's back, absolutely. Helga looks at them, the spyglass hanging from her right hand, her shoulders drooping slightly, which is unusual, perhaps she also needs a shoulder to lean on but doesn't know how to ask for it, and what shoulder should that be; are there shoulders for everyone? Again she strokes Ólafía's back, firmly yet swiftly. My little darling, she says, and at that Ólafía sobs even more. Run down there, Helga says to the boy, and find out what's happened; I'll go and wake Geirþrúður. At that, Ólafía's sobbing lessens.

The boy intends to walk quickly down to the Lagoon, but before he knows it, he's running. A crowd has gathered at the Lower Pier, some unloading yet working slowly, looking out at the Lagoon, at the keel, the boats that row gently around it, and it's time for a coffee break, as well; a number of women from the drying lots stand in groups and watch. It's as if the ship is permanently fixed. It can't be budged, says one of the men who'd rowed out to it. The boy comes running up and the atmosphere changes. He comes running into the muttering, the presence of death, and everyone looks at him. He can't distinguish the faces, all the people are blended into one in front of him, a shapeless mass that stares at him and he asks all of them and none. The crew, is it certain that none of them survived? At first no one replies, some keep staring at him, some lower their eyes, but then a man standing right next to the boy, along with his two companions, clears his throat, clears it twice, spits. Did she send you here to ask? he says, glancing at his companions as if looking for support, and getting it. The boy says nothing, almost as if he hasn't heard, just looks and then the man adds, no, my man, you'll most likely have to do for her until the next captain comes along—wasn't that why she took you in? The hatred that wells up in the boy turns into two fists, but he can say nothing; the damn words are stuck inside him. Though you may be stupider than a cod, Guðmundur, says a woman standing beside the boy, you should still have the sense and taste to pay a newly drowned man a modicum of respect; if you had a dog, it would be ashamed of you. What now? I was just joking, Guðmundur says, moving a bit closer to his companions. The boy looks at the woman, tries to thank her with his glance, her name is Bryndís, she's had two husbands and lost them both to the sea, now she's alone with three children, yet is doing surprisingly well, which many people find difficult to understand. They all drowned, she says, addressing herself gently to the boy. Their eyes meet, some people never get to encounter those whom they ought to know.

XV

Let me tell you, the sun can shine so brightly here! And it can be so warm between the mountains that the cliffs sweat like the women in their oilskins washing the fish, they would probably take off all their clothing, every stitch, if they dared. With the light comes the bustle. Sleep is minimized as much as possible, life fills every moment and not even death manages to trouble us. Yet it did so, for the more than twenty days it took to right the *St. Louise*. The dark keel was always there to be seen, as if death itself were napping there in the water, its unblinking eyes half-submerged, just beneath the surface. "The bodies of the deckhands and helmsman have been found washed up at Eyrarhlíð; the captain's body has not been found." The deckhands and helmsman were brought back to the Village, Jón the joiner and others constructed coffins for them, and a letter has been sent to England, written in excellent English, the magistrate Lárus got Þórunn, the wife of Ketill the photographer, to help him with the letter, the two of them lived for many years in England, they're familiar with a different sky than the one that takes its character from the mountains, and thus they carry themselves differently. The letter is on its way to the ship operator in Hull, written by Lárus and Þórunn, signed by death. The body of Captain John Andersen hasn't been recovered, he was unable to escape from his cabin; he's lying there submerged, motionless, the cat beside him, like a satellite.

The Will of the People doesn't mention the cat. Yet it was just a kitten, full of joy, of sunshine. Nor was it mentioned, not one word, in the letter to Hull, even though the captain's youngest daughter had chosen it with great care and affection for her father, had searched for a long time until she found this black kitten with absolutely irresistible eyes and one snow-white front paw. Irresistible eyes that filled with fear when the storm's wail changed suddenly into a scream, as if the world were tearing apart, some woke up in their houses, turned over onto their other side and fell asleep. The boy listened, said something about raindrops and fell asleep, the terrified cat curled up in a ball but relaxed slightly when the captain leaned over and said, You're coming with me, I'm not leaving you behind. The final words of his life, which unfortunately turned out to be true, but in a more bitter, merciless way than they were thought and spoken; he reached over, picked up the kitten, and the storm capsized the ship, the *St. Louise*, swiftly, violently, turned everything upside down. What previously faced upward now looked down, the sky became the sea, the sea the sky. And he, J. Andersen, like a fool, wasted precious seconds trying to rescue the creature, unable to bear its piteous mewing, its poignant helplessness, and couldn't escape. He might possibly have saved himself, being a powerful swimmer, unflagging, strong, it was good to run her fingers along his arms, over his chest, feel his power, her fingers would never forget it. Helga went upstairs, woke her, told her the news. Geirþrúður got up from sleep and a dream, her hair hanging like darkness over her face, and she said, from somewhere within that night, Yes, I'll come down right away. Some prefer to take the blows alone, are unable to do otherwise, know no other way, possibly dare do nothing else. Whence springs man's misfortune? Geirþrúður got out of bed, opened the curtain, looked out at the dark keel, saw that death is a dark knife that sunders the daylight. She sat for several minutes at a small, sturdy table, bought in Germany. Sat there slightly hunched, looking at her fingers, which had immediately gone numb with longing.

"Had not taken care to ballast it," wrote Skúli in *The Will of the People*; he wrote, "horrific accident" and meant it, but also thought, horrific carelessness. Not to ballast the ship, because everyone and everything needs some sort of balance, ships as well as men. The ships need something heavy from the material world and it's easy to provide it, simple work for the body, it requires more stamina and sacrifice to acquire ballast in life; some call it happiness, others security, the words, as always, describe our inner selves. Horrific carelessness, because the sky had begun to darken with heavy-sailing clouds, the sunbeams disappeared, the lovely June light turned gradually into dusk, the breeze into wind, shouldn't all of this have given warning to tried and true sailors? Skúli was satisfied to think it, saying it out loud, perhaps, rather than writing it, realizing, being the intelligent man he is, that Skúli, that everything is clearer in hindsight, the storm and its consequences are clearer after it has passed and you're out of danger, when you can draw your conclusions in peace; then the mistakes become obvious. To some extent it's true, it was careless not to ballast the ship, but it was urgent that they move it away from the pier; Kjartan had been spurring the men on with reprimands and curses, he was raving, Lúlli and Oddur told Rakel that evening, as the three of them sat together and Oddur's left arm lay on the table, close to her right arm, probably not more than two inches between their fingers, even as few as three, allowing the fingers to nod at each other, possibly chat a bit, tell the news from inside their bodies, and if fingers can strike up an acquaintance, it's not impossible that the rest of a person might follow suit. Stark raving mad, that Kjartan, because another ship was anchored just beyond the harbor and needed to come in, carrying salt for Tryggvi's Company, and what is life without salt? Besides, the company bore something of a grudge against Captain J. Andersen and therefore against his ship, this captain had no interest in associating with anyone but Geirþrúður, lying with her like a damned dog. Kjartan practically drove the ship from the pier, hearing no objections from the crew members, who had looked forward to spending a peaceful evening, night and the better part of the next day on the Lagoon, and who had their first drinks as soon as they cast off. Perhaps Skúli was aware of the impatience of Tryggvi's men, who control everything at the Lower Pier; was aware that if it were possible to speak of guilt, it could be found in more places than were apparent.

J. Andersen had to be rowed out to the ship. *Bad wetter måske komming*, bad weather probably on the way, said the oarsman. Some people here are able to put together sentences in other languages; it's another matter whether the sentences can be understood, whether all the words belong to the same language. Just to be sure, the man had nodded toward the sky, which was gone, replaced with dark clouds, but J. Andersen simply smiled, distracted, it was his only reaction, he seemed preoccupied, his body might have been sitting in the rowboat, but his mind and consciousness were far away. He pulled himself up onto the ship, it had no ballast, which is something he ought to have given his attention to when the wind began blowing. The crew had some bottles of drinkable rotgut. Damn, those are some mountains, they said as they drank, while their captain sat or lay in his cabin, stroking a purring, adolescent kitten and thinking about Geirþrúður, allowing himself the luxury. How she moved; and his blood was on fire. We call it desire, love, lust for life, longing for happiness, but whatever it's called, whatever words we choose, it was the reason why he was so distracted, why he didn't feel, until it was too late, how unnaturally the ship was rolling, and then he drowned. Along with all those men. How dangerous it is to let yourself dream of passion, of freckles and eyes, let yourself dream instead of concentrating on the struggle for life. That's how it is. You think too much about poetry, forget your raincoat and freeze to death. You think too much about a woman, the scent of her hair, how she stroked your chest and belly, which is why you don't notice that the ship lacks ballast, it capsizes, men and a cat drown. This should perhaps teach us something. Something about the dangers of dreams, the dangers of poetry. And yet. Who remembers those who have seldom, maybe never, become distracted and lost themselves in dreams, not felt the spark and gradually turned gray, turned gray and paled and merged, with hardly a fight, into monotony, who have become monotony and vanished long before their deaths? Can we then ask for the spark, even though it might cost us our lives far too early? Let's take the risk, instead, and live.

If only we'd done so.

XVI

It took a good three weeks to right the *St. Louise*. A capsized ship is so heartrending, we felt it every time we looked out at the tranquil Lagoon, which reflects mountains, reflects the sky, reflects our existence and the clouds that so resemble man, rootless, transient, everchanging. A three-week tug-of-war with the seabed. Geirþrúður sat one night on the shore and watched, just watched, one entire night. June nights here in the north must be the most beautiful in the world, the luminance of the night sky can bewilder you with happiness, it washes away anxiety, stress, hatred, envy, all of these things that are like a blight inside humankind. All is tranquil, transparent. A June night is a bit like the breath of God, and for a moment all existence is soft and still. For a moment. The wounds of life certainly don't heal in one night, it takes more than that, but the luminance of the night strokes them carefully, and perhaps allows you to weep. Did Geirþrúður weep? Can something as clear and transparent as tears come from such dark eyes? She sat there all night. Not always alone; Helga came around one o'clock with a blanket, spread it over her shoulders, said nothing, just spread a blanket over her shoulders, though there were many words in that movement, then stood there silently, close to her mistress. Where language ends, closeness begins. Then Helga went home. Geirþrúður continued to sit through the night, in the silence, watched and thought and now and then flexed her fingers, had to do so; they were numb with longing, white from a lack of blood, perhaps they'll be damaged and need to be cut off; Helga has sharp knives. Anything is possible. Four hours later, around five o'clock, Helga returned, not with a knife to cut away longing but with coffee and cognac. They didn't drink much, just a little. The sun had started to warm the air, dry the dew, the flies had begun buzzing, we emerged from our houses and the dark keel sundered the morning light.

XVII

You can accustom yourself to anything, you've got to accustom yourself, unfortunately, thank God. Life goes on without stopping, nothing seems capable of halting it, a meteor shower, the wrath of God, threats of nature, human cruelty. Ships come and go. The schooners, the whaleboats of the Norwegians, smelling of train oil and profit, the big sailing ships, the wheezing steamers, come and go, skirting the *St. Louise*'s keel. The *Hope* arrives, chock-full of fish, full to its deck, admittedly with rather small cod, but fish is fish, especially if it's cod. Every man on board was smiling, those old seadogs; their tough, weather-beaten faces, wizened by the salt of the sea, are grinning from ear to ear, and besides, it's a treat to come home, even for just one night, while the cod is unloaded, to have a chance to pat their grandchildren's heads and hug their wives, though they too had started to wear down like the men, it's a long time since it was possible to speak of beautiful, let alone soft, hands, their sunken breasts resembling birds that have given up all hope of flight, the men themselves half-toothless, yet it's just as nice to lie together as it was thirty years ago, possibly nicer, though it may not be pretty to see two old, stiff bodies rubbing together, but sometimes what we see ought not to be heeded, the eyes can be so stupid, and in any case, no one is allowed to look, what we do for ourselves, in private, is no one else's business.

Snorri soon arrives, along with Björn and Bjarni, father and son. They've closed the half-empty shop, put a notice in the window and written carefully: *The* Hope *has arrived! Opening soon!* They board the ship, greet the men. Tomorrow, Snorri says, the boys and I will bring pastries, more than enough of them, and maybe we'll bring something good to wash them down with!

The next morning is busy for Snorri, and for the father and son; the food is made ready, seabirds' eggs that Snorri had bought off farmers from the coasts to the northwest. Eggs that he'd kept in cold storage, meat that they'd boiled and stored, plenty of water, and biscuits that endure everything, hard and nearly tasteless; early in the morning they bring this down to the ship, so early that the blue sky breathes silently overhead and existence welcomes them like open arms. The *Hope* rocks slightly, almost imperceptibly, at the pier, looking forward to getting back out to sea, like Brynjólfur, who receives the provisions; they converse and the ship's mast stands tall in the pure summer air. Snorri pats Brynjólfur on the shoulder; the skipper hardly slept a wink at home, lying beside Ólafía, who snored a bit, farted twice, sighed as many times and, around four in the morning, whimpered, not like a big, worn-out and aging woman but like a girl, or even a puppy that's frightened and misses someone. Shortly afterward, Brynjólfur got up, went down to the ship, and now receives a warm pat on the shoulder from Snorri, who produces a flask, Brynjólfur takes a swig and notices the summer light. The three of them then go to the bakery: Snorri, the father and his son.

The father and son wait outside, in the sunny morning, watching the women untying the stacks of saltfish and spreading the fish out on frames on the drying lot of Leó's Shop and Trading Company, both in their worn-out old clothes, with a hint of weariness in their faces. Torfhildur, the mother and wife, hasn't got out of bed for nearly four weeks; it's just a slight indisposition, she says, a stomach discomfort, laziness. They stand there in the summer, in the light, the calm, the women chat, they laugh, it's hardly possible to feel melancholic on such a morning, not a wisp of cloud in the sky, the father and son fiddle with the frayed sleeves of their jackets as Snorri asks for the ever-popular rusks, which are unmissable aboard the Village's ships. And a bit of Danish pastry, as well, not much, enough to please the men, he says; so that they have a sweet taste in their mouths when they set sail again. He smiles, not broadly, yet it's a smile. But there in the German Bakery, silence follows Snorri's words, his ordinary request for rusks and pastry, and then one of the sales clerks begins to blush, the other opens her mouth to say something, shuts it again and looks helplessly at her colleague. Snorri realizes right away, has perhaps been waiting for this. That bad? he asks calmly, deliberately, smiles again and they both nod—Tryggvi's Company has spread the word that Snorri is insolvent, and that no one is to sell him anything on credit until he pays what he owes or, more specifically, signs his company over once and for all. The clerk who blushed bites her lower lip hard but the other looks outside, sees the father and son standing there close together, as if wishing to derive strength from each other in the face of the darkening world.

Snorri stands pensively at the counter, this is the first time that he's been denied credit in all his long years, just over fifty; he's always been reliable, as far back as he can remember, and it's never entered his head not to honor his commitments, such moral putrescence doesn't exist in him, not a trace, and that's how he got that little shop of his going, his universe, through reliability, calmness, prudence. But now it's over. It's happened. Things changed, his wife left, God took her into his service, those who serve God sometimes betray men. Everything became more difficult after she left, the bookkeeping, the darkness, he wakes up alone and has no one to talk to. What's more, it isn't easy to be small in the face of the big companies, it's difficult to compete with Tryggvi and Leó, they siphoned off clients slowly but surely, that's how it happened, and he was too feeble, too lonely, too something, to react. Well, Snorri says finally. Well. He uses this important word to break the awkward silence, and the women sigh. Well, that's how it is, everything runs its course, and I should have realized it, of course, instead of putting you in such an uncomfortable position. Yet I would like, he says, fishing some coins from his pocket, to have six of your Danish pastries, for which I will pay cash, like a gentleman! Without a word, one of the women puts ten or so pastries into a bag, and the other pushes the coins back. Snorri takes four of the pastries out of the bag, places them next to the coins, smiles faintly. We'll do this by the book, he says.

The father and son see from Snorri's expression that something has happened, and notice that the bag from the bakery is considerably less bulky than they'd hoped, yet they say nothing and head off toward the pier. Snorri stops at the ice house that he helped to build before losing his share in it to Geirþrúður, sits down on the sunny side, signals the father and son to sit down next to him, takes out the pastries, and there they sit, facing the spit that's turning white with saltfish, watching the women and teenagers untying the stacks after last night's storm, spreading out the fish, changing the spit into a graveyard of angels. The men munch the pastries, look out at the Lagoon. The plan is to right the ship today, Snorri says. That's good, the father says, yes, it's unpleasant seeing the keel, the son says, it's so dark, agrees the father, if not black, says his son. The father and son have finished their pastries. Snorri finishes his, wipes his mouth with the back of his hand and says, I'm bankrupt. They all stare at the keel. I've lost everything, Snorri says, tomorrow or the day after, someone else will own the *Hope* and what's left of my shop. I don't know what will become of me, he says, but I'll try to find you work. Mother is poorly, says the son, she doesn't have much time left, says the father, I don't know, he adds, before falling silent, and they all fall silent. Then Snorri takes three more pastries out of the bag.

XVIII

June crawls along and early summer boats arrive from the north, loaded with seabirds' eggs, some farmers having had to row long distances with theirs, unless they had favorable winds, most of them landing on the beach not far from Geirþrúður's house, at the end of the street, then transporting the eggs in handbarrows to their merchants, trying along the way to sell as many as possible straight from the barrows to the maids of the better homes; the freshest eggs are boiled and eaten, the older ones used in baking, mostly for scones—not much in life is better than warm scones with butter.

The boy tries to keep track of the egg farmers in the hope of seeing Bjarni from Nes, hearing news of the children, getting a chance to see his face, say something about Hjalti, that they'd lost him, that he'd been kind, but June passes without any sign of Bjarni, the boy must have missed him, unless he went to Slettueyri, to Sigurður, maybe Hildur tied him down again? The boy runs five times, six times, seven times a week and now looks forward to the mornings, to sitting with Andrea and Helga, listening to them chat. Andrea has started calling him by the pet names she used in the fishing hut, when no one else could hear except Bárður: my boy, my little shrimp, my dreamer. How is my dreamer today? she asks one morning, and Helga says, You've hit on the right word for him. How is my dreamer? I dreamed that you were a princess in a distant land, with trees and sunshine and a beautiful pond; I was a valiant knight and swore to fight for you all our lives. Why do you need to fight for me? Your beauty and benevolence are so great that noblemen and ruffians alike would wish to possess you, the latter by evil means if necessary. Oh, in that case, you must protect me, and it's so nice of you to make me a princess, everyday sort of person that I am, with ugly red hands. Our dreams sometimes tell us who we are, the boy says, besides showing us how the world ought to be, and now we know that you are in fact a princess in a beautiful, sunny country. What Geirþrúður said is true, Helga says, you'll be dangerous if you lose your innocence.

That's how they spend their quiet, pleasant mornings, it's a weight on the scale of life, which is constantly teetering; on one side there's happiness, on the other unhappiness, and which is heavier? Andrea often goes to sleep late, she stares at the basement ceiling, her eyes as red as her hands, Kolbeinn seems to have more and more difficulty getting up at dawn, he's late coming downstairs, and is then like a clenched fist, a shipwreck on a dark ocean, and Geirþrúður rides almost daily out of the Village, in her mind's eye the black keel slashes the daylight, perhaps she dreams of a half-grown cat lying next to a man who came too close to her and drowned.

How is my dreamer?

I dreamed that you were a princess of trees and sunshine.

How is my dreamer?

I'm worried about Jens, I must write to him, and I also want to write to Sigríður, Bárður's fiancée, I think that Bárður would have liked me to, I'll never forget him, he's like the sky above me.

How is my dreamer?

I miss my brother, his name is Egill, but I don't know where he is.

How is my dreamer?

Well, I met Ragnheiður the day before yesterday, it was sunny and she was on horseback, just as she'd promised, going for a ride in sunshine, and when she said that, I thought that I was supposed to be something, the horse, the wind brushing her cheek, but when the time came I was nothing, almost nothing, a person on the street who had to step aside, give way to the horses, she was with three other women from the finer households, smelling of purity and everything that we don't have, they looked over, rather than down at us.

He'd leaned against the fence outside the house that has the garden with two little rowan trees and glanced over at her, nothing more, then looked down, as expected of him. Then he remembered the poetry, or rather, it seemed as if the lines spurted through his bloodstream like a powerful force, lines from a poem that he'd read in a periodical that Gísli had given him, a strange poem by an American poet: "I am the poet of the Body, I am the poet of the Soul." The boy was captivated, Gísli wasn't. Far too clamorous, he said, it lacks focus, it's too loose, it crumbles into bits that do you no good, don't waste time on this poem. Which, however, was exactly what the boy did, spent time copying it, from *Leaves of Grass* by the American poet Walt Whitman, in the translation of Einar Benediktsson. No rhyme, not a trace, just weighty sentences filled with unrestrained, unruly power, and something big, something that holds a promise of a wider sky, a bigger earth. He stood by the fence, where two little trees crawled up into the light; he looked down and the poem spurted through his bloodstream. "Have you overcome the others? Are you the President? / It is a trifle—they will do more than come, they will go—past. I bear the outcome of past events. In me dwells what is to be." He looked up with these words in his blood, they infected his glance, it was unavoidable, in me dwells what is to be; that's how he glanced directly at Ragnheiður. Who was undeniably self-assured, proud, beautiful in her self-assuredness, in a blue dress with white lace trim and a red ribbon in her hair, she outshone the others, absolutely outshone the others. Their eyes met, it was unavoidable, and her lips parted, almost as if she needed to breathe faster, he noticed her bosom rise and fall, her breasts that once brushed against him, as if they wanted to tell him something, but then she'd passed by, it was the briefest of moments, he stood there alone, and muttered, "Now here I stand with a robust soul."

XIX

There is perhaps no great difference between the merchant Snorri and the *St. Louise*, which has finally been righted and now lingers on the Lagoon, piteous and battered. The cabins have been damaged by seawater and almost everything that recalled the deckhands is gone; Captain Andersen, lover, husband and father, had waited patiently in his cabin, along with his cat, among the papers, books and sea charts that the sea had ruined. The two of them were buried in our cemetery, in something of a rush, it must be said. That damn cat was also given a place below the ground, without the knowledge of

Reverend Þorvaldur, who naturally would have forbidden it, or else fumbled his way through a well-worn sermon on how we all turn to earth, will be resurrected from earth, presumably as angels or something else beautiful, free of our bodies, that heavy baggage we drag along through life. They placed the captain's big hands over the kitten; it was lovely, less forlorn. Nor would John Andersen have heard of ascending to Heaven without this kitten, which his daughter chose especially for him because she always missed him so much when he sailed, and now the sense of loss will never leave her. Thus they went together, kitten and man, down into the ground, drowned together and will hopefully get to cross together into the land of eternity that must be waiting for us somewhere with a mug of coffee, a view over what is beautiful and a dainty bowl of milk for the kitten.

The battered *St. Louise* rocks on the Lagoon, a pitiful sight, a ship of death, pitiful yet not unprofitable, joiners were hired to smarten it up, repair it, clean it, restore it to sailing condition, the outfitter in England is paying, and a new crew is on the way, a new captain for Geirþrúður, some say; dead lovers are of little use, you can see that she needs it a lot, it's true, it's so clear, yes, just look at the corners of her mouth, it's obvious, yes, I've always said that she would bed the Evil One if she could. If she could, how do you know she doesn't let him fuck her regularly, fuck her silly, somewhere out in the tussocks? He must have a damned big prick, someone adds thoughtfully. The *St. Louise* is worked on, put back in shape by joiners and their assistants from Tryggvi's Shop and Trading Company, and they see Geirþrúður ride down the fjord toward Tungudalur, almost daily, even in rain and wearisome wind, then up and over to other fjords, lay down their tools, follow her with their eyes and say these words about her. She rides fast, straddling her horse, of course; she's already got her legs spread, one of them might say, rubbing his eyes, in the dry weather her black hair flutters like a raven's wings around her head. She's hardly spent any time at home since the storm capsized the ship and killed the sailors and kitten, rides out nearly every day, and those who encounter and greet her, those who don't shun her, receive no response; she stares straight ahead, rising and falling with the horse's movements, supplely rising and falling, is even dignified. Hard to deny it, mutter those on the St. Louise's deck, before adding, the Devil's getting himself a nice piece.

The boy fetches her a horse from Hansen's Field, gives it some bread, then gets a saddle from Jóhann and rides swiftly, almost at a hard gallop, up to the house, it's difficult not to do so, even if people have to hasten out of the way and shout curses after him, it's just so good to feel the power and become one with it. Geirþrúður comes out, thanks him with a smile, leans against the horse, perhaps, and lets the boy say a few words. At those moments it's as if he manages to be a bit closer to her, as if he's allowed to be a part of her life, as if she lets her guard down, unless it's been cracked, leaving her vulnerable. She asks about matters great and small, asks as if there's no difference between the two. The horse occasionally nibbles at the boy while he's talking, as if to draw attention to the fact that it relishes the bread and that the boy could give it more. The boy scratches the horse behind its ear, having already said so much, even about things he never mentions; he dares to ask where she's from, how she's lived, but Geirþrúður deftly avoids the questions and continues with those of her own, and once the boy recited the poem by Mr. Whitman, what he remembers of it, which is a considerable amount. It's good, she says, it's different, thank you for reciting it to me. Gísli doesn't like it, he says, it bothers him. Gísli's from that sort of family, she says, having mounted the horse; she looks down at the boy, who's never seen such dark eyes before, and he says exactly that: I've never seen such dark eyes before. Like a winter's night? she says. Yes, he says, and finds himself adding, without fully understanding why, they're also like time. She leans down to ruffle his hair and then rides away. Quickly, down the fjord, her hair like a raven's wings, her eyes as dark as time, several men stand on the deck of the *St. Louise* and say their words about Geirþrúður.

It isn't difficult to mend a damaged ship, all that's required are skilled hands, materials, funding, and Tryggvi's Shop and Trading Company possesses all of these things, or has control of them; naturally, it doesn't possess the joiners' hands, not directly, although it might as well, probably does, nearly. No, it isn't difficult to mend a ship, it just takes time, though hardly more than a few weeks, two or three in this case. Unfortunately it's not as easy to patch up a stranded and tattered person; for that not even the best jacks-of-all-trades will do, not at all, to put it bluntly, nor does it do to have fine-smelling wood and good screws, yes, even money can't do the trick, despite it's being the world's most widespread religion. That's why we can safely say that Snorri looks worse off than the *St. Louise*. It wasn't just one short-lived yet violent spring storm that damaged him, but time itself, many years, so very many heavy, dark moments, it was the events of his life: his wife, God, the disappointments, loneliness. He sits all day in a nearly empty house, staring into space, playing the organ that he's lucky enough to have at home but has to leave behind when he sails to Reykjavík in several days' time aboard the *Thyra*, into the arms of uncertainty. It couldn't go on for one more minute, say Tryggvi's men, and they spread the word that Snorri was insolvent, demanded that he not be allowed to purchase anything on credit, and few dared oppose this. Most of his debt was to Tryggvi's Shop and Trading Company; for years, far too long, he'd borrowed most of his capital, and he'd had to pay such high prices for his wares that he was unable to sell them for much of a profit, if any. Some people aren't cut out for business, said Tryggvi's head bookkeeper, Högni, and therefore it's kindest to cut them loose before they drag others down with them. Several of Snorri's most faithful clients have come off extremely badly, having to start up new business relationships with Tryggvi while mired in debt, with no real chance of working their way out of it. Snorri rises late, and in poor condition; he sleeps in fits and starts, tosses and turns in his clammy, sometimes soaking-wet bedclothes, plays two-hundred-year-old compositions on his organ, no longer bothering to tune the instrument, and why should he? Life, that great instrument, is neither sonorous nor fine-tuned by the Lord.

They're damn cowards, to be honest, says Marta from Sodom, who recently started visiting Snorri each day; she tries to persuade him to eat, hoping to hear some of those old musical pieces from down south in Europe. I don't understand, Snorri says, why you're wasting time on me, you have enough to do, I'm sure; it's summer, he adds, as if this had to be pointed out, because outside, the light and the smell of saltfish reach halfway to the sky. I'm not letting those rascals kill you without a fight, Marta says, and besides, I owe you as much, to which he says, in surprise, Owe me? What drivel, you've never owed me anything. Marta smiles, staring dreamily at the merchant, who is embarrassed and thinks for an instant that this rough, sturdy hostess might be attracted to him. He looks awkwardly at his hands resting on the keyboard. Is that so? he says, when he finally realizes what she means, and plays a short piece to please her.

Occasionally Helga sends the boy or Andrea with some little thing for the ruined merchant: bread, coffee, seabirds; others stop by as well, though fewer than when Snorri could stand tolerably well on his own two feet, our friends' true colors are revealed when ill winds blow. Marta cooks for him and curses Tryggvi's Shop and Trading Company, curses vanished friends. They think they're doing the right thing, Snorri says, though it's unclear whether he means the company or the friends, perhaps both, and he pats Marta on the shoulder to calm her, probably also to feel another person's presence. We're badly off if we never get a chance to touch others; it's as if our fingertips wither, become lifeless, like those of mummies.

Perhaps that's why Geirþrúður ruffles the boy's hair before she rides off; ruffles his hair and says something, then rides off down the fjord. Into the valley, up onto a heath where the snowdrifts are dwindling. Rides off without saying a word to anyone outside the house, as if she couldn't care less about anything because a foreign sailor, a ship's captain, drowned along with a kitten; couldn't care less about life, about her business ventures. Doesn't this show precisely how women aren't cut out for business, sad to say, for taking definitive action, for being in charge? They certainly know how to love, which is magnificent; they know that better than men do, which is precisely why they have trouble making carefully thought-out decisions, losing, for example, their rationality to sorrow, kisses, a toddler's babbling; that's just how it is, you can't change the laws of nature.

Gunnar the Mustache, clerk in Tryggvi's Shop, leans over the counter and chats with two faithful clients about Geirþrúður, says this about women, that they're better at feelings, while we men are better at bookkeeping, management, making tough decisions, for which we should be thankful. The others agree, and Geirþrúður rides into the light and the summer, the calm or the wind, the sun or the rain, to be by herself, alone with her sorrow, her sense of loss, or to let the Devil and his little demons take her. Sod it all, they say on board the *St. Louise*, and tend dutifully to their chores. Snorri plays the organ, tosses and turns, can't sleep, is waiting for a ship to take him away, utterly defeated, bankrupt, almost as if he wants to avoid going out in public, bowed down by humiliation, fearing perhaps that he'll meet the poor bastards who, due to his insolvency, ended up in the clutches of Tryggvi's Company, meet the wives or adolescent children of sailors on the *Hope*, which he still owns, albeit in name only, pumps the organ pedals and doesn't understand why Tryggvi's Company hasn't seized the ship as collateral for his debts. Perhaps Friðrik is waiting for Tryggvi himself, who is expected in due course; is at this very moment on his own ship midway between Iceland and Denmark, his old, splendid sailing ship, unless he's bought a splashing steamer. Friðrik may wish to allow Tryggvi to claim the ship that the merchant has long had his eye on, for the sake of both its name and its good fortune with catches. It doesn't particularly please Tryggvi's men, therefore, when Snorri finally slinks out of his house, several hours after Geirþrúður rode down the fjord, having just heard a long American poem, Are you the king? It is a trifle, when he comes, pale and stooping, looking far from bold, to Högni and pays the debts of the five families that have been hit hardest by his insolvency, broken families living in the old neighborhood. Just like that. He says nothing about where the money has come from, yet a rumor spreads quickly, perhaps started by Marta, who got it straight from Snorri's lips that that same morning, Jóhann, Geirþrúður's bookkeeper, had paid a visit to the ruined merchant with a cash offer for the *Hope*, a bit below market value, to be sure, but Snorri didn't care, agreed to the deal in order to unfasten the noose from around the five families' necks, as well as, perhaps—After all, I'm not above such things, he said to Jóhann with a faint smile—to get back at Friðrik, to needle him.

As it happened, Snorri's needling worked very well indeed; Friðrik wasn't at all happy to learn that the *Hope* had been snatched from him at the eleventh hour, and by Geirþrúður, who'd taken advantage of Snorri's desperation and acquired the ship at a discount, cold-hearted bitch, and probably with silver from the Devil himself. It smarts; Tryggvi certainly won't be happy. Friðrik has a temper, and it was a nervous head bookkeeper who brought him the news. Neither said anything about their meeting, so we don't know how Friðrik reacted; someone said that he swept everything off his desk: inkpot, pens, papers, files; someone said that he nearly screamed Högni's head right off his neck. This is just hearsay, speculation; yet we do know that Friðrik took out a pistol that he received last winter as a gift from a foreign ship's captain, a six-shooter, and emptied it at the wall. The shots were heard, albeit no one was certain of the number;

four, five, six, but the gun was indeed fired, there were holes in the wall, and we most definitely heard the reports. Gunshots are not an everyday occurrence beneath these mountains.

XX

If God were honest he would give them a vigorous kick in the ass.

Snorri and Marta are standing outside Snorri's Shop when the boy arrives with food for the ruined merchant. A man who can pay others' debts, Tryggvi's men had informed Snorri, must surely be able to find lodgings elsewhere.

In other words, Snorri has been evicted with just a few books, musical scores, photographs of his boys. If God were honest he would give them a vigorous kick in the ass, Marta says to the boy. They're on their way down to Hotel World's End, Snorri's lost the will to live, is completely apathetic, and the boy watches them go. Snorri has become thin, is now slender as a string on which existence plays its sorrowful song, while Marta, on the other hand, is nothing but life, an exclamation point in existence.

The boy walks slowly back up to the house, his mind on Jens, about whom Marta had asked, Is he feeling well? The boy said, He made it home, I'm planning on writing to him tonight, at which Marta said, as she set off for the hotel with Snorri in tow like a wrecked ship, Every single word always has to be dragged out of Jens, sometimes it's as if he has no mouth, but I miss seeing him, you can tell him that, and I saw the new mailman yesterday, there wasn't much to him, he was hardly anything at all.

I'll write to him tonight, when I'm in my room, I really must, the boy thinks. He passes the school, glances at an upstairs window and meets the eyes of Bjarni, painter and assistant teacher, who has his hands full with an order from Tryggvi's Company to paint all of its ships, and to complete the work before Tryggvi's arrival. They look each other briefly in the eye and the boy thinks, It must be satisfying to be able to paint, to capture the world, the mountains and the light with a brush, colors, it would be fun to ask him about the altarpiece in Sléttueyri, maybe tell him, as an aside, nonchalantly, that he, the boy, had looked at the painting with Vigfús, you remember, one of the Apostles in the boat, he would say, then add that a girl had been with them as well, just to be able to say it, though without mentioning her green eyes, red hair; how do you paint hair, anyway, which is so red that it can be seen through mountains that are thicker and denser than a man's life? It would be nice to talk about this, thinks the boy, or these thoughts flash within him, and his longing to talk to Bjarni, talk to someone who thinks about something besides fish and the commonplace, gives him a sense of solidarity with the painter in the window. He smiles and raises his left hand in greeting, at which Bjarni raises his right hand and abruptly closes the curtain.

I probably shouldn't have saluted him, thinks the boy, smiling at a woman walking down the street, Svandís, who lives in the Poorhouse but is considerably younger than its other residents, barely forty; something shattered inside her head when she lost her child many years ago, a two-year-old boy, and she often wanders around the Village from morning to night, in every sort of weather, as if in search of something that cannot be found, usually wearing nothing more than a torn, skimpy dress. Last week, the boy had scolded and chased away four eleven- or twelve-year-old boys who were following her, taunting and throwing pebbles. My boy, she says, stroking the boy's cheek, as he gives her the food intended for Snorri and receives a kiss in return, a cold kiss on the cheek.

As he approaches Magnus' Shop he spies a group of smoking sailors, coming from a Danish ship. The sailors stop when they draw near to the boy, who hesitates, feeling a stab of apprehension, yet it's not he who draws their attention but rather the shouts of an egg farmer coming down Sea Street, along with his son, the familial resemblance is clear; together they carry a handbarrow laden with eggs and dead seabirds, both stooping, a habit passed down for generations in their abodes to the north, for these are men of Strandir, who hunt their eggs on cliffs, sheer cliffs, which is not without its dangers, they descend on ropes after eggs, rocks tumble onto men's heads and they're hauled up dead, having left their lives behind on the cliffs, their memories and desires among the birds' clamor; the dwellings in that place are so ramshackle and low-ceilinged that grown men cannot stand upright inside them, and it marks them, they're always hunched over, looking as if they have too much respect for life and God to stand upright, they walk hunched over like that in happy sunshine, calm weather, and dark, violent storms, hunched over but many of them tough as whips. The father and his son have come late with their eggs, most likely the last of the egg farmers for the season, something delayed them and hopefully the eggs haven't gone bad. They set off from home with hope in their hearts and wish lists from those waiting there, requests for something small from the realm of the trading companies, and every now and then the farmer calls out loudly, Eggs, good eggs for sale, on his way to Leó's and Tryggvi's shops, but knows that since he's late, the shops will pay less, it's the law of supply and demand, so he calls out, Eggs, good eggs for sale, and sometimes adds, And fresh seabird, in the hope of being able to sell his wares directly and thereby put a little more in his pocket. Fresh seabird, he shouts, though it's hard to see what's fresh about a dead bird; death is never fresh, but often merciless and boring. The Danish sailors call out, wave the father and son over, and the latter hasten their steps, so pleased with the luck that seems to have come their way that a trace of a smile appears on the son's lips, though such muscle movements abide much deeper within the father. They have reason to rejoice; it's a large group of sailors and they pay in cash, what a lucky day, now it will be fun to go home, maybe the son is imagining his younger siblings, itching with anticipation, God help us, this could be a memorable day. Not so fast, the boy hears the farmer say hoarsely to his eager son, just as well that he does so, it would be a painful misfortune if they went too fast, tripped over a rock, of which there are enough on the street, and the eggs were hurled from the handbarrow. The boy loiters to see what happens, the Danes handle the eggs, the farmer shows them how to check their freshness, holding them up to the sun and peering into them through curled fingers; like new, he says loudly, the Danes pull out their money and the sun is yellow and big and the sky beautiful.

But as it turns out, this isn't the last egg farmer of the summer.

The boy has reached Geirþrúður's house, his refuge and shelter, his mind on the son's expression, the joy that shone in his face no matter how he tried to disguise it, on Svandís' vulnerability, his shoulders more hunched than those of any man in Strandir, completely lost in thought; he nearly passes the house and, before he realizes it, meets an egg farmer, senses someone's presence, no more than that, as he passes the house his head suddenly clears, he looks around and sees the farmer waddling there, carrying a trough laden with eggs. This farmer is alone and doesn't shout; he walks silently, stares straight ahead, stiffly. The boy recognizes the cast of the man's back as he walks past, yet it takes a long time for a light to click on, for him to realize, so surprised is he to see this man here in the Village, as if meeting someone from another life, that it's in fact Bjarni from Nes, far away from his bay, from the Polar Sea, from his four children, the bitch named after a man, the Minister for Icelandic Affairs, far away from his bedridden mother, who apparently doesn't know how to die. Bjarni, the boy says quietly, hesitantly, but the farmer waddles on, doesn't stop until his name is spoken a third time, almost shouted, stops, stares as if lost in thought, lays the heavy trough on the ground, turns around slowly.

An entire world has disappeared since they last saw each other, said goodbye at the verge of a mountain, over a coffin, with the Polar

Sea on one side, the wilderness on the other, and a darkening horizon all around. Suddenly, the boy's memory of Hjalti strikes him so vividly that he nearly breaks down and weeps, out there on the street, in broad daylight. A distance separates them, the boy takes a few steps yet doesn't go all the way, respecting both Bjarni's space and his own, leaving three, four yards between them. The summer sun is in the sky, the ever-present brightness of the month of June, the smell of saltfish in the air; the distant sound of working folk, women cleaning and drying saltfish, men unloading, can be heard all the way up here. You've got eggs, the boy says finally, because it's natural for people to put the obvious into words when they don't dare ask about the absolute; are you sad, are the children alive, do you miss Ásta very much? Yes, Bjarni says by way of acknowledging all of these. I expect that Hjalti hasn't returned? the boy says, giving up on stating the obvious. No, Bjarni says. There's been no word of him? No. We simply lost him. Bjarni says nothing, stares, and the boy dares to continue. Jens blew and blew his trumpet; we shouted, but it was useless, we could barely hear ourselves think, could hardly see each other. Your wife, Ásta . . . I know, Bjarni says, to the boy's relief, though he doesn't know what Bjarni means, what he knows, because she blasted her way out of her coffin and stood over him like a guidepost, was a guidepost; she'd been inside his head, menacing, cynical, coarse, cruel, weeping, does Bjarni know all this? No, hardly, but there's also the fact that sometimes you know without having any idea of what happened. Life isn't incomprehensible, just inexplicable. How . . . how are the children? They're at home. Yes, at home, that's something; where are you going with the eggs? To Leó's. You're too late. Probably. Which means you'll get less for them. Probably. Do you have many trips left to make with your trough? Four, I guess. I live here, the boy says, gesturing toward the big house with his thumb. Bjarni glances at the house, then looks down at the eggs. Would you like some coffee? the boy says, somewhat agitated, not wanting to lose Bjarni, not wanting that at all. Coffee, exclaims Bjarni, why? I don't know, the boy admits, but you served me coffee. That was different. And maybe Helga will want to buy eggs from you, the boy adds, happy to have come up with this idea, she pays better than Leó's men, and in cash.

Is it far to this Helga, and to the coffee?

We're standing right in front of her house, as I said.

Fine, then.

Good, the boy says, and he means it; let's go in. Through the front door? Bjarni says over the eggs, stopping in his tracks. It's better. How can that be? Otherwise we'd go in through the café, where there's bound to be quite a few people. There are too many people here, says Bjarni, almost despairingly. That's true, agrees the boy, before adding, almost involuntarily, yet there are still far too few.

Helga buys all of the eggs in the trough; this is Bjarni from Nes, the boy had said, from Nes, repeated Helga, surprised, and she may have been alarmed but hid it well, and the boy nodded. Helga paid fairly, yet on the moderate side, knowing that anything else would upset Bjarni, counted out the coins, Bjarni thanked her with a nod. Andrea makes coffee, starts rinsing the eggs, happy to have work to do, at times it's as if there are too many hands in the house, too little work. Ólafía is out in the café along with Áslaug, a woman of nearly forty who is starting her third summer at Geirþrúður's, wife of a boatwright, she can't bear the brine, the wet and cold of the fish tubs, besides having a nine-month-old boy at her breast whom her two daughters, six and eight years old, bring to her twice a day, their expressions obstinate after enduring the taunts of several boys who follow them the whole way, shouting, What's it like, having a cow for a mother? Áslaug takes the children into the kitchen, gives them something to drink while the girls suck on boiled sweets from Helga, the sugary taste slowly softening their expressions. If there's not much to do, the women gather around the kitchen table, Helga, Andrea,

Geirþrúður, Ólafía, and watch the boy at his mother's breast, watch in silence, each in her own thoughts.

Luckily, Áslaug isn't in the kitchen when the boy comes in with Bjarni, she's out in the café, looking after the customers with Ólafía, while Andrea has finished rinsing the eggs and doesn't feel too well. Pétur was with her last night.

He came here for the first time a week ago, walked quietly into the café, which was nearly full at the time, spotted an empty seat in a corner, slunk over to it, sat there with his hands on his knees, looked at her or down at his lap and missed the sea, there's freedom in looking up from the fishing lines and seeing only the endless, leaden sea, problems become remote, and everything becomes small. Andrea didn't see him immediately, many things need to be done, coffee, beer, liquor, bread, soup, she was busy, focused, listening, sometimes smiling, Pétur looked at her and stopped thinking about the sea, looked at her and something trembled inside him, softening him, yet he maintained his tough, serious expression, held firm, and that's how it's supposed to be, one shouldn't give anything away, but why doesn't she smile like that around him? She used to do, often, and she smiled like that when Bárður and the boy were in the fishing hut, otherwise not. Why? Pétur's hands opened and closed on his knees. He recognized three sailors in the café but pretended not to notice them; they glanced over at him, once, twice, thrice, said something in low tones but didn't dare greet him first, not this tough skipper known for his good hauls. Pétur shook his head slightly, as if to clear it, stopped up as it was with the chatter in the café, mostly foreign babble, completely unintelligible, but when is it possible to understand another person, anyway, even if they speak the same language? It's possible to understand fish when you pull them up from the deep, it's possible to understand sheep, both in the sheep shed and out on the moor, it's even possible to understand the sea, but who understands someone when she's like a fish one moment, a butterfly the next? Pétur looked at his rough, scarred palms, looked up and met Andrea's eyes, she was holding four beers. You're here, she said, countless minutes later, when she had time to go over to him, when she worked up the courage to do so, sticking her hands in her apron pocket, sticking them like a scream into her pocket. Yes, Pétur said, straightening slightly, he's always been tall, not particularly strong looking at first glance, but his long arms possess enormous power. Is Guðrún looking after you? Guðmundur and I agreed that that wasn't a good idea. That what wasn't a good idea? For his daughter to spend a lot of time in my fishing hut. Do you mean that you and Guðmundur spoke to each other? Andrea asked, so surprised that her hands stopped trembling in her apron pocket; that would be for the first time in twelve years! People don't need to discuss things to be in agreement, Pétur said, the corners of his mouth stiffening slightly. I brought in a woman from the countryside, he said finally, as Andrea stood there silently, her hands deep in her apron pocket, as if she couldn't care less. So you did, yes. It's Elínborg. It can't be very tidy then, Andrea said, almost laughing. She works hard in her own way, and does what's most important. And doesn't go filling her head with nonsense, he added, when she said nothing. That's fine, Pétur; does she get to go out to the salting shed with you, perhaps? Out to the salting shed? he exclaims, aghast. She's soft and plump, and has never been shy, said Andrea, smiling incomprehensibly. Pétur swallowed, had to, what was happening with the world, merchants forcing people to sell their fish wet, English trawlers hauling in load after load of fish by steam power, plundering Icelandic fishing grounds in defiance of the laws of the land, as if they don't exist, even fishing within the fjords and just sailing over any small boats in the way, and a man's wife says things like this; where is the world headed? Soft and plump, never shy. A vision of Elínborg flashes through his mind, her firm, almost violent movements, broad hips, big bottom, roundish mouth that never takes anything from anyone, and then it was as if something were thrown through him, abruptly, violently, his eyes blazed, for a fraction of a second it was impossible to sit still, and then it was over, and he looked, uneasy and uncertain, at Andrea, who has never spoken this way before, has never been this way, but she's also never left him before, that possibility has never existed, people don't leave each other, not healthy people, they just die, and there's not much one can say about that. Pétur looked at her, tried to stir himself to anger because she was the one who left, she was the one who changed, not him, he's the same. Why do people change, isn't it treachery, or weakness, and why is he sitting here like, yes, like a beggar, he hasn't done anything wrong; he's entirely in the right!

When are you coming back? he asked, turning his hands over and gripping his knees; he has big hands. Can I get you something? This is a café after all. I came for you. I'm working. You're my wife! I don't know who I am, Pétur. I was telling you; I just told you who you were. I need to work. I don't like you being in this house. You don't? People say bad things about that woman. What they say falls back on them; Geirþrúður is twice the person that we are put together, and she dares to live her own life. What's got into you, what the devil's got into you? he said in a low, yet fiery voice; they spoke softly, just loud enough for the words to be heard through the babble of voices. I don't know. The men don't understand you. Have they dared to talk to you about me? Talk, talk, do you think everything needs words to be understood? Andrea looked to one side and met Helga's eyes, inquisitive eyes, smiled faintly and shook her head, I'll handle this, said the smile, the head movement, but she was relieved to know that the boy was in the house with Hulda, working on his English, hard to say how Pétur would react if he saw him. It was nice to see you, Pétur, give my regards to Árni and Gvendur.

He stood up, how tall he was!, put on his hat, wanted to say something but couldn't, didn't dare to, didn't want to, you're my wife, he said, just to say something, and returned two days later. Sat, watched her, left without speaking to her, she served him coffee, almost without thinking about it, as if out of habit, which can make life both beautiful and slavish. Then he was gone, stalked back to the fishing hut, taking long strides, made his presence known as he drew near, spat, cleared his throat vigorously and spat again, causing Elínborg, inside, to fall silent, her deep voice had carried out into the calm, perhaps she was talking about Pétur and Andrea because everyone looked down when he entered, and he could do nothing about it except clench his fists behind his back.

Then he came a third time, last evening, the evening before the boy showed up with this egg farmer, Bjarni, whom he'd told them about, of course; the woman who died, the farmhand who vanished into the storm, the children who lived with a dog. The boy came in with the egg farmer, whom he'd described so thoroughly that Andrea felt as if she'd met him before, as if they knew each other already. Pétur didn't come in, not the third time; instead he waited for her at the corner of Sea Street, how long she didn't know, but he was soaking wet, it had rained and he waited for her, he was drenched and oddly fragile, she felt, unable to say a word, she slowed down when she saw him, and then they walked side by side, silently; what were they supposed to say, anyway? Something incomprehensible had happened between them, something unthinkable. She allowed him to accompany her to the house, allowed him to come inside, down to the basement room, because he was sopping wet and so unlike himself, but it makes such a difference to have come in, not to be out beneath the sky any longer, among the mountains and houses and people. There was so little space between them in the basement room, and it was harder to say nothing, harder to hide their hands and eyes, and she couldn't even make coffee, which would have helped a great deal. I just sleep here, she said, as if to make excuses for the plainness of the room, just a cot, a simple chair, small mirror, wash bowl, chamber pot, two books, a textbook in English and a Russian novel that the boy had chosen for her, and two small pictures on the wall.

You need some joy, Helga had said, handing her the two pictures, paintings from abroad, two little fragments from the fantasy world. Pétur stood there wet and cold, far too big, tall and bulky in this little room, then sat down uncertainly on the cot, absentmindedly picked up the English textbook, immediately put it down, as if he'd burned himself, Andrea looked away and pretended not to notice. Then she too sat down on the cot, nearly an arm's length between them, their hands in their laps, resting there negligently, the ceiling creaked when someone walked past above them, a woman spoke sharply, a child cried, then laughed a moment later as they sat there, barely an arm's length between them and slightly more than twenty years. I just sleep here, she said again. Yes, he said. I go to work in the café at six and am there until eight. Eight, yes. Yes, eight.

That's fourteen hours.

Yes, fourteen, there's plenty to do.

We've had good hauls.

Yes.

They want to force us to sell the fish wet.

Yes. I know.

They're tightwads.

Yes.

I don't take Elínborg out to the salting shed, he said, louder than intended. No, I didn't expect that you did, she said with a faint smile. He laid his right hand on her shoulder, and they sat there like that. Then she looked at him. You're shivering, she said. It's nothing, just the wet. It's not good, she said, then stood up and began rubbing his shoulders, and his chest, quickly, to warm him, and he lifted his long arms, hugged her tightly, pressing her against him, pressed tightly, his head lay fast against her chest and he breathed her in, her scent, that familiar scent that penetrated his life, familiarity that made the world more reliable, but there was also a new scent, something completely new, and he sniffed inquisitively and she stood still as stone, and then he stood up and was so much bigger than she, and stronger, and she knew the power in his arms. She lay down on the bed, and he was out of his wet clothing, his disgustingly sodden garments, and had pulled her underpants out from beneath the blue dress that Helga had given her, made of soft, warm material over which Pétur ran his hands, so soft, he said hoarsely, but she said nothing and he kissed her neck clumsily, unused to doing so, then pulled up her dress, lay down on top of her and she parted her legs, did it without thinking, and he moaned softly and entered her, shoved his way in with that big member of his that always hurt her a bit unless she lay in just the right position, which is why she tried to reposition herself beneath him, tried to make herself more comfortable, which made him even more eager; he grabbed her arms, spread them and pressed her hard, fervently, into the mattress, as if he were fastening her down, and she stared at the ceiling as he worked like thunder, focused on counting the knots in the wood, concentrating so much on them that it was as if she left her body, as if this body that lay beneath the panting, fervent man had nothing to do with her; the only thing that mattered was to count the knots, she'd made it to nineteen when he shouted into the mattress.

Andrea is quick to clean the eggs from Bjarni, far too quick, because now she's got nothing to do, there's no particular need for a third worker in the café right now; Bjarni is sitting there at a table, having coffee and bread, he politely refuses pastry. Yes, yes, it'll do you good, Helga says, pushing the pastry toward him, and he dares not refuse it, takes a bite, glances at Andrea, she'd cleaned the eggs quickly yet gently. Pétur isn't coming today, no, perhaps tomorrow; he shouted into the mattress and she felt his warm semen inside her. Nineteen knots, she thought. He hauled himself off her, making it easier to breathe. She had to find something to wipe herself with. That semen had never kindled life, which is my fault, I suppose, she thinks, brushing an unruly lock of hair from her face, notices Bjarni looking at her, as if by coincidence. It'll probably be nice for you to work in the café during the summer, Pétur had said, charitably, as he slipped into his clothes, or until we stop fishing, in a fortnight; people these days feel they need a change now and then, such peculiar times we live in. Yes, she said. It would be terrible to send Elínborg away so soon, he added. Yes, Pétur dear. She sat on the bed, having wiped herself as well as she could; he stood so tall before her. He'll come tomorrow or the day after, and shout into the mattress. He's a good man, she thinks, in his own way, honest, wishes everyone well, he hasn't ever hurt me, can't help how he is from one day to the next, but he hauled in too many lines and that's why Bárður froze to death. Pétur should have known better, he should have hauled in fewer lines, that's just how it is.

She looks at Bjarni. How are your children? she says. They're at home, he says, forgetting to be surprised that this unfamiliar woman knows about his children. Her ash-blond hair has just begun to gray, and there's something about the corners of her mouth that causes him to think foolish thoughts about himself and about her; who's a master of his own thoughts anyway? I assumed as much, says Andrea, smiling gratefully as Helga hands her a cup of coffee. Bjarni glances at the two women, one standing straight-backed, so determined in her movements that she seems almost ruthless, the other slightly hunched in the shoulders, gentler, with weathered skin. Yes, there are four of them, Bjarni says, before taking a sip of the warm coffee, he can hardly say more, suddenly feeling a lump in his throat. Hopefully I'm not coming down with something, he thinks apprehensively, aghast, because what if worst came to worst, it's happened to others, he knows many examples, someone starts to cough, and then that person's dead. What would become of the children then? They'd be separated, settled far from one another, and who would want to take his mother in? I've got to get home, he thinks, to where it's safe; I'm too vulnerable around people. He drinks his coffee, hears this Helga tell the boy to go to a certain place to fetch a handbarrow, there's no sense in you transporting eggs bit by bit, all by yourself, for half the day, she says, and wearing yourself out, when you can bring them in one trip with the right equipment. It does me good to carry them myself, Bjarni protests, but says nothing further and doesn't move when the boy starts getting ready; he doesn't have the energy to say more, and besides, it seems pointless to make objections in this big house. He reaches out and unexpectedly finds himself holding another pastry, the name of which he doesn't recognize; he doesn't dare to leave it behind on the tray and eats it, accepts it like any other job that can't be shirked, yet grimaces instinctively. I'm sure your children would appreciate such a treat, says Andrea with a smile, and he smiles back, can't help it. Where did his self-control go?

By the time the boy returns with a handbarrow, a large plank four inches deep and with handles like jawbones at either end, Bjarni has told the women the names of his children, all four of them, and answered questions about them. It was a bit odd, as well, because something seemed to happen as soon as he said the names: Steinólfur, Sakarías, Jón, Þóra; as if the lives of his children became less remote by saying their names in the kitchen. Or was the pastry muddling his head? The boy brings the handbarrow, brings a smile, having come across Lúlli and Oddur, who'd finished unloading a Danish ship and then been given the rest of the day off, he spoke to them for one minute, which was more than enough to put a smile on his lips, and it's still there when he enters the house. Some people are precious in their everydayness.

I'm not used to talking so much, says Bjarni after he and the boy have finished loading eggs into the handbarrow; they've fitted them all in and arranged them so that the ones at the bottom won't break, put lifeless seabirds on top, the handbarrow is fully loaded, it must weigh a hundred pounds, said the boy, standing over it, at which point Bjarni said that he wasn't used to talking so much. The boy asks, What? They've been working in silence, haven't said a single word since leaving the house, which was a bit difficult, there was much that the boy wanted to say to Bjarni, but he couldn't bring himself to do so, the farmer from the Polar Sea seemed lost in thought, distant. In there, says Bjarni by way of explanation. Did you talk a lot in there? asks the boy; I'm not surprised, it's good to talk when you're with them, the two of them, it's easy, you don't need to . . . you don't need to watch what you say. Andrea, adds the boy when Bjarni says nothing, was the Custodian at the fishing hut. Fishing hut, repeats, or echoes, Bjarni, gazing into the distance as if he were elsewhere. Yes, the boy says, but Bjarni interrupts him, saying, The one with the gray hair? Huh? Is that Andrea? Yes, that's Andrea. Yes, Bjarni says, again looking as if his mind is elsewhere, and then the boy says, without being able to help it, suddenly so full of affection for Andrea that his voice breaks a tiny bit at the word, the big adjective, Yes, and she's precious. Precious, Bjarni repeats, having come back from wherever he was, precious, he says a second time, strange to say that about a person. You should probably talk more, says the boy, smiling. That's what Ásta used to say, says Bjarni, hurriedly bending down to grab the barrow's handles.

The eggs are heavy. They walk in silence past the café, the boy leading, it's difficult to talk to someone to whom one's back is turned. Hopefully you'll get a good price for the eggs, the boy says when they reach Sea Street, not wanting to walk in silence any longer, wanting to hear Bjarni's voice. I'm late and will hardly get full price. Yet still a decent price, the boy says; these are good eggs. Yes, I should be able to pick up a few things, Bjarni says, finding it good to talk to the boy's back. Will you buy something for the kids? the boy asks, unafraid to ask so directly. Some raisins, maybe, Bjarni says, should I get them something else? he adds unexpectedly. I, the boy says over his shoulder, would buy some blank sheets of paper and pencils, see, if you really wanted to surprise them and make them happy. Blank sheets of paper, Bjarni says, a pencil, and he tightens his grip on the handles, the children's joy, what I wouldn't give for that; blank sheets of paper, he says again, loosening his grip, oh, right, I believe I have a letter for you. For me? says the boy, so surprised that he stops and turns around to look at Bjarni, having forgotten the handbarrow between them; before he realizes it, they're revolving in a circle, like dunces. Of course, it's unnecessary to revolve in circles because of a letter, or even ten letters, because letters are just letters, sheets of paper with words, and though you might have different opinions about the words themselves, they don't go anywhere after you've put them down on paper, but instead wait with inhuman patience for someone to come and release them from their fetters, for a time. Shouldn't we be on our way? Bjarni says, but the boy doesn't move, twists himself around to get a proper view of Bjarni's face; he's stuck in place, doesn't want to keep going, can't. A letter for me, are you sure? Of course I'm sure, Bjarni says, surprised, impatient, it isn't good to stand so long in the middle of the street in the Village, holding onto a barrow heavy with eggs, it attracts attention, people soon begin to stare, it's bad to stand out. So you have a letter for me, says the boy, as if he's come to a remarkable and unexpected conclusion. Yes yes, I'd just forgotten it.

The boy: Forgotten, yes, you'd nearly forgotten.

Bjarni: Let's stop standing here.

The boy: From whom; did you stop at Sléttueyri, by any chance?

Bjarni: Why on earth would I have done that?

I don't know, the boy admits, not daring to mention a freshly dug grave on the east side of the church. From whom is the letter, I mean, if you haven't stopped anywhere; it's not from the Polar Sea? he asks, trying to calm his heartbeat with humor, it wouldn't be bad to get a letter from that!

So it's not from the Polar Sea, says the boy when Bjarni doesn't answer; the eggs are growing heavier, you feel their weight more while standing still, you've got to move, otherwise your mind numbs, and your blood, existence presses you down and you become stuck. No, Bjarni says finally; the doctor and his wife sent me a maid, temporarily, which was unnecessary, although it was helpful. Does she have red hair, by any chance? asks the boy, far too loudly. Yes, it's safe to say.

They're near the intersection of Sea Street and Main Street, people pass them by, two men carrying a handbarrow laden with eggs, apparently having forgotten their errand. Let's be on our way, Bjarni says. Is the letter from her? asks the boy, without moving. It's not from me. Nor is it from the Polar Sea, the boy mutters, and they continue on their way. The boy and the man with the letter. The boy is so distracted that Ragnheiður has to greet him twice and say his name loudly the second time, otherwise he wouldn't have noticed her, would have just plodded past with the ridiculous handbarrow, as if she didn't exist; he would have missed her completely, in her yellow dress, with long white lace gloves that reach above her elbows, holding a green parasol and stepping so delicately, with disdain, really, in those fine, shiny boots of hers, amidst the dust, the cowpats and people who smell of saltfish or eggs. You have the audacity to greet him? Lovísa says, it's almost a reprimand, after they've passed by on their way to tea with Guðrún, Reverend Þorvaldur's wife. Lovísa, the wife of the district magistrate, is dressed in a roomy, light-colored walking dress; men doff their hats to her from far away, she's superior to us, both of them, in fact, yet dust still settles on their dresses, their boots, that's how difficult it is to transcend one's environment completely. He's got no business passing by without noticing me, Ragnheiður says. He's nothing, that boy, and besides, he lives with Geirþrúður. I do as I please. I know, says the other, but don't do anything stupid, soon you're going to Copenhagen, where another life awaits you. I know what I'm doing, Ragnheiður says calmly. That's exactly what I'm afraid of, her elder mumbles.

In a yellow dress, shiny, pitch-black boots. He's never seen a woman in a yellow dress before, it has to be her wearing it, of course. They approach Central Square; Ragnheiður, Friðrik's daughter, took the liberty of greeting him. She, the daughter of authority, of superiority, dressed like a woman from another world, and he just an ordinary porter. They've come to Leó's Shop, put down the handbarrow, shake their arms. She said hello to you, Bjarni says, looking at the boy. We know each other slightly, the boy says as if apologizing, as if he'd betrayed Bjarni, not been forthright with him. Those people aren't accustomed to greeting anyone except themselves. You think that's true? the boy asks hesitantly, startled by the harshness in Bjarni's voice. Yes, says Bjarni, before falling silent, glancing around; his jaw looks taut. Well, begins the boy, but Bjarni interrupts and says, as if he's biting the words into pieces, They don't greet people like us without reason, and hardly a good one. You're just cruel, says the boy in surprise. No, it's not me who's cruel; fortunately I don't have the energy for it, but here's the letter, Bjarni says, reaching into his jacket for the envelope. They must see something in you, boy, he adds, looking thoughtfully at the letter before pursing his lips, as if to refrain from saying something, then handing the boy the letter, speckled with grease stains from his clothing, smelling of his sweat.

The boy smells the sweat as he sniffs the envelope, having found himself a place in the sun, his back against the Tower House of the Norwegian Elias, for many years the owner of a whaling station in one of the fjords, but who now lives here in the Village with his Icelandic wife, the daughter of a tenant farmer, thirty years younger and so vivacious that Elías' hereditary depression—his brother shot himself, his father hung himself, his grandmother swam out and drowned in the sea, their uncle cut his own throat, another ingested poison, his aunt tried to hang herself in the woods but the tree branch broke, as did both her legs, after which she lay helpless for twelve hours, in the cold rain, before being rescued and taken home, where she died of pneumonia—practically vanishes, as long as he sticks close to her. The boy hears her singing through the open window, and her voice reminds him of a brook in sunlight. He chose himself an inconspicuous place, Bjarni went into the shop to negotiate a price for his eggs and to put a few things on his account, various necessities and, hopefully, sheets of paper and pencils for the children. The boy sniffs the envelope again, but smells only the odor of the laborer's sweat. What does she want, why did she write him a letter, well, except maybe to ask about Jens? Of course she's asking about Jens, she's only interested in him, thinks the boy, relieved, yet not at all happy, staring blankly into space. Why did Ragnheiður greet him? I wish she were naked beneath that yellow dress, in those boots; no, that's not what I wish, or yes, or no, but dear God how red Álfheiður's hair is! I would willingly work myself to death just to be able to look at it, smell its scent, fall asleep to it and wake up to it. The boy regards the bustling life of Central Square, folk processing the saltfish, folk coming and going from Leó's or Tryggvi's shops, which stand opposite each other, or from the German Bakery. He holds a letter, his name written by her of the red hair, and suddenly he couldn't care less about this letter. Such freedom, not to care! I'm not going to read it, thinks the boy, surprised, happy, triumphant, and he puts the letter in his pocket. Wads it up, I'm not taking a step toward that life, he thinks, or something to that effect; I'm not letting red hair condemn me to utter poverty, probably having forgotten his conclusion that the letter was one long question about Jens.

Live!

The last word from his mother. The final cry. Live, get an education, don't let hardship suffocate you, disappointment diminish you. He's going to live, get an education. Thus he shoves the letter deep into his pocket, stands up, thinks of the yellow dress, the translucent white gloves that reach above the elbows, thinks about how she said his name, that she'd actually wanted to say it out loud, that his name, his existence, had quivered momentarily on her lips, or between them, those warm, red lips.

Those people, Bjarni had said, *those people*, almost as if he'd wanted to spit.

Friðrik has forced Snorri to his knees, threatens Geirþrúður, and Ragnheiður is on her way to Copenhagen, where it's probably easy to forget everything having to do with Iceland. Even if she didn't forget him, even if she wanted to continue to say his name, longed to do so, even if she, for some incomprehensible reason, wanted to have him with her day and night and offered him access to her world, a world of comfort, security, would he want to go there? Does he want to stroll around here and greet Bjarni as one of *those people*? What would the trinity say, how would Geirþrúður look at him, would Lúlli and Oddur continue to greet him in their cheerful way that makes everything brighter, and what about Gísli, whose expression becomes dark and rigid when he brings up his brother or else becomes cynical. The boy leans against the house, observes life in Central Square and tries to forget the letter.

It would be splendid if you would help me carry these things, Bjarni says, suddenly beside him, and the boy apparently answers in the affirmative, at least it's he who's holding the handles of the handbarrow, staring at Bjarni's back as they leave Central Square behind; it's nearly three o'clock and women rush past on their way home for quick bites to eat as they prepare food for their husbands, if they aren't out at sea, straddling the waves as if in a dance with the horizon.

The boy in fact read the letter.

Or glanced through it.

Seven times.

It happened unexpectedly, shouldn't have happened at all, his hand moved by itself into his pocket; besides, you've got to find a place to keep your hands, and then he found himself holding the letter, reading it.

The handbarrow is heavy. Loaded with necessities: flour, sugar, wheat, coffee, rice.

I'm holding the handbarrow, the boy thinks, there's Bjarni, which means that I'm no longer sitting up against the Tower House. Bjarni slows down, looks over his shoulder; I bought ten sheets of paper and four pencils, he says.

The boy had read the letter and heard Elías laugh twice inside, like jovial darkness. Read the letter, two pages, densely packed with words.

They don't meet any yellow dresses, any lips, moist and warm with life, saying his name, which is lucky, she'd probably have had to shout, so distant is the boy, who stares at Bjarni for a long time because they've stopped and Bjarni is saying something about sheets of paper. Ten, he says. No, the boy says, there were only two. No, I bought ten, says Bjarni, surprised, and then the boy understands; ten sheets of paper, four pencils, four lives behind all the mountains, in a little bay, and then the Polar Sea. Sorry, I was distracted. I can see that. I read the letter.

Bjarni: I expected that you would.

The boy: Did you know about it?

Bjarni: About what?

The boy: The letter.

Bjarni: I brought it to you.

Yes, of course, the boy says, his head clearing; he laughs, remembers the smell of the man's sweat on the envelope, the heavy sweat of a laborer, which smells entirely different from the sweat of anguish, the sweat of desire.

Bjarni: She's peculiar.

The boy: Who?

Bjarni: Álfheiður.

The boy: Yes, the letter was from her.

I know that, Bjarni says patiently, as if speaking to a child.

Is she peculiar?

Yes.

Do you think that's bad?

I suppose that depends.

On what? the boy says, and Bjarni thinks it over; they don't move, now it's Bjarni who twists around to look at the boy, women hurry past, glancing at these two men who stand there holding a handbarrow, motionless and for no apparent reason.

Bjarni: I expect it's bad to be peculiar in this country; people are punished for it.

The boy: Yes, I know, they forget their raincoats and freeze to death. But it was good of you to buy the paper.

Bjarni: Yes, and irrational, as well.

The boy: It's just this damned life that's irrational.

Bjarni: Hmm. Well, yes, I'm sure it's dangerous to overestimate common sense; it can suck the life out of so much.

Someone should kiss you, the boy says. I hardly think so, Bjarni replies, and they continue on their way. Yellow dress, black boots, supple yet incisive, determined movements, no, nowhere in sight. But here's a question: What are Friðrik's realm, and a yellow dress, compared to receiving a letter from the Polar Sea?

"I'm terrified of the sea here; it wants to devour me. Swallow me and change me into a cold fish. I have memories that are cold fish, they occasionally swim through my blood and make me cold. Do you have such memories? The kids here have fun teasing me about the sea. If my fear helps them, so much the better. Here we are, then, Salvör and I, where you were, before you crashed into the doctor's house. You and that big man. Do you think he has gentle hands, do you think they can be bad and harmful? Are your hands bad, by any chance? Not that it's any of my business. Don't let my thinking of you now and then go to your head. You don't know what other things I think of, anyway, or how I think. How strong are you? Not in your arms, but inside? People think it's easy to tell who's strong and who's not. People are just stupid. You know that life can be heavier than the mountains. It can be more dangerous than the Polar Sea, and much more savage than a polar bear. You don't know it, but I'm little more than misfortune, just red hair and utter poverty. You're quite silly for thinking about me. Do you think about me?"

They go straight to the boat without stopping at the house, put the things that he bought into it and cover it well; they have to cross a big, wide sea and mustn't get wet. It's fine for crossing, the boy says to the wind and to Bjarni, who straightens up, the blue sky is over the world and there's a bit in the eyes of the farmer. He offers the boy his hand; thank you for everything. I wish I could do more, the boy says. You've done a fair amount; I'm taking ten sheets of paper with me. Won't you come up to the house for a bit? I've stayed long enough, says the cottager; wait a moment, says the boy, as he notices Ólafía approaching, as fast as her stiff legs can carry her, she's panting and her face is red, which suits her. She clambers down to the shore, keeping her balance on the steep rocks by holding out her stocky arms like a big, dismal bird that life has deprived of flight. You mustn't go, she says to Bjarni, without coming up to the house first. I thought I would just leave my greetings and my great gratitude, Bjarni says apologetically, letting his eyes wander to the west, whence night comes; you have to take advantage of favorable winds when you can. Ólafía says nothing; here no one objects to arguments involving the wind, to which we've bowed for more than a thousand years, yet she doesn't agree, she just stands there, beautifully awkward, waiting for them, as if she can't imagine anything other than that Bjarni will come. One generally does what Helga asks, the boy says, seeming to speak to the boat, and she doesn't delay anyone without good reason. Is that so? Bjarni says resignedly.

People are waiting for them in the kitchen, and something is afoot; the boy senses it as soon as they step in, there's something in the air, the way the women carry themselves. Geirþrúður has joined them, she sits at the table, smokes a cigarette, her legs are crossed and one foot dangles in the air, but there are shadows on her face, perhaps from lack of sleep, sleep has shown her little mercy since the ship capsized on the Lagoon. Bjarni hesitates in the doorway when he spies Geirþrúður, immediately guesses it's her, forgets his manners and stares, then looks away, clears his throat, says nothing, uncertain. Helga is sitting at the end of the table, while Andrea stands next to the stove, looking slightly as if she's about to be shot, but she thrusts out her chest. She's changed clothes, having borrowed a simple brown dress from Helga, very plain, the commonplace incarnate, but she wears it well. Some people can bear the commonplace better than others, and thus are blessed, possibly.

He just took me, Andrea had told Helga, having started to boil the eggs, and it was as if the odor of Bjarni lingered in the kitchen; he and the boy were down at the boat, loading eggs into the handbarrow. A nice man, Helga had said, yes, Andrea said, fiddling with the eggs. A shame, Helga said, that such a man is denied any happiness. Andrea looked up, surprised by these words coming from Helga's lips, and said, unintentionally, moving the pot a few fractions of an inch, said, He just took me, and Helga knew immediately what she meant. When? Last night. But he didn't come here, not that I noticed. No, he was waiting for me outside, and I felt sorry for him, he was so wet. He walked with me down to the house, I felt sorry for him and invited him in, and besides, he's my husband, I couldn't forbid him. Then he took me and I didn't dare say anything, though he hurt me, without knowing it, he always hurts me if I'm not ready, and I felt as if he were tying me down and I could never get up again. I just lay there and counted the knots in the ceiling. But I also thought about Bárður, it was the only thing I could think about, I don't know why. He always smelled so good. It was nice to be near him. Everything became easier somehow. And I thought, Why did Pétur wait so long to return to shore, why did he haul in so many lines, all of them except for Einar's, he knows, of course, what it means not to have your raincoat at sea, let alone so far from shore, I thought, would he have waited so long if someone else had forgotten his raincoat? I know I shouldn't think like that, but I did, and I nearly asked him, but then he shouted into the mattress. And why ask when Bárður is dead? Neither questions nor answers raise the dead. I can't go back, she said. I don't want to go back to him, she said. He isn't a bad man, she said, but I would rather die than go back to him, she said. Then Helga said once more that Bjarni was a likable man. No, I couldn't do it, said Andrea when she realized what Helga was thinking. Our lives, Helga said, are shaped by what we want. And if you want, then you can.

That's why Bjarni was sent for.

Come with me, he repeats, astonished; he's sitting at the end of the table, as far from Helga and Geirþrúður as possible, watching the women, surprised, confused, wary and possibly frightened as well. Can we offer you some coffee? Geirþrúður asks amicably, having smoked her cigarette. Yes, please, Bjarni says immediately, relieved, because it's so much easier to accept a cup of coffee than a woman. Geirþrúður gets up and fetches coffee for the cottager, who has no idea how rare it is to be served coffee by this woman. The boy covers his eyes for a moment, as if trying to comprehend all this, to regain his composure, the world swayed when Helga said that Andrea had considered going with Bjarni, what did the farmer make of that? Bjarni opened his mouth, but no words came out. You have four motherless children, Helga says, your mother is bedridden, summer is coming, and there's a great deal of work to be done, you live far from everything and it's difficult to find decent farmhands in such a place. You can't handle everything on your own, you've either got to send some of the children away or take Andrea with you. You won't ever get a better offer in this life. You mustn't be so cruel, continues Helga when nothing comes out of Bjarni's mouth; he just sits there, his hands resting on the table, useless, his coffee cup empty. Or foolish, Geirþrúður adds, with a slight smile, almost as if she's amused, and she refills the farmer's cup. His hands come alive; one gets to lift the cup, the other can follow along. The boy looks at Andrea, their eyes meet, which is good. Finally, Bjarni says, because sometimes one is forced to speak, My oldest daughter, he says firmly, yet feeling it safer to keep his eyes on his coffee cup, will be thirteen soon. Then he drinks his coffee. Or rather, is going to drink his coffee, but it's finished, his cup is empty again, and there's something so stupid about raising an empty cup to one's lips that he adds hurriedly, Her name is Þóra. But I'm sure I've already said that. She's industrious, he says, as if by way of an explanation, when no one says anything; he's simply stared at. She's still a child, Helga says, and there's no need to burden her, she's endured enough, all of you have, life is tough enough without adding things to it. Doesn't she cry at night? Geirþrúður asks unexpectedly, and Bjarni looks down, those two useless hands of his resting on the elegant kitchen table, for how do you comfort a girl who's nearly thirteen and cries into her pillow when she thinks no one can hear? Yet he hears, wants to do something, but just lies in his own bed, unable to rise to the challenge.

Andrea: I'm used to hardship. I'm used to work. I'm not unused to children though I have none myself, but that's the Lord's decision, not mine.

Bjarni now permits himself to look at her openly, as she is speaking, though it's only three sentences, two of which are short; but she spoke slowly, looking directly at him the entire time and he back at her. She's beautiful around the eyes, Bjarni thinks, unable to help himself, and there's no trace of bitterness around her mouth. More coffee? asks Geirþrúður, focused on this new role of hers. No thank you, mutters the cottager, though he hardly remembers ever having refused the black drink. Give him a drop of whisky, she then says to the boy, stepping out of her role. Bjarni doesn't drink. Is he boring, then? asks Geirþrúður, as if the farmer isn't present.

The boy: No, he bought ten sheets of paper for his children, and four pencils.

Bjarni: I only came here to sell eggs, dead seabirds, put a few things on my account. I said that I would return by nightfall.

Andrea pats her hair, which is greying slightly: I've lived for forty years and have never, apart from once, done anything unexpected. Or unusual. Never made a decision that challenges my existence. I've lived like a sheep, docile and conscientious, have always done what was expected of me.

Apart from once? Bjarni says, again taking the opportunity to look at her and, who knows, maybe to imagine her in the tiny family room, amidst the children, his mother, to imagine that . . . It's hard to control one's thoughts, at times they tell us what we want but don't dare to admit.

Yes, Andrea says, returning his gaze as if she wants to see into his thoughts, fears, dreams, and maybe she sees it, the helplessness regarding the children, their eyes, the regret. Yes, apart from once. Bjarni looks, doesn't ask, nor is it any of his business, and Andrea adds nothing. Geirþrúður and Helga glance at each other, Geirþrúður takes out another cigarette. When you left Pétur, she says, your husband; when you showed courage. When was that? asks Bjarni, when nothing comes from Andrea. Five weeks ago. I'll be damned. Yes. You're married, then? Yes. The boy here wrote her a letter, says Geirþrúður from behind a cloud of tobacco smoke. A letter? And then Andrea came here. Why a letter? To change the world, Geirþrúður says; is there any other reason for writing? Bjarni looks down at his hands. They're industrious, they're heavy, they're mute. I'm a refugee, Andrea says, I have the right to live. Did he hurt you, your husband? asks Bjarni, without looking up from his hands, cracked by toil. It's rather everything that he hasn't done. So he's never beaten you? the farmer asks his hands. Pétur is a decent man, and reliable, but his heart is a piece of saltfish. Maybe I'm no better, Bjarni says, maybe my heart is a dead seabird. I don't think so, Andrea says. Bjarni looks at the boy, as if he's responsible for all of this. Don't be so pigheaded, Geirþrúður says finally; Andrea can come back here in the autumn if it doesn't work. Man wasn't brought into this earthly life to be on his own, Helga says. Bjarni sighs, Bjarni curses, then Bjarni says, it's a tiny tenant farm. It's a hard life. Surely it's a question of attitude? Andrea says.

Bjarni: Huh?

Andrea: Nothing is difficult if you're free.

Bjarni stands up, he has arms, two of them. Arms were put on people to enable them to embrace others.

XXI

The world is never nice, which is why it hurts to see a good person go, Gísli tells the boy the following day, as the boy sits hunched over the biography of an ancient Greek. It always hurts to see a good person go, the boy knows immediately that Gísli means Andrea, even though they haven't said anything about her. The headmaster is standing, as usual, by the window in the outer parlor, and he says into the light, Why did she have to leave us? She could do no other, the boy says, looking up from his 2,500-year-old wisdom. Could do no other, repeats Gísli, what can we do, what must we do? It's impossible to say, one makes a decision or doesn't make a decision, but in the end it doesn't matter which one; we're not in charge of our lives.

The boy pores over the old thoughts, concentrates, and it goes well sometimes, sometimes horribly. Nor is it always easy to receive letters. Why doesn't she go away with that damned Norwegian? The weather's better in Norway, it must be, which must make it easier to live.

"These sheets of paper are ridiculous. Far too small to write on. There's no room for anything. I got five sheets from Steinunn, gave three to the boys, the other two are for you. Salvör is outside with them, I can hear their laughter from here. You looked at me, did you know that? You shouldn't waste your gaze on nonsense. I saw immediately that you're hopeless, and that's why I think about you. You don't even have wide shoulders, nor are you beautiful, except maybe after I've thought about you a long time and haven't got much to do. Mother once wrote to me that you should never love a man. You start to trust them, but eventually they ruin your life. Unfortunately, however, I come from both my father and my mother, which is why I have such a low opinion of myself. I think you know how to write letters; I saw it in your eyes, your hands, I saw that they know almost nothing and don't belong anywhere. I don't know how to write letters. I also think that most words were invented by men, and that's why I can't use them about me. I don't understand them and they don't understand me. Do you see what I'm saying? And now this ridiculous sheet is finished. I'm redheaded and the dog sends you his regards"

That's how the letter ends.

No full stop.

But she'd drawn a tiny, grinning dog in the lowermost corner; amazing that she managed to fit it in, the boy's index finger is broad enough to cover it. Worst of all about the letter was the lock of hair she included with it, as if he didn't fully appreciate that she's redheaded, as if he'd forgotten. The only sensible thing to do was to throw away the lock of hair, which is what he did, after going up to his room that night. Threw it away. And then spent half the night trying to find it again. The boy yawns. Should I have done something? Gísli asks the day. Done? asks the boy, distracted, such as what?

Well, I don't know, to tell the truth; perhaps offered to marry her. You, marry Andrea? the boy says, so surprised that he forgets the lock of hair; why? Well, to prevent her from leaving. And I live alone, I'm alone, that's how it is, he who is alone has no one to talk to. She's married, the boy says, but Gísli doesn't seem to be listening, he simply looks out the window and the boy sinks back into ancient Greek thought. There's sunshine in the cloudless sky, it floods the mountains and the faces of men, shines on the blind eyes of Kolbeinn, who's sitting outside, against the wall of the house, listening to life. The boy had promised to tell Kolbeinn about the Greeks, so he goes on reading. Gísli then asks about the text the boy is reading, both of them so distracted that Gísli says, almost in midquestion, Well, that's enough for today. All the women leave, he adds, and I grow old amidst schoolchildren, books, words and whisky; how is Geirþrúður doing? he asks suddenly, nearly interrupting himself, and at first the boy thinks that he's asking how she feels: how she's sleeping, whether she's dreaming of a drowned cat with a ship captain next to it? He hesitates to answer and Gísli asks, How do you think she'll react? React, react to what? Oh, the ban, of course. What ban? She hasn't mentioned it? This ban? Yes. What ban? Then I suppose you're the only person who doesn't know about it, Gísli says, shaking his head, having crossed the room to the bookcase; he's grabbed a book, thin and tattered, and has started to read it. What ban? the boy asks again, as Gísli continues to read. She's been banned from unloading her fish on the Village's drying lots. Why? My brother arranged it. Why? He wants people to heed him. But he doesn't own all the lots. You mean Tryggvi doesn't own all of them, yes, but Friðrik is good at getting others to do what he wants, I know something about that, people most often give in to what's bigger than them, otherwise everything becomes far too difficult.

What can she do with the fish from the schooners, then? That's precisely the problem; have you read this? the headmaster says, holding up the thin book. No. Well, read it for the next lesson; you have five days. Gísli hands him the book, which is light in his hand. Is it serious? The book? No, the ban. Don't think about that, just the book, it's necessary for someone to think beyond the saltfish and toil, otherwise they might as well just shoot us, right away. What's it about? asks the boy, peering at the first page, haltingly reading the Danish words, or is this Norwegian? What do I know? Gísli says, taking the English coat that he'd been permitted to put on his account last summer. For what? Friðrik had asked, looking at his brother from deep within his thoughts, it was in Friðrik's office, where Friðrik sat at a large, heavy desk, and Gísli stood on a soft rug, forced, as before, to swallow his pride and ask his brother for permission to put such an expensive item on his account. Not everything has an explanation, dear brother, he'd said. Oh yes, everything does, Friðrik said, the only question is whether one has the sense to discern it, and the courage to accept it. But Gísli got the coat, just as he expected he would; it's great to have a good, high-quality coat, it makes one feel important. But how often, he thinks, putting on his coat in Geirþrúður's parlor, can a man bend his knee without it taking a toll? Doesn't it become ever more difficult to stand up straight again, stand upright? It may not matter what books are about, Gísli says, about to button up his coat but deciding not to, it being sunny outside; but like all significant books it concerns how to be a human being, which is damned difficult. But come out into the sun with me, we'll bring beer and drink with the blind creature; we'll drink in honor of Andrea, the woman who went out to the end of the world.

XXII

Everyone misses Andrea; she sailed away with a cottager who has four children, a decrepit mother, little more than the remnants of a life, a dog, a few beasts, a little turf-roofed farm facing the Polar Sea, behind the world's mountains. The end of the world, or where the world begins. The cottager, Bjarni, calls it freedom. What can we say?—But there went Andrea, with uncertainty in her blood, a refugee from her previous life, in search of a new one. A different one. You come right back if you feel the need, Helga had said, if you're unhappy. Yes, Andrea said, yet they knew that she wouldn't return anytime soon, not until autumn, anyway, perhaps later, perhaps never. The boy had described the place thoroughly, the four children, their defenseless-ness, their exuberance, described the dog, and Bjarni, that gentle yet unshakable man, with a touch of pain in his face, how he read books, how his father had gone into a burning house after books, these people have dreams, their hearts aren't dead seabirds, or pieces of saltfish, not at all. Perhaps Andrea sailed away with the cottager, Bjarni, because of dreams. It says something about the soil, if dreams grow from it. I've lived long enough without dreams, she said to the boy down at the shore, a large chest having been loaded onto the boat, filled in haste by Helga, Geirþrúður and the boy, clothing, fabric, for-eign biscuits, raisins, dried figs, paper, books; Andrea's protests were ignored, she had no say in any of it, and Bjarni stood shuffling his feet uneasily in the kitchen, wanting to leave, to make it home before nightfall, restless, but there was also something in his blood for which he couldn't find the words, perhaps music, slight dizziness, anxiety, a smidgeon of joy, it's no small thing to sail home with an unfamiliar person, an entire life, a woman who will lie down to sleep near him in just a few hours, and he will listen to her breathing. Promise to write me long letters, she said, hugging the boy as if he were some-thing precious, and then they rowed away, Andrea and Bjarni, rowed for half an hour until they reached the wind, when they raised their brownish sail. I do quite a bit of trade with foreign fishermen in the summer, Bjarni said, Frenchmen, Americans. I thought you were far away from everything, Andrea said; it had been good to row so hard, it held back the tears, it takes an effort to change lives. Well, yes, but fishermen need water, and ice for icing their catches; we have a good spring and there's a huge drift on one slope that rarely melts, it's a steady source of income. The kids find it fun to see foreigners and to hear them talk, Bjarni adds, though it was probably unnecessary for him to speak so much, what must she think of him? But then she smiled that smile of hers at him, out here on the sea. It's certainly true, what's been said—that it's possible to subsist on one smile for a very long time. Years, even. They sailed north and saw the mountains rise from the sea, saw the coal-black cliffs, saw green bays open up, deep fjords, a man and a woman in a boat, the sail above their heads like a wing, or freedom.

The boy begins his letter the next morning; he sits at the inner-most table, Kolbeinn's table, a smattering of people in the café. One transport ship, Danish, at the pier, a whaler on the Lagoon, taking on provisions; two schooners from the northern part of the country had arrived during the night, their catches bought by Tryggvi's Company. Five Danes and four Norwegians sit at two tables, and all the windows are open because of the stench of train oil from the Norwegians. The boy gets up now and then to help Áslaug and Ólafía, but it's mainly for show; they can cope, and just before nine he's sent with a message to the bookkeeper Jóhann—despite the bustle at the drying lots, the day is calm and it's tranquil between the mountains, almost a dreamy tranquility, as if the world has shut its eyes momentarily. But then a big steamship steams into the Lagoon and the calm is broken.

T. Jónsson is inscribed on its hull: Tryggvi Jónsson. He's here, then, Tryggvi himself, and he's bought himself a steamship, against the recommendation of Friðrik and Högni, the company's head book-keeper, who preferred a good sailing ship, far cheaper and just as adequate. But Tryggvi takes bigger steps than others, he doesn't want to have to rely on the wind, as we've always had to do, continually asking the wind to blow in our favor, while it simply blows and takes whatever is in its path with it; birds or ships are one and the same to the wind. It blows words and memories into the distance and ships between countries. Now, however, Tryggvi has purchased a big, powerful steam-powered vessel and is no longer dependent on the wind, almost as if he's conquered the powers of nature, and the three masts that rise tall and majestic from the deck are a sign that the wind is in Tryggvi's service; flouted in a headwind, utilized in a tailwind.

It seems as if the arrival of this ship, this 849-ton, twenty-year-old ship that Tryggvi purchased in Scotland, the first steam-powered ocean-going vessel to be owned by an Icelander, has unfettered latent forces—the Village is literally quivering when the boy comes from Jóhann. The great ship is lying in the Lagoon; *Little Tryggvi*, a 30-ton steamboat purchased last year, transports the V.I.P.s to land—Tryggvi himself, his wife, two grown children and father-in-law, an elderly general and former War Minister. The foreman Kjartan has driven men down into the holds of two sailing ships anchored at the pier, shouting and cursing them back to work after they'd had their fill of staring at the big steamer, because now is the time, in the Devil's name, for us to get these rotten old barges off the pier, the steamer *T. Jónsson* needs to put in, as shiny and magnificent as the future, laden with salt and coal. Saltfish is to be loaded onto this ship, but not until the men have spent the next day and night emptying and cleaning its hold, wiping away the coal dust, after which they'll ascend from it blackened like devils from Hell. Kjartan spurs the workers on with his shouts, pausing only when the little steamboat docks and the people step ashore, and then starting in again with his curses when the distinguished folk are far enough away; one doesn't yell when elegant ears are nearby. And now they walk together through the streets of the Village, Tryggvi and Friðrik, alpha and omega, Friðrik in his blue jacket, which is snug across his broad chest, nearly a head taller than Tryggvi, yet not nearly as threatening as usual; everything is diminished in the presence of some people. They stop once or twice to inspect the saltfish, Friðrik bends over to select a fish that they then examine together, holding it up to the light, checking whether it's well cured; if they can distinguish the fingers of the other hand through the neck, the fish is suitably dry, they can sail with it to Spain, toward the sun, and be paid for it, so as to survive, to tug this country, this scorched, windswept island, into the future. Out of darkness and death into light and prosperity. Friðrik hands Tryggvi fish after fish while those standing nearest to them feel a peculiar pressure inside their heads; they're relieved when he walks away, but also proud as anything to have been so near to him who keeps our Village alive, the earnings of thousands depend entirely on him, his resourcefulness. Tryggvi transforms our toil and gray everydayness into gold that pays for steamers, that pays for his life in the city of Copenhagen, pays for his clothing, pays for the lives of his children and grandchildren; we receive one share to the approximately nine that he receives, that's the way it is.

The boy yields to the temptation to head down to the Lower Pier to take a better look at the ship, that colossus, that token of victory, detours in order to avoid drunken sailors, passes the school and then hears his name spoken gruffly. He stops, turns around and stiffens when he sees Friðrik rushing toward him, striding along and soon blocking the sight of Tryggvi, who waits along with his entourage at the school building. Friðrik comes straight up to the boy, eclipsing everything, even making it harder to breathe, as if he's sucking up all the oxygen. The boy tries to think, now here I stand with a robust soul, groping for this line as if it's his last thread of hope, but it doesn't help much. Friðrik's eyes are deeply sunken, like caves, and power ascends from their depths. There's been mention of you at home, Friðrik says, his eyes drilling into the boy's head, and the boy feels his brain growing hotter. Ragnheiður has mentioned you thrice for no reason. I don't like it. A man who abandons his place on a fishing boat with a good skipper in the middle of the fishing season isn't worth much. I don't know whether anything has happened between you, but I know my daughter, and she wouldn't mention you unless something were going on. Friðrik pauses, looks contemplatively at the mountains above them; the boy is relieved, his brain begins to cool down, but then Friðrik, who is uncomfortably composed, looks at him again and says calmly, If you so much as touch her, or have the gall to address her, I'll scorch the earth beneath you. I'll have your balls cut off and fed to the dogs. She's leaving for Copenhagen in three days, and until then it's best that you run for cover if she so much as looks in your direction. Useless rapscallions come nowhere near my daughter.

XXIII

Evening falls over a banquet as a sparse crowd of curious individuals gathers outside the hotel to watch the guests arrive. Ragnheiður is wearing a distinctive red dress, with her white neck, with those eyes and the space between them; as she walks into the hotel everyone turns to look at her, the women at the dress, the men at the body beneath it. Draped over her shoulders is a brown shawl fastened with a black velvet rose, her dress hugs her bosom tightly, which is enough to cause most of the men to lose control of their eyes; they're so easily conquered sometimes. Gunnar, the mustachioed clerk, wasn't invited, of course not, but he did get to see her in her dress. He stood there in the shop like a specter, a quivering string, and stared at her. He felt too restless to remain at home, went up to the shop, found himself something to do, tried to calm himself with work. Go and pay him a compliment, Friðrik had said to his daughter, and she went over to the shop, dressed like that, red dress, as red as madness, walked in and Gunnar changed in an instant from a specter into a quivering string. I'm supposed to pay you a compliment, she said, and her lips were red, yes, they certainly are red, thinks Gísli inside the hotel, leaning against a column, not socializing with the chattering group, wanting wine but even more to be sitting at home, with the curtains closed, holding a book, sitting with a universe in his grasp. Gísli watches his niece pass through the room with a smile not entirely free of pride, the dress arrived on board the steamer, custom-tailored. It's the latest fashion, Ragnheiður says to the women, do you know Worth?, he has the finest styles, everyone who's anyone in London and Paris wears dresses made by him. Ragnheiður nearly steals the spotlight from the guest of honor, the reason for the banquet, the lord and savior of our Village. The weather is calm, the mountains darken slightly in the evening, and the sea is so peaceful that some of the drowned rise to the surface, float there like foam or mysterious jellyfish, dreaming their salty, bitter dreams, while the spaces between the stars are invisible doorways to Heaven.

There are, however, no mysterious jellyfish at the banquet, where Anna, Friðrik's wife, plays her piano, which she'd had brought over to the hotel the other day, reprehensible that Teitur and Ásgerður haven't invested in a proper instrument, other than the wreck that Hulda occasionally plays to herself. Anna plays in the grand salon, where Bjarni's paintings of Tryggvi's ships hang on the walls. What an armada! All the paintings are first-rate work; Tryggvi was elated and no one said a word as the merchant strolled from one to the next, accompanied by Friðrik, Reverend Þorvaldur and two important captains; they peered at the paintings, scrutinized them to check whether all the details were correct, everything in its place, and Bjarni passed inspection with flying colors, it's as if one is standing on deck, Tryggvi said, and these words still echo in Bjarni's ears when he rises the next morning. Such praise from none other than Tryggvi, that he'd passed with flying colors—but hurry down to the Lower Pier with your things right now and start sketching the steamer; it's sailing in two or three days, what a lucky man you are! That day hasn't come, though, that moment; we'll allow Bjarni to sleep on, exhausted, allow him to look forward to painting the summer light that the steamer has yet to take from him.

Anna sits back down at the piano after dinner, plays Mozart, and the music carries down to the basement, down to Snorri's room, where he has settled in with what little he wished to and could bring with him, which wasn't much, and why take mementos of a failed life? He's lying in bed in his threadbare silken pajamas, photographs of his sons on a little table, a few books, a knee-high stack of music scores and one on his lap, Chopin's *Nocturnes*, but now he listens with half-closed eyes to Mozart, coming from above, his eyebrows quiver every time that Anna fails to follow the composer, and that's how Hulda finds him when she enters, after knocking softly, hesitantly. Snorri answered distractedly, she was spared the banquet, was given the night off, and now stands there in Snorri's room, a bit tall, a bit ugly, excessively miserable, I'm sorry, she says. It's alright, he says, I'm sorry, she says again, there's no reason to say sorry, he says. Yes, for barging in on you like this. Her eyes are too large for her face, as if they don't fit completely into their sockets, and perhaps she's never seen a man in bed before, except for hammered sailors, some of them as randy as imps; randy due to their conviction that her lack of good looks makes her easy prey, takes whatever she can get; look here, doll, see what I've got for you. Nothing to worry about, Snorri says, by way of consolation, yet she still says sorry, for the third time, and then he says, It's Mozart. I know, she says. Anna should relax her shoulders more, Snorri says. Yes, Hulda says, she plays a touch too firmly. Would you like to sit down? Snorri says. Yes please, she says, and sits down.

Snorri: I didn't know you were such a music expert.

Hulda: No.

Snorri lays his hand gently on the open score on his lap. This, on the other hand, is Chopin, he says. Hulda looks at the notes and says, Aren't those the *Nocturnes*?

Snorri: Good heavens!

XXIV

It is so clear that the person who shapes our destiny has come. Tryggvi takes long walks in the morning, between seven and eight, threading through the streets of the Village; we hardly dare to greet him, and never without being greeted first; he does, however, greet everyone, asks children their names, and his steamer lies docked at the Lower Pier. The morning after the banquet, a great iron piece is brought from the ship to the Village well, an iron pump the height of a man, and Tryggvi's men go straight to work attaching it. It's Tryggvi's gift to us. No one asked him for it, and what a difference, what a blessing; even Skúli praised him in *The Will of the People*. Finally it will be possible to pump clean water, free of salinity. Until now, those who've accepted nothing less than clean drinking water have had to fetch it from a brook, which takes an effort, being quite distant, especially in winter, when the world is iced over and it's difficult to live, let alone carry cold water long distances as it splashes on you in the cold. Now this inconvenience is behind us, thanks to Tryggvi, and the pump, quickly christened Tryggvi's Pump, fetches clean water for us from deep within the earth, almost effortlessly. As the workers struggle to fit the pump to the well, word comes that others are busy laboring at Tryggvi's house, whence a telephone line is to be strung over to the shop, and later from Friðrik's house as well, a slender line suspended in the air, well above our heads, which is supposed to carry voices from house to house, a line no wider than a stream of urine, one might think we were being mocked, but this is the modern age, and this is how the future will be; what's impossible to imagine becomes commonplace. In addition, Tryggvi is preparing to string a telephone line all the way over to Þrengsli, a tiny village 12 miles from here, standing at the mouth of a valley no broader than a knife blade, the mountains high and sheer, where in winters the roar of avalanches is heard far out at sea. It's there that Tryggvi wishes to string a line, because from Þrengsli it's easier to read the weather, to predict it over the coming hours, to determine whether it's safe to go to sea; such information can save lives, without question. This innovation will be a type of lifeline, tossed to us by Tryggvi.

Tryggvi's children stay mainly indoors, tinkle at the piano, read novels, lie on fancy sofas, tell Ragnheiður about Copenhagen, while his father-in-law, the old general, sits outside by the wall of the house, staring out at the spit, which is covered with saltfish and people stooping to turn the fish over so that it doesn't bake in the sun. The old man appears intimidating, with bushy gray eyebrows, piercing blue eyes; he's a general in charge of the saltfish. The empty chair next to him is intended for Gísli, who's running late at the moment, but that's alright; the man's blue eyes seem to penetrate people and reveal their essences. This is why he knows that Gísli will come, as expected, and then they'll chat in French about historical battles, the events of the world. The old general looks out over the spit; he watches Ragnheiður walk quickly away from the house, not stopping until she comes to Sea Street, where she stands above the shore and focuses her will on calming her blood, rocks on her feet, as if impatient; the sea purls beneath her, eider ducks rise and fall on little waves. She inhales deeply and notices movement on the opposite shore, squints; yes, no doubt about it, it's the boy, running, he's easy to spot, there's no one else who runs like that, except to save his own life, and even then not so fast, or with such stamina. Ragnheiður watches, her hands open and close, as if they're gasping for air.

* * *

He runs like a scream. Flies buzz, birds sing, cows swing their tails, contented in the grass, and the taste of blood is in his mouth as he passes the cottage where a dog was frightened of a walking stick, runs over puddles and swampy ground, can't be bothered to avoid them, is muddy and wet up to his knees.

What's she going to do? he'd asked Helga when she finally came downstairs, unusually late, around seven, the boy having already made coffee and buttered bread for Kolbeinn, who was silent as stone in his darkened world. They'd stayed up unusually late the night before. Yes, now it begins, Geirþrúður had said when the boy announced the arrival of the steamer, although he made no mention of Friðrik and his threats. What begins? he asked. Geirþrúður smiled for an instant, her white neck still soft though perhaps just starting to dry up, to crack, because without kisses, the skin ages quickly. If only there were more people like you, she said, and Kolbeinn gave a snort. Go on and snort, you old dog, said Geirþrúður, still smiling. Sometimes it's as if you understand nothing, he said to the boy, sometimes you're such a damned nincompoop that it would be an act of charity to chop you into bits. That's precisely why he's so precious, Geirþrúður said. The boy didn't dare look up, but asked again, What begins? Then he got his answer, got to hear from Geirþrúður what Gísli had told him, that the fish from her schooners could not be dried on the Village's drying lots unless she abandoned her pride and her corrupting behavior, sold the *Hope* to Tryggvi's Trading Company, as well as her share in the ice house, joined the Women's Club Eva, attended Mass regularly and—married with all speed. She threatened the community with her lifestyle, completely flouted tried-and-true values, confused young girls, filled them with delusions concerning their positions and duties. Or, in the words of Friðrik: Those who question the rules of society undermine it, and what, then, is the difference between them and criminals?

What will she do? he asked when Helga finally came downstairs. She's thinking, said Helga, sitting down in her place at the end of the table with coffee and a slice of bread.

The boy: Can they . . . ?

Helga: Bend her? Force her to her knees? Well, they're not lacking in strength or will; the question is whether or how well it suits their interests.

Why can't we simply be left in peace, asked the boy; why can't she live as she wishes?

Kolbeinn: Because no one is allowed to stand upright. It's because these people are bullies, and it disturbs their digestion if they're unable to control everything. It's a disease. And Geirþrúður disturbs them.

Their digestion? asked the boy.

Kolbeinn: It would be best to shoot them, chop them into bait. Then the cod would certainly bite well. These men are as ravenous as cod, swallowing everything that isn't bigger than them, it's their nature. You know the cod.

The boy: I once counted 150 capelin in a medium-sized cod, and two stones.

Kolbeinn: You'll never make a capable sailor; it's out of the question. If these rascals manage to ruin Geirþrúður, it would be a humanitarian act to shoot you. First you, then me.

Stop this chatter, Helga said, we'll think of something.

Something—sometimes this word is of no use at all.

He has to stop. He isn't exhausted but is almost out of breath and, besides that, needs to pee, is on the verge of bursting, having forgotten to relieve himself before his run. It takes time to pee when you're panting after a furious run; he stands with his legs spread and waits, closes his eyes, hears nothing but the rush of his blood and his heartbeat. He's sheltered from the world, beneath the verge of a hill, his eyes closed, listening to his blood, which is saying something about Geirþrúður, about Friðrik's threats yesterday, about the fear, the anger. He opens his eyes, it's beautiful here, tussocks, grass, shelter. The forceful, foaming stream flattens the grass and the mild odor of urine rises to his nostrils. His heartbeat slows, but the rush of his bloodstream is so intense that he doesn't hear the hoofbeats in the soft grass. The horse is sweaty, Ragnheiður had ridden fast; what a sight it was to see her gallop out of the Village, bareheaded, her expression determined, wearing a light blue dress with white lace gloves, straddling her dusky horse like a man, like Geirþrúður, so damaging is her influence. Ragnheiður rode so heedlessly that some people practically had to leap out of her way, she's frenzied, the emperor's daughter, someone said, getting up from the dusty street, watching her ride away, hunched over in her saddle, her hair blowing freely; it was as if she were galloping to war. The boy looks down and senses something in the atmosphere, hears the horse, maybe, as it shakes itself slightly, as Ragnheiður dismounts, as her black boots trample the grass. Hardly more than three, four yards separate them; she stares at him, red-faced from her violent ride, her hair falling over her shoulders. She says nothing, just stares. Stares in front of him, and sees. He's finally done peeing but is rigid, frozen in place. He was going to shake out the final drops, as he always does, give it a thorough shake, otherwise the drops would just drip down into his pants, more than once he's been ridiculed for this prudery, even Bárður had shaken his head, thus the boy generally pees alone, goes off by himself, pees and shakes it until nothing's left. But now he's being watched. By a woman. By she who'd sucked on a piece of rock candy, stuck it in the boy's mouth and then come naked to him in a dream, causing him to sneak down to the basement to clean his sticky pajama bottoms; later she'd kissed him, her lips were warm and moist. He remembers all of it. It's his blood that remembers in one explosive flash, and some of it enters his penis, which swells a bit, hardly at all, yet a bit, and not imperceptibly.

For how long does the boy hesitate?

And for how long does she watch?

The blood has an independent will, an independent memory, and its memories have paralyzed him, changed him into a purely sensory being who recalls only her tongue, the kiss, the firm breasts whose outlines can be seen so uncomfortably well beneath her shirt, unless it's called a blouse, he doesn't know, and he also recalls Friðrik's words from yesterday, the violence in them, the iron that was meant to bend, smash, pulverize, terrify, and did so, but that also aroused anger, stubbornness, hatred that burns, is dangerously hot. The blood has its own will and the boy is there beneath the verge of a hill, having just peed, his pants still down and Ragnheiður watches and his blood continues to recall, it continues to paralyze him and change the moment into something infinite. Álfheiður had also kissed him when he dozed between existences, she'd sat right up against him in the church, he recalls so well the warmth of her thighs, and they sat so close together as the dogs humped beneath the coffin, which was ugly, which was sad, which was none other than life itself, its unstoppable power, the blood remembers this and some of it flows into his penis, which hardens a little more. And then it happens.

The boy manages to constrain the blind will of his blood, is about to put his half-erect penis back in his underpants, bring it to shelter, save himself from more embarrassment, but is too late; Ragnheiður comes to him, jumps on him.

Reaches him in two steps, two bounds, and her right hand grasps the back of his neck, clamps onto a handful of his hair, one boot sweeps the boy's leg from behind and he suddenly finds himself lying on the ground, in the grass, strangely vulnerable, astonished, maybe fearful, also because his pants are down, which deprives him of quite a lot. She falls with him, or lets herself fall, they're both in the soft, succulent grass on which the horse has begun to graze, ripping it with its strong teeth. Ragnheiður stares at the boy, her eyes so resolute, so fiery, that it's almost unbearable to look back at her, she bites into the glove on her right hand, tears it off, says, I'm going to Copenhagen in two days; I rode after you, she says, I saw you running. I rode after you and straddled my horse like a man, because no one tells me what to do, I straddled it, no underwear under my dress because I do what I want and what I need, I'm leaving and everything will be different when I return. I hate the way you look at me sometimes, as if you're afraid of it all, as if you're incapable of anything, yet as if you know everything, or something about which the rest of us have no clue, and yet you know nothing, and I'm taking what I want to take, I'm leaving, she says, I'm leaving . . . but then it's as if her voice breaks, no more words come, she looks away, as if uncertain, and then sees his organ, stiff, slightly quivering, slightly ridiculous. This isn't right, the boy says, sitting up. Ragnheiður breathes rapidly, as if out of breath, breathes shallowly, as if frightened, but her fingers are quick to unbutton her shirt, that's not my concern, she says, maybe more to herself than to him, she has strong arms that push or shove the boy back down into the grass. This summer, she'd said in April, I'm going for a ride in sunshine. It's summer, there's golden sunshine, she rode a horse and she sits astride the boy, straddles him, pulls up her dress, he sees her black boots, sees her bare legs, but not all the way up, she closes her eyes, as if to recall something as her hand moves down, gropes, grabs his penis tightly before she settles on him carefully, as if sitting down on something fragile—and she hesitates. She continues to hold him tightly, her eyes closed, breathing deeply, and he lies still, feeling her softness, wetness, feeling it with his entire consciousness. Ragnheiður's breasts lie close against his chest, her ear on his shoulder, her hair covering half his face, and he breathes in its scent, pure but also heavy, an intoxicating aroma that stings a bit. If you so much as touch her, or have the gall to address her, I'll scorch the earth beneath you, I'll have your balls cut off and fed to the dogs. I didn't address her, thinks the boy. Go to hell, Friðrik, you and your violence. I think I don't want to be here. Yet I do want this.

Ragnheiður places her hand in the grass right next to his head, breathes heavily, hard, then lets herself sink, and he never suspected that it could be so good. She lets herself sink, settles on him completely, he slips into warmth and wetness, but is quickly stopped by some obstruction. She straightens up, sweaty, a lock of hair plastered to her forehead, her upper lip taut; again he sees her bare chest, her breasts barely half-covered, she opens her eyes, stares at nothing, focuses, nearly looks angry, lifts herself up a bit and lets herself fall, heavily, and then something tears, he hears her suppressed scream, something tears inside her, and her small, hard fists pound his chest violently three, four times. Then she raises her head and lifts herself carefully, sinks down again, hesitantly, but the obstruction is gone, and the hesitation as well. She moves, but he looks away, the blood roars in his veins, yet still he looks away, sees the sky between the blades of grass and the tussocks, sees the horse, hears it ripping the grass, the blades of grass barely move and the boy hears Ragnheiður gasp, unless these sounds are coming from him; his blood streams fervently through his body and he feels it, senses the current, it's as if he's about to burst.

Then she's no longer on him.

It happened abruptly.

The boy hardly noticed it; he was looking at a horse, and had just started thinking about Jupiter, which is a planet 365 million miles away, except that she's no longer on top of him, but on all fours next to him; her hair falls over her face, she stares at the ground as if lost in thought. Then she gets up, buttons her blouse, he sees her face, and it isn't always easy to say what sort of pain it is that makes us cry, whether it's the pain of life, or pain of the body.

XXV

Next morning he's sent on a journey.

Another journey.

Over heaths and mountains. Down to a fjord. As if he hasn't had enough of such things. It's summer, of course; it will be a gentle journey, just a long walk. It's good to get away, more than good, even; to be alone up on a heath, up in the mountains. You think more clearly in mountain air, view life from a different angle, because of the air itself or the distance from people and settlements. He's sent with a letter, written by Geirþrúður, addressed to a merchant in a village of three hundred people on the neighboring fjord; the boy knows this village fairly well, he's nearing the place where he was raised after his father drowned. He's to deliver the letter and wait for a written response. He can make it there in one day, but will have to spend the night. He doesn't go alone any more than he did before, but now it's not Jens, with whom it's hard to keep up, Jens who'll be receiving a letter from the boy; are you alive, you rogue, with all your limbs intact, are you managing to pass the time without having me nearby? No, not Jens, but Snorri, former merchant, current ne'er-do-well in a hotel basement, skinny and pale; it's hardly possible to say that they're making this journey together, each in his own world, his own memories, his own uncertainty. Ásgerður, the hotelkeeper, had come up to Geirþrúður's house to ask whether it would be possible to borrow the boy for two days, to accompany Snorri south to this particular village, the former merchant not being much of a walker, unused to such trips, he would lose his way and won't hear of making the journey on horseback, hasn't wanted to mount a horse since riding south to Reykjavik in one go, only to discover that his wife, Aldís, loved God considerably more than him. In any case, Snorri is supposed to go south to the village to have a look at an organ, to purchase it for the hotel if it seems in reasonable condition; it simply doesn't do to be without music, we're not much more than fish without it. And we absolutely cannot afford to lose a man like Snorri, the hotelkeeper adds. Not that I'd lose any sleep over it, Helga said, but Friðrik won't be happy with Snorri around. Music is bigger than Friðrik and Tryggvi's Shop and Trading Company, Ásgerður said.

It was no problem for the boy to accompany Friðrik, and was in fact a remarkable coincidence, since the plan had already been made to send the boy south to that same village, and now they walk up Tungudalur, Snorri and the boy, hardly ever side by side, most often with dozens of yards between them, the boy forgets himself, forgets Snorri, forgets the purpose of the journey, his errand, it's good to be traveling, to feel the land rise, let his feet think for themselves; all the same, he doesn't feel well.

She'd ridden away. At first she crouched there, on all fours, as if paralyzed, as if lost in thought, then she stood up, looked at the boy, the lock of hair plastered to her forehead and barely visible moisture in her hard eyes; the two of them looked at each other and nothing was heard except for the sound of the horse pulling up grass. She reached for her glove, stood up, smoothed her dress, fixed her blouse, unless it was a shirt, he doesn't know, ran her hand through her hair, cold in her beauty, for how long can cold be beautiful? And then was gone. Rode away fast and quickly disappeared; he was in something of a hollow, anyway, hidden from view, in a pit, in a grave, but then he discovered a stream running clear between grassy banks. He wanted to wash his face, splash cold water on it—he felt so befuddled, or rather, as if his head were clogged—wanted to wash himself down below, wash off the blood that he'd seen when Ragnheiður abruptly lifted herself off him with a half-stifled cry, and whether it was because of the blood or because Ragnheiður crouched there on all fours, as if she were crying or cursing, his penis shriveled, softened up in a flash.

He knelt by the stream, pulled his pants all the way down in order to wash himself properly, and the blood had congealed; it was solid, almost in clumps, and smelled, and he remembered how everything tore inside her, how she hissed, how she stared, focused, at nothing, as if he weren't there, and instead of washing himself he crouched on all fours and retched and vomited and the stream received this despair, fear, anger, shame, like any other blade of grass that it's been entrusted with carrying to the sea.

Is it possible to forget everything amidst tussocks, closer to the sky than everyday reality? The day sprinkles birds over the heath, those musical notes between the sky and the earth, the tussocks are sleeping dogs, the stream's music pure as silver; on such days the heaths are like a slice of eternal Paradise. They'd set out around five in the morning, walked up from the lowlands, walked up into the beauty of air and tussocks, and for a long time it's unnecessary to remember, unnecessary to possess consciousness. The boy forgets yesterday, forgets uncertainty, forgets violence, forgets Snorri as well, and comes to his senses high up on the heath, stops, looks back, sees a speck in the distance and then lies down in the sun-filled grass, which is darker and brighter than his life, watches clouds sailing and life comes to him. The boy focuses on the clouds, as if he hopes that they might take him away with them, these clouds that travel over the fishing huts where five men stand on the shore and finish gutting their catch, while the sixth, none other than Pétur, enters Geirþrúður's café, fresh from a brisk walk. He'd set off as soon as they put in to shore, let the others tend to the catch, gave himself a few moments to down a bit of food prepared by Elínborg, who was in somewhat of a huff about his haste, urgent business, was the only explanation he gave them, before striding off in the direction of the Village. Where's Pétur going? Elínborg had asked the men as they cleaned the catch, looking at Árni, who shrugged. People have business to take care of, was all he said, but Einar blew his nose, putting a finger to each nostril and blowing hard to clear each one. He went to fuck Andrea, of course, he said. Shut up, Árni said. What do you mean? Elínborg said, without taking her eyes off Einar. Just what I said, replied Einar.

Elínborg: What do you mean, hasn't Andrea left him?

Even more reason for Pétur to fuck her, said Einar in an excited voice, it'll do her good to be fucked silly; all that reading and pretentiousness muddled her head long since!

Árni: Shut up, you scoundrel.

The others had stopped working, the giant Gvendur and the two itinerant fishermen who'd replaced the boy and Bárður.

People can say what they want, Elínborg declared, and it's true what Einar says; what sort of woman is it, anyway, who leaves a man like Pétur? I'm simply asking, what sort of woman is it?

What sort of woman, what sort of life? Pétur goes into the café, winded from his walk; there's considerable chatter inside, he looks around the room, recognizes several people but can't be bothered to greet them, glances around impatiently for Andrea; tell them, he's planning to ask her, that you need to step out for half an hour or so. He'd had such trouble sleeping the last few nights; their time together in the basement kept running through his head. He'd noticed another scent on Andrea, she was wearing a new dress, she was different yet the same. It had taken him ages to fall asleep last night, and then he'd started thinking about it again as soon as he awoke; when he got out of bed in the half-light of the summer night, he was fully erect. Elínborg was awake and probably saw it, but that was alright, she could look, his size was nothing to be ashamed of. Pétur puts his long arm around Ólafía's shoulder. Where is Andrea? he asks. She turns to look and says, Oh.

A few minutes later he's on his way out of the Village.

Ólafía had gone to get Helga, who told Pétur to follow her, led him into the house, into the uncomfortably elegant parlor, where stood this Geirþrúður, and they told him that Andrea was gone. Something along those lines; he wasn't in his right mind, received a folded sheet of paper from them, a few words that Andrea had written in haste, as if on the run: Dear Pétur, I've left. You're not a bad man, but our life together is over. I can't imagine returning to you, if I did, I would start hating you, and hate myself as well. Life is too short for hatred. Hopefully you'll find someone who is better than me. You may throw away all of my things.

Something along those lines. He read it quickly, struggled to concentrate. Read it in haste, crumpled it, wanted to toss it aside, but didn't dare. Where did she go? he asked. Is it written in the note? Geirþrúður had asked. No. There's a reason for that. At that he left. Like a miserable dog. Yet Andrea is his wife; she has no right to behave so . . . unnaturally. He could go to the magistrate, have her brought back, it's his right. Instead he slunk away, and now he's walking hastily, fleeing. He'll be ridiculed, to let them treat him this way, to be such a paltry wretch. People will say that he couldn't satisfy her.

God damn it. Why didn't he ask, at the very least, to be allowed to have a word with that damned boy? It was he and Bárður who made Andrea so confused. Bárður is dead, yet that improved nothing; quite the contrary. He should have asked to see the boy. And then given him a good thrashing!

It's little use, however, to ask down in town to see someone who's up on a heath.

Snorri and the boy had eaten some of their provisions where the boy had lain down among the tussocks and sun-filled grass. I'm entirely unaccustomed to this, the former merchant had said, making a sweeping gesture to indicate the tussocks and mountains and stream pure as silver. They drank cold coffee from glass bottles, the boy with a packed lunch from Helga, Snorri with one from Hulda. It was her hands that put the bread together, which is why it's so good, thought Snorri, this bankrupt man with his failed life. Her hands, he thought, as he bit into the bread, and the view around him was beautiful. Sunshine, and everything incredibly fine beneath this blue sky, especially after the boy had taught him to avoid the wet patches, swampy ground, allowing his feet to dry, his socks, everything is fine and this land and this day are like a playful yet heartfelt melody by Mozart. They walk down into a wide, deep fjord containing count-less valleys, sometimes side by side, and Snorri tells the boy about Mozart, stumbles thrice over tussocks, is caught the same number of times and saved from falling by the boy, who listens, drinks in the words and the melodies that Snorri whistles when the words stop short in their feebleness.

The hours pass, the boy and Snorri walk up from the fjord, up to another heath, walk in silence, thinking about their troubles, their wounds, unexpected happiness. Ragnheiður will probably be leaving on the steamer tomorrow or the day after, along with a great quan-tity of saltfish; she'll leave and that's good, he feels it so clearly now, here in the tussocks, as he skirts wet patches, helps Snorri up from one. Thinks of her, lets her pass through him, and what remains in his blood?

To his surprise, it's not anger, even less spite; no. Is it pity? Maybe a bit of shame?

He's standing at the edge of the heath, looking down into another fjord where the village is, with its merchant, and the letter from Geirþrúður is in his pocket. He hears Snorri panting; he'd fallen behind. Not far now, the boy says, no, Snorri says, winded. They stare at the fjord for some time, the sky above them like a blue wing. I thought that life was finished, Snorri says, but perhaps it simply never began.

The boy: I don't know much about life.

Snorri: One probably doesn't have to know much about life; one just has to step into it. And know how to welcome it when it comes.

XXVI

On their way down, they see the village across the fjord, but it quickly
vanishes from view, the fjord being deep and sinuous. Hardly less
than four hours, the boy says. What? Snorri exclaims, trying to maintain his footing on the slope, his mind entirely on the hotel's basement room. Good Heavens, he'd said last night, when he realized that
Hulda not only read music but recognized Chopin's *Nocturnes* after
seeing just a fragment of the score. If we're going around the fjord,
it'll take at least four hours, probably five. Evening will have come,
Snorri says; night will have come. We should be able to row across in
an hour, the boy remarks. Then let's find a boat, the ruined merchant
says, and that's what they do, go to find a boat; they traverse the slope
down from the heath, their nostrils assailed by a particular stench as
they approach the shore, damned Norwegians, the boy says, and they
turn right, up the fjord, moving away from the whaling station that
stands on a little headland or bank jutting out into the fjord, see the
tall smelter near the shore and the heavy chains extending from it like
the arms of a monster, used to drag the carcasses into the building.
Twice they need to detour around rotting pieces of whale muscle, the
lingering stench of the bowels, everything swarming with maggots,
and it's nearly half an hour before they've come far enough away to be
free of the smell and din of the smelter, but then they're surrounded
by silence, the purl of the waves, shells that crunch beneath their feet,
moors above the shore. They come across a little fishing hut, old, one-
storied, a fourareen on the beach. Do we need to row the entire
way? asks Snorri, looking over the broad fjord, toward the village
on the other side. There's a strong wind out there, the boy says, so
we can raise the sail. They knock on the door, having had no easy
time reaching it through the pile of shells left over from the spring,
the fishermen apparently having cleaned mussels inside the hut
before shoveling the shells out the door as the hut started filling

up. It must have stunk, thinks the boy, frowning, as Snorri knocks on the door.

A sleep-swollen face appears, curious and annoyed all at once; it's awful to have your sleep disturbed, rest is precious. Ferry you across the fjord, the face says, why the hell should we do that? There's a reason for everything, Snorri says calmly, adjusting his footing on the shells. It's also invigorating to be beaten, the face says, looking at the boy and waking fully as he does so. I highly doubt that, says Snorri.

The face: Doubt what?

Snorri: That it's invigorating to be beaten.

Why can't we have any peace to sleep? shouts a voice from within the hut, don't we get to rest anymore? Another deep voice lets loose with profanities. There's two morons out here, wanting us to ferry them over to the village, yells the face into the house. What the hell do we care? shouts the first voice, tell them to shut their traps and fuck off! We'll pay, Snorri says; he may be a derelict merchant, but he still knows the magic word, and takes out some money. Wait, says the face, looking from the money to the boy and back, and keep your damn mouths shut.

Five minutes later, the face has become a short man with ash-blond, greasy hair, eyes that give them only hasty glances. Short, but with strength in his shoulders. Quick as a flash they push the boat out to sea, he and the boy, as Snorri raises his hands, not knowing what to do with them, but they're soon given a role when the man holds out his hand. Payment, he says. The boy sits silently next to the man, they row, Snorri sits in the stern, absolutely useless after making the payment; he stares at the mountains, at a bird diving for things to eat, but not happiness, Snorri thinks, not happiness. They've come quite far out onto the fjord, the surly man raises the sail and they catch the wind, he steers, chewing tobacco, spitting red, as if his life were bleeding away. Where the hell did you come from? he asks, as if with contempt, should I know either of you? Good question, Snorri says; he watches the village approach and the houses become distinct, and then explains that he's Snorri, a bankrupt merchant, on his way to this village to have a look at an organ for Hotel World's End. An organ, says the man, scandalized; what an errand! I hardly expect you to be a down-and-out merchant, he says to the boy several moments later, after sticking another plug of tobacco into his mouth and chewing it with gusto. No, the boy says. But you must be called something. Hardly, the boy replies, before saying his name, and the man chews. Red lines trickle down the corners of his mouth, he wipes them quickly with the back of his hand, smearing some juice onto his left cheek. Are you by any chance the one who lives with the dames and the blind man? I don't live with dames, but with women. They've all got cunts, says the other, before adding, when the boy says nothing, just looks down at his feet, and your friend froze to death because of a poem! Their eyes meet momentarily, the boy feels a stab of pain, and then it's gone. You're famous, the man says finally, steering the boat. But what might your name be? Snorri asks courteously. I, what's my name, huh, my name's just Shitbag Giantson, the man says curtly, before shutting up for the rest of the trip, foregoing farewells when they step ashore below the village, saying only, The hotel's the building with the green door, and then sailing away.

We have a vacancy, one room out of ten, there's plenty to do here, says the man at the hotel, tall, gaunt, stooping, as if his body can't handle its own height, buckles beneath it. Three rooms are occupied by patients from American halibut schooners, two sick as dogs with influenza, the third in bad shape after a fight; they have machetes, the tall man says, coming right up to the boy, his breath so bad that the boy has to hold his own. The man with the bad breath points upward and they hear a moan, as if controlled by his finger. I just hope he holds out a few more days, these Americans pay damned well, but one of you will have to sleep on the floor, I don't suppose you're too good for it? No, the boy says, he's certainly not too good, and then they turn to their business. Snorri to try out the organ, the boy to take the letter to the merchant; his errand has to do with power, money, which is of course worse, because, as the verses say, "There are two poles in Hell/one is called money, the other power." They stand outside for several moments, gazing at three American schooners out in the fjord, sleek ships, and clean, it's obvious even from far away, and then it starts to rain. From a sky that is virtually blue, although dark clouds are gathering; the boy looks automatically at Snorri's shoes, his feet are going to get wet. You're going to meet the merchant, Snorri says, after listening for a moment to the raindrops falling on his head, that's right, says the boy to the rain, in the direction that the boat sailed back; where had he seen this tobacco-chewing man before? Christian isn't bad, says Snorri, but he's not particularly good either; life for him is either profit or loss.

The shop is in a rather large building, on two stories, with a deep basement. The premises are tidy and well swept, but the rain is slowly changing the hard ground outside into mud that people will bring in on their shoes. The boy goes in and announces his business. Meet the merchant, says one of the shop clerks; who doesn't want to meet the merchant, it's another thing entirely whether he wants to meet you, why should he want that? The boy says that he's come from Geirþrúður, he's there to deliver a letter, and the clerk's attitude changes from utter disinterest to curiosity blended with a touch of uncertainty. The merchant's office is upstairs, in a big corner room with three windows, the American schooners rock out in the fjord, a Norwegian whaler churns toward the station with a whale in tow. *Du kommer frá Geirtrúd,*[1] the merchant says. Yes, the boy says, and

---

1. *Du kommer,* etc.: The merchant speaks to the boy in a blend of Danish and Icelandic as follows: *Du kommer frá Geirtrúd*: Geirþrúður has sent you; *Hun vil faa brev tilbage*: She wants a reply; *Kender du erindid*: Do you know what it's about?; *Fanden*: Damn it. *Hun skulle ikke deila med Friðrik, det er dumt*: She shouldn't oppose Friðrik; it's stupid; *Hvad?*: What?; *Du faerd svar á morgun*: You'll have your reply tomorrow.

he stands there as the merchant reads the letter; he is not offered a chair. The letter isn't lengthy, little more than a page, yet the merchant takes a good long time reading it, smacking his lips, finally puts the letter down, lights a cigar, turns his chair to look out at the evening, the chair creaks beneath the man's weight; the boy doesn't realize the size of the merchant's body until the man stands up, his belly distended as if he's pregnant, his neck thick, his shoulders hunched, resembling shapeless heaps attached to his back. The boy can't help but stare. What are you going to be when you grow up? we asked the boys here in the Village sometimes, no need to ask the girls, they had no chance of becoming anything. I'm going to be fat, replied those who set their sights furthest and highest. *Hun vil faa brev tilbage*, says the merchant, looking out, a boat is being rowed out to one of the schooners. Yes, the boy says.

Kender du erindid?

Yes.

Fanden.

Yes.

Hun skulle ikke deila med Friðrik, det er dumt.

No, says the boy, far too loudly, perhaps, but so much boils up within him; maybe it's the tone of the merchant's voice, how he smokes his cigar, which the man now removes from his mouth before exclaiming, *Hvad?*

It isn't stupid. We should stand tall, we can't live otherwise.

Christian stares at the sea, mutters something unintelligible. *Du faerd svar á morgun*, he says, waving the boy out.

Something brushes the window and the boy wakes up. The middle of the night, no doubt; it's still raining, a dense rain that obscures the sky. It's chilly sleeping on the floor wrapped in a blanket; Snorri snores softly in the bed, he'd retired early, satisfied with the organ, and

that the *Hope* should be anchored here, the cook Jonni had broken
his arm and Brynjólfur said that he would ferry the organ and Snorri
back to the Village the next day, turning a deaf ear to the objections
of the ruined merchant, who knew that the *Hope* was supposed to be
catching fish for Geirþrúður, not ferrying an organ from one fjord
to another, yet it'll be good not to have to walk back, Snorri's legs
are completely worn out, they'll be stiff and sore tomorrow. You're
coming with us, Snorri said that evening, hardly intelligible through
his yawns, and then he was asleep. The boy read a bit but then lay
awake, listening to the rain and life stream like a heavy flow of blood
through his consciousness. Eventually the rain put him to sleep; he
sank into confused dreams but is now awakened by a hand rubbing
the window.

It's the fellow from the fishing hut, Shitbag Giantson, standing
outside, motioning to the boy to come out; he puts a finger to his
lips to signal that the boy should proceed quietly, which he does,
slinking to the front door, where he's startled to meet the eyes of
the tall, bent man sitting on a chair, watching the boy silently. At
first the boy wants to say something, explain why he's sneaking
out into the rain and night, although he doesn't know why himself,
but the lanky man seems disinclined to hear anything, completely
different than the way he was yesterday, people are one thing during
the day, another at night, and thus the boy says nothing, although he
does make gestures that are meant to explain something, but which
don't at all. He's welcomed by the rain, the tranquility of the night,
and the tobacco-chewing man sets off silently toward the shore, sig-
naling the boy to follow him. What? he asks, but the other silences
him with a glance, and there is the boat on the shore. What? the boy
begins again, but the other says, I need to talk to you, we'll row out
onto the fjord, and he starts preparing to launch the boat. It's as if
a fog lifts from the boy's mind, lifts from his memory. You're Egill,

he says hesitantly, and adds, stammering a bit when the man says nothing, merely straightens up slowly, as if he's afraid of breaking, we're brothers, I mean, you're my brother! Yes, Egill says finally, and they row out onto the fjord. It's dark with rain and night; all is quiet and calm.

THAT OPEN WOUND IN EXISTENCE

Sadness at not having lived well enough. At being dead, but unable to escape. At being unable to stop believing in what's beyond all distance, what we call God, call forgiveness, call hope. Sadness at it being less of an effort for a person to avoid the truth than to stand up for it in this imperfect world. At how minor unpleasantries in everyday life can cause one to forget that elsewhere in the world, hands are cut off people, children are raped, life is defiled. Sadness at how the living are no better than we were, how you don't fight enough, at times hardly at all, due to inconvenience, time constraints; at how you're able to live your lives and call that happiness, without ever having to look your consciences in the eye. Fear at the thought that one day you'll wake up like us, distorted shadows between life and death. Sadness at how thoughtlessly you munch the berries of Hell and allow Hell's poison to infiltrate your blood. Prejudice. Greed. Cruelty. Violence. Selfishness.

Five words in one berry; five words from one root.

That's why we've told these stories.

Yet it's not only the stories that ought to build this bridge to God or into the land on the opposite side of death, that ought to stir you and waken you, but rather, and no less significantly, the breaths we take, how our hearts beat, our blood roars; our fear, guilt, smiles, longing for happiness. All of these we sling with force into the world of imperfection.

Now we'll bring this to a close, our deaths and thirst for life, we'll bring it to a close. Let's follow the boy, that open wound in existence.

THIS GODFORSAKEN WORLD IS
HABITABLE SO LONG AS YOU LOVE ME

I

A SHIP THAT SAILS IS MUSIC. THE *HOPE* CLEAVES THE WAVES, WHICH were nearly mirror-smooth within the fjord but are more dynamic beyond it, as they sail out onto the ocean in the rain. God help us, how it rains! The ship sails past the mountain range, which ends so abruptly it's as if the land is plunging into the sea, then skirts two fjords and enters Djúp. Not a hefty catch in the *Hope*'s hold; Jonni stupidly broke his arm, forcing them to abandon the fishing for the time being, they did manage to haul in the lines with Jonni wincing; this man has never been able to suppress his pain or his emotions, nor to prepare decent food, but the men pin their hopes on his broken arm improving the situation. The organ is tied down tightly amidst the fish, and Snorri sits at it the entire trip and plays, unable to help himself, filling this fortunate ship with Bach, the boy lets it rain over him, listens to the raindrops dispersing on his forehead and to the music that streams up through the deck, the men lie or sit in the forecastle, on their damp bunks, staring at nothing, the music makes them remember, it fills them with a longing they don't understand, makes them melancholy and happy at the same time. Art is dangerous, it can stir up dreams of a better life, more equitable, more beautiful; it can arouse guilt and menace everyday existence.

The boy couldn't care less about getting wet; the temperature is fairly mild, if not warm, and it's risky to stand there wet for a long time on a ship's deck, wearing no protective clothing. Do you want to get sick, boy? says Brynjólfur, after coming out to join the boy, putting his arm awkwardly around his shoulders. The skipper smells of alcohol; it was too easy to get hold of liquor in the village, it literally lay in wait for him. No, the boy says, I'm going down to the forecastle, right away, he says, without looking at the skipper; he stares out into the rain, toward land, toward the fishing hut hidden within the dense rain, hears Brynjólfur go back inside, having stood with him for a while, for no reason, stood right up next to the boy, almost as if he were waiting for something.

The boy had smelled a similar odor of alcohol on his brother as they rowed away from the shore and into the semidarkness of the rain. Rowed out into the fjord, until they no longer sensed the land. This is fine, said Egill, drawing in his oar, moving over to the next thwart. The sea was so tranquil that the boy saw the raindrops sink. Egill handed him a raincoat, then a cask. Have some, he said, it's damned good moonshine. The boy put on the raincoat but shook his head at the cask, having not spoken a word since they were on shore. Egill stared for a moment at his brother, then swore into the rain; are you so paltry, not to drink? I just don't want to right now. Why not? I don't know. Maybe it isn't good enough for someone who lives with a rich dame? I drink everything, said the boy, obstinately sitting up straight. Oh, then drink! Geirþrúður isn't a dame. Don't be so sensitive; she's hardly an angel, people say she's lively with those who please her. She's, Geirþrúður is . . . Now then, interrupted Egill, no need to get angry, but you could still have a drink with me, we don't meet every day, you know, huh, we brothers! I don't want to drink; I might stop seeing the raindrops sink. Egill had raised the cask to his lips, but stopped before taking a drink, lowered it, stared at his brother, looked out into the rain and swore. There they sat. The boat hardly moved, only the rain between them, as well as many years, perhaps more than it's possible to tolerate. They said nothing and the sound of the eider ducks was a peculiar blend of loneliness and still-ness. It had been so long since they'd lain in their parents' bed, the two of them, Lilja, their mother; it was on the world's final night and the next morning the family was broken up. The boy had awakened with Egill's fingers in his hair, the same ones that clenched the cask in the boat; calloused, scarred fingers. The same? Or can a person change so much that he more or less dies, withers away, turns into nothing or, better put, into something entirely different?

You didn't recognize me, Egill said, and he smiled, or smirked, and raised the cask to his lips once more. The boy looked away, and it was as if he were losing his memory of that final night, a memory that he'd stored inside himself like a consolation, a painful delight. I remember so little, he'd said, I'm not even certain how many years it's been since Father drowned, is it ten or . . . Ten? It's thirteen! I remember *everything*, said Egill, almost reproachfully, and I knew as soon as you woke us that it was you, knew it immediately! I don't remember the events, the boy said, but I remember how I felt. He was going to add, I remember your fingers in my hair, but decided not to. I remember everything, Egill repeated, more quietly this time, looked out into the rain, took a drink. He'd heard stories of Bárður, two different versions, of the raincoat, and that afterward someone had walked up a valley, over a heath, with a book, a book of poetry, and he knew right away that it was his brother. I knew it right away, always knew that you were like Mother, and Father too, with that damn poetry nonsense, your damned dreams, you see how it went with them! Anyway, you were always exactly like Mother, constantly hanging onto her, and she hardly ever let you go. You've got to be careful with that nonsense. What nonsense? the boy had asked, looking at his brother. The stupid books, that damn poetry; that damned drivel will make you soft, you'll be plowed over, a man shouldn't give in, not an inch. To what mustn't we give in? To all of it, the entire stinking bunch of it, you've got to be tough, it's the

only thing that anyone understands. No, the boy said softly, looking
down to hide his eyes. Too bad you don't want to drink, his brother
had said. Were you beaten where you grew up, did you get enough to
eat? If someone's bothering you, you let me know, and I'll take care
of the bastard, I've survived, I've never had to bend, I know the ways
of this goddam life.

II

The *Hope* sails out onto Djúp; the boy is soaked to the skin, thoroughly drenched, and Bach wafts up from the hold, slips through the
deck. His face is wet with rain, not tears, yet it would be so good to
be able to cry, to shrug off this weight, this wound, this desperation.
He'd finally found his brother, only to lose him again immediately.
They'd said farewell onshore and the day had dawned within the rain,
though nearly invisibly; the drops seemed to grind the daylight into
half-light. The boys and I will come to the Village soon to lift our spir-
its, Egill had said; surely we'll get a discount on beer there, you must
have connections! The boy had merely shrugged. We'd like, Egill said,
to air out our little friends a bit, they've grown damn thirsty during
the winter, you don't fuck codfish and the dames here don't look at
anyone but those damn Yanks, they're the only ones fine enough for
those cunts. We'll do some stuff together, huh, brothers on the make!
Then the boat had vanished with him into the rain, the boy had stood
for a long time on the shore, raindrops splattering on him, which
they're still doing as he stands on the deck of the *Hope*, the merchant's
reply to Geirþrúður in a parcel down in the hold; he cannot, will not,
dares not assist her, the boy knows this, no need to break the seal
and read the letter to find it out, and what now, what roads are open
to Geirþrúður, might everything be ruined, and what will become of
him then, his education? The *Hope* crawls slowly through the rain;
Ragnheiður had pummeled his chest, he'd been inside her, she'd done

it, then left him lying there and he'd vomited. "How does your heart beat?" another woman had asked in a letter, she who thinks about a Norwegian, about Jens, they're both tall and strong like Brynjólfur, who comes out into the rain, walks over to the gunwale, heaves himself ponderously over it and disappears into the sea.

Tryggvi's steamer is gone. It's on its way to Copenhagen, sailing the high seas beneath the broad sky, fully loaded with saltfish, as well as Ragnheiður, who was going for a ride in sunshine, when the boy was supposed to have been something, he didn't know what, but knows it now. For a time he dreamt about her, ridiculous dreams, and not free from treachery; it's her people who are going to do Geirþrúður wrong, attempt to force her to her knees, at the very least hurt her, *those people*, Bjarni from Nes had said, his tone of voice indicating that anyone who had anything to do with Ragnheiður would no longer be welcome to greet him. Yet he can't hate the space between her eyes, the coldness in her expression, maybe because he'll never forget how she trembled after pushing him down, after taking him. He can't hate her, but can never love her; whatever that is, to love.

The sea is so still that the *Hope* hardly rocks as the boy walks from the pier up to the house. The sea into which Brynjólfur had disappeared.

At first the boy had merely stared. Stared as the skipper walked over to the gunwale and cast himself overboard, like an unfledged bird. Brynjólfur had stood there, weighed down by his life, his memories, and then he was gone, there was only the rain splattering the deck. A long time seemed to pass in that way. Yet it couldn't have been more than two, three seconds, though they were long, not much shorter than life. The boy stared, then leapt into action. Shouted something about drowning and death and the men barged their way like profanity up from the forecastle, turned the ship around in a big, endlessly slow circle, shouting the name of their skipper, praying, cursing, and Snorri stopped playing the organ, came up, stared into the rain that connected sky and sea, thought, this is my fault, my fault. Brynjólfur was dredged up like any old debris from the sea, drowned men saw his legs dangling and said to each other, Another one's come to join us. But this proved not to be true: Brynjólfur had kept himself afloat by flailing his arms, flabbergasted to have ended up in the sea, but also hesitant, because why fight it, isn't it much better and more honorable to sink, thereby to find peace, get away from everything, escape life? Then he heard the men's cries, heard them shouting his name, and those voices and that shouting kept him afloat until they managed to heave him aboard. What the devil were you thinking? they exclaimed, standing over him on the deck, furious; only their joy at the fact that he was alive prevented them from giving him a good thrashing. I don't know, Brynjólfur said, shaking with cold down in the forecastle when the boy goes ashore, the letter in his pocket. Few people are out and about, the drying lots look desolate in the rain, the saltfish having been stacked and covered over.

The boy walks up to the house, through the Village, and it's good that she's gone, that the big ship carried her away, it's fine with him, a bit as if he's free, although from what, he doesn't know. Yet he doesn't feel particularly well. "Can you brothers arrange to visit each other?" his mother had written in her letter. "You mustn't neglect it. You mustn't let the world tear you apart!"

Yet that's what happened. They didn't visit each other, were unable to do so, weren't allowed to do so, lost each other, two brothers, alone in the world, there were two letters, then nothing more, Egill moved to another district, then to yet another, the world sundered them, mountains and distance grew between them, and when they finally met, when Snorri pounded on the door of a filthy fishing hut and Egill opened it, it was too late. The boy had talked about Lilja, their sister, as they dawdled on the boat in the middle of the fjord; remember how happy she was whenever she woke up, how she laughed when she saw us? Egill just snorted and said, The things you claim to remember! I remember how I felt, the boy said, composing himself after an abrupt, violent wave of anger. They're all dead, Egill said, they're all gone and will never return, what good does it do to remember? It doesn't help anything, remembering just makes you soft, you're too soft, I saw it immediately, and you'll be plowed over unless you spit in your palms and man up. Well, and unless you get to stay there under the wing of that dame, damn good job I must say, wriggling your way in there, said Egill, spitting red overboard.

III

It's still raining when Geirþrúður opens the letter in the parlor. They're all there, Helga, Kolbeinn and the wet boy, who said he'd come on the *Hope*; Jonni broke his arm, yes, Snorri decided to bring the organ, was satisfied with it, he played it the entire way, it was beautiful, I was out on deck listening to the rain and Bach, at least he said he was playing Bach, and sometimes it was as if the music were bigger than the rain. Snorri played as we sailed and didn't stop until Brynjólfur jumped, or fell, overboard, no, he didn't drown, luckily, and seemed not to know how he ended up in the sea. Yes, drunk. He can't handle his liquor, Geirþrúður says.

Helga: All this unhappiness.

Geirþrúður: All this weakness.

But how did you like Christian? she says, after reading the letter; it dangles from her hand, which is resting on the arm of her chair. He's fat, the boy says, I had no idea that people could eat so much. There are signs hanging in his shop, all of them with the inscription *Time is Money*. That's why it's going so well for him, Geirþrúður says, those who think like that succeed; I'm sure you know what his answer is?

The boy: I didn't read the letter.

Geirþrúður: You read the man, you know the answer.

You knew the answer ahead of time, says the boy in surprise, as if having come to an unexpected conclusion. I could have written both letters, she says. Then why did you send me on that trip? It does you good to walk over mountains, it does you good to be near such men; wasn't it a good trip? Yes, says the boy, but weakly.

Helga: Did something happen?

You met a girl, hopefully, says Kolbeinn, knocking the floor lightly with his cane. Then the boy says it, that he'd met his brother and more or less lost him in the same moment, and that's why he'd been standing out on deck, in the rain, that's why he saw Brynjólfur disappear into the sea. One man's misfortune, Geirþrúður says, is occasionally another's salvation. Why did you send Christian a letter if you knew that it was useless? He's attracted to me. That fat bastard? the boy exclaims. Christian has a huge appetite, she says with a smile, as if she's talking about something amusing; unless it's just greed, she adds. He's a reprobate, Kolbeinn says hoarsely, a married bastard who keeps his wife locked up in the finery of Copenhagen. He's written me several letters, Geirþrúður says, and hasn't been shy, either; perhaps I wanted to torment the poor fellow by reminding him of his big words, I was sure he would never stand up to Tryggvi and Friðrik. He's offered to conquer the world for me, presumably assuming that he'd win me that way, and I couldn't withstand the temptation to needle him. There's a huge difference between talking big and being big. We're not often given the opportunity to demonstrate it. Sometimes I think we're controlled by big words spoken by little men.

We? Kolbeinn asks, we who? and he turns his head, as if gripped by the futile hope of setting his eyes on something.

Helga: There's nothing to be expected from Christian, of course?

Geirþrúður: No. But he says that I have beautiful eyes, beautiful lips, and that he often lies awake in bed thinking about me. Though I think it's about other parts of my body than my eyes.

Helga: It's not like we can dry fish on his insomnia.
Kolbeinn: Nor on his damned lasciviousness. Wretch and reprobate.
You'll need to come to an arrangement with Friðrik, and Tryg-gvi, says Helga, in a tone that's stern, but also not stern. I suppose I'll need to join the women's club run by Guðrún, the priest's wife, says Geirþrúður with a slight smile, and make a habit of drinking tea like a sophisticated woman, not gulping coffee like a fisherman. Invite them here, Kolbeinn says, and after they've all parked their polished asses, I'll come downstairs stark-naked and scorch their sensibility with some filth. Then you'll be free of them. Why naked? Geirþrúður asks keenly. You don't understand? It's an awful thing seeing an old man naked, a blind wretch, it's horrendous, and I'll fart as well, you know I can smell like a rotting ram's carcass. Enough of this piffle, Helga says. Maybe piffle is the only thing that can work against this . . . all of this, says, or mutters, Geirþrúður, who then stares into space distractedly, as we tend to do, even when there's no longer anything to see.

The next morning the boy is sent to fetch Jóhann, and it rains all day from this eye that hangs over us. He returns with Jóhann, then has pancakes with Helga before she joins Geirþrúður and Jóhann in the parlor. Are you going to negotiate? the boy had asked Geirþrúður. If I do, I've got to find my own way, she said, and touched him unexpect-edly, gently stroking his cheek, so delicately that he was nearly moved to tears. I'm afraid, however, that one defeat will lead to more defeats; that's their nature. Helga gives him pancakes, sits with him, watches him eat, asks about his brother. It isn't certain that you've lost him again, she says, he may not be the one you dreamed about, and may even be an entirely different man, but your blood is the same, and blood can be stronger and pull harder than anything else. He's says he's going to come here, says the boy, with his friends, and expects to get discounts for them all. We'll welcome them when the time comes,

Helga says, but it isn't always easy to be connected to others by blood; sometimes it takes more than it gives.

Toward evening the rain changes into a dense mist. Then fog. A dark fog, and everything disappears, even the mountains, as if they didn't exist, yet they're considerably larger than our lives. With the fog comes silence. People retreat into their houses and there's no one out on the streets apart from a few sailors, Danish devils who trickle ashore near midnight, wander in the fog in search of Sodom and run into their Icelandic counterparts, who want to fight, take these damn Danish wretches and send them all packing, you've got no mountains in you, fists fly but strike only fog, which swallows all blows, it puts up no resistance but causes everything to vanish. It's so strange when everything vanishes, we hear our own breathing, hear that our hearts are beating. There's so much silence in the world that it frightens me; come and lie with me, feel the warmth of my fingertips, feel the softness of my lips, when the world falls silent and vanishes, I call on you, with you I'm safe. This godforsaken world is habitable so long as you love me.

IV

The day is gone and will never return. It came, we filled it with our mistakes and triumphs, our treachery and dreariness, then came evening and the boy sits in the hotel with Gísli, who'd been there since standing up without a word and walking out of Tryggvi's house, despite his having agreed to spend some time with the old general. The old man had gone to bed and Gísli was supposed to have been available, yet he left. You can never be trusted, Friðrik will probably say to him. Damn, Gísli mutters. What? the boy says.

Gísli: I'm afraid your lessons won't amount to much anymore. I'm a miserable wretch, a cur that sits when it's supposed to sit, rolls over when it's ordered to do so, fetches a stick from the sea if the right person throws it. What good are poetry and knowledge if you have no dignity?

The boy probably isn't meant to answer this, they're not in class, this isn't an essay question but life itself, no grades are given, no diplomas are awarded. The boy has had a bit to drink, four beers, he's feeling tipsy, and the fog has taken away the world. No chores need doing up at the house, he wasn't needed in the café, nothing to clean, to fetch, he could of course keep translating, but was too restless to do so, I'm going to check whether the organ's been put in place at the hotel, he'd said, and Helga replied, Do what you want.

What he wants, apart from the impossible: to revive the dead, to crush Friðrik, make Andrea happy, cure coughs on Vetrarströnd, to have María come and join him in his lessons sometimes? If Gísli ever teaches him again, if he sobers up, if he's allowed to continue teaching him, if he doesn't get fed up with being a miserable wretch and a cur and leave, escape; maybe to become a cur and a wretch elsewhere.

What he wants—he has a letter from María in his pocket. A single sheet of paper that's an envelope on the outside and a letter on the inside; a few sentences, those that fit. It's closer to being a slip of paper rather than a sheet, and where are we to put our words if we have no paper; what will become of them if we live on a little turf farm beneath a mountain, a stone's throw from the ocean, and there's no paper, there's almost nothing but the struggle for life? A few sentences, thanks for the books, she would be so happy to discuss them with him, if only there weren't this sea between them, I read them and recite them to my poor Jón, thank you dearly, but tell me what I owe you, and in the corner delicate children's drawings, the entire page used, which is an indication of poverty but also of a thirst for life, without which one is lost. The boy watches Gísli, who reaches into his coat for a flask, refills his glass, winks at him. Thank you dearly, but not a word as to whether the little girl is still alive, how black her cough is, wouldn't María have at least hinted at it if the worst had happened, thank you dearly, I adore reading, yet life could be better—something along those lines? What he wants: to write to María. To ask, Is everyone alive, to ask, What do you dream? What he wants: to borrow the dory from Marta and Ágúst at Sodom and row like a madman over Dumbsfirðir, so hard that the skin peels from his hands, the calluses that have softened slightly this summer, row in the direction of red hair, green eyes. Row! Fair enough. But for what? To be defeated? Is it you? she would say, surprised, she who loves Jens, a damned Norwegian, loves big men that the wind has difficulty shaking. Is it you? Yes, I was sent here, he would reply, like the wretch that he is, I had to run some errands, now they've been taken care of; I just wanted to say thank you for the letter. Then he would row back, just not as hard, without caring one bit whether he were carried off course, even into a fjord that doesn't exist. But why did she write him a letter, even two? It would be most sensible, of course, to write to her and simply ask, Why are you sending me letters? I honestly can't bear it, your hair is so red, your eyes are so green. Write to her in a poised, deliberate tone. Yes, of course it's perfectly ludicrous to row alone across a fjord so wide that it's practically an ocean, to make such a journey in great uncertainty, possibly to encounter humiliation, total defeat.

Gísli reaches once more beneath his coat for the slender silver flask, glances around furtively, adds whisky to his glass. Drink up, he says, let's drink all damn night. It's good to drink with such a young man, full of poetry, I had no idea that such a thing was in store for me, nor did it ever occur to me that I would find him here, of all places; there now, drain that damn glass of yours, let's drink and be merry, like mice in the pantry! He drains his glass, a generous double, at one go, puts the glass down, now we're having fun, he says, although nothing suggests that he's amused; he looks distractedly at the boy and mutters again, as if to himself, as if quoting a proverb, rather than asking a question, what use are poetry and knowledge if one has no dignity? He expects no answer, has no interest in one; he merely stares at the boy with a look of pity, perhaps at how he's so young and inexperienced, how he has yet to experience the disappointments of life, to waste away in the toil of everyday life, he doesn't ask for an answer, yet is given one anyway. You can't blame it on poetry and knowledge, the boy says apologetically.

You ought to be ashamed of yourself for saying such a thing, says Gísli, who seems to have aged by several years; he turns his glass, which is sadly empty—perhaps you're nothing but questionable company for me.

Night approaches, fog distorts the world, but here we have a question to wrestle with: Bárður dies and the world becomes impoverished, but it's precisely because of this that worlds opened up to the boy, the possibilities that his parents had let themselves dream of, even as if Bárður had sacrificed himself; and how can one live with such a sacrifice, *how* is he to live? Bárður dies, and the boy's talents come to light. Now I die so that you can come to know happiness. I change into darkness, but you step into the light. It can't be right, the boy thinks, and it's why everything is falling apart now. Or can happiness dwell in the sorrow, can light emerge from darkness, and is it then justifiable to welcome it?

The boy sips his beer, it's as if the fog has paralyzed him, the fog and doubt, and maybe that's why he didn't go up to the house but continued to sit at the hotel. Nor is he any use to anyone; when Geirþrúður is threatened, he proves to be a good-for-nothing whelp and, even worse—part of her misfortune, yet another reason for Friðrik to crush her, she who looks after the person whom Ragnheiður has mentioned with interest in front of her father. This boy, who abandoned his place on a good fishing boat, who buries his nose in books, yet somehow manages to prick his daughter's interest. It's intolerable, but he's under Geirþrúður's wing, of course; yet another reason to clip those wings of hers. Worthless. Useless. Like the man opposite him, the headmaster. Is it their desire for poetry and knowledge that makes them so worthless?

Useless. Yes. Worthless. Maybe. Yet not completely, not absolutely; he's able to help somewhat, and in his own way. He has a letter from María in his pocket, or a note, the only thing that she could send, a few words expressing her gratitude and desire. That it could be nice to talk to him about those books, but the sea is between them, the ocean that we live on, die in. Wasn't she asking for companionship, the companionship that is, despite everything, to be found in words? There are few things to equal receiving a letter. There's intimacy in letters, they bridge distances, are precious companions that last a long time, warm you, long after they're read. I'm going to write to her, the boy says out loud, and Gísli stops talking to himself, raises his glass to drink, but it's empty, like life, everything ends up the same way; he looks at the boy, who was saying something, something about writing a letter, as if that would change anything, make any difference. Write, write to whom? the headmaster says wearily, his flask is empty, he has to buy himself his next drink, or rather, have it put on his account, increase his debt. The boy smiles at Gísli, insensitive to his fatigue, surrender, the drink—the same word written in different ways. María, he says, on Vetrarströnd. Who is María? Gísli asks, and then the boy says it, although he'd planned only to say, She lives there, I send her books, I'm going to write to her, but he suddenly feels that she deserves so much more, that she deserves to be told of, deserves for her life to be known, her struggle for life, her thirst for books. Jens and I nearly died of exposure below her farm, begins the boy, before telling of the evening, the night, the morning at that farm, which was buried in snow at the time but has now emerged and drinks in light and sun.

V

Don't leave me, Gísli says. They've come outside, the boy had written his letter to María, got paper from Hulda, called to her when it looked as if she was on her way down to the basement. Don't leave me, Gísli repeats. I'm just going to run up to the house, the boy says, let them know where I am; I'll be back. No, no, everyone in the world is asleep and you can't go anywhere in this fog, you'll lose your way and end up in Hell, believe me, I have excellent diplomas from the University of Copenhagen, says Gísli, gripping the boy's arm for extra emphasis, in case he didn't put full stock in university diplomas from Copenhagen. They're not sleeping, just stay here, I'll be quick. You won't find your way back, not in this fog, the headmaster says hopelessly, groping in his coat pocket for some solace, but the flask is empty and the book of poetry that he pulls out is worthless. Sometimes the deepest and greatest poems are nothing more than useless words on paper.

The boy was right, they're both awake in the parlor; I'm a bit drunk, unfortunately, he says, but I was sitting with Gísli at the hotel, I wrote a letter to María on Vetrarströnd, a long letter, while Gísli played chess with Ásgerður, I noticed Hulda going down to the basement, she was smiling, Snorri has a room in the basement, I remember him mentioning her up in the mountains, but Gísli is waiting for me in the fog, he's hoping I'll go with him to Sodom. The women glance at each other; Geirþrúður is barefoot, with incredibly beautiful toes. The captain had told her, Out in the world you'd receive awards and endowments for them, you could rule kingdoms, I can't get enough of them, wiggle them for me one more time, and she does so, wiggles them a little in the parlor, even though he's dead, down in the ground. I'm sorry I didn't come earlier, the boy says, I don't know why I didn't let you know where I was, was Kolbeinn angry about missing his reading? He said he was going to let you feel his cane, Geirþrúður says, but he's experienced greater disappointments, don't you worry, and you may certainly go back out into the fog, spend time with Gísli, absolutely, but don't drink too much, we'll probably be making a trip tomorrow morning, so be sure to come to the house in good time, if you want to get some sleep, and bring Gísli with you, it's important. Bring Gísli here? he asks in surprise; a trip, he asks, where, all of us, perhaps? Yes, we four are one, you see, haven't you realized that? The world has seen to it, has herded us together. But what, the boy says, but what? he asks again, feeling so sluggish, numb, but what, he asks or says for the third time, staring at nothing, as if desperately trying to remember something. This trip, he says finally, is it far, is it because of Friðrik, and Tryggvi, is it because of them, because of what they're planning to do, and are we going far? Maybe not in miles, she says; and figures are useless, anyway, for measuring anything in a human life, but yes, we wouldn't be going were it not for Friðrik and Tryggvi. I think, however, that their names and characters are irrelevant, because those who rule are shaped by their power, and their power by tradition. So we're wrestling with something considerably larger than those fine men. Enough of that, the evening is passing, go and spend time with Gísli, but don't come home too late.

He runs the shortest route down to the hotel, to find Gísli waiting exactly where he left him, at precisely the same point. You may have this, he says, handing the boy a little book, the poems of Hölderlin, I have no use for it. It's in German, the boy says, or asks. Yes, that's likely, at least last time I checked. I don't read German, says the boy, disappointed, which he's allowed to be; it hurts not to know languages. We'll change that when I'm free of that damned general and no longer have to be a dog, one can't live without knowing German, *da ich ein Knabe war*, life would be a wasteland if we didn't have poets, says Gísli, looking pessimistically into the fog before setting off in the direction of Sodom, the tavern owned and run by Marta and Ágúst, and whose name is actually Bifröst, but is never called anything other than Sodom.

It takes some time to pass through the old neighborhood, and they lose their way twice despite Gísli knowing it like the back of his hand. This night won't end well, he mutters, and seems about to add something when they meet three sailors. People out at this hour, says Gísli in surprise; three, even! I thought we two were the only ones left in this world; what are you looking for in the fog? But the men don't answer, sailors from a schooner, the same ones who wanted to give the Danish sailors a beating, in their own private fight for independence; the boy is able to see one of their faces, just a glimpse of it, otherwise their eyes are focused on the ground, or to the side, they hurry past and are gone, say nothing of their business. What bustle is this? exclaims Gísli, who wanted to talk, ask things, hear new voices, but they're gone. Why rush? There's nothing awaiting us at the end of life but death, Gísli half shouts, walking on but turning to look back, as if calling out to them; remember that people should go slowly, not flee in the belief that escape is possible; no one escapes, man doesn't have . . . Damn it all, he blurts out as he stumbles over a hump, some sort of shapeless mass, tumbles head over heels and lies there on his stomach, like a melancholy seal. Did the Devil fell me? he says to the ground, but the boy kneels next to the heap, which turns out to be a person, which turns out to be Svandís from the Poorhouse, lying curled up in a ball as if she wants to change into a conch, and who didn't move when Gísli fell over her. Svandís, the boy says delicately, and she opens her eyes, those two lonely moons, looks at the boy. My dear boy, she says finally, hopelessly, are you going to as well? Am I going to what? the boy asks, but she doesn't answer, just curls up tighter and starts abruptly when he tries to adjust her flimsy dress, which is torn and pulled up beneath her hips, and the boy feels something cold touch him. It's so obvious. The flight of the men in the fog, the way that she's lying there, how she is. Svandís, he says soothingly, tugging irresolutely at the torn fabric, at which she gives another start, curls up tighter. Don't, she pleads, don't. I'm just going to fix your dress, I . . . Not you, too, she says softly, hopelessly; the boy swallows and doesn't dare to touch her again, as if he's unclean, and then smells the stink of alcohol as Gísli bends toward them, and Svandís starts to cry. You're putting on my Englander, Svandís, Gísli says, having stopped feeling sorry for himself; he takes off his coat and the boy helps him to put it on her, that's better, my poor dear, the headmaster says soothingly, before helping Svandís to her feet, like a scared, hounded little animal in his arms, but wearing the fine, costly coat that Gísli acquired by kneeling to Friðrik. This Englander is yours now, you hear, this coat, I mean, it suits you better than me, anyway. Svandís' arms are wrapped around Gísli's neck, her head and dirty hair rest on his shoulder. Gísli looks down at her and suddenly it's as if he doesn't know what to do. What now, says his perplexed expression, what do we do now? Should we take her up to the house? the boy asks. What house? Gísli says.

Geirþrúður's, the boy says.

Geirþrúður's, mutters Gísli, as if he's testing the name, but then it seems to dawn on him. No no, it's shorter to mine, I'm sure Rakel is at home, she's the person you want, Svandís, my poor dear; how do you feel about that, he says, more than asks, and sets off. I begged them to stop, she says to his shoulder, why didn't they stop when I asked them to? May the sea take them all, says Gísli, holding Svandís tighter, and we're close to saying the same thing, may the sea take those three sailors, even though it's unforgivable to wish the death of another. Or, as it's said: "Power can turn a man into a devil, and that's why men are at times the worst thing to be found on earth."

VI

This is an evil night, Gísli says.

They'd brought Svandís to Rakel but are now sitting in Sodom, where there are four Danish sailors, hammered and boisterous; Marta is sitting with the Danes and has a formidable air. An evil night, Gísli mutters at the table.

But what is good, what is evil? The difference isn't as obvious as we'd wish. What is good can bring us misfortune, what is most difficult will someday become a solace. But this night doesn't look particularly good; that's true. In Rakel's room in the basement, Svandís stares at the ceiling, the sailors had come across her in the fog, wandering alone, wearing hardly more than her flimsy dress, jabbering incoherently; one of them had greeted her cheerfully, even merrily, but then grabbed one of her breasts, as if accidentally, and that was all it took, the merriment vanished. They couldn't bear it, those three sailors, couldn't bear the fog, their own superiority, contact with her bare breast, something snapped inside them, they were no stronger than that. They pushed her down, pulled up her dress, she said no, once, twice, thrice, but didn't fight back, except perhaps with a few tears, otherwise she just lay there, her eyes stretched wide. What fucking eyes are these? the first man said before covering them with his big hands, taking her while the others waited impatiently. Then they fled into the fog.

This is an evil night, and I don't know where it's come from, Gísli says, pouring a beer down his throat, pouring it over his life, those ruins, as the boy merely sips at his own and waits for the chance to bring the headmaster home, as he's been instructed to do, although he has no idea why, and isn't certain that he wants to know, isn't certain that he cares to take Gísli with them, because what trip awaits them, and who is coming along, hardly Gísli, no, of course not, but then why does Geirþrúður want him to come to the house? Ágúst brings another beer for Gísli and avoids looking at his wife, who turns in her chair to watch him. Damn wimp, she says, uncomfortably, deliberately, damn nobody, *ynkelig mand*, she says, *udueligt menneske, jeg behøver en rigtig mand, er I det?*[2] she asks the Danes, and the man next to her leans forward, says something quietly, she throws back her head and laughs. She's devilish tonight, mutters Gísli, and tomorrow will probably never come, he adds, when the Dane who'd whispered something to Marta grabs one of her breasts, a bit hesitantly at first, prepared to make it look as if it were in jest, but then continues greedily when she does nothing but turn her head and look her husband in the eye. *Jeg har to,* she says calmly to the sailor. *For helvede, det er sandt,* he says huskily, as his comrades watch, rocking in their chairs, as if impatient. You want to write poetry, Gísli says to the boy hoarsely, looking away from Marta, there you have something to write about, there you have life! I'm not a poet, the boy says, not wanting to look over at the other table. The Devil knows who you are, Gísli says, but we already have plenty of poems about mountains and the old gods, old heroes, you should write about this here, just remember to make it rhyme with what never comes; how can you put up with this? he then says to Ágúst, who has brought a beer for himself. She's just drunk, the landlord says, it'll pass. I'm not sure, Gísli says, I'm not sure that anything passes.

The boy: We should go.

Go, Gísli moves his head a bit to the side to avoid the shot glass that Marta flings at her husband, too drunk to aim well, it flies past Gísli's forehead and breaks against the wall; go, he repeats, go where, we're stuck here for eternity, and how can you put up with

---

2. Marta speaks to the sailors in Danish: *ynkelig mand*: pathetic man; *udueligt menneske*: inept person; *jeg behøver en rigtig mand, er I det*: I need a real man, are you one?; *Jeg har to*: I have two; *Forhelvede, det er sandt*: dammit, that's true.

this, this damned nonsense, huh, Ágúst?! Marta goes and gets a new bottle and a shot glass to replace the one that she threw at her husband, refills the Danes' glasses and empties her own. The sailor leans back, parts his legs and looks at Marta with half-closed eyes, so voraciously that he looks almost cruel. She's humiliating you, man, Gísli says. Are you certain it's me who's being humiliated? says Ágúst, without looking up from the table, and Gísli swears, curses his answer, curses Marta, curses life, but then the door opens and Gunnar the Mustache, the clerk in Tryggvi's Shop, staggers in. He's drunk, and a joyless smirk plays on his lips. Ágúst fetches a beer, hands it to Gunnar, who accepts it wordlessly, staring over at the other table, where Marta is in the lap of the sailor, who managed, for a fleeting moment, to bare one of her breasts. Damn it, Gunnar says, damn it, man. Drink more, Marta says in Icelandic to the Dane, filling their glasses yet again; you fellows certainly can drink, you have that in common with all the other miserable fools, being able to drink. She stands up, pats down her blouse, looks almost sarcastically at the bulge in the man's crotch, then leans against the wall, smokes.

She's gone, says Gunnar, looking at the boy. People don't go anywhere, Gísli explains, as if talking to a child, just their purpose; and we're left with beer, bad jokes, lecherous sailors and fog. Gunnar continues to look at the boy, almost helplessly, causing the boy to ask, Who? You know, of course *you* know!

The boy: Me? No.

Gunnar: Yes, you do.

The boy: Who is gone?

Gunnar: It's her, don't you understand, *her*, you know which, there's just one her, I think I'll kill myself.

Gísli: How?

Gunnar: By ship, of course.

Gísli: Is that possible?!

Gunnar: Are you an idiot? Of course it's possible. Ships sail away with people.

Gísli: I meant, how are you going to kill yourself?

Gunnar: How the hell should I know, I've never done anything like it before.

You mean Ragnheiður, the boy says; of course, says the other, why should I mean someone else, why should I be talking about anyone else, I hate everything that reminds me she's gone. What reminds you most of her absence? Gísli says. Everything! Then you can kill yourself now, Gunnar, says Gísli, as if reassuring him, you'll never get her, Friðrik may think highly of you as an employee, you're just enough of a rotter for him to do so, but he'd rather have Ragnheiður end up a spinster than wed her to the son of a carpenter; his son-in-law will have to be grander than that. I know, says Gunnar, as he watches Marta smoke another cigarette, and it's as if the air quivers around her. Jesus was the son of a carpenter, the boy says. That doesn't help me, the other man says. No, says Gísli, quite the contrary, neither Friðrik nor Tryggvi would care to have a fellow such as Jesus in their inner circle, a man with ideas like his would lead them straight into bankruptcy. In all probability, he adds, just as Marta puts out her half-smoked cigarette and goes into the small side room, followed by the Dane, it's considerably quicker getting to Hell than to Heaven.

VII

It's nearly three, says Geirþrúður, who is still awake when the boy returns with Gísli; they'd made their way through the fog from Sodom, through the dense fog that still seemed to cling to the head-master, making him look hazy. They'd come all this way, and it was nearly three o'clock. Helga is sleeping on the sofa, covered with a blanket, but wakes up when they arrive and the boy asks what time it is, wakes up, gets up, with an unexpected look of vulnerability reminiscent of loneliness, but perhaps it's a misunderstanding, it hardly lasts a second, and then she has recovered, then she's fully awake. What a sight you two are, says Helga, as she stops folding the blanket, leaning forward for a better look, were you in an accident? Gísli straightens up, looks down at his torn sweater, raises one arm as if he's surprised at the back of his hand, which is bloodied. What a damn disaster that was, he says.

The sailor had followed Marta into the little bedroom just off the bar, as his companions watched in silence; the door was left half-open, perhaps to invite others in? One of the Danes, wide-shouldered and completely bald, stood up hesitantly, took three, four uncertain steps toward the room but stopped, even stiffened, and smiled apologetically when Ágúst stood up from the table, as if the sailor wished to say, I'm sorry, but I just want it so damned much. Ágúst, however, paid him no heed, went straight to the bar, returned with a whisky bottle and four glasses, sat down, filled them, emptied his and then stared blankly, the corners of his mouth quivering mildly. The bald Dane looked uncertainly from Ágúst toward the room, and when the landlord made no move, simply continued to stare into space, he went the rest of the way, pushed open the door, watched, hunched over, like an animal. The boy looked at Gísli, questioning, pleading, but the headmaster shook his head, whatever that meant, and the boy swallowed, wanting most to rush out, away from the vulgar sounds that came from the room and tore apart something deep within him. Ágúst refilled the shot glasses, pouring evenly into all of them, seeming not to notice that the boy had hardly touched his drink, causing most of it to splash out and form a yellow puddle on the rough timber. The landlord put down the bottle and they all stared at their glasses, as if it were too much for them to do more than stare, than sit there like condemned criminals as the sailor grunted in the little room; the bald man, having undone his pants, held his heavy penis and stroked it like a pet. Ágúst reached for his glass and drained the whisky, down into his slender neck, then wiped his mouth with the back of his hand, glanced around as if inspecting the place with surprise, almost as if he wanted to ask, Where am I, in what life am I?

Ágúst, Gísli said once more, after the bald man stepped into the room, holding his swollen penis, that profanity, stepped into the braying moans of his companion, into Marta's curses and giggles, and the third Dane had stood up, was licking his lips, his expression like a mask; love can deprive you of your judgment, lust of your conscience.

Then everything happened very quickly.

Ágúst was at the door of the room; he slipped in and pulled the bald man out backward, it was easy, the man had trouble keeping his balance with his pants down around his ankles and the landlord threw him effortlessly to the floor, reentered the room and pulled the other sailor out by his hair, the man swore and tried to find his footing but it went badly, since he also found himself tangled in his pants, and he may have been bewildered, as well, to have been torn so violently from the ecstasy of the flesh. The sailors were quick to recover and knocked Ágúst over. Castrate the bastard! shouted one of them, waving a knife. For fuck's sake! exclaimed Gunnar. God damn! shouted the boy, something burst inside him and he grabbed the neck of the whisky bottle, raised it like a club, because now the fight was on, now fists would fly and the cursed bottle would smash someone's head, God damn, raised the bottle so high above his head that the whisky poured out the open neck and down his arm, I'll be a laughing stock until my final moment, he thought, and put down the bottle. I've never been in a fight, Gísli said, as one of the Danes tried to pull down Ágúst's pants. Damn it all! Gunnar shouted, and all three of them leapt from their seats. Hopeless at fighting, yet their action came as a surprise, came like an explosion, furious because of all that life had done to them. Gísli was quite hefty; he'd never had to apply his weight to anything besides drinking and reading poetry, but he threw himself on one of the Danes and they rolled across the floor, taking down two chairs and ending up beneath the table, with Gísli partly on top, shouting incomprehensible lines of poetry, swinging them like clubs, while the boy ended up under the bald man, the damned devil was strong as a bull, and he grinned snidely as he slapped the boy's face lazily, glancing around. Look at how much fun I'm having! declared his expression. But those who are weaker fight with everything they have, they have no choice, and the boy managed to bite into the man's little finger, bit with all his strength, as if life depended on his biting damn hard, the finger made a crunching noise and the bald man yelled at the same time as Gunnar managed to bring down his sailor, taking the Danes' table with them as they fell, along with all its bottles and glasses, and Gunnar howling curses because Ragnheiður's gone and he'll never get to kiss her, let alone anything else. What, then, was the goddam point of living this life? he howled at the Dane, who didn't understand Icelandic and thus was unable to answer such a pressing question, while the one who'd been in the room with Marta, who'd entered her and didn't have long to go before he was torn out of her by his hair, had pinned Ágúst to the wall, hoisting him up by his neck and causing his throat to rattle. The landlord could barely hear it when the Dane raised his knife and shrieked, Now I'm going to cut off your balls, you fucking twat!, yet he certainly saw his wife come rushing over, naked from the waist up and brandishing a heavy saucepan. After Águst pulled the Dane off of her and all hell broke loose, Marta had gone and lain in bed, just lay in bed, as if this had nothing to do with her, pulled the cover over her, having thought, perhaps, of going to sleep, but then her heart started beating furiously and she began to cry. It had been good having the sailor inside her and she'd seen the other one in the doorway out of the corner of her eye, knew that he was waiting for his chance, but she couldn't care less, didn't give a damn about any of it, it was good, but also ridiculously funny, she couldn't help but giggle, which confounded the big man on top of her, but so what, he didn't matter one bit, the only thing that mattered was what he was doing, and then everything went as it did. Ágúst had torn the sailor off her, Ágúst, who could be so wet, so intolerably vapid, always so careful, scraping money together, saving for a house and a future instead of living in the here and now, that damned prudence of his that could be so suffocating, Ágúst who never budges no matter what she does, how she behaves, doesn't even attempt to get back at her when she's behaved badly, belittled him and then lain sick as a dog in bed the next day, vomiting, with a piercing headache, he just sits beside her with a bucket, a wet cloth, strokes her hair, humming something silly, intolerably, incomprehensibly good to her; it was just then that she started to cry. It's damn useless to lie here while the best man in the world is in trouble, the best, so pitiful that he is lost without her! And she threw off the cover, grabbed the nearest piece of clothing, a pair of his pants, slipped them on without thinking of putting on anything else, rushed out, grabbed a heavy saucepan, saw this Danish piece of shit roughing up her husband, saw only that and struck as hard as she could, aimed at his head but was probably too drunk, too excited, only hit his shoulder, but hard, the right one, he screamed in pain, then doubled over when she kicked him viciously in the groin. The Dane's scream and Marta's curses changed everything, the others stopped tussling, the Dane got up off of Gísli, having gained the upper hand yet still half-flabbergasted by the words that had poured out of the headmaster, there stood Marta in the middle of the room, Ágúst beside her with the sailor's knife in his hand, she swinging the pan as her big, heavy breasts bobbed up and down; the Danes stood huddled together, uncertain, hesitant, one with a damaged shoulder, another with a maimed little finger, the third befuddled by poetry, the fourth, however, more or less unscathed, his shoulders broad, having overpowered Gunnar after he'd recovered from the unexpected attack, and looking sneeringly from the bobbing breasts to the saucepan, though more at the breasts, he found it hard to keep his eyes off of them and got his come-uppance, realizing it too late when Marta stepped up to him and cracked the pan across his jawbone and nose—and a few moments later the sailors fled, ran out into the night, a damaged shoulder, maimed little finger, broken nose. The fog engulfed them.

VIII

We can't see a damn thing in this fog, I can hardly see my own toes, Gísli says. Then all of us are blind, says Kolbeinn, sitting foremost in the boat, dilating his nostrils, he can't get enough of the smell of the sea, because the briny smell aboard a boat and out on the sea is entirely different from the one you notice on land. Kolbeinn's expression could well resemble a wound, but he turns his face away from them, out toward the invisible sea, the incomprehensible tranquility.

It was late in the morning when they rowed out from the Lagoon, past motionless sailing ships, they couldn't see the masts, only the hulls, which the fog transformed into age-old whales, toughened by the years. It was nearly nine o'clock yet all was quiet except for the oars, except for the boat's prow cleaving sea and fog. The two men row slowly through the channel below Sodom and the boy is relieved not to smell any smoke, they'd feared that the Danes would return with reinforcements, with more fists, with vengeance, perhaps even burn the building to the ground. But there was no smell of smoke, so Sodom is likely still standing in the fog, undamaged and empty. The boy and Gísli had taken the couple with them up to the hotel. Ágúst was reluctant to leave everything behind, the liquor, the furniture, their belongings, but it was better to protect their health, save their lives rather than their things. The boy had helped them right the table and chairs, sweep up the broken glass, but there was little help to be had from Marta; she wouldn't leave Ágúst's side, stroked him, held him. My poor dear, she said, my poor little thing, my hero, my man, held him tightly, still bare-chested but it didn't matter, it was natural. Life, breasts, tears, broken bottles, the night was a night and there was little else to say about it. But Gunnar had watched. He muttered something, gazing at the heavy breasts as they pressed against Ágúst, then bent down to the boy, whispered, God damn, what jugs that woman has, we should get something in return for our help, but then he was gone, vanished into the night and fog with his mustache and longing for her who left with the steamer and took everything that you can imagine with her, perhaps more. Not much later the four of them walked out into the same night, the boy, Gísli, the landlord and his wife. You're far too good for me, far too good, that's why I behave as I do, I'm bad, you're far too good, pattered Marta. I'm so boring, so colorless, and you're so vibrant, in comparison with you, I'm nearly dead, he said in return, and they walked so close together that it was hard to see who was supporting whom, sometimes both crying, Gísli and the boy following like an honor guard, like interlopers, like record keepers. Teitur let the couple in, frowning at his own drowsiness and the reek of alcohol from the group, yet he let them in, gave them shelter, as Hulda slept close to Snorri in the hotel's basement; they were both naked, he woke up and stroked her hair as tears trickled down his cheeks, took a meandering course through the bristles of his beard. They lay nestled together, resembling two interlocking notes just beginning to form a melody. Gísli and the boy continued up to the house. You're so vibrant that in comparison with you, I'm nearly dead, the boy repeated in the parlor; Helga had finished folding the blanket, but Gísli could no longer stand upright, he fell into a chair, his head teetering from the drink and the night, but the boy remained standing, smelling of whiskey, and he told about the evening, the night, the fight, of the lustfulness or, what else shall we call it, what word should we use for it when lust turns into lewdness: the man who stood in the doorway had unfastened his pants and stroked his swollen penis as if it were the Devil's pet.

* * *

There's no smell of whisky on him now, in the boat that crawls past the mountain, that will soon be out on Djúp; although they see nothing in the fog, it's almost as if they aren't moving, the only change is deeper waves indicating a deeper sea. He managed to sleep for just over three hours, without having expected to fall asleep; everything spun inside him, he had no idea how he should feel, sometimes it's impossible to respond sensibly to life. Let alone deliberately. What a blessing to be able to fall asleep. Something blessed him, he lay down on the bed and nodded off, slept soundly until Helga nudged him, it wouldn't do this time to knock on his door, she had to go in, nudge the boy, at the same time saying something soft and sweet, a man's life would be lighter and less toilsome if he were awakened in such a way more often.

The giant Gvendur and the boy row hard now, having reached shelterless Djúp, dozens of yards of dark sea beneath them. Gísli is seated in the stern, looking tired, his eyes lowered, Geirþrúður in the bow. It's our turn to row now, Gísli, says Helga. Row, he echoes, wearily, I haven't rowed in twenty years, and are we sure that we're headed in the right direction? We can't see a damn thing in this fog, I can hardly see my own toes! Then all of us in the boat are blind, Kolbeinn says. The boy takes a deep breath, it's good to become one with the tugging of the oars, become a movement, become a boat that crawls slowly over the ocean, from time to time he directs his gaze to where Vetrarströnd should be. You mustn't forget to send your letter to María tomorrow, Helga had said during the night. There were four of them in the parlor, Kolbeinn having long since gone to bed, and Gvendur as well, he slept in the room where Jens usually slept, two big men, yet different. Gvendur's here? the boy had asked, astonished, after telling the story of the evening that turned to night, he wrote a letter, came here, went back to Gísli, they wandered through the old neighborhood, Gísli stumbled over Svandís, damned beasts, the boy said. Some people deserve to be castrated, Helga said. It's might and power that does that to them, Geirþrúður had said, looking over at Gísli, who teetered between memory and oblivion, having slept little, drunk far too much, a lethal combination, though once or twice his head cleared. Power, he said, might, he said, and tried to straighten up, felt her black eyes, placed one hand on his thigh, a bit as if he were going to make an announcement. Yes, Geirþrúður said inquisitively. There was a long silence, they waited for something from Gísli, the parlor clock motionless as usual, the large pendulum an upside down, condemned criminal. The Devil gets his claws into people through power, Gísli finally said, the headmaster, a man from an important family. I hardly think so, Geirþrúður said, I think it's power that makes a man devilish. Damn it, Gísli said, and his head teetered from the drink, with fatigue, perhaps with concentration, or because the black eyes remained fixed on him. Go on, Helga said to the boy, and he did. They brought Svandís to Rakel, Oddur was there, and Gísli gave Svandís his coat. The English one? asked Geirþrúður. Yes, the boy said, and then night came over those in Sodom. He had the letter with him the whole time, it wasn't damaged in the fight. Letter, said Gísli, trying once more to sit up straight; damn, now I've got to write to Reverend Kjartan, what a crazy night this was, almost as if we were alive! The women looked at each other, the boy saw it, but most of all he wanted to sleep, to get out of his whisky-smelling clothes and fall asleep. But then Helga said, A big, fidgety man has come, in search of you. Me, in search of me? exclaimed the boy in surprise, why should anyone seek his presence, but then it dawned on him, from the concise description, a big, fidgety man; is his name Gvendur, maybe?

Yes.

Gvendur is here?

Me, too, Gísli was then heard to mutter, nearly dozing; his head had sunk down, his chin rested on his chest, it hung on the end of his neck like an inessential weight that his body wanted to get rid of as quickly as it could, yet he started when the boy half-shouted, Gvendur is here?!, then looked up and around, surprised, and said in an astonished voice, Me, too! Many a strange thing happens, Geirþrúður said. The boy looked from the women to Gísli and back; it had slipped his mind that it wasn't normal to have the headmaster here for the night, that he'd been entrusted with bringing him here, but for what? And Gvendur was here, sleeping. Well, the boy said, and then nothing more, just raised his hands as if to say that he understood nothing.

They must be out in the middle of Djúp by now, heading due north. Gísli is still sitting in the stern. Kolbeinn wanted to row, Now I'm alive, he said at the exertion. A bold assertion, said Gísli, as Geirþrúður sits in the bow, looking over the boat from time to time, at the four people manning the oars, this peculiar assembly of hers: a giant who's afraid of losing his life, a blind skipper who put himself in harm's way with books, Helga, her faithful companion almost from childhood, and then the boy, such a strange delivery. She shuts her eyes for a moment.
Gvendur had come to the Village the previous evening, looking for the boy. The fishing season was finally finished, having, truth to tell, dragged out unusually far into the summer, but it was as if Pétur simply didn't want to stop. He hardly spoke to anyone anymore; Árni was very impatient to get on with his farm work, and the atmosphere had become heavy and strained in the fishing hut—and then Pétur brought Elínborg out to the salting shed. They were gutting a catch when, without a word, Pétur put down his knife, went up to the hut, came back out with Elínborg and disappeared with her into the shed. Einar had laughed as if the Devil were in his veins and then said something about Andrea, something very ugly, so ugly that Gvendur saw red and didn't know it until he'd knocked out his leader and master of many years' standing. Knocked him out cold. Árni had quickly checked to see if Einar was still alive and then dragged him aside. It's

no good working amidst garbage, he said. They finished gutting the fish and then Gvendur left the fishing hut, encouraged by Árni, who told him to go find the boy and Andrea and then see what happened.

The boat rises and falls on the heavy waves, crawls onward to the north. Kolbeinn has an internal compass. There's Núpur, he says suddenly, with a nod of his head, they see nothing but fog, yet hear the waves as they rub and break against the dark, steely cliffs rising hundreds of yards into the air, as sheer as a scream. Gísli shuts his eyes, longing for sleep, longing for rest, the slow movements of the boat ought to put him to sleep, it's good to shut one's eyes and vanish from everyone else. He shuts his eyes and even the breathing of the rowers begins to fade, perhaps this is all a dream? The fog, this strange trip, this reversal of the world?

Life is misfortune, he'd said in the night, in Geirþrúður's parlor, the boy had recounted the events of the evening, of the night, but insomnia and weariness weighed down all of Gísli's limbs and his eyelids were transformed into shutters that sank slowly over his eyes, no matter how hard he tried to hold them open; he stirred slightly when the letter was mentioned and found his mind wandering to Kjartan, he needed to write to him, to visit him, I certainly won't be making it abroad this year, any more than any other, and he has no desire to go to Reykjavík, that pitiful little village. I'll go to Kjartan, he thinks, half-submerged in sleep, to sit in his little room, in the smell of books, drink and talk about what's important. But first of all, to fall asleep. Then his name was spoken, perhaps more than once. What? he said, and had the feeling that Geirþrúður was asking, What is life, Gísli? Life is misfortune, he replied. Isn't that the excuse of those who have given up? Something in her tone woke him. The women both looked at him, inquisitively. I'm a coward, said Gísli, raising his hands apologetically.

Geirþrúður: Honesty can make a person courageous, but life isn't misfortune; it may be difficult, sometimes degrading, which is why far too many give in, too soft or too sapless to keep heading toward their dreams. They bend, accept what they shouldn't accept. You and Reverend Kjartan know each other, don't you?

Gísli opened his mouth, sat there with it open for a while, struggling to answer a simple question, whether he and Kjartan knew each other, because he suddenly got the feeling that his existence had been summarized in a few sentences that revealed his betrayal of life, of himself, the dreams he once had; they were beautiful dreams, he feels, and there was no Friðrik in them. Finally he nodded his head, said, Yes, yes, we know each other well. The parlor was silent; the boy had sat down, tired, but looked from Geirþrúður to Gísli, sensed something, felt disquiet, even fear. The long silence once again weighed the headmaster down, and he stared into space, his head teetering a little, Helga didn't take her eyes off Geirþrúður, who smiled at the boy, and then looked at Gísli. That's splendid, that you know each other; I was thinking of getting Kjartan to marry us, you see. Gísli stared silently into space, before finally saying, Damn, I'm drunker than I thought, and he shook his head, obviously done with paying heed to his ears. Which prompted Geirþrúður to say, I'm going to marry you, Gísli Jónsson. And when he said nothing, just looked blank, she added, as if she'd forgotten it, That is, if you agree. Gísli continued to stare into space, Helga crossed her arms, just a hint of impatience in the motion, but the boy said the obvious thing, swallowed and said, I don't understand, and Gísli looked at him, childishly grateful.

Geirþrúður ran a finger lightly over her lips, between them my life, Captain J. Andersen had said, before parting them carefully with his tongue, with his kisses. Between them my life, and perhaps his death too? She stroked her lips gently and shut her eyes, just for a second, only the boy saw it, that moment of sorrow. We don't understand much, she said, just a little, in fact, but this is the only way. To marry you, she added, looking at Gísli, and you me. You'll gain freedom from your brother's tyranny; I'm not a poor woman, as you know, you'll have the chance to go abroad regularly, buy books, you won't have to wear worn clothing, won't have to kneel to your brother to buy an English winter coat, won't have to sit with an old, arrogant general unless you feel like doing so. You will of course be called various names; people don't take well to the idea of the husband being so clearly the weaker party. A woman shouldn't provide a man with competition but with solace, and she absolutely must not exceed him.

They've rounded Núpur and turn slowly eastward; they couldn't be far from Vík, it opens somewhere like a green embrace in the harshness of the mountains.

I don't know how I feel, thinks Gísli, dipping one hand into the sea, just to feel something distinctive. Once I wanted something, didn't it have to do with poetry, achievements, a home? My Lord, those dreams, what childishness! He pulls his hand out of the water, it's cold from the sea, that's something, at least for now. He surveys the boat, the four rowers have been sweating, are red from the effort, and the blind skipper wears a peculiar expression, that amusing curmudgeon, an expression reminiscent of pain but also joy. Will that joy subside as soon as they step ashore? Helga looks down, as if in thought, one never knows precisely what she's thinking, is she happy or does she not need happiness; is such a thing possible? Behind her the giant smiles, Gísli can't remember his name, someone the boy knows, obviously enormous strength in those shoulders of his, yet nothing but gentleness in his face. The giant doesn't take his eyes off Helga, but next to him is this boy. "Was he sent here by God or by the Evil One?" Kjartan had said, or asked, in a letter written in the spring. Damned if I know, thinks Gísli, slipping his hand back into the ocean before directing his gaze at Geirþrúður, sitting foremost in the boat; Gísli gets the feeling that they're all heading in her direction, that it's she who is leading all these souls, this peculiar assembly of variously hounded souls. He lets his hand dangle in the sea and they row toward Reverend Kjartan, toward a wedding.

Marry you, he'd said last night, following Geirþrúður's announcement that she'd been considering having Kjartan marry them. Marry you, said Gísli when he could finally speak again; well, why not? He'd shrugged as if undaunted, but then had shaken his head and exclaimed, almost as if he were relieved, You must be crazy! Not to bend, to refuse to live as I'm expected to do, not to let scoundrels lord it over me, not to let narrow-mindedness dictate how I live. Yes, maybe, Geirþrúður said, and she smiled, weakly, wearily. She'd considered this possibility, this ridiculous idea, before, and had taken time during the day to speak to Jóhann and Þórunn, a friend of hers and Helga's and wife of the photographer Ketill. Gísli is weak-kneed, Þórunn had said; Friðrik will get to you through him. I think I can prevent that, Geirþrúður had replied; I know that I'm fully capable of it. But do you trust Gísli? Not his weaknesses, no, but I think that I can keep them at bay. Is it enough to think that you can? There's no better offer; life is uncertainty, the outcome generally depends on us. Are you certain he'll agree? He's given me looks, I'm not blind, and I know what I have, he's intelligent and will realize that he'll gain a measure of freedom under my wing. Yes, I can accept living with him, the house is big, I'll send him abroad if I grow tired of him, the best has never been on offer, anyway, John was married, and . . . but now he's gone. Besides, Gísli isn't a boring man, he's no numskull, no stick, no dried saltfish; that's no small thing, and hopefully he's a competent lover. Don't look so shocked, Jóhann, everyone has needs. Afterward she spoke to the editor, Skúli.

Skúli! exclaimed Gísli, that thief, for what?! What he writes about this, matters. About what, this marriage?

Geirþrúður: Yes.

Gísli: I haven't said anything, neither yes nor no; well, nothing at all!

Geirþrúður: I know, Gísli.

Gísli: And what of today? When all I did was sit with the old general, the old rascal, listening to his boasting, with not a clue about anything, while you were off discussing the idea of me marrying you with others—including that bastard Skúli, no less!

I know, Gísli, Geirþrúður repeated patiently, almost as if she were speaking to a child—and then said that she'd gone to see old Karólína. *Mother?!* shouted Gísli, throwing up his hands in despair, not knowing whether he should be angry, shocked or frightened, and consequently doing the only thing he could think of: he threw up his hands again. But then asked, just in case, or else to maintain some semblance of self-respect, So you are actually crazy? No, she said, merely focused on my struggle for independence; some might think it madness, that's true. She spoke to the old woman; the meeting didn't last long, half an hour, they were both deliberate yet not exactly cold to each other. The three schooners in which Karólína owned a substantial majority, and which Gísli was to inherit, would be placed in Geirþrúður's name on the old woman's death; Jóhann will be drawing up a contract to this effect with Högni, the head bookkeeper of Tryggvi's Shop and Trading Company, tomorrow. My ships, Gísli said feebly, meaning, my freedom. Your mother knows as well as I do that you would squander everything on nonsense and lose the ships to your brother, but they'll be yours if we divorce; it's in the contract. I didn't know we were married, Gísli said torpidly, like someone who has no control over anything.

He withdraws his hand from the cold sea. The boat crawls onward and Geirþrúður looks at him. Damn it. She's beautiful, he thinks, sticking his hand back into the sea.

* * *

Love, someone may indeed have said this word in the night. Someone? It could hardly have been Helga, a mountain doesn't go and wonder about love; possibly the boy. Did he say that word, *love*, that cruel noun, that comet? No, the boy didn't say anything, just stared with those helpless calf's eyes of his, those peculiar membranes that make one remember various things. Was it he himself who said it, perhaps? Gísli moves his hand in the sea, leaning over to reach the water. Then it was me; I haven't learned anything in this life.

Love, Geirþrúður had repeated, I know nothing about it, but I suppose there's not enough of it in the world, meaning it's impossible for everyone to receive a share. I respect your intelligence, your learning, some aspects of your disposition; on the other hand, you're weak-willed and your brother will continue to try and push you around, both of them, in fact, then zealously, unwaveringly, as soon as your mother dies. You're her favorite, I might even say her beloved, having sat opposite her and spoken with her about you. You're her weak spot. Friðrik envies you for it, may even hate you for it sometimes. He has maintained and expanded your father's empire; everything rests on Friðrik's shoulders, and he's certainly received praise from her, respect, but hardly warmth, I would have a hard time believing that. I could almost see Karólína moving here just to be near you as she takes her final steps, yet I hope not; the house is big, but not big enough for that. Because of all of this, Friðrik will try everything he can once she's gone. Of course you know that as a man, you could easily appropriate everything I own, the law allows it, but Friðrik would immediately claim it from you, along with whatever remained of your self-respect. We'll marry, I'll grant you your freedom from your brother, you won't be allowed to come anywhere near the business side of things, but can ask as much as you please, share ideas, yet first and foremost, you are to hold yourself as upright as you are able, continue teaching, both here at home and at school; you are to bring your education and knowledge into this house. We shall attempt to deal with your weaknesses when they flare up, but for now we'll sleep, we need to get up quite early. And she'd stood up, in those downy nightclothes of hers that hugged her body. Will we be happy? he asked the blanket, imploringly, apologetically. Don't be silly, she said calmly, but hopefully there was something resembling a smile on her face; he didn't dare look up. You'll have your own private room, of course, but I trust that I'll see you some nights. Gísli looked up and blushed. Blushed despite the drink, the fatigue, despite having survived all these years, despite the sadness of life, the shattered dreams, despite having crawled along the bottom of heavy nights and drunk from streams that run from Hell. Blushed, which must be the reason why he dared to ask the questions that seemed to hang in the air: But if I can't stand up to Friðrik, if I can't live without betraying you, what then, if I haven't the strength within me? If you betray, you die, is heard from the boy, yet in an astonished tone, as if he'd come to an unexpected conclusion. That's that, then, said Helga, before bending over and handing Geirþrúður the flat, slender box that had been lying on the parlor table; Gísli noticed it out of the corner of his eye, although he kept his gaze fixed on the boy, the twelfth article, he said, it's the twelfth article of the Constitution, you've got it, you know the answer better than I do! Geirþrúður opened the box and pulled out a pistol. This was Guðjón's, she said reflectively, he was given it as a gift and was going to kill himself with it; it was before he met me. He gave it to me with the instruction that I was to use it only if I had to, in an emergency, if I were seriously threatened. He said it in jest. But perhaps in earnest, as well. She weighed the gun in her hand, without looking at Gísli, who said, You're cruel!

Geirþrúður: No, merely a woman in a man's world.

IX

They come ashore near the mouth of the river that runs down from a heath, curves past the vicarage and out to sea; the river finds its way despite the fog. Midday in summer, yet the world is silent, the fog has silenced it, they hear only the purl of the river, which carries the lives of grass blades, the dreams of tussocks, an enchanting, singsong murmur that dies out in the sea. The group stands by the boat, quite close together, as if waiting for someone, for someone or something to give them a signal and confirm that they exist, confirm life, that there's something left of the world besides this fog and the purl of the river flowing past. They stand there just as motionless as in the morning, when Þórunn came and took a photograph of the group. A photograph, Gísli had said; he'd been startled, was barely awake, hungover, tired, muddleheaded. A wedding photo, my dear, said Geirþrúður, smiling, as if it were all good fun. But she didn't smile in the photo; she and Helga sat there looking resolute, the men stood in a semicircle behind them, Kolbeinn, who appeared to be attempting to smile, or perhaps growl, the boy serious, looking directly at the lens, as if staring into the eyes of the future, time itself, Gísli looking weary, uncertain, with sadness in his right eye, something else in his left, but Gvendur grinning as if at that very moment he'd sighted great happiness.

Now we must navigate the fog, Geirþrúður says. I've no mind to stumble over tussocks, announces Kolbeinn; helplessness, the insecurity of the darkness had welcomed him at the shore. I'll lead you, Helga says, I'm no damned wretch, he says, yet he takes hold of her arm. Gísli is the only one who's been in this place before, apart from the boy, but that was just once, when he was barely conscious from fatigue, in heavy weather, darkness and snow. We'll start by following the river, Gísli says, leading the way. The boy is carrying a box of wine bottles. Helga has tied a bag around her waist and leads

Kolbeinn, Gvendur brings up the rear, carrying supplies, food for the feast, and other things. I thought we were supposed to be on the right side of the river, mutters the boy as Gísli tramps off to its left, leading them inland. We'll let him decide, Geirþrúður says, for once, it won't take long to backtrack, and it's good to walk. I'm sure the fog will lift soon, says Gísli after they've walked a considerable distance; he found a path to follow but now they're lost, there are no landmarks and the river's purl is nearly silent. Aren't we on the wrong side of the river? the boy asks cautiously, and Gísli looks at him. Yes, he says, with a sigh. Geirþrúður takes a bottle out of the box, French red wine, which makes the rounds three times before it's empty. There's a house, says the boy after walking away from the others, and then Geirþrúður is knocking on a door that the boy is familiar with, except that it was covered in ice when Jens pounded on it that April night, a horse between them. The mailman's blows had awakened dogs that responded with barks, but they don't bark now, perhaps because of the fog, and stay behind the housewife who opens the door, with her radiant hair, that sunshine, and she and Geirþrúður stand face to face, dusky and bright. The woman seems unsurprised, yet it's not every day that one opens the door to find such a group on one's doorstep, six people, two well-dressed women, four men, two of them carrying heavy loads, the third with eyes like black windows, the fourth, yes, now she recognizes the headmaster. Hello, Gísli, she says, bowing instinctively, because he's a distinguished man. You'll hardly find your way alone in this fog, unaccustomed to this place as you are, she says, following Geirþrúður's explanation about where they're heading, and offers them her husband, Jón, as a guide, not expecting Gísli to be able to find the way, distinguished man that he is. They welcome the company of the farmer, who holds his seven-year-old daughter by the hand as he walks beside Gísli; Jón smiles because it can be such a treat when something unexpected happens. Father and daughter accompany them to the cemetery gate, from there they make out the faint outline of the vicarage, almost as if it were a misunderstanding. Let me give this for your help, Geirþrúður says, taking a bottle of wine from the box, which Jón tries to refuse, you don't take payment for such a self-evident thing as escorting people from one farm to another in a murky fog, if so, the world would be perverse, but something in the manner of this woman convinces him to accept the bottle; he bows slightly, it's not polite to stare, he says softly to his daughter, who has trouble taking her eyes off Geirþrúður, her clothing, manner, then they return home, the girl's heart beating fast as she holds the pin that Geirþrúður drew from her hat and gave her, he holding the bottle of red wine, although he unfortunately hadn't dared to ask the question that was plaguing him: How do you drink red wine?

X

Later that night the fog turned into dense rain. So dense that it was almost entirely dark between the drops, which are transparent as innocence. The boy got to sleep in Reverend Kjartan's office, breathing in dust, breathing in books, breathing in tens of thousands of words, thoughts that should be able to free humanity from its chains but don't always do so. He listened to the rain, it was telling him something, but then he fell asleep. Even his heart couldn't keep him awake, that restless muscle, that musical composition, that dusky cave. The rain muttered something, the boy fell asleep.

Married, Reverend Kjartan had said, tilting back his head, which was his only indication of surprise, otherwise acting as if nothing were more obvious, while Gísli wiped his hands down his sides like a bashful boy; they were in the vestibule of the house, had barely stepped in. In a voice not entirely devoid of joy, Kjartan had said, To whom do we owe thanks for this great and remarkable visit; shall I bless the fog? No, Geirþrúður said, that would make little difference;

Gísli and I have come to be married. Married, Kjartan had said, tilting back his head, as Anna stepped out of the kitchen and discerned the guests as faint outlines. Geirþrúður introduced herself to Anna, a cold hand greeted a warm one. Pleased to meet you, said Anna, so earnestly that shyness appeared for a second in Geirþrúður's eyes, somewhere within the darkness. I didn't dare to hope, Anna said, that Gísli would marry so well, may God steer you clear of misfortune, and Geirþrúður bowed her head, as if to receive a blessing. The ceremony itself was brief, the fog so dense, even denser than before, that strangers could hardly have found their way to the church. Nothing was played, nothing sung. Shall we sing? asked Kjartan, although he knew the answer, and then did what he'd been asked to do. Only the boy, Helga, Kolbeinn and Gvendur were present, while the domestics prepared the feast. Trout soup simmered, meat roasted as Kjartan blessed Geirþrúður and Gísli in the church, blessed them from out of his own darkness, blessed them as husband and wife, and there was fog at the windows. Kjartan looked at the couple, he intended to say something, perhaps thinking, What word can be used to set life upright, what words conquer misfortune, but he gave up, somehow helpless, hollow, and blessed them better with old, dog-eared words of God, those overused, threadbare garments that we still wear because we haven't found others, while reality and the cold from outer space blow practically unhindered through them. Yet it was an excellent feast.

The fog lay siege to the house and afternoon turned to evening, evening to a feast, but occasionally Kjartan shook his head. Does your head hurt, my friend? Gísli asked. The other answered, Yes, every time I try to understand the world. The fog turned into rain and such good food had probably never been eaten, nor such good wine drunk, in the house of Kjartan and Anna. The farmhand who'd accompanied Jens and the boy up to the heath told stories of living and dead priests, laughed his whinnying laugh now and then, soon became drunk, was flustered by the variety of food, flustered by Geirþrúður's presence, he'd heard many stories about her, had told some himself, and there she sat, at the same table, straight-backed, and everything she said seemed carefully considered or right in some way. Her presence and the wine overpowered him, he whinnied twice, thrice, and was then carried out to the church by Gvendur, though it was before the fog turned into rain; he carried the farmhand like a sack. Not much stamina there, said Geirþrúður, half smiling, that's the effect you have, Anna said, and just then it started to rain. A first-rate wedding feast. No one knew, of course, what had blessed the newly wedded couple: the hope of a better life, some sort of freedom, unhappiness, the absurd? Whatever it was, the unfathomable had happened: Geirþrúður married Gísli, married into an important family, this woman who'd provoked everyone and flouted everything, married the weakest link in the strongest chain, enticed him with promises of independence, threatened him with a pistol, if he betrayed her she would load the gun with the darkness of her eyes and aim it at his heart. After half a bottle, Gísli dared to look at her, and he'd never been further from understanding life. From time to time she returned his glance and then he thought, My God, she despises me! Then he noticed her freckles; the light fell differently on her face, perhaps, for a moment, and highlighted them, and then he thought, No, she pities me, is that perhaps even worse? He looked at the freckles, thought, What became of my dreams, can I find them somewhere? But then the boy stood up. He'd hardly drunk anything, had just finished mumbling to himself, life, it's glittering stars, but what then is the darkness between them? Stand up, murmured his heart, and he did so. Everyone fell silent at once, almost as if they'd been waiting for this, fell silent and stared at the boy, who directed his gaze upward so as not to lose heart, gripping his nearly empty glass, looking up as if he were speaking to the roof, or what was above it, the evening, the raindrops, the sky,

God. Life, he began, should be glittering stars, not bitter misfortune and sorrow.

Those who gather shoes in order to make an important journey mustn't die. Death shouldn't be their journey, because where does it lead us except into the darkness? I always thought that books and knowledge made a person happy. Now I know that that's incorrect, but it's also the only thing I know. Life is hard, but it's still easier than death, which is a scoundrel that steals everything from us. I mean, all the possibilities. It takes our eyes so that we can't read, our ears so that no one can read to us, takes our arms and you can never embrace the person who matters most, never again touch those whom you want to touch, far too many hands are gone. I don't know where they went, I dream of them often, but they can't touch anything anymore. Once, and it wasn't so long ago, I thought that the way to come nearer to them would be to die as well. Yet I knew that that was wrong. And once I received a letter that said I was supposed to live. But I didn't know why. You ought to know that you can't live just because you're not dead; that's fakery. You ought to live like a star, and shine. I know that now. But I don't really know why I stood up. Today, Geirþrúður was married. To Gísli. They both know a great deal, and she's so strong, yet that hasn't helped them enough. I feel that for them, life ought to be something besides unhappiness. I don't know where the darkness comes from, yet I think that it comes from the same place as the light, and I think it grows dark because we let it happen. I think that it's difficult to attain the light, often very difficult, but I also think that no one attains it for us. Not God, not Jesus, who maybe should have been a woman because then the world would have been different and better, not the governor, not farming, not ships, not books. If we don't set out on our own, life is nothing. We ought to live to conquer death, that's the only thing that we know how to do and are able to do. If we live as we're able, preferably a bit better, then death will never conquer us. Then we won't die, we'll just become something else. I don't have the words for it, to describe it, I mean. Maybe we simply change into music.

Then he stopped.

He sat down, suddenly noticed the glass in his hand, stood back up, held it out, as if irresolute, started to sit down again, but then everyone stood up, raised their glasses, and the rain told ancient tales on the roof.

I can't ask for a better blessing than that, Geirþrúður said; now it's up to us, Gísli. Yes, he said. Damn it, he said, draining his glass inadvertently, and Jakobína, the maid who had pulled off Jens' clothes at the start of April, rubbed life into him, a bit too much, perhaps, though it had been so terribly nice to put her hands where they weren't supposed to be put, became surprisingly drunk, unused to red wine, astonishment and melancholy seesawed in her beautiful face. Kjartan leaned over the table. I thank you for your unorthodox speech, he said to the boy, it was perhaps unnecessarily atypical of a wedding speech and could have been more Christian, you mustn't say such things about Jesus, but it was inspiring. You write, Geirþrúður said to Kjartan. I do? So I'm told, and you also translate, which is, admittedly, more widely known; so you're a writer. No, no, said Kjartan, aghast, flattered, and he emptied his glass. I immerse myself in books sometimes, that's all, he said, looking away. Gísli muttered something at the table, but the giant Gvendur drank his wine like water, now and again looking around him, perplexed, his big heart struggling, he emptied two glasses before he knew it, which proved to be too much; he stood up, sputtered some nonsense and just managed to make it outside before throwing up all the wine, all the food, that terribly fine food. Such a disgrace. Everything has simply collapsed, is gone, torn apart, existence that for years had revolved around Pétur, Einar, Andrea, the fishing hut and the farm, that most dependable thing of all that is dependable, a mountain has suddenly been snatched away to reveal something dizzying and incomprehensible. He vomited bile, fear, incomprehension, vomited anxiety, and it was as if he were dying, he retched, was on his hands and knees, shaking, but then felt a hand on his cold, sweaty forehead. Are you death, he asked, a bit piteously, with vomit in his nose, bile in his mouth, tears in his eyes. No, Helga said, I'm not quite so bad. And then she helped him up to the room of the farmhand, who was snoring in the church, helped the big man up the stairs, after wiping the tears and vomit from his face. Oh, oh, Gvendur more or less whimpered. Yes, said Helga. There, there, said Helga. She undressed the giant, pulled off his clothes and put him to bed. First him, then herself, and lay down beside him, that beautiful woman, calmly and deliberately, with a touch of austerity in her gray eyes. She undid her hair and it spread out like open arms, over her bare back, somewhat over her small breasts; her palms, softer than clouds, stroked his arm, stroked his chest, stroked his belly, his groin, moved lower, good that not all of you is so terribly big, Helga said, but Gvendur shut his eyes out of shyness, and who knows, perhaps happiness—is it possible to understand this life?

XI

The boy pushes the dory away from the shore, gaining leverage on the gravel, and it slips into the tranquil sea. It's morning, hardly past seven o'clock and the raindrops work together to pulverize the light, change it into semidarkness. He hops into the boat, grabs the oars. There's nothing like the sea, Kolbeinn says.

It had been clear.

Maybe he'd made the decision long ago, but hadn't had the guts to admit it. Afraid that he was misunderstanding everything, afraid that it would turn into misfortune if he admitted it.

He'd stood up last evening, something inside him had instructed him to stand up, which he did, and said all of those things about life, energy, death. He'd spoken, and at the same time made a decision, or rather, admitted it. To take a small boat, row north to Sléttueyri, row in the direction of red hair, toward what he doesn't know. It simply has to happen. His heart demands it. He who disobeys his heart turns into a gray shade. No trouble finding a small boat. Just take the dory, said Kjartan, pointing out to him where to find it; are you going far? I don't know, said the boy, hopefully all the way. I'll be damned, the priest had said, but the evening turned to night and the rain fell ceaselessly on the roof, each drop an accusation, and Kjartan couldn't sleep, lay in his little room just off the master bedroom, each drop a reprimand. The word of God? Or of life? There probably aren't any answers, thought Kjartan, continuing to lie there instead of joining Anna in their bedroom; she may have been waiting for him, hoping that he might dare to come, that he might be able to overcome what separated them, overcome the disappointments of life. I'm rotten hay that the Lord has tossed aside, thought Kjartan, and he closed his eyes. Sank into self-pity, one of the mortal sins, instead of going to her and hearing her say, Kiss me and kiss me, let the kisses be no fewer than the raindrops on the roof, change your fingertips into kisses, kiss me and touch me and we'll make the world habitable, kiss me and we'll transform rocks into flowerbeds.

Did Geirþrúður and Gísli kiss each other? Let me know when you leave, Geirþrúður had said to the boy; it was near midnight, the rain was rain and he heeded her, snuck out at first light, nearly tumbled over Kolbeinn, who had fallen asleep in the vestibule and was curled up in a ball like a dog, the skipper was determined to go with the boy. No freaking way, the boy had said, before noticing, to his horror, something akin to vulnerability in the old wolffish's face, as if a wound were opening, at which point he hastily agreed. Slunk up the stairs, Gísli and Geirþrúður shared the maids' room, and the boy was just going to whisper something into the room, that he was leaving, but Geirþrúður was awake and got out of bed in the half-light, stood up naked, he averted his eyes. I'm going, he said after she'd come out, having thrown on a robe, Gísli was sleeping on his back, as if dead, except that he snored, which the dead never do. I know, she said, to Sléttueyri. How did you know? It's probably my misfortune to understand mankind; go, otherwise you'll always regret it, revenant dreams can play awful games with people. Go, but come back, don't leave me behind. I, can I leave you behind? he asked, surprised. Gísli's snoring, he said when she made no reply, and the headmaster's snores grew significantly louder, became clamorous. Should I shoot him already? Who would teach me, then? That's right. Instead, pour a bit of water into him; it'll startle him so much that he'll turn over onto his side, which will reduce his snoring considerably. There, you see, Geirþrúður said, I need you, and she went downstairs with him for some water, then said goodbye to them in the vestibule, kissing the boy on the forehead; it was like a blessing. You're going too, you old seadog? Are you certain it's the right thing to do? Let me go, he said, he pleaded. I'd rather not, she said, yet hugged the wolffish as if he were something precious, embraced him like a sorrow, then went back up with the water to stop Gísli's snoring. Not even a winter night had eyes black as hers.

There they went at the break of day, the boy and Kolbeinn, the old skipper, blind amidst his books, within the phosphorescence of words; his strong paw held onto the boy's shoulder and they inched their way along, heading toward the sea. Two men, almost the only things connecting them being their course toward the sea, and the old man's paw on the boy's shoulder.

The boy was quick to turn the boat upright, the dory. I've run my hand over bigger coffins than this, said Kolbeinn. In other words, you want to go with me? said the boy, swallowing something difficult. I've long since stopped wanting anything. But you're going with me? Are you done untying it? Yes. What are we waiting for, then? Nothing, replied the boy, without moving; he simply couldn't, as if the size of the sea had overcome him, or his fear of what awaited him, humiliation or a new life, but then what kind of life, days of toil and disappointment? *Live.* The prayer of his mother, whose name was Elín but who wasn't allowed to live, who was forced to witness her three-year-old daughter die before her. They died as spring returned to the world. Died as the snowmen melted outside, the entire family, five snowmen who melted into the earth along with their smiles, their whiteness, disappeared without a trace into the dark, wet earth. When are we leaving? asked Lilja, meaning, When are we going to visit my brothers, yet she asked so faintly that the question was barely heard. Tomorrow, my dearest darling, Elín whispered, and I'll hold you the entire way. Lilja grasped her mother's index finger and slept, glad that everything would be good again tomorrow, grasped it tightly, out of pure love, but possibly also out of deep fear of life that senses the presence of death, feels the darkness. Held tightly, but Elín rested her forehead against Lilja and thought with all her strength, with every cell in her living body, You're not going to take her, you may not, I beg you, spare this life, this light, this little girl, show her mercy, I beg you!

But death steps over our wishes, our prayers, our despair and strength, it does so whenever it pleases.

"Björgvin and I were going to do so much. We were convinced that we would gradually work our way out of the daily grind, and have a decent life. A life with you, with books and knowledge, a life with joy. We weren't asking for much, not for riches, but rather what we could create with our own hands. Perhaps it's too much to ask for love and happiness in this life, on this earth? My dear, my dear boy, I've been crying so much that there are no tears left, and what is there to do? Lilja is with me in bed, close to me. If only you'd got to see her again! She was always so happy, she was always so brimming with life! A touch mischievous. Chirped so irresistibly when she was happy. Lovelier than all there is. If only you could see her now, incredibly small and defenseless, the beautiful corners of her mouth so lifeless. She is lying so close to me and yet is gone, is so terribly far away, she who was always asking about everything. How can the world hold so much cruelty? Now I am going to lie down to sleep beside her, and sleep a heavier sleep than life can bear. It isn't fair. Lilja and I had so much within us, and Björgvin, and soon it will all have come to nothing, as if it had never existed. As if we had never lived. Never laughed, embraced, never told each other what matters more than a thousand ships loaded with gold. Now it will all vanish. Gold never vanishes from the world, just life. Yet gold is nothing but a cold metal, and the cold can neither comfort people nor make them happy. Is this the world you wished to see, God? Where does all our love go, where does everything that we do go, where do all the incidents go that lit up the world and made us happy? My dear boy, if only you manage to do what we longed to do, then perhaps there was a reason for all this . . . I'm so terribly tired. My beautiful boy. If only Lilja could wake up again. Where are you, God? Live, as you are able, *live!*"

Kolbeinn had pushed the boat into the sea, stood with his old legs in the sea and enjoyed feeling the salty cold chill him, but only at first, he quickly became too cold, turned his blind head in what he thought was the boy's direction. Are you dead, you dimwit boy, are you going to let me freeze to death here? he hissed, before stepping carefully into the boat, finding his footing, sitting down, groping for the oars, muttering something about poltroonery, that he would just go alone, then, nothing else to be expected, but then the boy had joined him, grabbed the prow with his right hand, the left opened and closed in its mitten as if to catch its breath. Regret for the dead can play cruel tricks on us. There's nothing like the sea, Kolbeinn says.

The boy rows and everything runs together, the air with the sky, the rain with the sea, and that's why it's hard to know whether their tugs on the oars are bringing them farther out to sea, higher into the air on their way to the sky, or down into the sea, toward the seabed, where everything ends. He rows. The two of them, he and Kolbeinn, are all that remain in a world of half-light and disappointment, which is probably why the boy dares to say it out loud, that he's no longer certain what direction they're headed in, because he can no longer tell the difference between the seabed and raindrops, sky and semidarkness. Kolbeinn sits hunkered in the stern, as if he's cold, his thick tongue emerges twice, thrice from between his teeth, a blind snake in a dusky cave. People can rarely tell the difference, he finally says, there are so few who ask and even fewer who care to know. The boy stares into space, so lost in thought that he forgets to row. Keep rowing or I'll suffocate, Kolbeinn says. Sorry, says the boy, and rows so that Kolbeinn can breathe, even though the purpose of it seems quite vague at times.

The boy: Now I understand.

Kolbeinn: An idiot would congratulate you, a wise man would offer you condolences. I'm neither.

The boy: What?

Kolbeinn: Hardly anyone has eyes in order to look squarely in the face of understanding; few eyes can tolerate it.

The boy: Is that why you're blind?

You're almost fun to be around, says the wolffish, clearing his throat and spitting, though it doesn't go overboard. What do you understand? he asks, as the boy rows on in the direction of the unfathomable. What Reverend Kjartan said to me in the spring, that people like Kierkegaard were dangerous because they cause us to question, and even rethink, the world.

Kolbeinn: He's good at thinking.

The boy: Kierkegaard?

Kolbeinn: Reverend Kjartan.

The boy: Even so, he doesn't feel well. Nor Gísli, either. And Geirþrúður doesn't feel well, though no one is bigger than her.

Kolbeinn's dead eyes are directed at the rain and half-light. It isn't enough to think, it isn't enough to understand, he says, licking his lips to taste the salt of the sea. No, says the boy, or asks, it's likely that they've rowed out of the world and into another in which Kolbeinn actually speaks. You also have to be able to live with what you see and understand, but that requires more guts and more stamina than most people have, which is why misfortune hunts us down. I should have been dead long ago. The boy starts rowing again. Rows hard, in the direction of the seabed, raindrops, the sky, rows in a direction that might not exist. The boat crawls along and it rains, between the drops is semidarkness, and the boy has begun to row hard, very hard, in fact with the fervor that deprives a person of his thought, his senses, he's soaked with sweat but takes no notice of it, his hands ache but he rows on, as if fleeing from the questions of the world, fleeing from the reason why Kolbeinn wanted to come along, fleeing from the invocation of his mother, that he must live so that light might shine on the dead, live what they didn't have a chance to live. He rows fervently for a long time, until Kolbeinn asks gruffly, What's your heading, boy? The boy looks up, exhausted, and spies the outline of something big and dark within the rain. Land, ho, he says, with surprise in his voice, even astonishment, as if he's forgotten that something besides the sea exists. The boat bobs on gentle but rising waves, the boy leans forward, rests on the oars, which hang in the sea, two long arms that reach out toward the seabed. I wonder where we are? says the boy after recovering for the most part; his sweat has stopped pouring and his heart pounding, pumping energy into the oars. Where did you want to go? asks Kolbeinn reluctantly, as if no longer caring to hear an answer, and then the boy says it—albeit not saying: to her who writes peculiar letters; she has red hair, its color passes through mountains, she has a small child, is poor, I'm afraid that life with her will be difficult, that I'll end up toiling at sea with useless hands, shredded dreams, no—he merely says: to Sléttueyri. But of course the word contains everything that we mentioned, which is why his voice trembles slightly. You should have headed north, not northwest. I know; do you mean that we've gone northwest? Kolbeinn doesn't answer, can't be bothered to, the answer is too obvious, he also needs to think about other things, they're not so simple. The boy turns the boat, then rows in the direction of this word that makes the vocal cords sag. Follows the land, which is a heavy, dark shadow, rows hard, but it's slow going, he's lost in thought; so now's the time.

It has begun to blow. The waves rise beneath the boat, the raindrops become a flail with which the wind beats them. Kolbeinn smiles. An impenetrable smile that transforms his face, a smile that is a sparse row of teeth beneath dark, dead eyes, the boy has never seen anything resembling this smile, he felt a chill, a chill of fear. He says agitatedly, It's blowing. Kolbeinn smiles even more broadly. We're just offshore, he says, or asks. Around fifty yards, the boy says. It isn't as dark as before, as if the wind has managed to blow life into the light, the boy is unable to discern small details, rocks and tussocks become one, but he catches a glimpse of a shadow, a human, a sheep, something. He needs to work hard to hold the boat steady. Is it deep here? Judging by the waves, yes; several yards. Kolbeinn is still smiling, hardly anyone could feel well with such a smile. The boy starts to row again, hard, feeling something in his stomach, anxiety, nausea, fear. Then you're safe, the old man says. Am I safe, from what? You keep the books. Books, why should I keep them? asks the boy, rowing even harder, instinctively approaching land. I'm not going any farther than this, says Kolbeinn, almost triumphantly, before adding, I belong in the sea.

The boy: No one belongs there except the fish. You're not a fish.

Kolbeinn: What am I, then?

You're a person, the boy says, and he stops rowing. A person, just listen to you. I'm a blind rogue, a helpless wretch, no one should live like that. No one belongs in the sea, repeats the boy.

Kolbeinn: Belongs, as if anyone belongs anywhere! We two don't belong anywhere, it's been arranged. Be good to the books, they're all yours, except for one. Which one?, the boy asks automatically; one book suddenly makes him forget life and death. You, of all people, should know that, the old skipper says, I have it here, beneath my coat. I forbid you from trying anything, do me the honor of allowing me to depart with dignity. No commotion, no shouting, no damned hysteria. I've lived a long time as the most wretched man of all; no need to die as such. But, says the boy, but, begins the boy. There is no but, Kolbeinn says, not any longer; I've come to the place where there's no reasoning. He gets up, gets to his feet in the rocking dory, stands upright like a man with shreds of respect left, of dignity. The wind has started to chop up the sea, it sprays over them and Kolbeinn stands up, quickly but with authority, completely fearless, raises his right arm, perhaps in farewell, but then the boy stands up as well and says something resembling a prayer, a profanity or a persuasion, reaches for Kolbeinn, who suddenly grows agitated and hastily lifts one of his legs, intending to step overboard, step down to the bottom of the sea, where death will give him new eyes, those that sit in his head are utterly useless, so useless, in fact, that he miscalculates, fails to lift his leg high enough, it's a matter of a few inches, besides the fact that the boat is rocking sharply, making it difficult to calculate anything, and what does he do but put his foot down wrong, not into the sea, but onto the gunwale, they both lose their balance, the dory overturns and they're in the sea, two men who are unable to swim, shouting, cursing. Where is dignity now, does it not exist, either in life or death?

XII

When you're in the sea, you're in the sea. A simple fact and so self-evident that no one should have to put it in words. But there is of course nothing self-evident about being in the sea if you have no idea how to swim, besides having feared drowning and the sea's depths ever since you could remember, found yourself without any warning in the sea amidst the heavy waves, having possibly been on your way toward the purpose of life, well, or maybe just its lack of purpose, but end up instead in the sea, splashing, spitting, cursing, terrified, and the deep pulls you down toward the seabed where everything ends, where hands change into cold jellyfish. Not far away splashes a blind devil, an old carcass, with a precious book beneath his coat, and now it'll be ruined; words tolerate the sea, not books. Without any warning, they both tumbled into the sea, which received them like any other pebbles, raindrops, so unexpectedly that the old skipper is on the verge of desiring life again, that trash, that vulgar beast, which is why he sinks with curses, spits out black profanities, but perhaps also because he's played such a large part in the drowning of the boy whom life had driven into Geirþrúður's house, this boy who's an abode of dreams, sadness, regret, a voice that came into the life of the wolffish with tidings of death and poetry, a voice that was like a memory of something that Kolbeinn had never lived, yet still missed, as ridiculous as that is. Whatever it is, regret or stupidity, they're both on their way down to the bottom of the sea, an old, blind wolffish with a book beneath his coat, poetry that emerged from darkness with a great light. The light that killed Bárður and kindled everything that we've told you, that we've rattled off in order to change the world, to call on God, oblivion, a new seashore and dry socks—how appropriate it is that this book sinks into the cold sea. In the month of August, in hammering rain, sinks into the silence of the sea along with these two lives that were drawn to words by an incomprehensible force, isn't there beauty and harmony in this tragedy? Yes, appropriate. Beauty. Harmony. And four groping hands, twenty fingers, shouts, curses, staring eyes, memories that sink and change quickly into darkness, into yet another black hole. Yes, perhaps appropriate, yet still a damn shame, and unbearable, because, for example, why doesn't this boy get to live any longer? So replete with dreams, why doesn't he get to grow, challenge himself, even become something and transform his environment with dreams, with his longing for beauty, with those eyes of his, of which Steinunn of Sléttueyri wrote in her diary that "it would be difficult to forget them"?

He flails his arms, doesn't get to live, absolutely not, kicks out with his feet. So this was how my father died, he thinks, and I'm going the same way. But I don't want to die, don't want my hands to become jellyfish, you can't comfort anyone with such hands; Mama, where are you, help me!

Kolbeinn shouts something in the direction of the boy, who cries out, What?! in return. Damn it to Hell! yells the old curmudgeon, though he's barely intelligible through the seawater that's sucked into his mouth as soon as he opens it, it isn't good to die shouting profanities, thinks the boy, as he tries to flail his way toward the old man, perhaps to allay his loneliness, because it's so hard to die alone, but the waves sweep them hither and yon, taking no account of the men's fear and loneliness. *I'm sorry!* shouts the old man, or seems to shout it; *I'm sorry*, shouts this old crust, this curmudgeon, at least that's what the boy thinks he hears. He hopes that he's hearing correctly, that it's "I'm sorry," not "Aw, screw it." Kolbeinn shouts, *I'm sorry* and the world suddenly becomes beautiful, the loneliness dwindles, the boy shouts back something that sounds like "Thanks" and "Goodbye," tries to keep his head above water, but it only becomes ever more difficult and soon far too difficult, yet he still manages to keep himself afloat, shouts Kolbeinn's name several times but receives no answer. He splashes, cries a bit but finally shouts at the sky, Nothing is sweet to me, without thee! He shouts it thrice, with all his might, sends it up like an emergency flare, like a farewell, like a declaration of love or just something to leave behind, because soon he'll be gone, completely gone, and then it will just be the sea with its waves, the rain that beats on the sea's surface, the ponderous land close by, yet still so distant. He shuts his eyes, flails his arms with dwindling strength, yet continues to flail because it's our duty to fight against death as long as we can endure it, or preferably even longer; those who leave, never return, we've lost them and all that was theirs, their eyes, smiles, the movement of their fingers, how they slept, stared distractedly into space, how they wept, kissed, touched, how they existed, all of this vanishes as soon as death touches us. Vanishes and never returns. Like these two different men, Kolbeinn and the boy, they vanish and then there's nothing left but the surface of the sea, a capsized boat, a wind that blows, rain that falls. What was sweet is gone; where are you, life, where did you go, mercy?

In the end we all change into silence.

WHAT WE MISS MOST IS EXISTENCE

What we miss most is existence. We haven't forgotten how it was to have the spark of life in our breasts. That is the greatest wonder we have ever known; whence comes that force, that tremendous light? Stars twinkle above us, birds fly through us, and now we've told this entire story. Retrieved words from the abyss of death, the expanses of life, hearts beat, wounds were opened, we recalled how it all went, or how it didn't, we traveled so far to seek the words that there's almost nothing of us left—we are now nearly silence. Yet no story can ever be told completely, or, how shall we say it; we inhale in the nineteenth century and exhale in the twenty-first. Time is an illusion; the only useable unit of measurement is life. People never change, regardless of the passage of time, what we call the years; fashions change, not mankind. But what pains us most is that we no longer exist, except in these words; they're as close to life as we can come. The seabed keeps those who were supposed to live; the boy sinks slowly thither, with his powerful dreams, with poetry churning in his veins and the hesitation that made him beautiful, eyes that were sometimes open wounds, he sinks with all of this. Sinks, waves his arms, manages to scramble up to the surface, where the weather welcomes him. That was the second time, now I'm sinking for the third, he thinks as he feels the deep tug him down, looks around for the final time in this life, calls out for Kolbeinn but receives no response except for the whistling of the wind. And then he weeps.

Weeps at the death of Kolbeinn, weeps at his own death, sinks, weeping, with sorrow and a lust for life, but not fear. Those who have never betrayed life do not fear death. Then it's finished, we say no more. Soon someone may wind up the music box, and then perhaps we'll hear the faint notes of eternity.

WHERE DOES DEATH STOP BUT IN A KISS?

DAMN IT, SAYS THE BOY, RETCHING.

One moment he was in the sea, about to sink for the third time, and the next he was on all fours, shivering in the darkness, spewing seawater, astonishment, sorrow, the seabed. He sat up with his back against something hard and rough, shut his eyes, thinking, Is this eternity, then? Is it so dark, cold, and me vomiting on all fours? No, he's probably still dying, it just takes longer and is more difficult than he expected. It's best to close his eyes. Which he does, and sinks again. No, I don't want to drown, he thinks, starts waving his arms and one arm strikes the face of the woman crouching in front of him, dressed in very little, her red hair wet. He stops struggling and says, I thought it would be different to drown; is this death, then?

He retches once more.

This time little comes up but bile and astonishment. Are you really alive? he asks. Why? he asks, but is unable to say more, sits up again with his back against the hard, rough surface. She's shivering as well. Kolbeinn! The boy tries to get to his feet but is unable to, there isn't enough energy left in the world for him to stand upright. Kolbeinn, he says weakly. I know, she says, there were two of you in the boat, but it was just you in the sea, the other one was gone. Kolbeinn, says the boy, not the other one, his name is Kolbeinn, he's blind and old and miserable. Or was, I don't know, I should have saved him, I should have known why he wanted to come with me. He shuts his eyes, hears the sea, the wind close by, where are they, why are they sheltered, how did he get here, what is she doing here, are they both drowned? He opens his eyes and asks about all of this. You certainly ask an awful lot of questions, says she who swam out after the boy and then again after the other, whose name is Kolbeinn, then, or was, she saw no one, just waves, it was all she could do to make it back here. Here, he asks, asks in order to escape from thinking about Kolbeinn, to stifle his tears, here, where are we? Why are you here? How is it that you can swim?

She was taught to swim by an old man, long before she came to Sléttueyri. This old man swam sometimes on calm and sunny days in shallow water, and many people had asked him to teach them, but he always refused, hoarding his knowledge like a treasure that no one could touch. But he taught you? Yes, and never forgave me. Why, then? He thought he would see my breasts, and preferably something more; several times I needed to fight him off, men are beasts. I'm a man. Are you? I don't know; then I wouldn't have swam out after you. Why did you want to learn to swim, you're not a sailor? It's so stupid to live on an island and not know how to swim, and I knew that it would come in handy; that's why I took the trouble to let that filthy ram teach me. And he never forgave me.

First for not allowing him anything, and then, which inflamed his hatred even more, for teaching others, and he started spreading the rumor that she'd allowed him everything, that she was like that, crazy with lechery, ravenous for men, young as well as old, he wasn't sparing in his descriptions. A short time later she became pregnant, apparently proving the old man right. Pregnant, the boy says. Yes, with Salvör, she says. A farmer's son whom she taught to swim, beautiful, as men can be, with strong, trusty arms, a gentle voice and solid words. He intended to take responsibility for the child, of course, but that was before he spoke to his parents; then he denied everything, and it turned out that he wasn't strong, after all, men think it's enough to have powerful arms and solid words to be called strong. She was made to give up her position or, rather, was exiled here to the north, to Sléttueyri, far enough away. But it was worth it, the whole stupid thing, the betrayal, the poisoned words, the humiliation; without Salvör, her life would be nothing.

And otherwise, you would have drowned.

She sent him the letters almost on a whim. Was perhaps calling out to him, to see whether he dared to answer or, in other words, dared to come. That's why she'd gone out numerous times a day to watch for him, ignored Þórdís' scolding and reprimands for this damn vagrancy of hers, went down to the shore, stared out to sea as if expecting something, like a jackass because no one came, not to her. She stopped going down to the shore to stand there in plain sight, decided to go out beyond the village, and that very afternoon walked out into the rain, felt she simply had to go, without being given leave to do so, her bones were restless, walked a long way and then saw the dory, saw Kolbeinn stand up, first him, and then the boy, saw them tumble into the sea. Without hesitation, she dived in. Was out of her coat before she knew it, was in the air before she knew it, but on her way down thought, Oh, hopefully I won't land on a skerry. In fact, it was a close call; she grazed against something, scraped herself. It took time to find him, the sea is so big, a person so little, but then she heard him cry out, though not for help, rather as if he were reciting something. We're in a cave? Yes, she says. A sea cave? Yes, she says. And we're trapped? asks the boy, after listening for several moments to the surge of the sea outside. Yes. Can't you just swim for help? Not against these waves, they're so heavy out here. You just dived off a cliff? Yes.

Semidarkness around them, darkness further inside the cave, damp and cold, and outside the wind rips apart the rain, tears up the sea, now those in Vík are worried, perhaps standing on the shore, Geirþrúður, Helga, even Gvendur, peering out to sea but spying nothing through the rain. She's still crouching before him, shivering slightly, her hair wet with seawater, drenched by the sea, she dived off a cliff and nearly killed herself on a skerry, in order to save him. She'd gone out daily, sometimes numerous times a day, to watch for him. What about the Norwegian? What about Jens? Those big men. She shivers. If only he dared to put his arms around this girl, this woman. But he's at a loss. The smell of vomit is no good, and he's starting to feel horrendously cold; how long does it take to die in a sea cave? Álfheiður has a little girl, people mustn't die and leave their children alone, that's the heaviest thing in the world, and this is why he says it, that she mustn't die, that it's forbidden for her to die and leave her child alone, he puts it like that, that it's forbidden. Says this trembling from cold as well as from something else that we, who are nearly silence, have lost the words for, then she raises her eyes, looks at him.

The smell of vomit isn't particularly nice, she says.

He: No.

She: You seem to have eaten quite well yesterday.

He: Very well. There was a wedding.

She: I wonder if it's fun to get married; were they happy?

No, he says. I'm not certain there's enough happiness for this world, because many people have to live without it. I don't like breathing in the smell of vomit, he adds, and for this reason they move farther in, it's possible by inching along the wall, by scraping themselves a bit; inside is darkness, the darkness of the earth. It's soft beneath them and so low that it's nearly impossible to sit up. We'll lie down, she says. Yes, he says, lying down.

She: We're soaked to the skin.

He: There's a reason for that.

She: You're shivering.

He: You too.

It's not just the cold, she says, and he says, I know, and she says, We should take off our clothes, they're so wet, she says, we're inside the earth, inside a cliff, in darkness, what use is clothing that doesn't protect against anything? I don't know, he says. Then let's get out of it, she says, which they do, in the confined space, and then they lie there naked, shivering with cold and life, as they hear the surge of the sea so clearly, and it's the surge of death. The world is very far away right now. Yes, he says, almost as far as Jupiter. How far is that? Three hundred sixty-five million miles. Jupiter, she says, Yes, he says, and has suddenly begun to tell her of his mother's letters. He'd never told anyone about them. Not even Bárður. But he's also never lain naked within the darkness of the earth, shivering with cold, the sea outside, Kolbeinn drowned and he himself soon dead. He tells, she listens. But then she says, It's cold, and moves closer to him, puts her arms around him and he does the same, because life demands it, we demand it, his blood demands it, it says, put your arms around her. He puts his arms around her and soon something happens that we no longer know how to describe. He tells her everything, his life streams from him, as if he wishes to put it all into words before it's too late, before the cold and his weariness silence him. They all died, he says. Jens, he says; you wrote that he'd made it all the way home, how do you know? Then she says, or whispers, they're lying so close together that it's enough to whisper, so close that it's almost enough to breathe. She breathes this about Jens, that he'd paid a visit to Salvör.

He stopped there one night, on his way home. Salvör had slept restlessly the preceding nights; Jens should have been there long before. A storm had raged, maybe it delayed him, yet not for so long. Maybe the storm killed him, or—even worse—maybe he didn't dare return to her, she'd said too much last time, said words that she thought no longer existed in the language, let alone between a man and woman— what if she'd scared him away? She'd woken to the agitation of the dogs, went down, looked out and saw two horses a short distance from the farm, and a big man on one of them. Have you come to kiss me? asked Salvör. No, Jens said, and she looked down, because her entire life had been filled with disappointments, and it wasn't certain, wasn't certain at all, whether she could endure any more of them. I came to bring you with me, he said, finally daring to say it. He'd had to go through all of what he did in order to dare it.

How do you know this? asks the boy, realizing the answer at the same time; your daughter, he says. Yes, she says. Her name is Salvör—like her grandmother?! Yes, she says. Yes, says Álfheiður, who'd received a letter from her mother, "so, he didn't come to kiss me, but rather, to live with me. His sister was so frightened when she saw me that she ran off and hid. But she's recovering, the dear." That's why you asked about Jens' hands, whether they could hurt someone. Yes, she says. They don't hurt anyone. I know. Is he in bad shape? He lost two toes, one finger, but got a woman. Not a bad deal. No. It seems the sea's drawing closer, says the boy, because the surging has grown louder. Yes, the cave floods when the tide is high, like now. Will it flood completely? One never knows. You can save yourself. Maybe, though it's uncertain in this weather. Don't try to save me, you mustn't die and leave your daughter, you mustn't die and leave your mother; write to Geirþrúður and tell her how it all ended. When does it all end? she asks, before kissing him unexpectedly, and she starts kissing him and it's good, much better than good, in fact. She strokes his face with her fingertips, strokes it as if her fingers were memorizing his face. They lie merged as the sea slowly fills the cave, and the boy thinks of all that he's experienced; he remembers all of it, it all piles up on the moments that he's inside of her, and everyone who has died comes to him, everything that he's lost and regretted, and out in the sea Kolbeinn's body tosses and turns, the skipper who had shouted *I'm sorry*, those beautiful, poignant words, and then drowned with a volume of poetry on life and death beneath his coat. He cried out to the boy, perhaps to life as well, and we do the same, cry out *I'm sorry* to life, to the sky, to what we don't understand, and they lie there entwined and the boy weeps, unable to help himself, the tears stream down and her lips drink them, those transparent fish, those transparent pearls, that glittering string of pearls by which we pull ourselves up, up from the mysterious depths, toward what is hopefully bigger than all else, pull ourselves up and leave the words behind in death. Thank you for weeping, she says. Now I'm ready to die, he says, as he hears the sea approach, hears as it's sucked into the dark earth, like death, like what we don't understand, like what is impossible to understand. Just kiss me again, she says, and the cave will stop flooding. Yes, he says, understanding; yes, he says, because where does life begin and where does death stop but in a kiss?

A GUIDE TO THE PRONUNCIATION OF ICELANDIC CONSONANTS, VOWELS AND VOWEL COMBINATIONS

ð, like the voiced *th* in *mother*

þ, like the unvoiced *th* in *thin*

æ, like the *i* in *time*

á, like the *ow* in *town*

é, like the *ye* in *yes*

í, like the *ee* in *green*

ó, like the *o* in *tote*

ö, like the *u* in *but*

ú, like the *oo* in *loon*

ý, like the *ee* in *green*

ei and *ey*, like the *ay* in *fray*

au, no English equivalent; but a little like the *oay* sound in *sway*. Closer is the œ sound in the French *œil*

JÓN KALMAN STEFÁNSSON was born in Reykjavík in 1963. He is the 2011 winner of the P. O. Enquist Award and his novels have been nominated three times for the Nordic Council Prize for Literature. His novel *Summer Light, and then Comes the Night* received the Icelandic Prize for Literature. Spellbound Productions are making a film of his trilogy of novels—of which *Heaven and Hell* (2010) is the first and *The Sorrow of Angels* (2013) the second—for release in 2015.

PHILIP ROUGHTON is a scholar of Old Norse and medieval literature and an award-winning translator of modern Icelandic literature, having translated works by numerous Icelandic writers, including the Nobel-prize winning author Halldór Laxness. His translation of *The Islander*, a biography of Laxness by Halldór Guðmundsson, was published by MacLehose Press in 2008.

ABOUT THE TYPE

Typeset in Minion Pro, 10/14.25 pt.

Minion Pro was designed for Adobe Systems by
Robert Slimbach in 1990. Inspired by typefaces of the
Renaissance, it is both easily readable and extremely
functional without compromising its inherent beauty.

Typeset by Scribe Inc., Philadelphia, Pennsylvania.